THE LIGHT IN THE TREES

Jeff Van Valer

The Light in the Trees

For more information, contact:
jvvtricycle@gmail.com

This is a work of fiction. Names, characters, businesses, organizations, places, events and song lyrics are products of the author's imagination. Any resemblance to actual persons, living or dead, is coincidental.

ISBN: 9781980576822

First edition
Copyright © 2018

For anyone who remembers going away
to summer camp.

August, 1970
Loon Lake
Benzie County, Michigan

WHEN THE BODY crashed into the fire, a startled flock of orange sparks took flight. Two levered sticks twirled their tiny flames far outside the clearing as the spilling blood hissed and steamed off the coals. One stick lit the pine-needle blanket of the forest floor. Its flame spread concentrically, like a viscous fluid poured from a spout. The other tangled itself in the rust-colored web of a dead cedar's branches. In one breathy yawn, the tree stood fully ablaze. The smoke thickened. It would soon reach White Birch Camp across a mile of placid water, obscuring the utility light above the beach house. A chorus of snaps, pops, and sizzles joined the reek of burning hair, the sputter of boiling fluids, and the current of a stiffening breeze.

CHAPTER 1

June, 1968
Opening Day
White Birch Camp

JUST MINUTES BEFORE Mom and Dad drove four hundred miles south without me, Dad and I sat on a bench atop a sandy bluff. Delicate waves danced across Loon Lake's lazy, afternoon surface. Dad wrapped his arm around my shoulders, and I leaned into him as much and for as long as I could. A little sailboat far away glided on a distant breeze. The opposite shore's trees were tall, each a different height. The forest wasn't anything like those alongside the highways on the way to camp, around towns named Bear Lake, Benzonia, and Honor. The groups of trees around those places looked more like planted cornfields at home, not the thick and mysterious place hiding God-knows-what across a mile of water.

I was ten. Dad's shirt smelled half like a mix of aftershave, laundry detergent and a hint of cigarette smoke. The other half smelled just like Dad himself. Mom was up at the place they called Headquarters, talking to the man with the funny mustache, Mr. Dinwiddie.

"Just look over there, Ted," Dad said, pointing across the water. "Lake like this, and other than the camp and the state park, not one house or building on it."

"Are there bears, Daddy?"

"Bears? No." He pulled me tight for a second. "Least I don't think so."

"You don't *think* so?" A forest that big seemed like it'd have some bears in it.

"Can't say I know for sure. After we get home, I'll read about bears in Michigan and write to you. You ask around up here and let me know what you learn. Sound like a deal?"

I didn't speak.

"You just do what the counselors say. And always tell the truth. Long as you do that, you'll be okay."

My dad was a lawman. A prosecutor at home. He was always after the truth.

"I always tell the truth," I said.

"Pretty much," he said. I swung my dangling feet, pointing my toes, trying and failing to touch the ground.

"Let's *hope* there are bears out there," he said.

"How come?"

"To scare away the builders."

I didn't understand.

"Yeah," he said, "so that forest can stay…natural like it is now. Be nice to preserve it, you know."

I pointed to the far shore with one foot. "What do you think it's like over there?"

"Oh. Can't be sure. Like it is on this side, I imagine, but with—well, who knows? It's too far away for you to ever know."

We were silent for a minute, until I said, "Daddy, I'm not sure about staying here."

"I know, and I understand. But I'm convinced you'll like it. It's about the best thing you can do with your childhood."

"But why does it have to be way up in Michigan?"

"I don't know. That's just where the camp is. Best camp I know of. It'll give you a break from all the violence in the real world."

Violence made me think about pigs in Cuba, missiles, riots, churches exploding, and Martin Luther Kennedy Vietnam.

"Hey, Ted?"

"Huh?"

"If you get lonely, just picture your mom and me waving at you. We'll always be on the other side of those trees."

"Nuh-uh," I said.

"No? Why not?"

"Because that's east." I pointed off to my right. "Indiana's down that way."

"Smarty-pants. That how you're gonna be?" Dad pulled me tight again. I giggled as he rubbed his knuckles on my scalp. Mom was coming. She walked toward us alone, up Cabin Row. That surely meant they were leaving soon.

"All you have to do," Dad said, "is remember to enjoy it up here. Have fun. Have an adventure. You'll love it. Every now and then, come out here and have a seat, right here on this bench."

The trees next to us rocked in a sudden gust. "Watch the trees, Ted. They're already waving their leaves at you." Another gust whooshed through them. "And now they're talking to you. What do you think they have to say?"

I hummed the way kids do when they mean to say *I dunno*

without bothering to open their mouths.

"Pretend that's your mom and me out there, across the lake, waving and talking to you. Talk to us. Just give it a try."

I listened for the trees' voices and thought I might hear them.

"Okay. I'll give it a try."

CHAPTER 2

June, 1970
Opening Day
White Birch Camp

IT'S MY THIRD summer, and I'm late for camp. For that, there'll be a stiff penalty. All the top bunks, chosen on a first-come-first-served basis—those'll be gone. Hell, they'll have been taken by noon, and it's almost four. Taken by kids I don't give a damn to meet, and the jerk who sleeps above me—whoever he ends up being—he'll step on my blankets all summer long and put sand in my bed every time he wants to get into his. And what does Dad care? He's not the one who gets screwed with the bottom bunk for two months.

He pulls to the top of the waterfront and cuts the GTO's engine. The V8 shivers for a little bit before it finally shuts up, and a very uncomfortable quiet sets in. After what seems like a whole minute, I figure it's probably time to say something. I just don't know what.

See you later seems too casual. *Good-bye* sounds too final. *See you at the end of the summer* sounds about right, but trying to say it drops a lead weight in my stomach.

What if he doesn't want to see *me* at the end of the summer?

I can still hear mom's voice after so many months telling me I'm being silly. *Of course Dad wants to see you at the end of summer, sweetie,* she says. But she's gone. She died on a

5

pretty Friday afternoon last October.

Drunk driver. Couple blocks from my house just after school. That man killed my mom and the wife of the county prosecutor. Things didn't go well for the guy, but it was still a lot worse for Mom. I heard the crash and rode down to it on my bike, the Schwinn Lemon Peeler Mom and Dad gave me on my twelfth birthday. It happened at 25th and Washington Streets, and it didn't take a minute to ride down there from the park to see what the excitement was. From a block away, I realized it was Mom just before her car burst into flames.

"Well, B—" Dad says, stopping to clear his throat. He sniffs, like he's caught a cold. "Buddy Boy," he manages to say from behind the wheel. "What do you think? Time to get your duffel?" He's decided to talk, but he doesn't even seem interested in me.

I'm alone up here.

Dad's always been a family man, never out for anything other than Mom and me, but things have changed since she died. Eight months seems like plenty of time to lose closeness with your son and want some freedom. Dad's not married anymore, and I'm the only one left to get in his way.

And guess who he's just about to leave at camp?

When he fires up the GTO and speeds away in that V8 Majesty he talks about, I won't be in the passenger seat, and he'll taste his freedom. After two months of *that*, maybe he'll want to keep it.

My duffel's in the trunk, and since Dad doesn't seem to be moving—he's just sitting there with his handkerchief in his hand—I decide to get it myself and open the door.

"Let me," he says suddenly, getting out in kind of a hurry. A speedboat way out on Loon Lake spews a plume of water twice the length of the boat and three times as high. Dad pockets his handkerchief and pats me on the shoulder as he opens the trunk. Just like that, his sudden head cold is gone, and he seems to realize the freedom he's given himself. No way am I gonna look at his face. Because if I do, the right thing to say might be *good-bye*. And then my stupid chin will start to quiver. And then?

I'm just sick of the tears, man.

Cabin Row is to my left, starting with Cabin 1. Behind it, just like always, is the big white birch tree. It's pretty much the same as it was the last two summers, but the—whatever it really is, the something that made the camp so different from home— isn't there. Maybe just a *few* things are missing, maybe a whole lot. One of the things missing is my excitement to be there. The giant pine trees, the lake, the sandy dirt at my feet. They're all there. Maybe *I'm* one of the things missing. I'm afraid to ask Dad just to take me back home. Kind of afraid, really, of what his answer'll be.

But since in the past couple of months I've learned to fake a smile or two, Dad's come to the conclusion that spending the summer of 1970 in my...Very. Favorite. *Place*...will do me some good.

It'll recharge your batteries, Ted. That's what he told me.

Recharge my *batteries*. Okay. What does that even mean? Does watching your mom burn in a wrecked Corvair drain batteries? I don't *have* batteries, Dad.

The only thing I know, next to that big fat birch tree, is that being eleven in 1969 is a lot different than pushing thirteen in 1970 with a dead mom.

White Birch Camp. *Whoop-de-Doo.* Looks to me like I no longer *have* a favorite place.

~~~

That's how I was that day, and that memory is just as clear as my first at White Birch. It may be even clearer. If I'd written it down like I wanted to but never did, that's pretty much how I would have stated my position. Now that I'm grown, with graying hair and occasional back pain, I guess I might be a little less flip about drop-off day in 1970. I might have seen things a little—or a lot—differently. After all, the bottom bunk issue wasn't exactly at the core of my woes.

I've read that memories tied strongly to emotion last the longest, especially if they come from childhood. That's what White Birch Camp was to me (and to almost everyone who ever spent a summer there), a bundle of stark, childhood memories. My indelible, emotion-tied experience there is a packed, canvas duffel bag that hangs on my shoulder to this day.

It took me thirty years to realize I'll never be able to shrug it off. Just how *that* little revelation came to me, though, is a story for another time, and it's a big one.

This particular story, as it needs to be told, began when I decided not to talk before getting out of Dad's GTO. Loon Lake's surface gleamed. In its late afternoon, the water was green in the shallows and midnight blue further out. The ribbon of unmolested forest stretched across the other side, reaching

8

around to the state park on the right and all the way around to the seven cabins on my left. The sky—or at least the part the enormous pines and oaks let me see—was deep and vast and full of playful white cumulus clouds. The cool breeze carried the smell of pine sap.

Mr. Dinwiddie, the camp director, stood from a picnic table near the front of Cabin 1. Campers signed in there with him when they arrived. His lumberjack physique, barbershop quartet face (complete with his funny, handlebar mustache), and gregarious nature were synonymous with what I once considered magical about that camp. In my first two summers, I learned to respect and admire him. He was the kind of guy who, after ten months away, I'd normally jump out of a car to greet. But not that day.

Right then, outside of the car, it happened after all. My chin quivered. I didn't know what was wrong with me. It'd been eight months, but the tears still seemed to come from time to time.

As Dad hefted my duffel out of the trunk, I busied myself watching a pair of swans paddle past the far end of the waterfront's dock. The structure was big, like field goal uprights lying on top of the water.

I was glad no do-gooder waltzed up and called the day beautiful.

It was time to step into Cabin Row, a lazy arc made of seven cabins and a larger cabin-like Headquarters. In '68 and '69, those cabins lived and breathed with boys running in and out. They sheltered us, ran water, and burned lights when we needed them. They were dynamic, living things. But that moment in 1970, those cabins might as well have been solid blocks of wood, props on a stage or display.

It was as though I'd come, not to White Birch Camp, but to a life-sized model of it, a diorama in which the artist failed to capture the camp's essence. And sure enough, in front of Headquarters, stood a model of the giant white birch tree that had been in a dozen of my long-vanished, happiest dreams. Steadfast, its branches moved around in the same wind that chopped the lake's surface into whitecaps. In previous summers, the birch's leaves waved at me, but not that day. Not anymore.

Will Dad be lonely at home with me gone? I worried about him. But then came Mom's voice. *Don't be silly, Ted. That empty house is just what he wants.*

CHAPTER 3

MR. DINWIDDIE WALKED toward us, leaving a young woman sitting at the table. When I faced him, he said, "Hi, Ted! Glad to see you!"

I managed to wave. Dad shut the trunk, my duffel over his shoulder. He gave Mr. Dinwiddie the old-fashioned, cheerful *Good afternoon!* he kept in his back pocket at home.

"Safe drive?" Mr. Dinwiddie asked. "Up from...where in Indiana?" His smiling eyes were the shapes of two rising suns. They were deep, full, and true. You might think our hometown was going to be the most exciting thing he'd ever heard.

"Blue River," I said, and I couldn't help grinning a little.

"Blue River!" he said with even more enthusiasm than I expected. "*Blue* River to *White* Birch. How silly of me to forget." He extended a hand for a grip that'd impress Dad. "How have you been, Ted?"

The sincerity in his voice compelled me to answer in some way I wished was enough. But whatever I said to him that day, I'd spun up from an expanding warehouse of pat phrases designed to appease.

Mr. Dinwiddie shook hands with my dad and stepped back to the picnic table, as though to get something.

"You ready to go, Buddy Boy?" Dad said.

Nope. I wasn't ready to go at all.

"All right," he said, "let's go."

"Dad. Wait. I should just go." I was not going to let my

11

chin quiver again. At least not in front of people.

"You sure?"

"I'm sure." I wouldn't dare hug him, or I'd cry.

"Okay."

He put my duffel on the ground and reached to hug me. *He has to hug me, doesn't he? As a dad?* His motivation in doing so was unclear, but I hugged back and squeezed hard. Just in case. It took all I had to still those tired muscles in my chin and the glands in my eyes.

Mr. Dinwiddie returned to us with the young woman. "Ted, this is Karen," he said. "She'll walk you down to Cabin Seven. I'll see you at dinner line-up in a short while." His rising sun eyes sparkled when he said, "Welcome back to White Birch."

He and Dad walked to the picnic table. I slung my duffel onto my shoulder.

"Hi, Ted," Karen extended her hand. "I'm Karen Dinwiddie."

"Dinwiddie?"

"Yep. Mr. Dinwiddie's daughter."

I took her hand in mine. She, too, had a fine grip. When the breeze tousled her red hair, I smelled something like perfume, but only faintly. It was a good fragrance—nothing like some old lady's, and nothing that makes you want to wave your hand in front of your face, saying *Eeeww*. It was nice. It may have been a lotion of some kind or maybe just the lingering scent of shampoo.

She released her grip and pushed the blown strands of hair out of her face. With the other, she held a notebook and a paperback with a faded cover, its edges yellow.

On the book's front, beneath a title I couldn't quite see, a giant crustacean stood, as though roaring, on a cratered planet. The creature had an anguished man in one claw and a frightened, mini-skirted woman in the other. A round UFO whisked away somewhere. It seemed strange for a woman like Karen to read the kind of science fiction Dad shared with me.

"Crawdads from outer space?" I asked, pointing at the book.

"I think they're more like lobsters," she said, handing it over. "Do you want to read it? I just finished."

I took the book. Her gesture brightened a dark world for a second, like a struck match. But it didn't seem to last. I stepped off, toward Cabin 7.

She came along dutifully, asking questions her dad probably told her to ask. *Where are you from? How long was your drive?* Usually tiresome to answer, the questions seemed okay coming from her.

We passed the front of Cabin 1. To my left, between the cabin's rear and Headquarters, stood the big birch. For a second, maybe it waved to me. Maybe not. A black squirrel, a mythic beast unknown in southern Indiana, skittered up a red pine's trunk, pausing at the clothesline tied to the tree. Off to the right and down the bluff between the big dock and the boathouse, a million slivers of sunlight glinted from the shallow water. A couple of one-man sailboats tacked along in the distance. From another gust, I caught a little of the fragrance again. The trees above up whispered.

I got the impression Dad was talking to Mr. Dinwiddie about Mom. Somewhere around Cabin 2, I stopped to see, and sure enough, there he was with the director.

He lifted his arm in a wave. "Love you, Buddy! Take care!"

Something like happiness played in his voice. No doubt about it. Normally, Dad wouldn't say *I love you* in public. And normally, I'd be embarrassed. But under the circumstances, I was damned glad to hear it.

Until I felt like a hobo leaving home. The duffel resting on my shoulder might be a four-foot stick with a red, polka-dot bag hanging off its far end. It was as though I walked the tracks leading out of town, waiting for the next train to hop, being told to go see what the world has to offer. Dad might be saying good-bye, after all. Maybe that happiness in his voice was because I was in White Birch, and he was finally going to be alone, all the way down there, in Blue River.

A part of me pictured him in his GTO, its top down, wind in his hair, laughing all the way home.

That's why I answered the way I did. *"I love you too, Dad!"* I waved at him with my free arm. And then, I blurted, "I'll miss you!"

Karen waited patiently. Before I turned back to finish the trek down Cabin Row, I heard something. It was a high-pitched, sing-song kind of voice with a fake lisp.

"Love you too, Daa-deeee! I'll *MITH* yoooooo!" said one of the sixty-odd strangers I'd meet that summer. This one, who stood outside Cabin 5, was extraordinarily tall. He had one hand on a perversely jutted hip and his opposite leg turned out. His other arm was high above his head, wrist flexed severely, waving with just the fingers. If the kid had been in a tacky dress, he'd look like what my dad and his policeman buddies might call a two-dollar street-walker. The son-of-a-bitch was mocking me.

I had no choice but to continue walking toward him, since my cabin was down that way. The kid strutted over to the bench—*The* bench I shared with Dad in '68—and stepped up on its seat. There, posed, arms akimbo, one foot out front, toes tapping. "Yooo-*Hooooooo!*" he shouted, waving one set of fingers from his hip.

"As long as he's not in Cabin Seven," I said out loud.

"One can only hope," Karen said.

I wanted to turn to see Dad one more time, but I didn't, because I knew he'd probably be gone.

CHAPTER 4

THE KID HOPPED over the back of the bench. Dusty clouds poofed up at his feet as he landed and jogged away, into Cabin 7. Fresh disappointment weighed on me.

As though reading my mind, Karen said, "Aw, *man*," and became my instant ally.

"It was really nice of you to say that to your dad," she said.

That's when I first really saw her face. Her eyebrows were the same dark red as her flowing hair. Shaped like wings above her green irises, the left had a streak of blonde in it. Her lips appeared soft and pillowy. They stretched gently and parted a little as something inside told me I was staring. It's hard to know how long she let me study her face as we strolled.

Some kid leaning against the doorframe of Cabin 6 whistled at her, and she didn't even seem to know the whistle was for her. Karen was built almost like a grown woman, her shoulders back with good posture. But otherwise, she carried herself like a kid who wasn't aware of her looks. If somebody put me to the task of describing her, I'd've found the word *pretty* didn't do the job. It didn't even come close.

"Most kids would be afraid to say that in front of a bunch of strangers," she said, her gaze on mine.

"To say what?"

"'I love you.'"

My throat parched when she said that. In a reflex, I swallowed with my mouth open.

"To their *parents*, I mean," she added hastily. "In front of a bunch of *strangers*."

"*Oh*. Yeah. I imagine they would."

I know what you mean, because I'd normally be the same way. But Dad's all I have now. He's a good dad, and I probably don't say so enough. That's why I stopped to say 'bye.

I was glad I said 'I love you' to him. Just in case.

The duffel strap slipped off my shoulder and I shrugged it back up.

"Are you really just twelve?" she said.

"Be thirteen in September." It was anybody's guess how old she was. I wasn't sure how old college girls were supposed to be. But by then, I didn't think she was in college.

"But you're so tall," she said.

"Mmm-hm."

"Not so tall as that kid who just ran into your cabin, but you're just, kind of...*big* for your age."

When an awful silence fell, she deftly took on another subject, narrowing her eyes. "You know...since you're a what? Three-year veteran of White Birch? You need to tell the new kids about The Sloth."

I stopped and faced her, as though she didn't have my full attention already. The Loon Lake Sloth. The number-one camp legend of White Birch. The man-eating, ground-dwelling, prehistoric beast that lives only in the woods of northern Michigan and cleaves down massive trees—and unlucky boys—with one swipe of its giant, two-toed claws. It was what boys at White Birch came to fear once setting their imaginations on what might live out there, in all those woods.

The Loon Lake Sloth was ten times as frightening as any bear. Especially at night, when they turn out the lights.

"How do you know about The Sloth?" I asked.

"Well," she said, rolling her gaze upward. "I *am* the director's daughter." She mimicked certain women on T.V., primping her hair with the upturned palm of one hand.

And she's also funny. My God.

I wanted to be close to her, maybe to hug her or touch her hair or something. Not that I was, at twelve, interested in girls in the slightest. An image of Mom—smiling as proudly as she ever could—popped up in my mind and embarrassed me. The only answer I could come up with was, "Hmm. Then I bet you know all kinds of secrets around here." I peeled my gaze off her and stepped once again toward Cabin 7.

The essence of the camp is what made the Big Birch wave at me. It's what Mr. Dinwiddie called White Birch Magic. And right there, that day on Cabin Row, Karen was awash with it.

As we strolled past Cabin 6 where that caterwauling jerk still stood quietly in the doorway watching, a gangly young man emerged from Cabin 7. He wore sandals, cut-off jean shorts and a bandana tied around his long, stringy hair. Matted, premature hairs dirtied his chin and upper lip.

"Good afternoon?" the young man said, lacking Dad's sincerity. "Ted or Cornelius? Ted, probably?"

"Ted."

The young man had a contrived enthusiasm. Dad might call him a hippie from the university.

"Cabin Seven counselor," the guy said, making his statement sound like a question. He pointed to my duffel.

"Name's Cliff? Help you with that?"

I dropped the bag off my shoulder, letting it slide into the crook of my elbow, then down my arm to my hand.

"Blue River?" he asked.

"Blue River, Indiana."

The way he made everything sound like a question felt like he doubted my intelligence. For someone so unkempt, he seemed a little...something funny I didn't know how to describe. He just carried an air of *I know more than you.* I immediately disliked him, but even then, the facts were on the table. That day, I hardly liked anyone or any*thing.*

He took my duffel by the strap. When I let go, its weight pushed some air out of him as it fell to the ground.

Karen gasped.

"Whoa," Cliff said. "Heavy. Let's go on in and introduce you to the guys," he said. I slung the duffel back onto my shoulder. Something inside gave me the good sense to thank Karen for walking with me. When an acute embarrassment grabbed me, I dropped her green-eyed gaze and climbed the stoop into the cabin.

CHAPTER 5

INSIDE, A FAT kid off to the right, in a kind of school picture pose, showed me all his teeth. It was almost as though he expected me. To my left, the tall smartass who'd mocked me from the bench leaned back, his elbows on the bunk and his legs crossed at the ankles.

He hummed a melody to the same words he'd sung to me moments before, *Love you too, Daa-deeeee! I'll MITH yoooooo!* I wanted to punch him in the face.

Cliff said "Hey guys! This is Ted. Ted? These are the other guys. We'll make introductions after dinner." To me, that meant Cliff couldn't remember the other guys' names.

The cabin was just like I thought it would be, like my other cabins in past years. The front section was reserved for the counselor, whose area was on the right as I entered the door. A thin wall of unfinished plywood and open doorway in the middle separated the counselor's area from the largest area, the bunk room. Another plywood wall in back separated the cubbies, sinks, toilet, and shower from the bunks. Above that back section was the loft, which stored the empty trunks, duffels, and suitcases for the summer.

The loft was as alluring as it was off-limits to campers.

The inside of the cabin was unfinished pine lumber from floor to ceiling. The graffiti of yesteryear's campers was everywhere: walls, rafters, cross-ties. All the way up to the ceiling's apex.

The living area was, of course, full of strangers, and I didn't want to meet them. Didn't want to know them, didn't want to spend two months living with them. One was off to the left, a kid I thought I remembered from another cabin in '69. He was well-groomed, regarding me with some genuine, non-threatening interest. Another couple guys of average size sat on a bottom bunk to the right, reading what appeared to be a *Mad* magazine. A shrimpy kid with white hair and pale skin sat on a bottom bunk, open-mouthed and staring off distantly. The smartass held a truculent glare. Heeding Mom's advice, though, I tried to ignore him. The happy fat kid had taken to digging in his suitcase.

"Any of these bunks strike your fancy?" Cliff asked me.

Each side of the cabin had two sets of steel bunk beds. Off in one corner sat an unclaimed, wooden, single-decker. It was the odd man out, like me. I staked the claim and dropped my duffel on it.

"Looks like a decision's been made!" Cliff said. "Okay, guys. Keep settling in. Make Ted at home." Cliff strolled toward the front of the cabin.

"Cliff?" I asked suddenly, pointing to the back wall of the counselor area. He faced me, his chin and eyebrows up, listening. "Is it okay if I move my bunk up to the other wall?"

"Sure?" he said, "I don't see why not? What's up, if you don't mind me asking?"

"I just don't want people standing on my bunk to get up into the loft. Gets sand in the sheets. I figured moving it up to the other end would fix that."

"Oh. I see. From what I hear, the loft is off limits anyway, but whatever floats your boat."

Just then, everyone stopped what he was doing and studied the loft. Amateur counselor. He probably had no idea how forcefully he'd just stoked a flame of desire to break the no-loft rule.

The serious, well-groomed kid—I remembered his name was something like Dan or Danny—appeared next to me at my bunk.

What's he want?

"Hey, Ted. Denny." He stuck out his hand. "Cabin Four last summer. Have a good year?"

Kid had a good handshake. Good grab, good squeeze. "No. Not really."

"Sorry to hear that." He didn't pry for information. "I just came over to help you move that bed. I'll grab this end, and you grab that one?" And just like that, after stepping over a duffel bag and a trunk lying in the middle of the floor, we had the bed moved to the place I'd wanted, on the front end of the living area.

"Call me Buck," he said, wiping his palms together after he set his end of the bed on the floor.

"Buck?"

"Yeah. One thing that went wrong last year is that we didn't have nicknames in the cabin."

"That didn't seem like a problem in my cabin."

"Wasn't in mine, either, but it just seems like we should have nicknames."

"Okay. Buck."

"How 'bout you? What should your nickname be?"

"Ted."

"But that's your name."

"You can call it my nickname if you want."

He looked disappointed but after a minute said, "All right."

Buck sure seemed to think he was God's gift to White Birch or maybe even all of humanity. But at least he'd come over to help. To what I figured was my own credit, I shrugged off the indignity of some other kid trying to decide whether he approved of my own name. And besides, he seemed nice enough.

Buck stepped back to the table and surveyed the bunks on my side of the cabin. "Hey, everybody," he said, pointing to the bunk with the *Mad* magazine readers but talking to everyone. "The cabin's lopsided now. Let's move this bunk off into the corner we just opened up."

Those boys seemed to check for the others' reactions, closed the magazine, and stood up. Buck recruited the fat kid to help slide the metal double-bunk into the corner from which we'd just moved my single. Buck, the fat kid, and the *Mad* readers were four boys at work with a foreman.

Next, the fat kid asked for help moving his bunk lengthwise, against the outer wall, just beneath the high-set cabin windows. The four of them did it.

Buck said to the fat kid, "I like your bunk like that, under the windows. Let's get mine!" The crew traversed the space and manhandled Buck's bunk (the shrimpy kid never got off the bottom bunk as they did) against the wall, mirroring the other side of the cabin.

"There," Buck said. "That's better. There's a lot more room

in here to boot. What do you guys think?" he asked no one in particular, and he got plenty of affirmative responses. It was a simple thing Buck did, helping move the bunks around and delegating duties, but he had everyone's attention, even mine.

Smartass never lifted a finger. Standing in his corner, he said with a threateningly deep, articulated voice and dismissive tone that all together suggested a great deal of intelligence, "My bunk's just fine, everybody. Thanks for asking."

"Nobody asked you," the shrimp said.

Smartass took a step or two, then a fake lunge at the little kid, who jumped and let out a yelp. Smartass laughed and went back to his corner. He took a prodigious leap from the floor and landed, sitting comfortably, on his top bunk. Then, he flipped open a pocketknife and sliced a curl of bark off the stick he'd been holding.

CHAPTER 6

I MOVED TO the foot of my bed a slender, free-standing set of stacked shelves that looked like a narrow book case. Each camper had a set to hold his clothes, books, and toiletries. Anticipating daily cabin inspections for rights to be the first to go to meals, I finished unpacking my duffel.

The fat kid dragged a chair from the table and stood on it, to spread sheets on his own, top bunk. He wore a navy-blue T-shirt with a little pocket on its upper, left front, jeans held up by a wide, leather belt, and brand-new tennis shoes, no doubt bought for camp. The legs of his jeans were turned up in six-inch cuffs. It was clear he had to wear pants cut for grown men just to accommodate his waist.

But he worked on his bed just the same, not seeming to mind any of it. He had the air of a man in his workshop. All-in-all, he radiated a contentedness I couldn't fathom. It was a wonder he wasn't whistling—the way Dad used to before what happened to Mom.

I watched secretly while ordering my shelves. He spread a bottom sheet, then a top sheet, carefully but quickly tucking in the corners as he went. Then, he took from his trunk a perfect, traditional, red-plaid wool blanket and spread it across his bed, arranging it around the pillow he'd put at the end closer to me. My own, unmade bed, a plastic mattress with parallel, blue stripes, gleamed in the light of the naked bulbs.

When he was finished, Big Cuffs glanced at me, and I

pretended to be busy. He returned the chair to the table and said to me, "I can help you, if you'd like. Make your bed, I mean."

No, I thought as pure reflex, *I don't need your help. I don't need anybody's help. I can do it myself, so go away.* I faced him, maybe to tell him to buzz off and mind his own business. His face was chubby, and the corners of his mouth were turned up naturally, in a neutral, friendly-appearing expression.

"Okay," I heard myself say. "That'd be nice. Thank you."

"I'm Zeke," he said without trying to shake hands. "From Missoula, Montana. You're Ted?"

I nodded as he stepped toward my bunk and peered through my duffel's open zipper. He pulled out two folded sheets and a blanket.

"I wonder who my bunkmate's gonna be," he said. Zeke's bottom bunk was the only one left.

"I think his name's Cornelius," I said.

Right then, I heard a squeaking sound. Buck seemed to take notice, too, and no one else. It was a sound the two of us had heard a thousand times, the squeak of the bell. Just north of Headquarters, a stout, wooden tower stood maybe fifteen feet tall with a bell on top. A rope ran from the top of the bell through one of two knotholes on the nearest wall of Headquarters.

From inside that room, someone pulled on the rope and got the bell moving. When it first swung, before the clapper engaged, it squeaked. At wake-up, call-to-quarters, and line-up, three meals a day, the bell would speak to us. *Bong! B-Bong B-Bong, Bong, Bong!* The sound was in the camp veterans' bones.

"What's that?" Zeke whispered.

"Sounds like suppertime," I said.

"I guess we'll make your bed after that." Zeke followed my lead up to Headquarters. It was tradition to run to line-up, so we did. When we got there, the big birch tree was different somehow. A few of its leaves waved. Zeke's face was flushed from the running, as he regarded the dozens of unfamiliar boys being directed, in their inattention and dusty footing, into seven lines for seven cabins.

We made the quarter-mile hike to the dining hall, and we ate the usual fare. Macaroni and cheese, quartered peaches that had come out of enormous cans, and hamburgers. It was pretty much school food.

After supper, Zeke and I walked back to the cabin. He asked how the days worked at camp, how much free time we had, how deep the lake was, things like that. The camp had no organized activities on that first day, so it was free-recreation (*free-rec* is what they called it) until call-to-quarters before bed. Cliff milled around the front of the cabin but didn't seem to encourage anyone to do anything. The *Mad* magazine boys took off to shoot baskets. Others played ping-pong behind Cabins 3 and 4, and some went to explore the woods, probably breaking boundary rules as they did.

A couple of boys with baseball gloves struck up a game of pickle in front of cabins two and three. It was a simple but fun game—two basemen trying to throw out a runner between them. It was a camp game nobody ever played at home.

Feeling vaguely lost, I wandered out toward my bench in front of Cabin 5 and sat down. Squared in my seat and leaning against the back support, my feet were flat on the ground. The far shore took on a majestic, orange glow from the sun in its descent behind me. I couldn't help but think it was pretty. The water's deep blue middle had calmed from earlier in the day. The whitecaps were gone. Only gentle swells and shallow troughs remained.

I sat there long enough for a few games of pickle to play out and to see a couple more swans paddle by. A small gust brought me the scents of pine needles and sap. A speedboat, too far away to make any sound, sped across the blue like an airplane in the sky, leaving a white, foamy trail.

The orange glow on the distant confluence of trees intensified as the near-shore's shadows crawled across the lake. A few white birch trees over there shined at me like neon lights. Since '68 and '69, I'd spent untold hours on that bench, thinking about (and even talking to) Mom and Dad, sometimes just thinking. And wondering what it was like over there.

Then there was the other thing. Mom. I didn't know if I was supposed to try to talk to her or not. Or Dad, really.

Twelve's too old, isn't it? Almost thirteen?

It was silly, after all, to talk across a mile of water to some trees that were supposed to be Mom and Dad. In '68, I believed in it the way a little kid might think he's invisible if he closes his eyes. In '69, I still talked to the far shore, but I quieted my voice, worried someone might hear me. Between then and the summer of '70, I'd experienced a lot of adult things, and I just felt too old to talk to a bunch of trees a mile away.

But I was there. I made sure no one was nearby.

"Hi," I said.

My own voice startled me. Then Mom's appeared and put

a familiar pain behind my eyes.

Come on, Ted! You can do it!

"Hi, Mom," I whispered. It didn't hurt. Not much, anyway. Except in my chin.

Hi, sweetie! she said, just as something new caught my eye. From the darkness behind a pair of stout birches, a short and round light burned. It was faint. I almost leaned forward to get a better look, the way you stand on your toes to see a dim star in the sky. It wasn't lost on me that I'd seen the new light in the trees right when I heard Mom's greeting. The tired old hand of grief massaged my throat, no longer choking me like it once did.

Then, the rhythmic squeak cut through the evening air. A few more of those, and the bell would ring.

"Call-to-quarters!" shouted a guy named Alex, Cabin 1's counselor. Dozens of pattering feet ran behind me and into the cabins. The sky's deepest blue seemed to darken one more shade, as though whoever rang the bell in Headquarters had just pressed a button. I left my special bench and headed back to Cabin 7, thinking of Mom and wondering about Dad.

CHAPTER 7

BY THE TIME I entered the cabin, Buck had taken charge of the roster Cliff left on the table. Buck held court, headlong into his nonsense of assigning nicknames. Cliff was nowhere to be found.

"Say hello to Teddy!" Buck said, as though I'd made a red-carpet entrance, wearing a tux.

"Call me *Ted*."

"But that's your—"

"Yes. It's my real name. I thought we covered this."

If Buck thought it wasn't reasonable for me to go by my own *name,* that was his problem. But I'd made the place quiet, and I felt the need to concede a little.

"*Ted* only has one syllable," I said, "and you can't do better than that in a nickname, anyway."

"For you," Smartass said from his corner, "I could do a *lot* better."

A hot flame ran through my neck, but I ignored it.

So, apparently, did Buck. "Good point, Ted," he said. "Okay, who's next?"

Zeke said meekly, "Um...*Zeke* only has one syllable."

Smartass made a *t-sick* sound and rolled his eyes.

Don't pick on Zeke, you asshole.

"Okay," Buck said. "Everyone okay with the name *Zeke*?"

"A kid's name is a kid's name, Buck," I said. "He doesn't need a new one, does he?"

"I think we can make another exception," Buck said.

Zeke leaned against his bunk with an incredulous, self-satisfied grin, like he'd just won a prize at the county fair. He cast me a glance. It occurred to me I liked Zeke. A kid from Sheboygan, Wisconsin, one of the *Mad* magazine kids, said something to me about my one-bunk bed being the couch in the cabin.

"Coach?" Buck said.

"No," the Sheboygan kid said. "Coach. Like sofa."

"Oh," Buck said. "You have an accent."

A Wisconsin accent. *Coach* is the way he said *couch*, so *Coach* is the name Buck gave him. And *Coach* seemed pretty happy to take the moniker. The other *Mad* kid, a muscular, sun-bleached guy from San Diego, seemed like your average middle-school kiss-ass, and *Sunny* became his name. A rail-thin and sinewy kid from west of Chicago became *Bones*.

The creep in the corner continued his whittling, creating a growing pile of shavings on the floor.

Buck said, "Not supposed to have any kind of weapon here. Mr. Dinwiddie'll send you *home* if he finds it. Right, Ted?"

"That's right," I said.

"In fact, a few years ago, they sent a kid home for it. Isn't that right?"

"Yep."

"That kid had a funny nickname, didn't he?"

"Toad."

"Do you know the story?"

Did I know the story. Of *course* I did. "I was *here*."

"You were *here*?"

31

"It was nineteen sixty-eight."

All eyes were suddenly on me. It seemed like all a veteran had to do is allude to a previous summer to gain special attention from the newcomers.

Toad was a weird kid with thick glasses that magnified the iris of the eye so much it was all you could see in the lenses. He had a few bumps on his skin, but not exactly warts. With his underbite and a flat nose, his face was shaped in a way that gave him a perpetual frown. Kids called him *Toad*.

"Did you *know* him?" Buck asked.

"Yeah."

"So what happened, exactly?" Buck asked.

"Can't remember exactly how it started, but since he was funny-looking, somebody gave him a nickname he didn't like."

"What'd he do? This Toad kid?" Coach asked.

"Got mad and pulled a knife. Almost stabbed the other kid."

All eyes were on me, as though I was telling a ghost story. All we needed was darkness and a campfire. And maybe some snapping branches in the woods.

"Other kid probably deserved it," said the whittler, making figure-eights in the air with his blade.

"What else?" Coach asked.

I told the story. Toad went to Headquarters after pulling the knife. I'd seen him through Mr. Dinwiddie's office window, sitting in a certain wooden chair. If you were ever in Headquarters as a camper, that was bad enough. But to be parked in Mr. Dinwiddie's chair meant you were probably being sent home. Toad sat there, indifferent-seeming. He wore his frown, the exact one he had when he ate supper, brushed his teeth, and slept. He would've had the same face when he stabbed at the other kid.

"Guess he didn't read the camper's handbook," Buck said.

Smartass piped in, "*What* camper's handbook?"

The handbook was a several-page, stapled-together set of behavior standards for White Birch Camp. But I'd never read it.

"It has the rules in it," Buck said.

"Is one of the rules 'No stabbing people'?" Smartass asked.

"Not exactly, but it says 'no weapons.'"

Smartass held up his little knife. "*This* is a *weapon*?"

"According to the camp, it is."

"Well, then..." Smartass pulled a sheathed hunting knife out of his waistband. Jutting out from the hilt, the blade was about five inches long and curved at the end.

"Better hide that knife," Buck said.

"Mr. Din-whatever doesn't have to know about my knife."

Dinwiddie, you jerk-off. The kid had no respect for the place.

The little, blond-headed kid spoke again. "Now we *all* know about your knife."

"You gonna do something about it?" Smartass asked. The white-blond kid didn't answer.

"What about you?" Buck asked Smartass.

"What *about* me?"

"Nickname, I mean."

We all watched. I could've ponied up a few suggestions, but they all had more than one syllable.

"I'll take a nickname," the kid said, "if there's a little something in it for me."

"Like what?"

"You let me pick my own nickname, and you let me pick his." He pointed the five-inch blade at the blond kid.

"No!" the shrimp said. "You're not gonna give me my nickname." His sudden indignation startled everyone.

"Whoa!" Smartass said. "What the hell is this?"

'No bad words in the cabin' is another rule, fuck-face.

The shrimp's scalp reddened beneath his crown of baby-blond hair. A sprig stuck up like an antenna from the top of his head and seemed to vibrate.

"Hey," Buck said, holding up two hands in a *stop* posture. "You guys—"

"No, *Buck*," Smartass said. "We can take care of our*selves...Buck.*"

"You're a bully," said the little kid. "You want to be a leader, but nobody ever follows you. My mom told me there'll be boys like you—"

"Boys like me?" Smartass said, now leaning forward.

The cabin quieted. If we'd been in a saloon, like on those westerns Dad and I once watched together, even the out-of-tune piano would've stopped playing. All eyes were on Smartass.

"Whadda you mean, boys like me? Tall? Strong? *Smart?*"

"*Smart?* You don't look very smart."

"Oh, no? Why?"

"Hey," Buck said again. "That's probably enough—"

"No. It's not enough. I want to know why this little bastard thinks I'm not smart."

The word *bastard* seemed to confuse the little kid.

Buck surveyed me again, a little worry on his face. I thought it might be a good time for a counselor to show up, but no one did.

The shrimp went on. "My Dad says long-haired kids are stupid."

"Your hair looks like the top of a fuckin' *corn* plant. How smart do you think *that* I—"

"Stop," Buck said. "You two knock it off."

The little kid's face—he probably didn't hear a word Buck said—reddened still. His corn-tassel shook.

Smartass sliced another piece off his stick—this time with the big knife—and chuckled. His shoulders muscular and broad, he raised his eyebrows in a mocking, sad-clown kind of face. "Talk about smart, your mom seems pretty smart, dumping your sorry ass up here at camp for two months."

The little boy pursed his lips, and his whole body quaked.

"I bet she's at home right now just *dreaming* about leavin' you here for good."

"No, she's *not!*"

The tall kid made the sad clown face again. "*No, she TH'not!*"

The little kid stood up and faced his new adversary from about ten feet away. His little fists clenched as he stepped nearer Smartass's bed. The little boy's size and apparent willingness to fight didn't fit together. It was as though he was about to reveal hidden super-powers. Either the shrimp was in for a hell of a beating, or the knife-wielding creep was about to die bloody.

CHAPTER 8

THE BIG KID reared up and hoisted himself off his bunk, landing on the floor with a definitive, wooden thump that resonated through the hollow chamber of the cabin. His fingers gripped his knife, the blade jutted out, toward the kid. Some gasps rang out, and the blond kid lunged at the creep. Just then, Buck jumped from the table to a position between the two boys. I slipped quietly behind the blond little atomic bomb and grabbed him by the shoulders.

Letting out a half-growl and half-wheeze, he twisted out of my grasp. I crouched and restrained him with a hug from behind. His breathing was fast and shallow, through his nose.

"You put that knife down *now*," Buck said.

"Oh," smartass said, in what might have been honest surprise as he glanced at the knife in his hand. "Yeah. No intent." He put the knife on his bed and held up his hands.

Buck said, "And keep your big mouth shut. Leave this little guy alone."

"Okay," Smartass said. "A knife fight wasn't on the schedule tonight, anyway. I never stab anybody while they're awake."

"Shut up!" Buck said to Smartass, facing the taller kid. I stared in disbelief as the little kid wiggled to try to free himself. I whispered to him everything was going to be okay.

Then, as though nothing had happened, Smartass hopped back up on his bed.

The atomic-bomb kid stomped again, and I held my grasp. My face was close to his, and he seemed poised to bite. He shivered. His eyes were wide and seemed not to focus on anything.

Buck faced us. "Hold him still, Ted."

Zeke stepped over and stood next to Buck.

"Hey, Bud," Buck said to the kid. "You okay?"

The boy said nothing.

"It's going to be all right, Bud," Zeke said. "Is his name Bud?"

"Don't worry about that big old Hoss," Buck said. "Listen to Zeke. It's gonna be okay."

"I like 'Hoss!'" Smartass said with a giant grin. "And my last name's even *Cartwright*! Get it? Hoss Cartwright from *Bonanza*?"

Everyone ignored him.

The shrimpy kid's breathing slowed some, and I loosened my grip. "I'm gonna let go of you now," I told him. He didn't move.

"Tell you what," Buck continued. "Me and Ted'll walk outside with you and get you some fresh air. You like that, Bud?"

"Bud sounds like a good name," I added, lost for what to say. Dad called me *Bud* plenty of times.

The kid nodded. "*Goooood*," Buck said. "Let's go get some fresh air." I let go of the kid.

Buck was able to get his arm around Bud's shoulders and guide him toward the door.

The creep—*Hoss*, his name was now—whistled

something. It was a melody I recognized from one of Dad's little, forty-five singles. "Floatin' Down the Mississippi" it was called.

The song was from the fifties, its sugary-sweet innocence hopelessly out-of-date and almost embarrassing by 1970. I'd sung it with Dad enough times—before Mom died, anyway—that I still remember the words:

> *Floatin' down the MISS-issippi*
> *With my Polly ANN*
> *S'm TIMES I think the boat gets tippy*
> *When she takes my hand—WHOA!*

It was god-awfully strange to hear Hoss whistle it. But at the moment, it struck me as far more odd that he could be so nonchalant after almost causing two fights.

"I like *Hoss*," he broadcast from his bunk. "Just in case anybody gives a shit. It's a good name. Who watches *Bonanza*? Anybody?"

Everyone seemed afraid to speak.

"I like the *Bonanza* Hoss better," I muttered to myself.

Hoss tilted his head to one side, tented his eyebrows, and put a sudden drawl into his speech. "Got sump'm you wanna say to me, *Boy?*" The way he said *boy* sounded like *bowah*.

Is he making fun of me again? Of the way I talk?

I faced him. His truculent eyes incriminated a sliver of enjoyment. Leaning forward and matching his stare, I spoke clearly. "*I said I like the* Bonanza *Hoss better.*"

"Whoa," Hoss said, his eyes immediately playful. His lips

stretched and slipped apart. "Don't be so trigger-happy. You goin' getcher self into a *fight*. Y'ought not *start* a fight so early after y' come tuh camp. *Hey, y'awl, this here's Ted. Look laak he wanna start a faaght!*" He took his drawl away and said, "Maybe you should see my brother's shrink." His grin widened as he got back to his whittling.

Jerk-off.

Buck and I walked Bud toward the door, and Buck said in broadcast format, "You guys start brushing your teeth and get ready for bed, okay? It's gonna be lights out in a few minutes, and Cliff's not here to—"

"Ah," Mr. Dinwiddie said from the doorway of the cabin, shocking the three of us. "Do you know where your counselor is?"

I said, "I figured he was at Headquarters or something."

The handlebars of his mustache drooped a couple degrees, and his rising sun eyes narrowed almost imperceptibly.

I bet Cliff's really gonna be in for it.

"Is this young gentleman all right?" Mr. Dinwiddie asked, kneeling down to Bud.

"Hi, Mr. Dinwiddie," Bud said, cordial as can be.

This kid's not right.

"Thank you, Mr. McDaniel," Mr. Dinwiddie said, "for taking the initiative to get your cabin mates ready for bed." His grin came back, and he stayed with us.

Bud took off and grabbed some pajamas off his shelves. I went back toward my area. Hoss had hidden his knife and kicked the whittled shavings under Bones's bed. Zeke milled around the living space with light-blue, werewolf foam oozing

40

down his chin. It startled me for a second, before I noticed the green-sparkled butt of his hard-at-work toothbrush.

Over the next few minutes, Cliff showed up. Mr. Dinwiddie told him the last kid for our cabin would show up in the middle of the night. He also invited Cliff outside for a little talk. I got ready and turned out my light before Cliff came back in.

Just before lights out, I noticed something I hadn't before. Near the foot of my bed, a few inches above my shelves, there was a hole in the partition. After lights-out, I quietly crawled down to see what that hole in the wall would reveal. The opening had been drilled into the thin plywood for a reason I'd never learn, but it was in a good position for me to be able to see through the glass of the front door, past the leaves at the edge of the bluff's cottonwoods, and across the lake to that matching pair of birch trees.

The light I'd seen earlier was still there. It flickered.

Campfire, I thought. Had to be.

CHAPTER 9

AT DINNER LINE-up on the second day of camp, some older man told us about something we weren't allowed to do. To this day, I'm not sure who the guy was. Severe, dark-headed, and slight, he had slicked-back hair and might have been right out of a detective movie from the forties. He may have been the camp's owner. He spoke for what seemed like forever, saying not one thing worth remembering, except one. He forbade us in a way I cannot remember word-for-word, but his tone said:

> *The Office of the Director at White Birch Camp has chosen to ban graffiti in the cabins. We feel the camp has reached a kind of nostalgic zenith we wish not to sully further with writings, drawings, and the like. In their current states, inside and out, these cabins are to be considered essential components to the camp's historic landscape. They are part of White Birch's glorious past and should remain so into the future.*
>
> *Any further graffiti shall be considered vandalism and punishable accordingly.*

And that was that. After I asked to see the dictionary at Headquarters to figure out what a *nostalgic zenith* was, there was no way in hell, after that line-up, I would exit White Birch Camp's 1970 season without leaving my mark in Cabin 7. This was one of those stupid rules I knew would make Dad proud of me for breaking.

At supper that night, I finished early and left the dining hall. By the time I made it back, the sun had begun its several-hour descent in the sky, and Cabin Row was peaceful, empty. I went back to the cabin and collapsed on my bunk, my fingers laced behind my head. The only thing that interested me was my own inertia.

But my attention went to the graffiti. Directly above my bunk were short poems, names, and drawings. Snoopy and Woodstock grinned next to a poorly drawn but recognizable Jughead from the Archie comic series and a testimonial to somebody's favorite band, *Moby Grape*. One name, an actual carving I hadn't seen before, caught my eye.

It said:

CAL OWEN '38

Surely, I thought, Cal Owen must have been somewhere around twelve when he carved that. And surely, no camp director had held him hostage in supper line-up to drone about *nostalgic zeniths*. Nineteen thirty-eight. Seventy minus thirty-eight plus twelve would make old Cal forty-four when I discovered his graffiti. I couldn't begin to comprehend when I would be forty-four, in the year 2002. I searched the other names up there. *Milt Sweet* put up his name in 1931. Next to his name was *Russ Barnes*, 1927.

After just a few minutes, I stood to find their names on the plaques. For each summer since 1927, a plate-sized board cut into the shapes of shields, hung in the rafters. Each plaque represented one year and recorded its cabin members' names.

Lacquers or stains preserved most of the records. Others were just old, untreated and graying boards, bleeding rust from where the nails had split them.

I hunted for the plaques from '31, '27, and especially 1938, and I found them. *Russell Barnes*, *Milton Sweet*, and *Calvin P. Owen*. Their names were written as they'd appear in school yearbooks. But the plaques didn't tell me those boys went by Russ, Milt, and Cal. The plaques held their records of attendance. But the graffiti, written or carved, in their own hands, showed something of the people they were. On the plaques were the lists, and in the graffiti, the proof. The continuity was pleasing, almost eerie.

At the end of camp, they'd hang a plaque from 1970. And now the graffiti—my proof of living—was forbidden. It wasn't fair. I was going to create my own *nostalgic zenith*, and that old man at dinner line-up could suck it.

Two voices came up from outside. It was Zeke and the camper who had arrived in the middle of the night before, Cornelius Shepherd. Neil, as he liked to be called, had gotten in too late to make his bed. I lent him my sleeping bag. Early that morning, he sat up and scraped his head on the mattress and springs above him, which sagged under Zeke's weight. Neil confided he'd never been to camp before as he thanked me for lending the sleeping bag. I told him I was happy to do it and that the kid above him was good at making beds.

I remember thinking immediately Neil was at least as smart as Zeke. He told me his dad was a University of Michigan history professor who had always been active in the civil rights movement. Like Zeke, Neil brought a box full of books. When he got to talking about something academic, maybe about public unrest or Vietnam, he sniffed, cleared his throat, and pushed up his horn-rimmed glasses as his speech accelerated.

He was able to convince Zeke to switch bunks. The three of us ended up eating breakfast together. I liked them both. That night, after dinner, as I stood reading plaques, the two of them walked into the cabin. Neil grabbed his swimming trunks from his shelves and pulled off his shirt. His dark skin stretched tightly over a solid stack of muscle.

"Your name is Ted, right?" he asked, "And not part of this *nickname* bullshit?"

Zeke was shocked at the language, and I reached a milestone: unbridled laughter. It was my first since Mom died. Neil put a signature on the conversation with his own, deep giggle.

"Yep," I said, my laughter calming slowly. "My name is Ted."

"That sounds good to me," Neil said. "I didn't know what to expect up here. My dad told me it would be good for me. Said something about it being an *opportunity to grow*. Which, from him, meant I'd probably be the only black kid."

I didn't know what to say about that. Neither, it appeared, did the usually chatty Zeke.

"But so far, it doesn't seem like much of a problem," He mocked shifty eyes at us and said, "You guys seem all right...so *far*, anyway."

I definitely liked these guys.

Neil went on. "There's that tall kid, Hoss. He's a smartass. We have them at home. And that bossy kid. Buck. Nickname-man. And that weird kid from Nebraska."

Bud. Neil didn't even have the pleasure of Bud's flip-out the night before, but he already knew something was wrong with the kid.

"Sounds like there are a lot of rules around here," Neil said, pointing up and around the walls. "No more graffiti. Why aren't we allowed to become part of this place's 'glorious past'?"

Zeke, sounding uneasy, said, "Rules are rules, I guess."

"Rules are for dummies who don't know any better," I said.

Neil snickered and said, "I'm gonna use that statement when I get home. I'm also gonna go swim. Who's with me?"

I was. So was Zeke. I glanced at Cal Owen's name once more. Already, I pictured my name up there, on the ceiling or wall, etched into the wood with Zeke's and Neil's. We'd leave our *proof.*

To hell with the 1970 plaque, I heard my dad say—and my mom's admonishing voice: Roy. Don't talk that way around Ted.

Zeke, Neil, and I got ready and headed toward the waterfront. A chilling scream would send two of us running back.

CHAPTER 10

I SPLASHED AROUND in the shallows with Zeke, and Neil swam laps. He told us "I need my exercise," but he got a lot more than what I'd call exercise. He swam expertly for around twenty minutes, back and forth between the field-goal-uprights part of the dock. Zeke seemed to prefer the shallows, where he could see the bottom. He asked me once if I'd ever seen the teeth on a northern pike, and I decided I didn't want to know about them. I took a prone position, my legs floating behind me, and pulled myself around on the bottom. Zeke sat cross-legged and hovered his arms over the undulating surface. He seemed fine with what would be his home for the next two months.

After Neil was done with his laps, he joined us in the knee-deep water. Zeke made an announcement.

"I have to pee."

Me: "Okay."

Zeke: "I mean pretty soon."

Neil: "Just go in the lake, man."

"I can't do that!"

"Sure you can."

"Nuh-uh."

Me: "*I* just did."

Neil giggled, and Zeke made a worried face. "I can't. It's unsanitary."

Neil: "Swimming in a *lake* is unsanitary."

47

"I'm gonna go back to the cabin," Zeke said, standing up. He seemed torn between running and standing still to cross his legs.

When Neil and I decided we were done swimming anyway, Zeke was already on the dock and half way to the beach house. As Neil and I climbed onto the dock, Zeke was half way up the bluff. He gained on Bud, who kicked up dust as he rambled from the top of the waterfront toward Cabin 7. Down Cabin Row, Hoss stood on the bench, facing Bud. He hopped down and ran to Cabin 7.

I knew immediately he was up to something.

Zeke made good time, like a kid in school who really wants to run but isn't allowed to. Something about the whole thing bothered me, and not just that my new buddy had to pee.

Neil and I left the waterfront, and a counselor who doubled as a lifeguard scratched our names off a clipboard. We headed for the cabin.

"When a man's gotta go, a man's gotta go," Neil said.

I grinned but didn't say anything. Neil was headstrong. Zeke was nice as anyone could be, but he struck me as fragile in some way. Down Cabin Row, where the cottonwoods wagged their leaves like a thousand puppies' tails, Hoss was nowhere to be seen. Neil and I were maybe two cabins behind Bud.

Zeke stole into the cabin door, unquestionably headed straight for the toilet. Somewhere around the time Bud wandered up past Cabin 6, I heard a toilet flush and the bathroom door slap shut.

"I bet Zeke's feeling better," I said.

"Mm-hm," Neil said.

What happened next I wasn't there to see. But according to what Zeke would tell Neil and me that night, it went this way:

Zeke finished his urgent business in the bathroom, as Hoss stood casually in the counselor area, peeking through a curtain. Zeke took the opportunity to take off his swim trunks and put on his underwear. Just then, Hoss tiptoed quickly back toward Zeke, jumped up on my bed, and hid behind my shelves.

"What are you doing?" Zeke asked.

"*Shhhh!*" went Hoss.

The door opened.

Neil and I were somewhere around Cabin 6 by then. Bud entered the cabin, and just as he passed from the counselor area to the bunkroom, Hoss poked his head around *my* shelves and let out a scream that sounded like a girl being murdered.

What followed, as far as I could tell, was another scream, then unintelligible, yelling speech that devolved into something like a young wolf's growl. Then, another scream, this one high-pitched. Then came an adult-sounding voice—Hoss's—yelling *Stop it! STOP!*

Neil and I took off, running to Cabin 7. When we dashed inside, Bud stood over Zeke, who had rolled into a self-protective ball on the floor. Bare legs crossed at the ankles, his fat rolls jiggled every time Bud's slapping and punching hands connected with his back. Zeke yelped in fear with each strike. He wore nothing more than his store-new tightie-whitie underwear and held his hands and arms to his face.

"Stop!" Neil yelled, just as Hoss finally got both his arms around Bud, pinning the kid's arms at his sides.

I was petrified for a moment as Hoss dragged Bud to the middle of the cabin. He spoke in soothing words to the little monster, trying to calm him.

Zeke convulsed with sobs, his rolls still jiggling. The back of his neck flushed beneath his fresh, summer haircut. Watery, red fluid seeped out of two linear streaks on his right cheek. He finally eased the self-protective ball he'd formed. Through his spastic, open-mouthed frown, red face, and dripping tears, I could just barely make out his words, "I...didn't do anything."

On his face was the shock of the recently betrayed. He met eyes with us all as he cried, devoting equal time to Neil, me, Hoss, and the restrained but still-kicking Bud. I got the quick idea Zeke didn't know who he could trust. He was more vulnerable than anything I could stand to see.

In almost perfect unison, Neil and I knelt down to help cover Zeke with our towels. Bill, the counselor from Cabin 6, burst through the door. In another few seconds, the footfalls of a running giant approached the cabin stoop. It was Isaac, Cabin Row's Assistant Director and Mr. Dinwiddie's right-hand-man. He had run all the way up from Headquarters.

Neil and I would learn in a few minutes Hoss had deliberately scared Bud, and Bud retaliated by mistakenly attacking Zeke.

Neil sat Zeke on his bed and gently urged him to get dressed. Isaac was about six-foot-six and three-hundred pounds. He knelt down by Zeke and checked him over. Something about Isaac, other than his size, made me feel safe. Zeke let out tears of relief when Isaac showed up.

Hoss escorted Bud to his bunk. The little albino boy's

explosion was finally over. Only the flame and smoke remained. He was red in the face and still breathing heavily by the time a half-horrified Isaac noticed the scratches on Zeke's face.

"Somebody get a wet washcloth," Isaac said. "And Bill?"

"Yeah?" said the Cabin 6 counselor.

"Go find Cliff."

Neil went toward the sinks as Zeke pulled on a T-shirt.

"Bud just flipped out," Hoss said.

"Did you see it happen?" asked Isaac.

"Yeah."

"Why'd he flip out?"

Zeke took a deep sniff, collecting himself.

"He got scared, I guess," Hoss said.

"What scared him?" Isaac asked.

Hoss was slow to answer as I noticed big, sandy footprints on the end of my bed, next to my shelves.

Isaac asked Bud, "What scared you?"

Bud's face was white, and he just kind of shivered on his bunk. He seemed miles away.

Zeke sat still and quiet, eyes locked with Hoss.

"I did it," Hoss said. "I scared him."

"Accidentally, I hope," said Isaac, who seemed to have noticed the big, sandy footprints. "Because scaring someone on purpose isn't so nice, is it?"

Isaac was an awfully big guy to appear as unhappy as he did at that moment. But he held still. "You gonna do anything like that again?" he asked Hoss.

"Never again," Hoss said, something like actual remorse

showing on his face.

He passed Isaac's test, but not *mine*. I flunked him. *Hard.*

Cliff showed up with Bill. Isaac thanked Neil for the washcloth and finished his counseling as he dabbed at Zeke's face. "Let's get you down to H-Q for some first aid. That sound okay?" Zeke stood with him. "And you," Isaac said, pointing to Hoss and never acknowledging Cliff, "tell your counselor what you did, and what happened because of it."

Isaac and Zeke left the cabin. By then, I was convinced Cliff wasn't all that smart. I couldn't see him at a university, and I figured he probably wasn't even a proper hippie. But coming from Blue River in 1970, I wouldn't know one way or the other.

My only real concern at the time was Zeke. The idea of making him aware he had Neil and me to trust was almost overwhelming. I supposed worse things have happened to kids, maybe even at White Birch. But considering Zeke, who only later took a deep breath and relaxed, I knew nothing mean ever happened to a nicer kid.

Later, the three of us chummed around in the woods, talked about pine tree species, watched the lake, and did whatever Zeke wanted. Those two made me realize fully the difference between the writing on a cabin plaque and actual graffiti. They were my friends.

CHAPTER 11

AFTER LUNCH THE next day, I got back to the cabin in time for the dubious pleasure of being alone with Hoss.

Bud recovered from his fugue sometime during the night. At breakfast, he made a face like something smelled bad, pointed at the scratches on Zeke's face, and asked, "Wha'd you *DOOO?*"

I wanted to throw that judgmental little pile of shit out the dining hall's window. But I knew his question meant he didn't even remember the incident. By that time in my life, I'd heard people can have complete breaks of memory from surprise, fear, or anger.

That morning, we had our first classes. Camp-crafts, swimming, or Frisbee up on the soccer fields, and a half-dozen other things. By lunch, the sun seemed to occupy the entire sky, and a haze of moisture hung in the air.

Some northern Michigan summer days can get warm. Others can be Louisiana-swamp hot with mosquitos and horseflies. When the air stands still, the heat can be brutal. It can also get cold at night. Some nights, it got so cold, we closed the cabins' indoor shutters. The windows were high enough on the walls that, to open and close the shutters, a grown man would have to stand on a chair.

Or a bed.

The night after Bud attacked Zeke, a minor thunderstorm left the ground wet and littered with twigs and dead, orange pine needles. When morning came around, the sun heated the moist air so much that by lunch line-up, our T-shirts stuck to our skin.

I entered the cabin after lunch. Hoss was inside, opening the shutters. He stood on the bedclothes of his bunkmate, Bones.

My shutter was already open. The blanket I'd straightened for inspection that morning was messed and twisted. In the center of the disarray was a big, damp, sandy footprint.

"Don't step on my bed," I said.

Hoss finished fixing his shutter into place. Then he stepped down to the floor to face me. "Excuse me?" he said, his eyebrows up and his jaw forward. He made fists briefly with his hands and narrowed his eyes. "I don't believe I heard you just right."

"I think you heard me just fine."

He didn't answer.

"Keep your feet off my bed. Gets sand on it. I didn't like you standing on it last night, when you did that to Zeke, and—"

"I didn't do shit to Zeke. Bud did it."

"—and I don't like it today."

"What makes you so sure I stepped on your bed?" He strutted over to me. He stood straight-backed and almost nose-to-nose.

I'd like to say I stood there, staring at Hoss because I didn't know what kind of message turning or sitting down would send. I'd like to say I remained calm and thought of enough good ideas to make Mom and Dad both proud. I'd like to say I was

54

charming. But the truth is, right then, I'd had enough of Hoss, and I wanted to face him. I didn't worry about what Mom would think, and the day's heat took the charm right out of me.

"You're the only one here," I said.

"So?"

"I think you need to keep your feet off my bed."

"What are you gonna do about it...*Teddy?*" he asked, giving me a little push with one hand on each of my shoulders. I flushed with adrenaline immediately.

"Don't push me." I leaned a bit forward, anticipating he'd push me back more forcefully. As a result, when he *did* push again, I didn't move much, but he rolled back on his heels. "*DON'T PUSH ME!*" I shouted, in a deep stab of sudden rage. With both arms, I shoved his chest as hard as I could.

His feet nearly left the floor.

My voice was deep and threatening enough to startle me. Call it flash fury, no good ideas, or just plain hate and fear— my push was no test. I used all my underestimated strength. I may have been pushing the guy who killed Mom.

Hoss half stumbled and half flew in a clumsy, low trajectory, to the center of the cabin. The small of his back hit the edge of the tabletop, knocking the entire thing over with a hollow crash. As he fell, his folding legs kicked one of the wooden chairs and sent it rolling across the bare floor.

Hoss rocked back and forth, one hand rubbing the small of his back.

The first parent I thought of was Dad, who said to me the week after Mom died: ...*you'll regret it. Once you let yourself get mad, it only makes you angrier.* Without any doubt, this little problem with Hoss let me know Dad was right.

At first, I didn't know what to do. So I just walked over to the downed chair and picked it up. Hoss rolled to a crawl position. He didn't cry, and he didn't curse. He just stood up. Once he did, I reached for the table to put it right-side up. And then, to my deep surprise, so did he.

By the time we'd righted the table and chairs, my fury was long-gone. I thought about telling him I was sorry, but I didn't, and I wasn't. At least not for him. I was sorry for ignoring Dad's advice and I was sorry for what having done so might do to me. For all the things I might have been sorry for, I didn't give a damn about Hoss.

The only thing that came out of my mouth, before I went over to wipe the sand off my covers, was, "Don't step on my bed." My voice was soft and calm.

CHAPTER 12

MY EYE JUST caught the cabin door closing as I jogged toward it from the bench. Who had entered didn't concern me. At the time, draining my bladder was my only want, my only need.

It was evening. Hoss's flight across the cabin had occurred just after lunch, and the event already seemed remote. A forgiving breeze blew away the humidity, and the promise of good weather had emptied most cabins. Boys flooded the outside of Cabin Row running, throwing footballs, heading down to swim, or just standing at the bluff, yick-yakking. I'd been sitting on the bench with Zeke and Neil.

Joining the pickle game behind us was a familiar voice. *Her* voice. Karen had shown up and stood in front of Cabin 5 in jeans and an H.R. Pufnstuf T-shirt. Holding a ball glove between her knees, she drew her hair into a ponytail. Those magic fingers married the hair and rubber band with quick, automatic movements I couldn't begin to follow.

She gloved her right hand and waved at me daintily with her left. Then, she slapped the inside of her glove and yelled to the kid with the ball, "Come on! Show me what'cha got!"

She jumped just enough to separate her feet and ready her glove. The kid delivered, his pitch fast and true, straight toward her middle. I admit I expected her to flinch, but she didn't. She pinched the ball right into her glove's webbing. At least ten of us bore witness to what in my mind was the most beautiful sequence that followed.

Karen stuck her left hand into her glove and grabbed the ball. As she took a couple of casual steps forward, she rotated to her left, straightening her throwing arm behind her. Her third step was a kind of sideways hop toward her catcher. Her left foot landed first, her right stepping far forward. Her pelvis, then her core, twisted to bring her face-to-face with her target as her left elbow flexed through a natural, forward-moving arc. All the momentum from the hop and twist shot like lightning into her wrist and fingers.

The ball flew arrow-straight. It sizzled past the bench and smacked the pocket of the catcher's glove with a dusty, leather-on-leather *POP!* I'd swear still echoes through those woods today.

"Wow," Zeke said.

"Impressive," Neil said, scrunching his nose and pushing up his glasses.

Karen shot me a glance but kept her face steely.

I suddenly had to pee.

She snagged the catcher's return throw as I jogged toward Cabin 7. The front door clicked shut as I went, and of course I made nothing of it. Until I went inside.

Two people stood by the table, facing me. It was Isaac and Mr. Dinwiddie. It's easy to say I liked them. I respected and never quite spent enough time with them. Hell. Over the years, it's come crystal-clear to me I loved those guys.

But just then, perhaps due to their location, their expressions (pleasant surprise, perhaps) or the power and magic both of them held at White Birch, I froze. I even quit breathing. The cabin seemed dark and lonely with those out-of-place men inside it.

"Hello, Ted," Mr. Dinwiddie said. His mustache straightened as he tilted his head and grinned disarmingly. His eyes became rising suns.

"Hello."

"Didn't mean to startle you," he said, "but Isaac and I were looking for someone."

"Who?"

"Mr. Cartwright. Have you seen him?"

Hoss. He was probably somewhere he didn't belong. "No. Not since supper."

"I wonder where he…it might be just as well to ask you a few questions, Ted. If you don't mind," Mr. Dinwiddie pulled out the chair Hoss had kicked down when he flew across the cabin. "Care to sit down?"

The fight with Hoss. They wanted to talk about it.

It was like one of the movies Dad liked to watch. Mr. Dinwiddie was the boss, and Isaac, the muscle. I felt lightheaded and sat in the chair. My rationale for the fight with Hoss was slow to come. In truth, I had no defense for it. *Please don't ask about the fight with Hoss.*

"How is your buddy, Zeke?"

Hoss started it. He picked on me, and—Wait. "What?"

"Is Zeke feeling better? After the other night when Mister, uh, don't you call him *Bud*? Had his little problem?"

"Oh. Yeah. Zeke's fine."

The director breathed in deeply and seemed to relax some. Isaac didn't move. "That is certainly very good to hear."

That can't be his question.

"Good, indeed," he said. "Isaac here did a fine job on the first aid, didn't he?"

"Um. Yeah. He did."

Another deep breath, and Mr. Dinwiddie said, "After the, uh, incident the other night, your friend Bud said something troublesome."

Oh, no. "What'd he say?"

"A few things. He said Mr. Cartwr—*Hoss*—who frightened Bud into his little, let's say *episode*, attacked him with a knife. I'd like to ask you. Since you're a veteran of White Birch. And since, frankly, I trust you,"—

Those words popped into an imaginary glove like Karen's pitch. I already felt like I was lying.

—"Did you see anything like that? Any attack with a knife?"

"No."

Hoss didn't attack Bud at all. He made a mess Buck and I had to clean up, but he didn't attack Bud.

Mr. Dinwiddie and Isaac exchanged glances.

"We need to ask you directly, Ted."

Please don't.

"Did Mr. Cartwright have a knife?"

"Yes."

"Can you describe it to me?"

A knife or knives? I saw two knives but took Mr. Dinwiddie's use of the singular *knife* as a choice of which one to describe. "It was a little folding knife. For your pocket. He was whittling with it."

"And nothing threatening happened?"

"Not too bad."

"So something did happen."

"I mean, they argued a little bit, while Hoss was whittling, and Hoss stood up, you know—"

"With the knife."

"Yeah," I said, "but it was just in his hand when he stood up, but then Buck—that's, um—"

"Denny McDaniel," Isaac said.

"Yeah. Buck said to put the knife away, and then it looked like Hoss forgot he was even holding it."

Isaac nodded slowly. "Okay. But Bud said he was holding a great big knife."

I shrugged, deciding I could dance around the edges of the truth a little, but I wouldn't lie. Not to these guys. If I did, I'd never forget it. It'd sort of change everything.

"All right," Mr. Dinwiddie said. "What happened next?"

"After Buck said to put it away, Hoss backed off and put the knife down."

"Oh. So no attack took place after all. Is that right?"

"Hoss...ran his mouth some, but he didn't attack anybody."

It was clear to me Isaac and Mr. Dinwiddie hadn't come to talk about the fight. Hoss might be going home from camp for having a knife, but I felt a little better.

Save for my about-to-explode bladder.

Mr. Dinwiddie leaned toward me and shook my hand. He thanked me for talking to them, and he and Isaac showed themselves out.

I ran to the toilet room just before I wet myself.

CHAPTER 13

THE CABIN SEEMED empty at the time. Right as I finished my business, Zeke and Neil came in.

"Hey, Ted," Zeke said.

"Hey, what."

"I want to ask you something."

"Shoot," I said.

Zeke: "What do you know about Mosquito Point?"

Mosquito Point was a sandy clearing hiding in the woods about a half mile north of camp. It was near the lakeshore and smaller than the bunk area of the cabin.

Me: "Why do you ask?"

Neil: "We heard somebody talk about it. They say it's a pretty place."

Me: "It is."

Zeke: "Where is it?"

I was apprehensive, but I figured I could tell Zeke and Neil. "You know that trail at the end of Cabin Row? The one that way?" I pointed toward the woods just north of Cabin 7.

Neil: "No."

"It's hidden. Even from here."

"So where is it?"

"Right outside the front door. Leads about a half mile down to Mosquito Point."

The trail started as a simple gap between a couple of red pines. At first, it ran narrow and parallel to the tree line. That way, no trail was apparent when seen from any distance. From Cabin 1 or even the bench, the great forest north of Cabin Row might as well have been a solid tree line. Most kids would spend the entire summer without ever seeing a trailhead. But saunter up to the trees themselves, and you might find the little path. After fifty yards or so, the trail widened as it wound down the bluff, nearly to water level. It was never mentioned, except in the White Birch Camper Handbook. An unspoken rule dictated that you never talk about the trail once you find it.

Unless, of course, you were talking to best-friend types like Zeke and Neil.

Zeke: "Can we go there?"

Me: "It's *way* out of bounds."

"Would we get in trouble if we went?"

"You can get sent home."

Zeke's mouth dropped open.

Neil: "What's the big deal about going there?"

Me: "It's close to the water, for one thing. No grown-ups here want us near the water if we're unsupervised. And also, if you went to Mosquito Point, no one could find you. Mr. Dinwiddie would get pretty worried if that happened." I wondered if the director was worried that he couldn't find Hoss.

Neil: "But you've been there?"

"Not this season. It's far enough away that you can't just sneak down there any time. You need at least…"

Zeke: "How long?"

Me: "Half hour or more. And that's if you stay down there only a couple minutes."

Neil put on his professor face, pushed up his glasses, and

said, "Yeah. I guess there's always gonna be a line-up or something."

Me: "Or call-to-quarters or rest-period or…" Or the organized and mandatory, pre-dinner recreation we called *forced fun*.

At White Birch, you didn't just not show up for one of those things. If you did, the camp would go instantly into a missing-person search. Just thinking about something like that brought up images of what my Dad and his police buddies called an A.P.B.

Neil: "But it's possible to go?"

I dropped my chin and spoke softly. "It'd be the greatest thing to have a campout down there."

"If we're gonna camp out somewhere," Neil said, "that sounds like the place."

"But we can't," I said.

"Rules are for dummies who don't know any better," Neil said before issuing a small version of his classic giggle. "Don't you remember saying that?" Not fair. My buddy had used my words against me. Zeke seemed a little nervous, but then again, no he didn't.

Neil gently slapped Zeke on the arm with the back of his hand. "C'mon, man. Let's find that trail."

"Don't tell anybody about it," I said.

Uninhibited glee radiated from Zeke. It surprised me—he seemed like such a rule-follower—but it also made me happy. I realized just then that my buddies—and Karen—were healing me. Going back to camp had been the right choice after all. White Birch was still my place. I belonged there.

65

The door slammed behind them. As its window rattled, I watched the cottonwood leaves wave for a moment. Before heading out to join them, I went to my bunk for something. When I turned back around, White Birch was no longer sacred.

Hoss dangled, spread-eagle, from the rafters. His eyes stared, and his mouth gaped, like those of a man dangling from a tight noose. If I hadn't just peed, I'd've wet myself for sure.

His hands let go of the cross-tie from which he hung. His feet contacted the floor, and he eased into a crouch, softening his fall. His landing—on those boards, in that hollow cabin—made no sound at all.

"'Rules are for dummies who don't know any better,'" he said, standing up. "I like that."

CHAPTER 14

"'S'MATTER, TEDSKI?" Hoss said. "Cat got your tongue?"

"Where were—how'd you get in here?"

"Loft. That's where I've been hiding my knife ever since you warned me about that kid, *Toad*."

"I didn't warn you about anything."

"Why didn't you say anything about my other knife?"

He'd heard the entire conversation with Mr. Dinwiddie and Isaac.

"Because he didn't ask," I said.

"You could have said something."

"But I didn't."

"But you could have."

"Still can. You want me to?"

Hoss's lips stretched across his near-perfect teeth. On his thin surface, he had the kind of looks girls might like, and he oozed a little charm. Something inside me warned that he might be interested in Karen.

"Nope. I sure don't want you to tell Mr. Dinwiddie—or Isaac—about my knife. I just want to thank you for what you said."

Already that summer, Hoss seemed bored with everything. Except me.

"I didn't say anything other than the answers to his questions."

"Then I want to thank you for what you didn't say."

"That doesn't even make any sense. All I did was tell the truth."

"Damn, Ted, that's gotta be about the first time in my life the truth ever got me *out* of trouble."

"You better be nice to Bud from now on."

"What are you gonna do if I'm not?"

I guffawed. "Nothing. I don't care what happens to him. But if you want Bud telling Mr. Dinwiddie lies to get you in trouble, keep on being mean to him."

"So," Hoss said. "About this knife. Am I really gonna get in all kinds of trouble?"

"Toad got sent home."

"But he tried to stab somebody."

"And Bud told Mr. Dinwiddie *you* tried to stab *him*."

"But I didn't, and you cleared that up."

"I'm not sure I cleared up anything." Hoss appeared lost for a second before I said, "If I were you, I'd run that knife out to Mr. Dinwiddie and hand it over."

"Really."

"Yep. For sure. Tell him you didn't read the camper handbook."

Hoss appeared to come around. He reached into his pocket and pulled out the folding knife. "Go now?"

"I would. Turning yourself in's gotta be better than getting caught."

"All right," he said with a confidence that impressed me. "Wish me luck."

Don't blame me if it doesn't work, Hoss.

"And when I come back," he said, "Me an' you are gonna

have a talk about this campout at Mosquito Point."

He bolted out the front door and ran toward Headquarters, whistling his favorite song.

CHAPTER 15

TWO DAYS AFTER Hoss's flight across the cabin and one since I became his buddy over the knife issue, Buck said, "Hey, Ted."

"Yep?"

"Hoss and I are headed down to Mosquito Point. You want to come?"

Nope. Not with you guys. And keep your voice down. Are you nuts?

Mr. Dinwiddie confiscated Hoss's folding knife, gave him a camper handbook to study, and a quiz the next day. Hoss passed the quiz. Somewhere between that and Cliff still being our counselor after his absence at the first call-to-quarters, Mr. Dinwiddie emerged as a man who believed in second chances.

None of it, though, made me trust Hoss.

It was after dinner, and the lake was fine. The mysterious far shore's green was brilliant in the evening sun. I was alone in the cabin with Hoss and Buck. With me, Hoss had gone from hostile, to civil, to fawning. It was as though I was an Indy 500 racecar driver or a movie star, and Hoss was a fan.

It was free-rec time. Zeke had taken the city slicker out to hunt pinecones or something. The other guys were off somewhere else. Hoss and Buck were in the cabin, wearing jeans, button-down shirts, and boots. Given that it was every bit of eighty degrees out, they were downright suspicious in their outfits. Their intention to leave the camper boundaries and tromp through the woods couldn't have been more obvious if they'd passed out fliers. I tried to gauge how loud Buck's announcement had been. Would his voice have spilled just outside the cabin or all the way down Cabin Row?

"Not me," I said. "I'm gonna head up to Headquarters and say hello to Isaac. Haven't talked to him much this summer."

Hoss pinched his eyebrows together and dropped his jaw. "Jesus, Square Meal. Come on. We need an expert guide. Show us the ropes. You know?"

"Nah. You guys can find it. But don't *tell* anyb—"

"You really wanna go up there and talk to *them* instead?"

"I guess so, yeah."

Hoss made a face that said, *Okay, Buddy, it's your funeral.* "You change your mind, you know where to find us."

Buck seemed to adjust something under his flannel shirt, but I ignored it and headed out the door. If they went to Mosquito Point, I didn't see them go. It was definitely better that way.

I ambled down toward Cabins 1 and 2. The shouts and splashes—happy waterfront sounds—carried up the bluffs. A distant crow issued an echoing *cawwww!*

Between the first two cabins, I could see the concrete steps at the Headquarters commerce window. Just behind the screen, there he was. Isaac sat in the office manager's seat. His Fu-Manchu mustache and mop of black hair completed his face.

I broke into a jog and bounded up the four steps to the window, leaning my elbows on the sill. On the counter in front of him sat a tattered copy of an open book, pages-down. *Crawdads from Outer Space.* I'd read it and returned it to

Karen. An old coffee cup sat off to the side, holding a couple of pencils and a shiny permanent marker. *King Size*, it said on the marker's side.

"Hey-hey, there, young man," Isaac said. He yawned as he opened the sliding part of the screen window.

"Young man?" I asked. "How old are you?"

"Plenty old enough to call *you* young." I think he was about twenty-five at the time.

He reached through the window toward me, his hand nearly swallowing mine in a semi-painful squeeze. Remnants of cigar smoke hung in the air. Rumor had it that Mr. Dinwiddie enjoyed the occasional cigar in the bowels of Headquarters. From my angle, I could see the armrest of Toad's chair through his office door.

Isaac and I talked about what we called the off-season, the ten months we weren't at White Birch. His accent placed him from the south, maybe Kentucky or Tennessee. I was openly happy to spend time with him. In years past, he and I talked for what seemed like long hours through that same window.

"Is that Ted?" said a female voice. *Karen*. I froze. She stepped in from what they called the lounge, the area off to the right, the one no camper could see.

"It is indeed Ted," Isaac said.

"Hi!" Karen said, holding a few pages of loose-leaf paper, sitting down in front of the typewriter.

"What are you doing here?" I said, with, I'm certain, stupid accusation in my voice. "I mean with the, you know, the…" I pointed and wagged my finger at the table as she sat down.

"Typewriter?" she said. "Just helping Dad with some

reports. He writes them by hand, and he pays me to type them."

"And she pays me rent for the typewriter," Isaac said.

"You wish." Karen loaded the machine with a single sheet, ran her fingers through her lovely hair, and pecked at the keys.

Isaac waved slowly, a few inches from my face as I stared. When he caught my attention, he grinned but didn't make fun.

"Making any friends?" he asked.

"Sure, I guess."

Isaac rubbed his temples and squinted, his eyes appearing sunken in.

"What's wrong?" I asked.

"Nothing much now. Just getting over one of my famous migraines." He waved a hand in front of his face in a way that suggested the cigar smoke bothered him. "These things take a while to get over if I can't go to bed right away. But it's fine now.

"I saw you palling around with Cornelius and Zeke. You have them whipped into shape yet?"

"You mean have I told them stuff like 'the lake is heated' and about the Loon Lake Sloth?"

"Precisely," he said, a crispness returning to his expression.

Karen's typing fingers hesitated when I mentioned the sloth, but with her dad's rising-sun eyes, she got back to work.

"You know," Isaac said, "I already overheard some kid tell a newcomer the lake isn't really heated. What do you suppose gives him the right to do something like that?"

I shook my head, not understanding.

"Ruining a camp legend is like telling a little kid there's no Santa Claus."

Isaac leaned toward me narrowing his eyes further. The typewriter dinged, and Karen pushed the bar to set a new line.

"You wouldn't do that," he asked, "would you, Ted? Ruin a legend like that?"

God, no. I shook my head.

"Legends are sacred, Ted. These kids want to believe them." He swiveled in his wooden chair toward Karen. "Ain't that right, Chief?" She nodded, and he swiveled back toward me. "And that means you, my good friend. You want 'em to be able to *believe*, don't'cha?"

I nodded, feeling reverent. No camp legend would *ever* die at my hand.

The King Size marker seemed to speak to me.

"Why is there no more graffiti allowed?" I asked. "That's not fair."

"Rules, my friend. Some people just gotta make up rules. They make sense, and they don't make sense. They're fair, and they're not fair. It's like the lofts. It's fun to get up there, and then it's risky at the same time."

Karen stopped typing, pulled the sheet off the roller, and said, "Isn't that what makes it fun?"

"Do not contribute to camper delinquency, young lady," Isaac said.

What happened next was ten times better than Karen's left-handed pitch.

She finished loading the next page. When she ran her fingers through that red mane again, it fell and covered her right eye. Something made me hold my breath. Expertly, she lifted that partly blonde eyebrow and said, "You hear that, Ted?" I

74

didn't speak. "Better stay out of the loft."
   And then she winked.
   Right then and there, I almost died.

CHAPTER 16

SOME DAYS LATER Buck declared, "We need to start winning inspections."

"Why?" Hoss asked.

Their speech was pressured, like when a local celebrity endorses a car dealership on TV. I knew right away it was rehearsed. Written and directed by Hoss. The commercial took place in the morning, as we cleaned the cabin.

Buck: "Because to go on a campout…"

Hoss: "We get to go on a campout?"

"Yeah. We do. But we have to earn it."

"How do we do that?"

Hoss did everything but say *Sounds exciting! Tell me more, Buck,* before posing sideways into a camera and showing his pearly whites. Some of the newcomers stopped making their beds. Coach stilled his sweeping broom.

"Win inspection three days in a row," Buck said. "If we do that, we'll be the first cabin this summer to go on a campout."

Neil seemed unsure.

"The other day," Zeke said excitedly, "in line for lunch. The first kid from the winning cabin got into the dining hall at eleven thirty-five. The last kid from the last cabin got in at eleven fifty-eight."

"We talked about that," Neil said. *This* particular dialogue was unrehearsed. "That's just about twenty-five minutes. Over three meals, that's an hour and fifteen."

"Holy crap!" Hoss said, receiving Cliff's tepid admonition. "That's more than eight hours a week!"

Coach's broom didn't budge.

Zeke: "Over eight weeks, that's sixty-four hours—"

Hoss: "That's like two-and-a-half *days* or something."

Zeke: "Two and two-thirds."

Neil: "That's just shy of five percent of the entire summer, ladies and gentlemen."

"Waiting in *line…*" Coach said, putting his broom back to work.

Neil grabbed the rake and headed out the front door to tidy up the cabin's outside. I'd never viewed inspection like that. Sponge in hand, I scrubbed the sinks and faucets. The whole job didn't take two minutes. Bones grabbed the toilet brush and yanked open the bathroom door. It slapped behind him. Even Bud got up off his butt and emptied the trash.

Through his office window in '68, Isaac dropped some prophetic words on me. *No one ever got hurt learnin' a little discipline and keepin' his crap in order.* I think it was *…a little discipline…* that I remembered most.

Cabin 7 won inspection that day and most days that followed. We avoided the wait in line and ate sooner. As a result, we were the first kids to return to Cabin Row after lunch. And because of *that*, the summer of 1970 took a hard turn.

Digesting a drab lunch of meatloaf and cut pears in syrup, Zeke, Neil, and I cut out of the dining hall early. Walking past the industrial fan blowing dank kitchen air into the heat of midday, we made it into the noon sun and downtime of early afternoon. A couple of motorboats left white trails on the distant, navy blue water. We watched them as we traversed the top of the bluff.

Neil adjusted his glasses on his nose and squinted. "How far do you think it is to the other shore?"

"Mile," I said.

Zeke: "Or maybe even more."

Neil: "How do you know?"

Me: "I don't. Just guessing. Seems like if a highway reached over there it'd be about a mile."

Zeke: "Do you think anybody ever tried to swim all the way over there?"

Neil: "I could do it."

Zeke: "Nuh-*UH!* Really?"

Neil: "You bet I can. I'll go that far swimming laps this afternoon, down at the waterfront. Bet I could swim that lake in under forty minutes."

Zeke: "But the fish…"

Me: "What about the fish?"

Zeke: "What if they bite?"

Neil laughed, softly at first, then more forcefully. "No fish out there's gonna bite you!"

"How do you know?"

"What the hell kind of fish you think is gonna come up out of there and bite you?"

"Northern pike."

Neil's stride broke as he laughed.

Me: "Have you seen the teeth on a pike?"

Neil: "No."

Zeke: "I have. I'd be scared to swim across that lake. You

couldn't see—how deep is it, Ted?"

Me: "Mile."

Neil stopped and hunched over. It was now his laughter that was funny.

Zeke: "No it *isn't*. Really. How deep? Do you know?"

"Nope," I said. "I don't. I heard around a hundred feet in some places."

"Isn't Cliff still at lunch?" Zeke asked.

"Yeah," Neil said. "Why?"

"'Cause our cabin door is open."

So it was.

"I closed it before we went," Zeke said. "Do you think somebody's in there?"

"Don't know," I said. "Who wants to race me back and find out?"

"Not me," Zeke said.

"Okay," I said to Neil. "How about you? Want to race?"

"I don't run after I eat," he said, taking off in a dead sprint.

"*Cheater!*" I said, chasing him. I overtook him at about cabin 3.

When we got back to Cabin 7, he said, "You're the cheater."

"How do you figure?"

"Too tall for me to beat." Just outside the cabin, we both heard a thump and a couple of hurried steps. We bolted inside to see who it was. From the far end of the sink room, the Emergency Door slammed. It was a foolish mistake to run back that way to find out who had been there. When we got back to the sinks, nothing but a closed Emergency Door stared at us.

Forsaking what was always a cardinal rule of White Birch Camp (and committing a victimless crime in the process), I burst through the door and jumped the stoop to the ground. Neil followed, slamming the door behind him. A linear cloud of rising dust led to the far side of Cabin 5.

Neil found the Emergency Door's outside had no doorknob, just a tarnished brass plate in its place.

"One-way door," I said. "Gotta go 'round front to get back in."

When Neil and I got back in through the front, I noticed something I hadn't before. A scent. It was like perfume, but only faintly.

CHAPTER 17

THAT NIGHT, WHILE the cabin was quiet, well after the three of us had stopped our whispering, after the late-June sunset of Michigan had squeezed out its last drops of twilight, I lay awake, thinking about Karen. Her silken blanket of hair, that pretty freckle-face, those shapely lips. Her green eyes burned brightly in the near-total darkness. But it wasn't so much those things that drew my thoughts. What captivated me was whether she had been in the cabin that day, and how close I came to missing it completely.

The Karen-fragrance was so faint I thought my own imagination might be playing tricks on me. After all, Karen was on my mind a great deal. Not even considering that killer wink she threw me from Headquarters. Maybe Isaac was right. Maybe I just wanted to *believe* she'd been there. One way or another, I hoped she had.

I couldn't sleep.

It was time to slip down to the end of my bed and peek through that drilled hole in the partition. Loon Lake's calm surface was a mirror reflecting the distant streetlamp of the moon. Right where those twin birch trees should be, it was there. The light's flicker was as dim as the Karen-fragrance was faint. Either one or both could've been imaginary.

But then again, in all that dark forest across the lake, there could be a little clearing. Just like Mosquito Point. If that light was anything, it had to be a campfire. *If* it was anything at all.

Imagination or not, the nighttime, moonlight, and lake got me thinking about camping and sleeping under the stars. It also got me thinking about another confrontation between Hoss and me, earlier that day.

As Neil and I sat at the table, after the post-lunch excitement, I decided to keep the idea of the Karen-fragrance to myself. I heard Hoss singing a familiar tune.

"Tokin' on the MISS-issippi with my Polly ANN," he sang, bursting into the cabin, rattling the panes in the door's window. Buck followed him in. I have to admit Hoss's colorful lyric changes amused me.

"S'm TIMES I think the boat gets tippy when she slaps my can—what're you girls doing?" Hoss asked.

We didn't answer.

"You missed a good hike to Mosquito Point yesterday, Tedski," he said. "Hope your visit to Headquarters was meaningful."

If he only knew. I'd take a conversation with Isaac and a wink from Karen Dinwiddie over a hike with Hoss any day of my life.

A little more seriously, Hoss said, "What about a campout there? At Mosquito Point."

Buck: "You can't camp there. When we camp out, we go to the campsite."

Hoss: "What campsite? Sounds boring already. Is it near the lake?"

"It's just on the other side of the road, next to archery."

The archery range was a weeded, grassy clearing in the woods about a hundred yards behind headquarters, across the double-track utility road and down a straight, hard-packed dirt path. The designated camping area, known as Campout Circle, was a similar area just north of there.

Hoss: "What? With this lake so nearby? What'd they do *that* for? The best campsites are by a lake. We want Mosquito Point, man. That's where it needs to be."

It didn't seem too painful to agree with Hoss on that one.

Buck: "We can't go there."

Hoss: "We just did yesterday."

"Yeah, but that was—"

"And you said staying away from there was a rule nobody even seemed to worry about."

Me: "Long as you don't get caught, that is. Besides, I think sneaking a whole cabin and counselor out there to spend the night's a little different."

Hoss: "Sure it is, but Cliff's kind of a pansy, and I think I can roll him over on it pretty easy."

Buck: "You think so?"

"Bet you a dollar."

Buck shook his head. Hoss paced near his bed.

Hoss: "Hey, Ted."

Me: "What."

"What size shoe do you wear?"

"Twelve. Why?"

"So you didn't make this footprint."

"What footprint?"

Neil and I stood up.

"On my bed," Hoss said.

We stepped over. The sandy outline was clear enough to

appear deliberate. Hoss's bed was otherwise inspection-grade.

"I wouldn't step on your bed, anyway," I said.

Hoss surveyed the other two with eyebrows raised.

Buck: "Not me."

Neil: "I didn't step on your damn bed."

Hoss swiped his hand over the footprint a couple times and cast the sand to the floor. "But anyway," he said, "I'll work on the counselor, and we'll get our campout at Mosquito Point. Best not say anything to anyone until we do, because if we're not supposed to go there, then we want…you know."

"For people to shut up about it," Buck said. "But I still don't think it'll work."

"Better yet," Hoss said. "Best not say anything to anybody else at all. They don't really even need to know, do they?"

Hoss leaned in toward us and said, more softly, "And I don't think Cliff's too excited about following the rules, either. Look. The guy's a moron. He left us unsupervised on the first night of camp, almost all the way through call-to-quarters— whattayou wanna bet he got an earful from Dinwiddie over *that?*—but anyway. Betcha a dollar. I can get us this campout at Mosquito Point."

Neil: "What do you think, Ted?"

I shrugged, trying not to give away how much I'd like to camp there. Later, Zeke, Neil, and I sat on the bench and talked about it. Zeke was instantly excited, and Neil was more reserved, admitting he'd never camped outside before. Much less in the deep woods.

The topic secretly came up before supper and in evening free-rec. Neil warmed up to the idea by call-to-quarters. Later, out went the lights and after them, so went the setting sun.

After I was done squinting through the drilled hole in the partition, I settled back beneath my covers. That's when the Karen-fragrance and the sandy footprint fit together in the same story. The print's toe had been pointed toward the cabin's back wall and had to be evidence of someone getting into the loft. The loud thump Neil and I heard just after our little foot race was Karen jumping to the floor. It had to be.

I suddenly trusted my sense of smell again. Karen's playful, winking admonition that I stay out of the loft, the Karen-fragrance, the footprint on Hoss's bed, and the thump all told me something: Karen Dinwiddie snuck into the cabin to hide something in the loft, just for me. Right before she winked, she'd all but told me something was up there for me. In fact, she may have timed it that way on purpose.

I wanted it to be true. I believed, and I hoped.

Belief and hope both, I told myself, are okay. They're downright healthy. Ridiculous as it sometimes is. I often hoped Dad missed me and believed I'd see Mom again some day. But that night, there was only one hope I could verify, and I was not going to sleep until I did.

CHAPTER 18

ON A FRAMING beam behind me, the same one Neil and Zeke used as a bookshelf, sat my flashlight. It was an old military piece with a sturdy clip that held it onto a pocket. After easing on a pair of jeans, I stood. My bare feet caused the floorboards to creak ever so slightly, but nothing near as loud as that groaning spring on the bathroom door.

I snapped my jeans, zipped them up, and clipped the flashlight on the back pocket as I tip-toed over to Hoss's area. When someone rolled on his bunk and let out a sigh, his bedsprings chirped out a flurry of what sounded like a couple of distant, warring blue jays at home.

Hoss's bunk seemed hard to navigate, especially since he and Bones were asleep. But curiosity and infatuation pushed me along, rational thought nowhere to be found. It would be too risky to climb up the long sides of the bunks, right over Hoss's body, and too loud to move their shelves, but I had another idea. Since my height had increased so much over the last year, I figured I could just jump up and grab the roof-supporting cross-ties that ran parallel to the floor, like a gymnast grabbing the parallel bars. Wondering how much the cabin might protest in creaks and groans didn't stop me.

Making sure my flashlight was secure, I jumped and grabbed the crossties. Silence. It surprised me how easy it was to tighten my stomach and hoist my feet up to those same boards.

Without too much trouble, I walked my hands up the diagonal struts that connected the ceiling rafters to the cross-ties. The loft's floor was comprised of one-by-six pine boards spaced about four inches apart. It would be all too easy to miss a step and fall through. From where I stood, as though hovering eight feet above the cabin floor, the loft was one quiet step away.

The cabin's front door opened. Cliff scuffed his way inside. The door shut behind him, rattling its window panes. He seemed mindless of the sleeping boys in his charge.

To my frozen horror, he headed toward the back of the cabin, a flashlight beam preceding him like a sniffing dog on the hunt. From where I stood, guilty of God-knows-how-many camp-rule infractions, my white T-shirt seemed to give off its own light. I didn't dare move as Cliff strolled almost directly beneath me.

He lumbered into the sink area, and without breaking stride opened the plywood bathroom door. The long, rusty, and tightly-coiled spring groaned like an old man in pain. Cliff let the spring slap the door back into its frame. The noise almost hurt. He pulled the string and turned on the toilet room light. The slatted beams shone through the loft's floorboards onto my shirt and face. For a second, I was as conspicuous as Elvis in a spotlight.

Even Cliff's zipper made noise. A splatter sound came next as his initial stream missed the toilet bowl. What followed was a better-aimed, roiling stream in the tiny pool of the toilet. The porcelain megaphone amplified the sound almost to comic proportions.

I took the opportunity to snake my way into the loft. As the urine stream powered on, I noticed the complete absence of graffiti up there. The loft would be a perfect place to hide our names. On the backsides of the rafters, we could most-assuredly enter the immortal world of former campers without being caught.

While Cliff waited out his prodigious stream, I noticed something else. Something small in the loft's corner interrupted the up-shining light. It was prism-shaped, the size of a Kleenex box. The urine flow weakened to a dribble. What was that thing in the corner? Couple pieces of scrap lumber? Surely it wasn't actually a box of tissues. Maybe it was something else, like a cardboard pencil box.

At the very end of Cliff's performance came two or three *Squirt!* sounds. Following the *Zip!* of his pants came the head-crushing toilet flush, the squawk of the spring, and the slap of the door. I took in absently, with some irritation, that he didn't wash his hands. But then, what kind of guy who would allow himself to make so much noise so close to nine sleeping boys would be conscientious enough to wash his hands after taking a piss?

Cliff's sandpapery steps headed back up front.

You left the bathroom light on, Cliff.

In my mind, Hoss said, *Cliff's a moron*, and I agreed.

He made it as far as the table before he stopped, cursed, and turned around.

I froze again. He scuffed his way back. *Squawk!* went the spring, *Click!* went the light, and *Slap!* went the door. At last, it was dark in the loft. Cliff found his flashlight in the darkness

88

and let its trail-sniffing beam lead his way. It could be minutes or hours before he fell asleep, allowing me to escape the loft.

But then, against all prediction, he headed back out the front door. I waited a minute for him to return, but he didn't. No one will ever know where he'd been, but he'd walked all the way into the cabin just to empty his bladder.

Why didn't he just pee outside? It's dark. I bet even Zeke would pee on the ground at night.

Cliff's kind of a pansy, Hoss said in my mind. With that, *Dad* would agree.

I dared to turn on my flashlight and train the beam on the mystery shape in the corner. It was a cardboard box, the kind with a flip-top, like a school box. I inched toward it, careful not to jam my head on a rafter or fall between the floorboards. When I lifted the lid, the box seemed empty at first.

Cigar smell.

Mr. Dinwiddie's cigars, I figured. Four, folded and ancient-appearing pages blended in with the tobacco-stained box. The unfolding seemed as loud as the toilet flush. But no one stirred. The first was a title page. In the upper right corner was the date June 6, 1953. About a third of the way down, in all capital letters, it said:

THE LEGEND OF THE
LOON LAKE SLOTH

The three pages that followed were a typewritten story. The paper itself seemed awfully old, but it was stout just the same, not friable like old documents might be. Deciding I wanted to read the story in bed, I clipped my light to a belt-loop and clamped the pages between my lips, careful not to let my teeth or spit touch them.

Dedicating one finger to hooking the box beneath the lid, I could still use the hand to support my weight. In some haste, I misstepped on my way out of the loft and almost fell completely between two of the cross-ties. If not for one of the support struts, I would have fallen three or four feet, right onto Hoss. The four pages fell out of my mouth. Sacrificing one handhold, I swept my arm and caught the pages before they fell more than a foot.

Elvis had left the building. From then on and all the way to my area, I was the perfect cat burglar. In bed, pants off, flashlight in hand, and blanket over my head, I was ready to read. But the title page was missing. I pulled the blanket away from my face to hunt for it.

"Tedski!" Hoss said in a harsh whisper. He was monster-like above the flashlight he held beneath his face. His surprise appearance may have taken ten years off my life.

"Hell you doin' up in the loft, *bowah*?"

Good question. I had to think of something pretty quick. "Tonight, brushing my teeth, I saw this cigar box up, between the boards. Thought I'd find out what it was."

"In the middle of the night?"

"Yeah. Had to. Or Bud'd prob'ly tell on me for going up there."

Hoss seemed convinced by that and said, "Well?"

"Well, what?"

"The *box*, man. Damn." He held up the story's title page.

"This all there was in there?"

"No," I said and held up the other three pages. "Here's the rest. Lemme read it, and you can have it after me. But give me the title page, so we can keep it all together."

He handed it over. "Thing is *old*. Very exciting. Nineteen fifty-three. You think it's been up there for that long?"

"May-*bee*," I said. But I knew otherwise. Especially with those pages in my mouth. In addition to the cigar smell, they had Karen-fragrance all over them.

CHAPTER 19

IN THE MORNING light, I could tell the pages of the sloth story were doctored, made to look old, maybe by being held just over a burner until they browned and seared at the edges. To say nothing of the captivating story itself, the creativity of it all made me long even more for Karen.

By then, I was sure the next time I saw her, I wouldn't be able to speak at all. It was a cool day, overcast, so foggy you could hardly see the lake. From the top of the bluffs, the boat- and beach houses were no more than darkish smudges. The dock wasn't visible at all. An entire cloud rested on the soccer fields.

But Karen made it the brightest day I'd ever seen. It was chaos at breakfast. Neil and Zeke talked feverishly about squirrels, trees, and the outdoors. Hoss and Buck were at the other end of the table, and in between, the four other guys were eating, yakking about something shallow, and scraping their silverware on the plastic trays. Cliff ate scrambled eggs and kept his nose in a magazine.

When Karen stood up from Mr. Dinwiddie's table to head out of the dining hall, I snuck a glimpse of her. When I did, I found she was already doing the same with me. That hair fell beautifully over her shoulders. My heart leapt, and this time, I held her gaze. Something, and I don't know exactly what, made her stop walking.

I went for broke and lifted my arm in something like a

peace sign, only I bent my two fingers slightly. Baring my teeth and swiping my arm in front of me, I was the Loon Lake Sloth, slicing through the bodies of two imaginary boys from Horseknuckles, Arkansas.

Karen seemed confused for a second, but then she laughed and covered her mouth. Her open surprise said she knew I'd found what she'd left for me. She sneered and returned her own swipe-of-the-claw. Before I could pass out from the greatest, star-struck confusion a young man ever knew, Karen ran away.

Mom always seemed fond of the word *smitten*. I knew I'd been smitten with Karen from the start. But that day, when she ran out of the dining hall, *smitten* didn't really cut it. Whatever it was I had for Karen was starting to hurt. I didn't so much get excited about the next time I'd see her as I worried whether or not there'd even *be* a next time.

Right when I wished I'd gotten up to talk to Karen about the story she'd written, Hoss moved down to my end of the table, holding the pages. Buck followed him, pulled up a chair, and sat down.

"What's up, Tedski?" Hoss asked, handing me the four pieces of paper. "Great story."

"It is."

"I wonder who wrote it," Buck said, "and if it's really been there since fifty-three."

I didn't say anything. Any secret between Karen and me would remain precious for all my days.

"You know how we've been talking about a campout?" Buck asked.

"Yeah?" I said.

"Well, this story is—"

"*Perfect*," Hoss said. "We gotta read it to the cabin."

Buck: "*During* the campout."

Hoss: "Or maybe we have it backwards. We gotta have a campout so we can read this *story*. We *have* to. Be a crime if we didn't."

I wasn't thrilled about how much I agreed with Hoss. "So when's this campout gonna take place?" I asked.

"Funny you should ask," Hoss said. "Just asked Cliff. He'll clear it with…Headquarters, I guess, but we get to do it later this week, maybe Friday night." That moment, Hoss carried a certain genuineness I hadn't seen. Maybe it was because he suddenly had something to care about.

Buck: "But we want to run something past you."

Me: "Okay. What?"

Buck: "Mosquito Point."

Hoss: "Yeah. Did you know there's a tiny path through the woods from Campout Circle"—the horribly disappointing camping area by the archery range—"to the Mosquito Point trail?"

Amateur. Of course I knew about it. I'd found the small, winding, easy-to-miss path in '68. It was deep enough in the woods that anyone at Campout Circle could steal away to Mosquito Point without being seen or heard.

Me: "What about it?"

Hoss: "On campout night, we need to start out toward Campout Circle."

Buck: "Like we're supposed to, because hiking to Mosquito Point as a cabin wouldn't work—"

Hoss: "It *won't* work, because the trails…"

Buck: "The trails start in different places."

Hoss: "People'll know otherwise."

The Archery Range/Campout Circle trail traveled west from Cabin 4 to the road, and the one to Mosquito Point headed north from near Cabin 7.

Hoss: "Look, man. Nobody else in the cabin knows those trails but us, and we wanted to hike from Cabin Row like we were going toward the right place, and then—"

"—Head out to Mosquito Point from there."

When did those two start finishing each other's sentences?

Me: "So we head to Campout Circle like we're supposed to, then take the little trail to Mosquito Point…I still don't know if that's gonna w—"

Hoss: "Hey. Great idea, Tedski. Glad you thought of it."

Me: "Shut up."

Buck: "Yeah. That's what we were thinking. If you were up for it, nobody else'd know the difference."

Me: "Not even Cliff?"

Hoss: "That's right." He leaned in and whispered. "I've pretty much decided Cliff doesn't know *shit*."

Buck: "We figure, carry all the gear, get it out to Mosquito Point, then act like we'd used the wrong trail by mistake. Then ask Cliff if we can just stay."

Hoss: "If he ever figures it out in the first place."

Buck: "That'll probably work." With a sinking stomach, I knew they were right. With Cliff in charge, the plan, as simple and fallible as it was, would probably work like a charm.

Hoss: "And you guys'll each owe me a dollar."

Me: "I didn't take the bet."

Cliff probably *didn't* know shit. To my diminishing surprise, Hoss and I were eye-to-eye on lots of things.

But being his friend gave me the creeps.

CHAPTER 20

ISAAC AMBLED UP to the Cabin 7 stoop, three or four military canteens draped over his shoulder by their canvas straps. He carried a cardboard box and had a pleasant expression, but he seemed to search for something. Every couple of steps, he bent forward to pick up a twig and put it in the box.

"Ready for your campout, fellas?" he asked Zeke, Neil and me as we sat on the stoop. Isaac bent over to pick up another dry twig, this one complete with a tuft of dead, rust-hued pine needles. The canteens clanked together as he moved. Those needles would burn nicely, I thought.

"Hey, Cliff," Isaac said with a booming voice meant to fill the cabin from behind a closed door. *"Need you out here for a sec."*

Cliff's sand-on-wood shuffle approached from the inside. As he opened the door, Isaac's face morphed into that of a stern businessman.

"You're going to need this box of kindling for your cabin, *if* you expect to have a campfire."

"Oh," said Cliff. "That's, uh, that'll be helpful. Thank you."

"Helpful?" Isaac said. "It's *essential*. Especially tonight. Might be pretty chilly."

He handed the box over to Cliff and took the canteens off his shoulder. "Get your bigger guys to carry these as you go.

You carry the kindling."

"All right," Cliff said. "I've got it under control."

I doubted that.

As a White Birch veteran, I knew what Isaac was up to. He didn't even have to say *Idiot Test*. After what I'd seen already, I'd bet all my weekly Coke-machine allowance that Cliff would carry that kindling box all the way to the campsite. That forest had enough kindling start a thousand fires. Or a *million*. Neil gave me a shifty eye. He seemed to know what was going on, too. Zeke was too trusting to suspect any trickery.

But either way, Friday night had rolled around. It was campout night. We were the first cabin to earn one—from all those inspection victories—and were about ready to go.

We would take off down the back side of Cabin Row, along the tree-line to a point just behind Cabin 4. From there, the designated trail would lead us west, across the dirt road, to a fork. The left branch led to the archery range. We'd head right maybe two hundred feet to another fork. From there, Campout Circle, our ostensible destination, would be on our left. If Mr. Dinwiddie had made the signs he said he wanted to make, Campout Circle would be clearly marked, and Hoss's plan would be kaput.

The smaller trail was a scantly visible path that made the one to Campout Circle look like a paved highway. It was lined with spider webbed maple, oak, and pine saplings. It snaked through the woods, well deep to the margin of forest behind Cabins 6 and 7. It was, of course, the path Hoss and Buck—and I, too, I must admit—wanted. In a couple-hundred yards, it would meet up with the main trail to Mosquito Point.

Cliff was lazy. We knew that.

Because of it, we knew if we made it all the way to our secret destination, Cliff wouldn't want to double back. The hope, at least with Buck and Hoss, is that the other campers would never know the difference between Campout Circle and Mosquito Point.

We took off, single file, from the cabin, heading toward the back of Cabin 4. Several members of Cabin 6 piled onto the top bunks to stare at us, through their windows, as we marched past.

Hoss greeted them happily with a middle finger. Marty, the privileged, north-of-Chicago kid (the one who caterwauled at Karen on the first day of camp), said something colorful in return and flipped both his middle fingers right back. Then Hoss stopped cold, turned to face Cabin 7, bent forward, and dropped his pants. He slapped his own, bare butt three or four times for those watching from Cabin 6. When Hoss pulled his drawers back up, we hiked.

Cabin 6's jeers fading behind us, we found the utility trail and crossed the double-track access road. After we passed a couple of green, fifty-five-gallon drums serving as trash cans, we were pleasingly outside any signs of civilization.

It didn't take long, though, to reach the split, at which we turned right. Hoss and Buck placed themselves in front, and I was in back, with Zeke and Neil. Their next planned move was to walk quickly into the right branch of the second fork, hoping to get Cliff to follow them blindly.

When we were maybe fifty feet from there, it was clear Mr. Dinwiddie hadn't gotten around to making any of the signs.

Cliff said, "I hope you guys know where you're going. How 'bout the White Birch Camp *veterans* guide us. Where's Ted?"

Crap.

It was not at all what I'd expected. First, Cliff all but *volunteered* he didn't know where he was going, adding to his growing list of first-summer counselor mistakes. But that wasn't the real problem.

"Yeah, Ted," Hoss said. "Which way do you think it is?"

You know good and damned well, you turd-puking asshole.

"I can't exactly remember," I said, tromping up to the split and pointing straight to Campout Circle. "Is it this way?"

"No!" Buck said. "I remember. It's just a few hundred feet down this *little* trail."

"All right," said Cliff. "Lead the way, Buck."

Hoss stood still for a second, shaking his head, his eyes narrow. A slight grin crept onto his face. I'm sure my expression was the exact same. He didn't say anything, but his face said *well-played.*

Yes. Yes it was.

As the members of Cabin 7 followed the winding, narrow path, Hoss fell back with me. He put his arm over my shoulders and said, "Never a dull moment with *you*, Tedski."

CHAPTER 21

THE MAIN TRAIL to Mosquito Point was another highway, compared to the one Hoss and Buck had duped Cliff into taking. The trail meandered through natural stands of red and white pine and the occasional oak or white birch. The path's floor was hard packed dirt and some dusty sand, like what we had back at Cabin Row. The ground was softer, though, almost springy, in its generous coating of dead pine needles. Save for any talking amongst us, only natural sounds occurred: the scratch of a small bird hopping on the forest floor, the skitters of mice and squirrels, or the echo of a distant woodpecker's painstaking work.

When the bounding of a startled fawn and two adult, whitetail deer shattered the relative silence, Neil bristled in such fear that neither Zeke nor I ribbed him for it.

The bluff gradually dwindled as the trail ran downhill to The Point, where dune grasses and horsetail grew around the clearing only a few feet above water level. As we hiked, an occasional gust brought the smell of the lake to us. When the trail spilled into the sandy clearing, the guys who hadn't seen the place—including Cliff—reacted with expressions of satisfaction and wonder.

In the center of the clearing, a couple of inert, black-charred, former logs poked out of the sand where a good fire pit should be. The forest sounds continued. A few yards away, past the dune grass and horsetail, lazy waves lapped at the shore. Otherwise, we enjoyed a degree of quiet worthy of outer space.

Wondering when the legend of the Loon Lake Sloth started, I tapped my flannel shirt pocket. The story's pages crinkled between my chest and fingers.

Cliff dropped the Idiot Box and said, "Okay, guys, all we have is kindling. We need bigger pieces of wood."

Bud asked, in a cutesy, cloying kind of way, "Cliff, what's kindling?"

With a contrived air of patience, Cliff said, "Small pieces of wood that burn quickly and help start a fire. So go get some bigger stuff, okay? And make sure it's dry."

We all exited the clearing, on the hunt for firewood. It had to be nine o'clock by the time we dropped our gear. The sun had fallen past the treetops opposite the lake and cast its orange hue on the other side.

I set out to find firewood like everyone else, but I got only so far before I realized the entire northern wall of the clearing was a bone-dry, fallen pine tree. It was ten feet from where we would build the fire. Everyone, including me, walked right past it, into the woods. The ends of the dead tree's branches alone would fill twenty Idiot Boxes. The rest of the tree, even the branches as big as a twelve-year-old's wrist, were brittle enough to snap under a little pressure.

I went to the tree's top to gather medium sized branches, and Cliff stepped out toward the water, glancing behind him quickly. When I dropped my first load of sticks next to the fire pit, I faced his back and heard a repeated click sound.

He just lit up a smoke. Mr. Dinwiddie would frown terribly.

No counselor was allowed to smoke in front of the campers. Sure enough, Cliff blew out a big cloud.

Click, click went the cigarette lighter. Why was he lighting it again?

He inhaled deeply, taking furtive glances to each side, missing me completely. When he put both hands in his pockets and turned around, he spewed out the next cloud like he'd just been punched in the stomach. Then I smelled the smoke. It was no cigarette. As though waking slowly, I realized I had just smelled my first marijuana. My father prosecuted people for possession of the stuff.

Dad's voice said, *No wonder the son-of-a-bitch is so lazy.*

Mom: *Roy. Honestly. Ted doesn't need to hear that.* She'd try and fail to hide a grin.

Dad: *He's gonna hear it from somewhere. Why not from me?*

And why *not* Dad? He could say what he wanted. When he was vulgar, it made me react like Mom. It was all I could do not to laugh.

But Mr. Dinwiddie wouldn't. Not at this. Facing a rogue counselor smoking pot on a forbidden camping trip, Mr. Dinwiddie would take a giant leap over frown-grade disappointment. This would get Cliff fired.

"I thought you were gathering wood," he said.

Nothing from me.

Then Hoss showed up with a handful of firewood. "Looks like you didn't need that box, Cl—" Stone-cold recognition washed over his face. With his backwoods drawl, he said, "Mary Jane come to visit, did she?"

As I tried to figure out who Mary Jane was, Hoss drew a sinister grin. It was the face you'd see on a cheater whose efforts had just won him the game.

"Welcome to Mosquito Point, Cliff," he said.

"What's Mosquito Point?" Cliff asked. He didn't know the rules of Hoss's game. He didn't know there *was* a game, until Hoss answered him.

"It's where you've brought us, Mr. Counselor. We're not supposed to be here, of course. It's against the rules. But it's beautiful out here...isn't it, Ted?"

I didn't answer.

"If you don't talk," Hoss said, "we won't, either. You have my word."

It became clear that Hoss lived his life cheating, lying, and sneaking around. His motto may have been *Play the game, lay the blame, clear your name.* Hoss had Cliff on a leash that evening, and they both knew it.

I resented being drawn into Hoss's game, but it was no matter. Cliff instantly recognized the blackmail. He didn't protest, but he gave us equally ugly glares. "Beautiful place indeed," is all he said.

"Hell of a lot better than that dumbass Campout Circle," Hoss said.

"I guess I wouldn't know." Cliff produced a Zippo lighter in one hand, and a small, purple pipe in the other. "As long as we're partners in crime, I'm just going to take the last hit out of this."

He lifted the pipe toward us as though making a toast before burning the last of his illegal stuff. Mary Jane, Hoss had called it.

"You bring enough for us?" Hoss asked.

Pipe in mouth, a tendril of smoke curling up from the bowl, Cliff hummed, "Hm-mm." Then he leaned his head back and croaked out the words, "That'd be crossing the line." In another few seconds, he blew out his final cloud of smoke.

"Where'd you learn to call it Mary Jane?" Cliff asked.

"Older brothers. One of 'em's in the slam for dealing."

I pulled twigs off the dead tree. The two of them talked like contemporaries. Cliff slipped the pipe and lighter into his pockets as Sunny and Coach showed up with some twigs and sticks.

Sunny sniffed at the air. "You light the fire already?"

Cliff didn't answer, but Hoss did. "Just tried to light some birch bark. Didn't work very well. Stuff doesn't burn near as well as they say."

In another five minutes, Cliff had a small teepee of kindling aflame. We worked to build a cabin of twigs, then sticks. Buck ripped a panel off the kindling box and used it to fan oxygen into the fire. He got to steady work, adding dead branches to the flames. Cliff told him to slow down once, but only once, before falling into his own, disconnected world. Buck had Coach and Sunny at his disposal to provide all the dry branches anyone could want. He waved the cardboard at the fire, and it grew quickly.

My buddies and I bored quickly. We took off down the fifty-foot path to the little beach. As shadows crept up the orange-tinted far shore, I dreamed of what it was like over there and if, after the sun set completely, the flickering mom-light might appear.

CHAPTER 22

BEFORE TOO LONG, the wonderful breeze chilled, and the stars came out. I told Zeke and Neil it was time to head back to the fire and tell a little story.

By that time, the fire itself was the biggest source of light, and the woods around us were dark enough for us to feel isolated and small. We sat on our sleeping bags, in a circle around the fire. Cliff was on some other planet. Buck took a break from his fire habit after some of the guys moved their sleeping bags back to escape the heat. The flames roiled and cast dynamic, expressive shadows on our unchanging faces.

It was time. Buck suggested I read the story. I pulled the pages from my pocket and cleared my throat:

June 6, 1953

THE LEGEND OF THE

LOON LAKE SLOTH

It was five years ago, June, 1948. The remains of two boys were found at Mosquito Point. And not much remained, other than a single boot with a rotting foot inside it. Half buried in the sand was a camping skillet and a hatchet. The last anyone had heard of the two boys was September, 1947. Some people thought the sand at The Point was magic and swallowed them up. Others thought it might be a UFO that took them. But nobody really believed those things. They wanted to believe something other than the truth, but they knew. The Loon Lake Sloth had struck again.

I read on with growing reservation. The intro alone piqued the boys' awareness of ambient sounds. No raccoon or skunk took a step unnoticed. Zeke sat cross-legged and rolled back and forth in clear anticipation of every word. Neil slowly eased into the protection of his sleeping bag.

Bud let out another cutesy yelp, and Hoss told him to shut up and listen.

I continued reading. The Sloth, a lumbering, cabin-sized beast with claws and tusks, stalked the missing boys of 1947. Its eyes were narrow and glowed red. It was, of course, as fearsome as any twelve-year-old could imagine. To me— especially since it was Karen Dinwiddie's work—the story was a science-fiction masterpiece. As I read, all I could see was Karen in profile, sitting at that typewriter. Her falling hair and smiling lips, every inch of her. Her image in my mind made me want to check the pages again for Karen-fragrance. One of the two most harrowing passages was this:

> ...Johnny Appleseed's blood trickled in spirals down the tusk's grooves before it poured down in sheets, like syrup over a stack of pancakes. His kicking and screaming body slid down the bloody spit on the tusks and hung there, head-first, in the monster's mouth. The jaws closed with all the force of a car crusher, and Johnny's head gave way with a pop, like the cherry tomato you'd find in a salad. The beast's tongue slithered through Johnny's middle, sounding like somebody trying to swim through a pool of macaroni and cheese. Johnny never knew his boot fell to the ground with his foot still inside it.

and the other was this:

> The Sloth's front leg flew with blinding speed toward Bobby, who could only stand there, paralyzed with fear. The claws whopped through the air like two, swinging golf clubs. They sliced through Bobby, like swords through a watermelon. One claw chopped off his legs, just above the knees. The other went right through his ribcage. The middle section, the one with the intestines, thumped wetly to the ground and wiggled like a bloody sack of enormous worms.

The passage including the slurped-up length of intestine whipping around "…like a piece of sauce-covered spaghetti," did some of the boys in. They hid in their sleeping bags with no intention to emerge before sun-up. And to my own astonishment, the story actually made Neil cry. *That* I didn't like. When I stepped over to comfort him, he quietly waved me off. He wouldn't accept any help from Zeke, either. I should have known. He'd been afraid of a squirrel and especially those deer on the way to The Point.

I hid the sloth story in my sleeping bag. Cliff had rolled up his sidewalks for the night. We were without a counselor. Buck stood to feed the fire again, tossing one eight-foot branch across the middle of the flames. Hoss stood and watched. Just as I stepped to the water's edge to search for the light in the trees, a stiff gust grabbed me by the face. The trees swayed and rocked lazily. The dune grass sighed.

Tiny waves slurped, one after the next, at the quaint shoreline. The unpleasant image of Neil crying passed through my mind again, and I wondered if he would have a hard time trusting me from then on. I wanted to be lost in the far shore. With the firelight behind me, I couldn't see well enough.

"Hey," Hoss said, startling me.

"Hey."

"Buck won't leave the fire. Wants to see how tall he can make it. Cliff's out like a light."

"Hope nobody's sleeping bag melts."

"Nope. They moved them away from the fire again. The fat kid—"

"Zeke."

"Zeke. Moved yours, too."

Good old Zeke. That kid had *best friend* written all over him.

"So what's up?" I asked.

"You're the only one doing anything interesting."

Hoss reached into his shirt and unsheathed the knife tucked under his belt. After assuming some kind of martial arts fighting stance, he waved the knife in the air. I ignored him.

"Not much to see," he said. "Not even stars."

He was right. Earlier, before I read the story, I saw what seemed to be all of them, but some cloud cover had slipped in. Neither of us seemed to notice the sudden temperature drop or labile winds. The whispering trees and dune grass tried to tell us, but we didn't listen.

No sound came from the campsite other than the occasional pop in the fire. Hoss was ready for action. He stowed his knife and pulled out his flashlight. It was one of those new ones, shaped like a lazy *L,* and waterproof. Zeke's was just like it, only yellow and with his surname—YASKO—scrawled on it in permanent marker.

Hoss shined his light southward, down the beach. I was

tired and losing focus until Hoss called my name and pointed out the eighteen-inch, flat strip of sand at water's-edge. The spit of shore held an irregular line of washed-up plant-life. It may as well have been a lit runway. Hoss took off walking.

"Where you going?" I whispered as loudly as I could.

"I want to see how far I can walk down this way," he said.

"Not sure you should be doing—"

"Come on."

Nuh-uh, I thought. *Not with him.* But I wondered. What if I got out there a few feet, maybe fifty or so, and out of the firelight, so I could see across the lake better? A short trip down the wet sand-walk couldn't do any harm, I figured, as long as nobody knew about it.

We tiptoed over a little tree, one about as big around as my upper arm. The tree had lost its hold in the knee-high cliff above the wet strip of sand. It was easy enough to step over, but when I did, my left foot, already a little wet from the growing wave action, plunked into ankle-deep water. The cold rush overtook my foot.

Dammit.

The last thing anybody wants when hiking is to get water down in his boot.

"Step in the water?" Hoss said.

"Yep."

"Me too."

I figured, even if we went as far as we could, it would only be a few hundred yards, down to a jut of land, from which we'd be able to see the beach house light. We went. The waist-high cliff reached eye-level, then ascended, steadily and quickly to

111

the better part of fifty feet.

My life up to that point had meandered the way any life should, but like with so many events in 1970, it was about to turn.

I pulled out my own flashlight and shined it on Hoss in front of me. Another gust blew all his hair to one side, and he forged onward.

CHAPTER 23

WE'D GONE MAYBE a football field on the spit of beach. Behind me, Buck's fire wasn't much more than a glimmer. The trees continued to whisper to us, and we continued to ignore it. I stepped on something raised on the beach, maybe three inches high. It was soft, and under my weight, my foot slipped off it the way it would slip from a debarked, wet log. My flashlight beam revealed a rotting northern pike about two feet long. My boot had just ripped scales and skin off its midsection. Its one visible eye socket was empty, and the fishy corpse appeared to vomit seaweed. An eddying breeze brought me its full, rotting stink.

Hoss was fifty paces ahead of me. I thought about calling his name, but by then, the waves and wind were loud enough that I doubted he would hear me. The trees high above had already exchanged their soothing murmurs for the admonishing *SHUSHes* of a hundred school librarians.

As Hoss and I got close to the point, a strike of cold blue lightning lit up the crescent of beach. I felt some pressure to return, but not without Hoss. By then, not even a full yell could catch his attention.

The beach became irregular as I went. Sometimes it was passable, like it was near Mosquito Point, and other times it required a walk in the water. Still others made me climb over ten-ton boulders. Another, milder strike lit up some of the bigger rocks poking through the water's agitated surface. I climbed over a boulder and slid down to the other side. By then, I couldn't see Hoss at all.

Instead of landing in the clear path of the sand-walk, I found myself in thigh-deep water. My flashlight quit working after being submerged. Another strike lit the area, and I stood in the middle of a triangle of boulders. They were too close together for me to walk between them. So I climbed over one of them in what I thought—based on the last lightning strike—was the right way to go to get to Hoss. The water around me splashed on the rocks, rose and fell, and moved in two-foot waves. As soon as I gained my footing on the next boulder, I lost it again, sliding down the rock's other side.

That time, I went completely under.

In a moment of terror, I kicked and scrambled, did my best just to swim somewhere. In two or three strokes, my body hit something big and flat, not entirely firm. I was on the sandy bottom of the lake. When I pushed up on all fours, my head easily broke the surface. I stood quickly, having realized when I fell off the far side of that boulder, I'd fallen more into a wave than into the lake. As I tried to find Hoss down shore, another wave smacked and almost knocked me down.

My flashlight was dead. The lightning was my only guide.

Another flash identified Hoss at the point, maybe thirty yards away. He stood there, silhouetted in the camp's distant beach house light. I made it there without further incident.

Wind harshly blowing his hair, Hoss sported a maniac's excitement. He yelled over the wind and waves. *"TEDSKI! What're you doing out on a night like THIS?"*

I opened my mouth to speak, but I closed it again and just

THE LIGHT IN THE TREES

bent forward, exhausted. So far, the adventure had cost me a
flashlight. "*Trying to keep up with you*," I said.

"You're all wet! You went over those rocks?"

"What. Didn't *you?*"

"Nope. I climbed the side of the bluff. Held onto the little
trees."

That sounded more dangerous than what I'd done. The
bluff by the boulders is no more than a cliff made of sand. Hang
on a sapling growing on that, and it can uproot.

"You could break a leg doing that," I said. "We need to get
b—"

"Not the way *you* went."

"Safer than climbing."

"Not if you don't swim."

"You can't swim?" I asked.

"I said I *don't* swim. Except during the twenty-minute
swim test. But on that, I found a concrete block sittin' on the
bottom by the raft. I just stood on *it*. Counselors never saw me."

Cheated on his twenty-minute test.

Dick.

"Let's go," I said.

The stern librarians had exited and ushered in an angry
mob. The tops of the trees swayed and creaked in the wind.
Sometimes, they even howled. Twigs snapped here and there.
Somewhere up above, a deep and hollow *CHOCK* echoed
through the trees. Immediately following, something heavy fell
from high up. The wind—a full gale by that time—had
officially split a dead tree in half.

"Hoss! We need to get—"

"I don't know what the hell you're doing out here, Ted, but we gotta get you back to camp!"

"Stop screwing around, and let's go!" I rattled off a whole string of Roy Gables expletives in my mind.

We headed back. The next flash of lighting showed the trees rocking to their very structural limits. Whitecaps had returned to Loon Lake, and the waves bludgeoned the cliff-like bluff, which at that area reached its full height. In thirty yards, we reached the rocky trouble spot. I climbed the first boulder and committed to being in the water. Hoss hesitated and decided to go the way he had come, grabbing the bases of some saplings growing from the cliff's sandy face. I climbed over the next boulder to the sand-walk, which was, by then, ankle deep. Only the sounds of splintering wood and waves helped me discern land from lake.

A lightning strike lit Hoss sliding down the bluff, one uprooted sapling in each hand.

When he disappeared on the far side of the first boulder, he said, "Ted! I'm gonna climb up the rock like you said!"

I let out a mom-grade curse: "Dang it." I climbed back knowing Hoss wouldn't fare well in the sloshing water between the two big rocks. The vague shapes of his white hands reached to climb up the first boulder. As they did, something high above released a deep and wet, earthy thump.

A longer flash lit Hoss's smiling face as he pulled himself up on the rock.

Suddenly, I fell—or was thrown—backward in a deafening, predatory attack from above. A mass of sand and roots the size of a small car struck and swallowed Hoss's boulder with a speed that could only mean it fell from the bluff's top. Driving the muddy root ball's downward trajectory was a tree as broad as Hoss's shoulders. Its impact cracked branches both big and small. In that violent, splintering mass, Hoss's long bones and skull wouldn't stand a chance.

"HOS—" I shouted as a wave smacked me in the face, choking me. I clambered to get up, stunned. *"HOSS! ARE YOU THERE?"*

With a series of pops and muffled cracks, the tree, which seemed determined to remain standing at first, toppled. Slowly and with gaining speed, all of its fifty-odd feet and crushing weight cracked and thumped into the rocks, splashing into Loon Lake.

The Volkswagen-sized root ball kept me from climbing further, so I struggled back to the top of the boulder behind me. Hoss was either pinned under the tree or just plain dead. It was the first time in my life I ever wanted more lightning.

A second or two later, a thin beam of light appeared on the other side of the fallen tree.

"Holy CRAAAAP, Tedski!!" Hoss shouted, laughing.

Jesus! "Are you okay?" How had that tree missed him?

"Yep. Sure am. But now I'm *really* stuck." I could hear him, but I couldn't see him. He was able to use his flashlight to investigate the new barricade. The tree's smaller branches, the ones that didn't snap off when it hit, might as well have been jail cell bars. What was left of the root ball blocked any hope of anyone using the saplings to climb, cliffside, over the boulders.

"I have to go around!" He said, which I almost couldn't

hear. His flashlight beam moved toward the lake. The kid who had to cheat on his twenty-minute swim test was headed into *that* water.

The living trees' windy expressions were by then a full-blown panic. The lightning snapped flash photos every few seconds. As Hoss headed out farther, I could see him through the new obstacle's naked branches.

He walked with no apparent fear into the lake. *"Be careful!"* I yelled, over the water and wind. At the downed tree's apex, Hoss stood in chest-deep water, waves slapping him in the face. I couldn't see his flashlight.

He rounded the tree's top. Between the lightning snapshots, Hoss moved about five feet. He was still chest-deep. The next strike showed me he was standing on a big rock, the water only up to his ankles. He beat at his chest, like King Kong. And at the next flash, he was gone.

CHAPTER 24

NEXT, I SAW two arms, maybe fifteen feet from shore. They flailed.

"HOSS!"

The next flash showed me a short movie of Hoss's wide eyes, open mouth, and slow, climbing movements.

I bounded into the water and went under, thinking he'd be sluggish—we'd both be sluggish—with our clothes and boots on. He was close, maybe five feet away. Something instinctual told me to grab his shoulders and flip him around, which I did in the deep, ten feet from shore. That way, when he grabbed for something, he couldn't grab me and take us both down. When I turned him, I reached around his middle with one arm and tried an underwater sidestroke. I made no apparent progress. But after two or three tries at kicking, my lower foot grabbed the lake's bottom. I pushed.

When I dragged him to shore, Hoss fell to his knees, lurched forward, and barked out the deepest cough I'd ever heard. I asked him if he was okay, and, coughing again, although not as horribly, he nodded. He put one foot on the ground, grabbed at my arm, and stood. His lit flashlight shined from its seat, deep in his pocket. He coughed again, pulled at my arm, and said, "We gotta get"—he made one more desperate cough—"back."

I pulled him up from his armpits. We stepped toward the glow of Buck's fire. "Wow," I said, pointing my thumb at the lake, "Another minute in there, and you woulda been in trouble."

He stopped walking. "*Woulda?* I *was* in trouble." I stepped toward Buck's fire, and he followed. "You saved my life."

No. NO. I didn't save your life. "Let's go," I said, walking faster. The lightning continued as we made good time. We were close enough to Mosquito Point for the fire to show us a leafed branch flying horizontally in front of us, shore to water. A second later, maybe fifty feet north of the first branch, another leapt off the beach and shot in toward Mosquito Point.

Only a tight whirlwind could make those branches fly in opposite directions like that. We'd seen a tornado touch down. A flaming branch flew maybe twenty feet skyward, then shot into the forest.

Amid all the spray and tree noise, I was glad for the fire; it gave us a clear direction. In less than a minute, we were back to Mosquito Point. The firelight showed us just how chaotic things were. The trees jerked and twisted, alarmingly unstable. The fire was an obscene pile of dead and dry logs, a misshapen, burning schooner, heading inland. The flames danced, grabbing in all directions, greedy for more oxygen. In the next big gust, it nearly exploded into an ocean of sparks.

Zeke and Neil both bent at the waist, shaking Cliff awake. It was the first thought I had that someone could be hurt. I ran to them. Coach, Sunny, and Bones stood off to the side. Bud stood, attending to nothing and no one.

Cliff jumped up, his feet apart, pointing at something on the ground. He seemed to give instruction to each of us. His mouth moved, but I couldn't hear anything.

The wind howled, and a few, fat drops struck the ground. With no more warning than that, we stood in a sudden, full torrent of summer rain. One cracking sound after the next came from high up as the storm yanked more large, dead branches from their trees.

"*Okay, Guys!*" Cliff finally yelled from somewhere. "*It's raining! We have to go!*" He bent over, maybe to pick something up or roll up his sleeping bag. No one seemed to get anything done.

Somewhere in the nearby woods, I heard something. It was a deep thump and two awful cracking sounds. Buck yelled. A big man with a Fu Manchu mustache stood at the trailhead, feet apart and knees bent, naked surprise on his face. He appeared to dance in the frenetic action of the firelight.

"*LOOK OUT!!*" Coach yelled.

A tall, dead, telephone pole of a tree, a straight shaft with short and spiky, broken branches, fell toward the fire.

And toward Cliff.

I lunged, judging, reacting, not thinking. Cliff took my shoulder to his gut. He let out an *Oooff!* as I hit him and fell to the ground. The tree cracked and thumped conclusively across the middle of Buck's fire. The full weight of it levered the flaming schooner's bowsprit and launched it, twirling, into the dense forest.

Cliff stood, surveying the wreckage from the downed tree's other side.

"*My God! You guys, okay?*" Isaac asked out of nowhere. Suddenly, I knew the downed man wasn't Cliff at all. I'd just tackled Mr. Dinwiddie.

"Thanks to Mr. Gables," said the director, who lay on the ground next to me. Zeke and Neil gaped. Hoss and Buck stared from another direction, Buck at Mr. Dinwiddie, and Hoss, in unmasked amazement, at me. Mr. Dinwiddie got up. His usually coiffured hair soaked and his mustache drooping, half-covered with wet sand, he was no less refined than ever.

The rain doused the satellite flames the tornado and falling tree had kicked out of Buck's fire.

"Line up boys!" Mr. Dinwiddie said over the rain and wind. *"Line up with me! Let's head back toward Cabin Row!"*

He spoke with urgency but was encouraging just the same. He gently pushed my shoulder toward Isaac, leaning down to my eye level and pointing where to go.

"All right," he said. "That's the way we go. Good job."

"Basement of The Hall," Isaac said, meaning that part of the dining hall no camper ever saw. Quickly, he walked the path away from Mosquito Point.

We went. The storm shelter was where we needed to be.

CHAPTER 25

MR. DINWIDDIE AND Isaac led us quickly up the trail. By the time we made it to the cabins, the steadying gale blew the rain into a spray that stung my face. It was the kind of rain even a twenty-year-old man wouldn't drive in. Isaac took us through Cabin Row, past the waterfront. Everything surrounding the beach house's utility light, for a radius of maybe twenty feet, was a bright-white haze.

In the dining hall, a flight of concrete stairs descended into a dim space behind a door I'd never seen opened. The basement was smaller than the dining space. It had no windows. Concrete block walls and concrete ceiling with I-beam girders ensured our safety in any weather. Four simple lightbulbs lit the space. Spiderwebs crowded every corner, and a pile of wood sat off to one side. All in all, it could have been one of those nuclear fallout shelters from the fifties. The strongest tornado in history could have swept the camp's surface clean, and from The Hall's basement, we'd never know. We spent the rest of the night down there. Karen slept, leaning on her dad's shoulder.

~~~

By the time we emerged from the shelter and slogged back toward our cabins, the sun was up. Twigs and leaved branches littered the waterfront and the grounds of Cabin Row. Some of the cabins lost a few shingles, but they'd survived. Only Headquarters came close to any serious damage. A century-old oak had fallen and smashed a picnic table just south of the building. I couldn't imagine what would have happened if that tree had fallen on a cabin full of boys.

The sand all around us was different. The rain had sculpted it into a peculiar landscape.

"Hey, you guys!" Zeke shouted. "It looks like the surface of the moon!"

The rain had made sandy craters. Craters within craters. It had erased all evidence of the mass exodus to the storm shelter. It could've been a place no one had walked in decades.

"I'm Neil Armstrong!" he said, taking big steps and willing them to appear in slow motion, like an astronaut in low gravity. "That's one small step for man, and one giant leap for mankind!" A ray of happiness—and a pang of sadness, too— ran through me as I wondered how much Zeke's mom must love him.

We were told to get back to our cabins and change clothes. All the morning's activities were cancelled, which suited us just fine. Isaac popped in to tell us about a special staff meeting going on, that we'd be alone in the cabin and to relax the morning away.

No one said anything for a minute or two after Isaac left, but then Buck got out of his bed, pulled a chair out from the table, and sat down. Before he even said anything, he had the cabin's attention.

"I think you all should know," he began, "that Ted saved Hoss's life last night."

Oh, no. Not this again.

Everyone expressed some form of amazement. Zeke and Neil both perched up on their elbows, facing me. Someone asked for the story, and Buck told it.

Zeke whispered, "Ted! You saved *two* peoples' lives last night!"

At the end of Buck's monologue, Hoss said, "Thanks, Ted."

Being in the spotlight was never my thing. But Hoss's appearance of sincerity made me sit up and acknowledge the whole topic. I checked him, as he thanked me, just to be sure he wasn't sticking his thumbs in his ears and waving his fingers. Or making faces and grabbing his crotch. He wasn't. Putting my head back on my pillow, I gave Zeke and Neil self-conscious acknowledgement, saying, "Shut up." Zeke grinned and Neil feigned offense at my brazen command.

"But also," Buck said. "If anybody talks about this, Hoss and Ted could get in big trouble."

No. More like Hoss broke the rules, and I had to rescue him. It reminded me of Bud's first flip-out. In that case, Hoss made the mess, and Buck and I cleaned it up. Later, I'd answered the directors' questions about Hoss's knife. And instead of being sent home like Toad, Hoss came out ahead. With this most-recent mess, I probably did save his damned life. I wouldn't have put it past him to remember it the other way around.

Buck added, sounding more like a politician than a boy-at-summer-camp: "We're a cabin, and we need to stick together as a team. And that means no talking about this. That includes with kids from other cabins. Okay? Let's keep our guys out of trouble."

Buck. Shut up before you make Hoss the president of the

Ted Gables Fan Club.

Tackling Mr. Dinwiddie was a different matter. I would put up with the other campers' reverence for days. Never again—I thought at the time—would I be anywhere so near *famous*.

The morning's laziness took hold, and everyone relaxed in his bunk. Neil and Zeke traded books: *To Kill a Mockingbird* for *America's National Parks*. I wanted *Crawdads from Outer Space* again. A part of me wanted Karen to fall asleep with her head on my shoulder. Everyone drifted toward sleep.

Sunny broke the silence, "I heard somebody told that storm to happen. Like the controls are in Headquarters or something. Do you think that's true?"

"May-*be*," Buck said. I waited for a scathing retort from Hoss, but it never came. Bud leaned up on one elbow, eyes wide, glancing from cabin-mate to cabin-mate, as though for some affirmation. Bud was a *believer*.

No one said anything more. Zeke fell fast asleep, probably before he was done with Harper Lee's first paragraph. Neil flipped pages showing the parks' pictures. I dreamt for a time about Cal Owen and what the camp would have been like in 1938. My surroundings faded from view.

Then I bolted into a sitting position.

I'd left Karen's sloth story in my sleeping bag.

CHAPTER 26

I WANTED THAT story. Losing it would be my young life's second-greatest tragedy.

The guys were almost all asleep. There had never been a better time to steal down to Mosquito Point. Figuring I might have an entire hour, I got up quietly, and as I tiptoed up front in my bare feet, nobody stirred. A peek through the burlap curtains told me it was safe. In one silent turn of the doorknob and a gentle push, I was on the stoop.

Over my right shoulder, Cabin Row was one of those old-west ghost towns. Even the cottonwoods were still. To the left, the trailhead to Mosquito Point was there, where it always was, twenty running steps away. I shut the door.

Bounding for the hidden safety of the woods, I didn't slow for twenty yards. At a portion of the trail that wound up to the bluff's edge, I stopped for a second in the inviting sand. A jaunt down the bluff to the water was just a couple of steps away, but I didn't dare. Down to my left jutted the unnamed point Hoss reached the night before. Further north would be the boulders I'd never seen in daylight and the dead tree that almost killed Hoss.

I smartly decided to stay on the trail and jogged again. It felt good to stretch my legs. The trouble I could get into for going was of no concern. Slowing to a walk, I enjoyed the squish of soft, wet pine needles between my toes. A distant woodpecker was hard at work, maybe the same one we'd heard the night before.

Yet another fallen tree crossed the trail. *Coulda fallen on us.*

I hopped over the trunk and made it to the clearing in no time. Daydreaming, I strolled into the sand. The Mr. Dinwiddie tree snapped me back into consciousness. A telephone pole with deadly spikes, it divided the clearing in two.

Its bulk pressed itself into the sand and to the bottom of Buck's ridiculous fire. One of those sharp, broken branches impaled Zeke's sleeping bag and drove it partially underground. Something in my imagination pulled up a photograph of Zeke inside the stabbed sleeping bag, his face white, a flow of maroon blood clot coming out of his mouth and nose. I squeezed my eyes shut to purge the thought.

The familiar green plaid of my own sleeping bag reminded me of my mission, and I headed to it. Lifting a flap from the open top, I guessed the entire waterlogged bag would weigh a hundred pounds. Sand, caked into the zipper, shot out in all directions as I pulled it open. The pages were still there, and they were wet. They'd lost all their crispness, but as I carefully peeled them apart, the typed words proved to be in good shape. Some were a little smudged, but that just added more age to the paper.

Holding two pages of the story in each hand and straddling my sleeping bag, I almost fell when Karen appeared at the mouth of the trail. Her face was red, her breathing heavy.

"Is *that* the tree that fell?" she said, "Almost landed on my *dad?*"

She followed me. She had to've.

"I thought you'd saved him from something little," she said. "Maybe kept him from being *scraped* or something. But..." she pointed at the downed pole of a tree. "Was that really gonna *land* on him?"

"I don't know. It's hard to remember."

"Dad said you kept a tree from landing on him."

I shrugged and stepped away from the bag to stand up straight.

Karen wore jean shorts cut off a few inches above mid-thigh and a faded, old yellow T-shirt. Her hair had fallen partially out of its ponytail and rested on those athlete shoulders.

Open marvel on her face, her eyes blazing green fire, she said, "You kept him from—" Her voice dropped to a whisper. "*You saved my dad's life.*"

I broke eye contact and swallowed hard.

"You really did," she said. "He didn't say so, but I bet he didn't because—"

Probably because he wanted to protect her. I understood that. Maybe I did actually save Mr. Dinwiddie's life. It was hard enough to process myself.

"Thank you," she said softly.

You're welcome could not have sounded more ridiculous in that setting, and probably for that exact reason, I said, "You're welcome."

Her expression softened, and she walked toward me. My legs felt as though they were eight feet long and pure, wet spaghetti. Her lips separated. She didn't stop until she was a half-step away.

Oh, my God. Is she going to…

"So what are you doing out here, anyway?" she asked, breaking the most pleasant tension I'd ever felt.

I held up the damp pages of the sloth story, two in each hand. Karen stepped back to see what I held. In a moment, incredulous surprise crossed her face.

"I left it here," I said. "Had to come get it."

"I'm so glad you found that. Did you *read* it last night?"

Ah. A question. Something I could muster the courage to answer. "Yeah. It scared them."

"Really?"

"Made most of them hide in their sleeping bags."

"You big liar!"

"No. Honest. Gave 'em the creeps."

She crossed her arms, leaned on one leg, and cocked her head to the side. "What about you?"

"What. Gimme me the creeps?"

"Well did it?"

"Wouldn't'a read it to 'em if it didn't." That felt like the correct answer.

"Did *you* hide in your sleeping bag?"

"Sure." I only wished I had. If Hoss and I hadn't been gone, we as a cabin would have organized ourselves and made it back to Cabin Row quickly. And if so, Mr. Dinwiddie might never have had to come to Mosquito Point at all.

Karen stared into my face with an indescribable air of confidence. I wanted to ask her what she was thinking just then. Maybe she was happy her story came off pretty well. She stepped toward me—my entire torso a pounding heartbeat—

and hopped over my sleeping bag. She stepped carefully over the fallen tree itself, her arms out for balance, then headed for the lake. Something inside told me to follow her, so I did. Karen picked a piece of horsetail to play with as she went. With great care, I folded and pocketed the damp pages of her story.

In another minute, we stood side-by-side at the end of the path to the lake, on the edge of the deep sand. When we got there, she started working her feet in little circles, burying them, getting down to where the sand was cold and damp. Her ponytail slumped forward as she bent to watch her feet.

One minute, she was like a grown woman. But the next, she was a girl just my age, someone I'd take fishing or to the park, talk to effortlessly for hours about absolutely nothing. I was pretty sure she'd ride bikes and play in the dirt with the best of them.

She let out a whimper as she flailed her arms, losing her balance. I reached for her hands, and after a few tries, she grabbed mine. Somewhere around all that ponytailed hair, a giggle emerged as she pulled hard on both of my hands to keep from falling. When I leaned back, she straightened, her feet together, almost toe-to-toe with me. The happiness on her face was pure and honest.

She had no apparent problem with close eye contact. When I broke the gaze and studied the sand at our feet, she took a step back, put her hands on her hips, and said, "You're tall, Ted."

I nodded dumbly.

"You're as tall as me, and I'm the tallest girl in my class. There are only a couple of boys taller—"

"What grade are you in?" I blurted.

"I'm starting high school in the fall."

"*High* school?"

"Yeah?"

"Just starting?"

"Sure. Why?"

"Um…never mind."

"What?" She shifted her weight to one leg. Her mouth hung a little open, and its corners crept upward.

"Well, a…" I stammered. "It's just that—"

As though biding the time it took me to answer her, she reached up to fix her ponytail with the magic fingers that threw the sizzler up by the bench.

She relaxed her arms, dropped her chin, and raised her eyebrows. "You were saying?"

"I—"

"Come *on! Tell me!*"

"I thought you might be in college."

Her mouth fell open in a gape of disbelief.

I luffed like a flag in the wind. Between the heaven of Karen's presence and the hell of self-consciousness, I said, "I'm sorr—"

"That's the sweetest thing I've ever heard."

She stepped toward me, took my right hand in her left, and faced the lake. My hand bristled but soon relaxed. In that moment, we were two young and perfectly innocent lovers, holding hands. I secretly wished someone would take a picture.

"I love my dad, Ted." There was no doubt in my mind. Mr. Dinwiddie was a great man. "Probably as much as you love yours."

"Yep," I said absently. She squeezed my hand. A soft wind came from the lake.

I also loved Karen, in a different way. And Neil and Zeke in a third. Trust was the thread that ran through all of them. Then, Mom. No matter how horribly I missed her, thoughts of her *always* made me happy.

"Have you ever been over there?" I asked pointing to the other side.

"Nope."

"I wonder what it's like. Always have. My dad says it won't stay that way."

"We should borrow a canoe and go."

Borrow a canoe and go. The glass-eyed daydream was immediate. I focused on those twin birches across the lake. *Borrow a canoe and go. With Karen. Yessir*, as my dad would say.

All of a sudden, Karen let go of my hand. I stood as though in shock as Karen stepped in front of me and blocked my view. She put her arms around my middle and hugged me. Painting by numbers in a foreign situation, I hugged back.

She squeezed for just a second and said, "What you did for my dad was...just...thank you." She backed away. "Gotta get back,"

I concentrated on her every step, every choice of foot placement in the sand, her care in crossing the downed tree, and the way her arms elevated to balance her. At the trail's head, she waved. That time, I held her gaze solidly until she took off in a gentle, bare-footed run up the trail. Her strides were long, and that ponytail danced behind her. When no trace of her movement remained, my heart ached.

CHAPTER 27

WHEN I GOT back to Cabin 7, no one was any the wiser about my departure. Except Hoss. He seemed to be the only one awake. One thing I knew was *Hoss is smart*. And observant.

In fact, the door latch's little click alerted him. I was who he saw, and the pages of Karen's story were what I carried. His mental wheels ground only for a second before his eyes narrowed and his tight-lipped grin appeared. It was obvious he knew where I'd been and that he respected the rule-breaking I'd just indulged.

I had the guts to sneak down to Mosquito Point during rest period. His expression and the slow shake of his head meant one thing. Hoss admired me. He was impressed. Proud. He accepted me as one of his own. There was nothing to do about it but hope he didn't deduce I'd spent a little time with Karen. I shrugged him off and laid the open pages of Karen's story underneath my blanket to finish drying.

That afternoon was all free-rec. I lazed around the cabin for a time. Later, Zeke, Neil and I watched three men with a big truck and chainsaws dismantle the fallen oak until nothing but a fresh stump and a heavy snow of sawdust stood in its place.

After supper, Mr. Dinwiddie got to work cleaning up the rest of the debris from the storm. The job would cost him three large watermelons, a cross-section of a downed birch tree, and about twenty minutes. He decreed "Everyone between the age of eight and thirteen" will don his swim trunks and place his towel on the waterfront beach at eight o'clock. When he held captive every inhabitant of every cabin—cheap and effective manual labor—he announced "Operation Pick-Up." All campers would pick up the twigs, branches, and a few pinecones the storm had littered onto Cabin Row. He said the cabin who picked up the most sticks would win the prize of one large watermelon.

It was an interesting social experiment. Some kids ran around picking up as many sticks as possible. Others ambled without aim, hardly working at all. Marty chose to lead Cabin 6 into picking up sticks and breaking them each into two or three pieces to double or triple his cabin's apparent yield. In no particular hurry, Zeke, Neil, and I picked up our share and dumped them in a growing pile at the top of the beach.

By the time Mr. Dinwiddie and Isaac revealed enough watermelon for all participants to share, the pile of picked up sticks atop the waterfront was the size of a ping-pong table and taller than I stood. Everyone gathered around the watermelons outside Headquarters.

Isaac disappeared between Cabins 1 and 2. He re-emerged on the south side of Cabin 1's front face, then disappeared again behind the stick pile, where he stayed for less than a minute. After hiding a pump-sprayer of some kind down at the beach house, he jogged back up the bluff to sit down, on an old, wooden box, next to Mr. Dinwiddie.

Zeke and Neil were off to the side, conversing intently. Sauntering past them and toward me, Karen grinned mightily when she heard Zeke say *sloth*. With the formality of a business executive in an evening gown, she said, "Good evening, Ted," before taking a big, wet bite out of her own slice of watermelon. In another half minute, she drew some eight-year-olds from Cabin 1 into a seed-spitting contest.

"Attention!" came a booming voice from near the pile of sticks. It was Mr. Dinwiddie with a megaphone. "May I have your attention...Please gather 'round. And yes. You may bring your watermelon. I have an announcement to make."

The boys gathered in one, big, watermelon-slurping gaggle to a rope on the ground. Isaac was there to instruct that no one cross the rope. The boys complied without question, standing in an arc running from Cabin 1 to the wooden box. Mr. Dinwiddie stood between the boys and the pile of sticks. With everyone quieting, he put down the megaphone and talked. He issued a few platitudes about the privilege of spending time in such an idyllic setting, the responsibility of pulling your own weight, and the virtues of mutual respect.

"Because when we work together..." he said theatrically, "giving everything we can...cleaning our summer home after an historic storm...we know the meaning of—" He took three steps to one side. "That *old...White Birch*—" He swept his arm slowly and gestured toward the pile of sticks. "*MAGIC!*"

The pile burst into a cone of flame shooting thirty or more feet in the air. Its heat spread to us in an explosive wave. Half the boys screamed, and the other half gasped. Genuine surprise touched every young face from Cabin Row. Neil, Zeke, and I...even Hoss. We *believed*. The magic was there. It was everywhere, and we'd never forget it.

CHAPTER 28

IN ONGOING CELEBRATION, the waterfront opened. Swimming—or lake-bathing, to rid us of all sticky watermelon juice—was mandatory, and we were happy to oblige. No one mentioned the vague smell of gasoline on the fire. I stood inside the waterfront and watched as Isaac pulled up two buried wires and wound them around his hand. Those wires led from the wooden box to the fire. I didn't know exactly how he did it, but I'd've bet Hoss a dollar Isaac had a battery in that box somewhere. The sleuth work was satisfying, but part of me wished I'd just jumped in the lake *believing*.

Mr. Dinwiddie found me.

"Mr. Gables," he said. "Ted. I have something for you, made it today. It's a token of sorts."

He held something like a large wooden coin just bigger around than a baseball. It was a cross-section of a white birch tree, maybe a half-inch thick. Through a hole drilled in the top, he'd put a ribbon that fit around my neck. Burn-etched into place were the words

**Integrity
&
Courage**

"A little thanks from me to you, my friend. I've never been so grateful to be tackled to the ground."

A couple dozen boys, including Zeke, Neil, and Hoss stood

nearby. Mr. Dinwiddie patted my shoulder before heading back to his office. A minute later, Karen appeared with an expression I'd never seen. More business executive than seed-spitter, she strode my direction until we were a foot apart, face-to-face. Everyone around us might as well have disappeared.

With no more than a second's hesitation, she planted a big, fat kiss right on my mouth.

She wanted to say something. I knew it. But her face reddened, and she ran away, toward Headquarters. What she almost said remains a mystery. The boys around me gradually reappeared and congratulated me like I was an astronaut returning from the moon. Karen's quick strides carried her all the way to the big birch.

Zeke and Neil stood by me. Cabin 6's Marty grumbled something vulgar and jealous-sounding. Hoss bullied his way past the other boys, shoving Marty aside.

A strange man, a tall, thin guy with a minor hunch in his back stepped out of the office's front door. His thin lips stretched and opened to reveal crooked, yellow teeth as he watched Karen run toward him.

Dread unfurled in my stomach.

"Jesus, Tedski," Hoss said. "You pay her *money* to do that?"

Karen, still in a healthy run, stopped cold. Her hair parachuted inelegantly, her foot slid on the sandy hard-pack, and she fell on her butt. Isaac stood from a picnic table nearby, as though to help her. Karen popped to her feet. Without so much as bothering to slap the dirt off her hands or rear end, she hurried into headquarters, giving the stranger a wide berth.

~~~

That night, Mr. Dinwiddie delayed call-to-quarters by a half hour. When the last swimmers dragged themselves up from the waterfront, having washed away the watermelon sugar, we found ourselves deeply tired and ready for bed. No one stood outside Headquarters. The stranger was gone. Zeke, Neil, and I walked toward Cabin 7, talking about sloths, tornadoes, and how Mr. Dinwiddie got the fire going. (I didn't tell them about Isaac's wires.)

Zeke and Neil debated with spirit the shape a raindrop might take when it falls from the sky. I was too tired to do much of anything but listen. The birch trunk medal hung around my neck.

"Hey, Ted!" Zeke said with sudden, ridiculous enthusiasm.

Me: "Hey what."

Zeke: "I called my parents this afternoon."

Neil: "Yeah, man. You're gonna like this."

Me: "So?"

Zeke: "They're gonna send me a book about sloths."

Neil: "And I'm gonna need to read it."

Me: "There'll be giant sloths in there."

Zeke: "They're extinct."

Me: "I bet whoever wrote that book's never been up here."

Neil: "Don't play like that."

"These woods have plenty of room to hide in."

"Shut up, man."

"Book won't say how fast the big ones can run."

Neil: "Sloths are slow, Ted."

Me: "Wait till the book shows up." Neil giggled. "Those big prehistoric ones can run thirty-four miles per—"

Zeke: "So what's it like to kiss a girl, Ted?"

We entered the cabin, our sandy feet scraping the old wood floor. It was deserted, and something was wrong. Cliff's bed was bare. Someone else's sleeping bag, rolled up tight, sat on the plastic mattress next to an uncased pillow. The shelves were empty. All traces of Cliff were gone.

"Where's all Cliff's stuff?" Sunny asked when he made it back, his towel bunched up around his neck.

Buck beckoned me to a meeting with Hoss in the front of the cabin. Before I went up there, I took off my medal and stuffed it in my shelves, next to the hidden cigar box.

Buck whispered, "You think they fired Cliff?"

Me: "I imagine so."

Buck: "Why do you think?"

Me: "Because nobody knew where we were during the storm."

Hoss: "That and him smoking pot right in front of us."

Me: "Did you tell?"

Hoss: "No. Didn't you see? Last night in that basement? Isaac got in his *face*. Moved in real close and smelled it on him is my guess."

Buck: "What? Smoking *pot*?"

Hoss: "Shhhh. He did it in front of me and Ted."

Me: "So Isaac found out about it on his own? *You* didn't tell on him?"

"Ted. You disappoint me."

"For real, you didn't tell?"

"No. I didn't. Said I wouldn't, and I didn't."

Buck: "You think Cliff told how we ended up at Mosquito Point?"

Hoss: "I think they probably put it together how we ended up there. They'll know it wasn't his idea. I bet if they want to make something of it, they'll talk to us real soon."

"You think we'll get in trouble?"

"No."

I wasn't sure.

Hoss continued. "Look. We're campers. Our job is to give the counselors shit and try to get away with stuff. *Cliff* is the one who was stupid enough to let us get away with it. And *Cliff* is the one who decided to smoke weed when he was in charge of us. We were just campers being campers. We'll be all right."

I whispered the words on my burner-etched medal. I knew what *Courage* meant. *Integrity* was more nebulous, and I didn't know it well-enough not to want a dictionary. Mr. Dinwiddie knew what we'd done. He had to. He gave the medal to the one member of the cabin who would know Mosquito Point from anywhere else on earth. And he treated me with respect anyway.

Dictionary or not, I knew *Integrity* well enough to know it didn't apply to me. Later, I hid the medallion in the cigar box and didn't want to see it anymore.

That evening, I was the cheater and the liar, and Hoss was the one who'd kept his word.

And a close eye on me.

CHAPTER 29

THE CABIN DOOR opened. It was Isaac.

"Fellas," he said in his booming-but-normal speaking voice.

Everyone stopped what he was doing. Coach took his nose out of his *Mad* magazine, and Zeke emerged from the sink area, foaming at the mouth with toothpaste.

"It's okay. Keep getting ready for bed. Mr. Dinwiddie's gonna be here in a few minutes to talk to you."

"About Cliff?" someone asked.

Isaac nodded. "Yeah. About Cliff. And some other stuff."

"Where'd Cliff go?" someone else asked.

"S'pose we just wait for Mr. Dinwiddie."

"Cliff's been fired and carted outta here," Hoss said. Some of the guys answered in gasps and murmurs.

Isaac blinked slowly and sighed. "Look. Let's wait and talk to Mr. Dinwiddie."

"Hey, Buck!" Hoss said. "What about that loony bin you told me about? The one in Traverse City? You think they dragged Cliff away and threw him in there?"

Buck didn't say anything, and I didn't know what Hoss was up to. He usually didn't draw attention to himself and was probably just bored. The guys sat on their bunks, ready for bed, listening. Zeke disappeared to finish brushing.

"No," Isaac said. "They wouldn't do that to Cliff."

"What loony bin?" Coach asked.

143

"Okay, hold on, now," Isaac said. " *'Loony bin'* is a pretty disrespectful way to put it. 'Insane Asylum' is the proper term for a place like that."

"Nut house," Hoss said.

"No. Not 'nut house,' either," Isaac said as Zeke returned and got in bed. "And they wouldn't put Cliff in there. That place is only for the truly insane."

The whole conversation was bizarre to me until I realized Isaac was changing. I'd seen his metamorphosis many times before—usually through the screen window at Headquarters—from mild-mannered Isaac to his legend-building alter ego.

"Truly insane?" Buck asked.

"*Criminally*," Isaac said.

The cabin went quiet. Zeke and Neil snapped their gazes at me. I narrowed my eyes and shook my head at them as subtly as I could. Those two guys were my best friends, and I decided I'd put them in places of prominence even higher than camp legend. For then and forever. I'd never deceive them. They already knew to let the others *believe*.

"Where is it?" Coach asked. "Where is the…place?"

"Traverse City," Isaac said. "'Bout twenty miles from here."

No one spoke, but everyone listened, including Hoss.

"They don't put many people there nowadays."

"How come?" Coach asked, unknowingly placing a baseball tee in front of Isaac.

"Well…same reason they closed Alcatraz."

Coach set the ball when he asked, "Why'd they close Alcatraz?"

"The inmates learned to escape."

TOCK! Base hit. Gasps and murmurs.

Zeke: "What do they do when somebody escapes?"

Isaac: "Catch 'em and put 'em back in, I suppose—"

Coach: "Where do they go when they escape?"

Isaac: "You mean the ones they can find?"

TOCK. That one went over the fence. Even Hoss seemed unsure. I wanted a bucket of popcorn like the ones Mom, Dad and I used to get at that old movie theater in Franklin, just north of Blue River.

"*Yeah*," Coach said. "Where do they *go*?"

Isaac rubbed his chin and smoothed out his Fu Manchu. "I dunno. Lotsa, lotsa woods out there..."

Another home run. I could almost hear the cheering crowd.

Someone knocked at the door and opened it.

"There's the Psycho now!" Hoss said. Bud clapped a hand over his mouth. His face white and his eyes wide.

"No," Isaac said. "That'll be Mr. Dinwiddie."

Just as soon as it started, the fiction was over. Isaac was instantly Isaac again. But the legend that night germinated in the fertile ground of idle, young minds.

"So now we got psychos out there too?" Neil said.

"Sloth'll eat 'em," I whispered.

He crossed his arms and shook his head, giving me a stern, professorly glare over the rims of his glasses.

Mr. Dinwiddie stepped in. Before he spoke, I heard the whispered word *psycho* no fewer than three times.

Isaac would stay with us that night, after Mr. Dinwiddie was done telling us about Cliff. Cliff had, indeed, been fired, and Mr. Dinwiddie, had, of course, avoided specifics. But we all knew, some of us more than others, that Cliff had been disposed to ignoring common sense, as well as a few rules. Mr. Dinwiddie used phrases like "amicable parting," and "Cliff and I agreed" when he told us "just because Cliff was a nice young man unfortunately doesn't mean he and White Birch Camp are fully compatible." What followed was the most negative thing I ever heard Mr. Dinwiddie say: "Cliff and I therefore concluded that each of us would benefit from going his own, separate direction."

I wondered why he'd given Hoss a second chance with the knife and had fired Cliff. But I supposed Cliff had screwed up plenty. After thinking of all the examples, it was a wonder our counselor lasted as long as he did.

Before leaving, our director said we should "have a pleasant sleep" and that "by lunch tomorrow, your new counselor should be ready."

CHAPTER 30

BETWEEN LUNCH AND rest period the next day, our new counselor showed up, a stranger I recognized. He followed Mr. Dinwiddie into the cabin. Isaac stood by, idly. Just like the night before, we sat on our bunks, listening.

"Aft...-men," the man mumbled. He cleared his throat and tried again. "Afternoon, gentlemen." The stranger then stepped a little to the side of Mr. Dinwiddie, but not quite all the way next to him. I wanted Isaac to be the counselor, but I supposed that wasn't possible. What we'd just been given was a man with a hunch in his back and crooked, yellow teeth.

"Gentlemen," Mr. Dinwiddie said. "Please give a warm greeting to Lloyd. Lloyd is a man who can teach you all manner of teamwork, leadership, and just about anything you want to know about the outdoors. He is your new counselor."

Lloyd stood a little taller than Mr. Dinwiddie, and a little thinner. That is, he was less muscular. Mr. Dinwiddie stood straight and true. Lloyd hunched a little and craned his neck accordingly. My bed being where it was, the two men appeared in near perfect profile. Lloyd's hair was dark with flecks of gray, and short, almost military. Mr. Dinwiddie's hair was gray with flecks of darkness, and wavy. The two of them had the same jaw angle and similar noses, although Lloyd's was larger. So were his ears.

They were brothers. They had to be. In profile, they could almost be twins. It was as though, as they grew, Mr. Dinwiddie had found the good spine and muscle, and Lloyd had found only used and mismatched body parts. Lloyd was younger, I figured. Older than all the other counselors, to be sure, but not as old as Mr. Dinwiddie.

The two men were the difference between a handsome man and his caricature. Mr. Dinwiddie carried an aura of greatness. Lloyd didn't. His eyes didn't smile. The director might break into song with his barbershop quartet, and Lloyd might bark at us for name, rank, and serial number. Something bad—hell if I knew what it was—lurked beneath his skin.

Why is Karen afraid of you, Uncle Lloyd?

"So," Mr. Dinwiddie said, his baritone voice filling the cabin, "you've got a lot to talk about, some getting acquainted to do, and—Oh! One more thing. Lloyd will be heading up, shall we say, a kind of outing for you." He hesitated for the nine, young, rapt faces.

"What kind of outing?" Coach asked.

"Ah!" Mr. Dinwiddie said, "Glad you asked. An outing at that. Let's call it a canoe trip."

Zeke grinned.

"Yes," the director continued. "It's a little something for you, a reward for being the first cabin in my entire twenty-two-year history of White Birch Camp…" he paused again, baiting us.

I took the bait. "First cabin to do what?"

"A-ha! Mr. Gables. You're the first cabin to win inspection twenty times in under thirty days."

Twenty times? No one seemed to believe it. We'd just become accustomed to working as a team and going to lunch first.

"For that reason, this week or next during a rest period, you'll get two hours, as a cabin, in the canoes," and then he added, lifting up his eyebrows and one index finger, "with appropriate waterfront staff, of course..." His mustache straightened like an eagle's wings. "...and with the concession that each and every one of you first passes his twenty-minute swim test."

All eyes beamed at Zeke, whose grin went away.

Neil leaned down from his top bunk to face his friend. Neil, afraid of the sloth, and Zeke, afraid of the northern pike.

"Safety first," Mr. Dinwiddie said. He swept a theatric arm in front of his body, patted Lloyd on the shoulder, and bowed to us before leaving the cabin.

Then it was just Lloyd and us. Cabin 7 was at another fork in the trail. Either this guy would warm up and want to show us everything there was, or he didn't want to be there at all. Zeke seemed eager to get to know him. Hoss's expression was a couple steps the other way past neutral. I didn't like Lloyd. If he'd given Karen a reason to fear him, I *concluded that each of us would benefit from going his own, separate direction.*

We went around the cabin, one-by-one, introducing ourselves. Lloyd wrote down our names and, it appeared, our hometowns as we spoke. Our short presentations were regimented. Especially for Neil, who Lloyd cut off after just a few words.

"That'll be enough, *Mister* Shepherd," Lloyd said to Neil. I wasn't sure why Lloyd treated Neil that way, but Neil clammed up in surprise, scrunched his eyebrows and pushed up his glasses.

"Very good," Lloyd said at the end, clearing his throat. "I suppose I'd better let you boys get on with your rest hour."

"It's rest *period*," Bud said. I rolled my eyes. Neil closed his and shook his head.

"Excuse me?"

"I said it's rest *period*. It's ninety minutes. An hour and a *half*."

"Thank you, Bud," Hoss said. "I've been wondering all summer how many minutes are in an hour and a–"

"Rest period," Lloyd said. "That'll be fine." And after about fifteen long seconds, he said, "Let's get a few things clear. It is my understanding that there are certain rules. These include a no-tolerance policy for swearing. There will be no swearing in this cabin. There are to be no weapons of any kind. And there will be no additional graffiti placed in Cabin 7.

"These are camp policies. You'll learn *my* policies as we go. For now, I'll be up front unpacking my things. It is also my understanding that you are to remain in your bunks for the entirety of the rest period."

Just as Lloyd turned the corner to his area, Hoss sat upright in his bed, opened his eyes wide, frowned severely, and mumbled the following: "It is also my understanding that you are to remain in your bunks for the *entirety*—"

In a burst of no more than ten, echoing, boots-on-hardwood footsteps, Lloyd made it from the counselor area to the far end of the cabin. "Out of bed, young man!" he said, in a harsh but unmistakable Dinwiddie voice.

"I thought we were s'pose to remain in our bunks for the

en-TIRETY of the—"

"*Now*, please."

Hoss jumped off his bunk in one big lurch and landed on the floor, feet planted. It was clear he'd tried to make all the noise he could.

"I will not be mocked in this cabin," Lloyd said. "That's rule number one."

The two were face-to-face, almost touching. Cords showed on Lloyd's neck, and Hoss slumped his shoulders and his eyelids, obviously feigning boredom. He faked a yawn, patting his open mouth.

Lloyd grunted.

When he did, Hoss suddenly stood up straight, perhaps more serious than I'd seen him. He leaned slightly toward Lloyd, the way he did just before I pushed him across the cabin.

"Is that perfectly *clear*?" Lloyd asked.

Buck shifted in his bunk and steeled himself. "Lloyd...um Sir? I'm sure Hoss didn't mean—"

"Oh, I'm quite sure he did mean it, Mister..."

"McDaniel."

Hoss seemed to age five years in an instant as he stared Lloyd down. Lloyd checked the clipboard and faced Hoss. "And I'm here to set a precedent. There will be respect in this cabin. Or there will be trouble. Is *that* clear."

Nothing happened.

"You will speak when you're spoken to, Mr. Cartwright."

Hoss gave no response other than to turn his head slowly from side to side.

"I said you will speak—"

"Whenever. I. *Want*." Hoss said.

Lloyd flinched. "I don't believe I heard you quite–"

"I believe you did. And I don't believe you're gonna do anything about it."

It was silent. Up to that point in my life, I'd never seen two people so quick to anger at one another. An adult and a kid. It was instantaneous. They repelled each other like powerful magnets.

"Oh, you just wait," Lloyd said.

"For *what?*"

Again, nothing happened.

"I'm waiting," Hoss said.

No one moved, including Hoss and Lloyd, for what seemed to be an entire minute.

"Back in your bunk," Lloyd said. "I will not be mocked or addressed in this manner. I *will*...make this a tremendously long summer for anyone who repeats this behavior."

He walked off without answering Hoss's question. Lloyd's exit seemed like nothing more than an escape. It set a precedent, all right, but probably not the one he wanted. My heart raced for the next five minutes. Not another word was spoken for the next hour, but the cabin buzzed with body language.

Facing Zeke, I pointed to the graffiti on the walls and Lloyd's roster on the table, mimicking handwriting. Zeke nodded in recognition. It was do-or-die on the graffiti. After the display Lloyd had put on, I was happy to break another rule, to commit another victimless crime. If Lloyd's roster was still there when the bell rang at the end of rest period, I'd jump at that table to get it.

Hoss sat on his bed, leaning against the back wall, legs dangling off the front of his bunk. I would have thought, after winning the confrontation, he'd grin and whistle "Floatin' Down the Mississippi." But he didn't. Instead, his face showed the most intimidating glower I'd ever seen. His hands were white-knuckled fists, and he did nothing but breathe for an hour. Lloyd had just drilled through Hoss's smug satisfaction, hitting a gusher of something nobody knew about.

Another question that tickled my mind was whether Mr. Dinwiddie had sicced his angry little brother on us, maybe as a punishment for Mosquito Point or as a tool to keep us in line. Or maybe, on short notice, Mr. Dinwiddie simply couldn't do better than Lloyd.

CHAPTER 31

ZEKE WAS UNDER pressure to pass his twenty-minute test. It took a handful of calm and perfect afternoons to get him down to the waterfront to do it. He'd shown us a hundred times how well he could swim, but it was the deep and dark water we knew he was afraid of. To pass the test, he would have to swim from the end of the dock, about twenty-five yards out to deep water, and around the lifeguarded raft. Next, he'd have to tread water while donning and removing a life vest. After that, all he had to do was finish the twenty minutes under his own power, protecting his airway. He could swim, tread, or float.

Zeke worried and complained as we walked along the dock. He even whined when a thrown volleyball splashed near us and got him wet. But he went with us and said something simple.

"I'll do it for you guys."

"Maybe it's an adventure," Neil said. "You remember?"

Me: "Remember what?"

Neil: "Something I said to Zeke about my Mom and Dad. They told me I work hard in school and someday, I'll probably be a professor or something. So I need to be a kid *now*."

Zeke: "They told him to have adventures."

That's precisely what Dad told me in 1968, the first time we sat together on our bench. My mind trailed off to what Karen said. *I love my dad, Ted.* I missed my dad that day on the dock, and I worried about what it might be like when I got back home.

Neil: "All three of us need to do that, and I'm not even sure if I've ever had one."

Me: "What. An adventure?"

Neil: "Yeah. How are you even supposed to know?"

Zeke: "My parents say when you're done with them, you're supposed to…"

Me: "Learn from 'em, probably. I imagine they're things that don't feel much like adventures when they're happening."

Zeke: "Like Tornado Night?"

I thought for a minute. "Yeah. I guess *that* would count."

Neil: "Oh, good. You want another night like that?"

A distant whistle blew.

Me: "There'll never be another night like that. Let's have a different one. A better one."

Neil: "Now that we have a cross-burning Nazi for a counselor?"

Me: "Gettin' away with sump'm'll be all the nicer."

Zeke: "Rules are for dummies who don't know any better."

Hearing Zeke say that made me proud.

Neil: "We're gonna have to sneak around just to do anything."

Zeke: "Hey, Neil."

Neil: "Huh?"

Zeke: "The canoe trip Lloyd's gonna take us on might be an adventure."

It was another simple statement. Typical Zeke. Saying things designed to help his buddies be happy. There's something about those guys I could never fully define. They lifted each other up. They lifted *me* up.

I'll do it for you guys.

The high, early-afternoon sun cast our stubby shadows on the murky water's surface. The sun's rays converged around them and shot deep into the lake. They burned my back. And as I watched our shadows, I felt the sun's warmth all the way down to my healing soul. We belonged there, the three of us.

It got me thinking about when camp would be over. In about three weeks, Zeke and Neil—Karen, too—were going to be gone.

"*Hey, ZEKE!*" shouted the guard from the raft, holding a stopwatch. "*You ready?*"

Neil: "All right. Here we go."

Zeke: "No."

Neil: "Oh, you baby. Get your butt in there."

CHAPTER 32

ZEKE PASSED. NEIL clapped him on the back, and Buck met him on the dock to shake his hand. After a congratulation from Hoss, something in Zeke changed. His eyes may have narrowed slightly. He may have chosen his words in a more measured way. Maybe he stood up straighter. I don't know. I'm not even sure if how he acted was any different after his trip through that deep, dark water. After all, how are success and confidence supposed to look in a twelve-year-old kid? I guess it doesn't matter. All I know is that after he passed that twenty-minute swim test, Zeke was rapturously proud of himself.

Now, it was Lloyd's turn. It was time to pony up our canoe trip. How to get him to do it was the question. How would we approach the man who nearly attacked a camper in his first ten minutes as counselor? The man whose leadership came mainly in the form of yelling at us without getting out of his own bunk? How gentle would we have to be? Who would have the finesse to do it?

Buck.

Buck was the answer, and we elected him. That evening after lights out, after we were all in our bunks, Buck said, "Hey, Lloyd?"

"Hay's for horses, Mr. McDaniel," Lloyd said, sitting at the cabin's table.

"Okay, sorry. But today, you know how Zeke passed his twenty-minute test?"

"*Yeh*-ess," Lloyd said in one of those sing-song, I've-already-heard-this-a-million-times voices. "I *know*-oh..."

"You said if Zeke—"

"I *didn't* say that. Mr. Dinwiddie said it. Not me."

"But he's the director," Hoss said, "and you're just a counselor."

"Ex*cuse* me?"

"Don't play the 'excuse me' game, Lloyd. You heard me. You're just a coun—"

"I can take care of this," Buck said to Hoss. It was a rare put-the-foot-down moment from Buck that said *Shut up, Hoss. You're about to blow this for us.*

Lloyd: "No, Buck. I'll take care of the troublemakers. Not you."

Buck: "Okay. Didn't mean to step out of line. But about that canoe trip?"

Lloyd: "We'll work on your canoe trip."

Hoss: "We'll *work* on the...what's that even supposed to *mean*?"

Buck: "Shut up, Hoss!"

Hoss: "Okay. But let's find out what it means to *work* on the *canoe* trip."

Lloyd: "You'll have to earn it. Your friend Hoss cost you two days, just now, with his sarcasm, and there are only two weeks left of camp."

Discontented responses wafted into the cool darkness.

Sunny: "Hey, you guys—"

Hoss: "*Hay's* for *HORSES!*"

Buck: "Hoss!"

Lloyd: "Two *more* days. Keep it up, Mr. Cartwright."

Hoss: "With pleasure...*Lloyd*."

Buck: "Dammit, Hoss."

Lloyd: "Language, Mr. McDaniel."

Zeke: "Don't make Lloyd mad, or maybe he'll—"

A loud thump startled us all. Lloyd's flat hand on the table. Something about an open-handed slap seemed worse than a fist.

"Maybe I'll *what*, Mister"—Lloyd consulted his cabin roster—"Yasko?"

Zeke held still as a mouse.

"Maybe you'll slap the table real *loud*," I said. *DON'T be mean to Zeke.*

Lloyd stood immediately. The chair slid out from beneath him, and his long thighs knocked the table forward a foot.

"Unless you want to cost your cabin the canoe trip Mister..."

"*Gables*," I said, as Lloyd paused to check his roster. "You want me to spell it for you?"

"...I suggest you shut your mouth."

"He has every bit as much right to speak as *you*, Lloyd," Neil said. His voice seemed unusually deep.

Lloyd put his hands on his hips and faced Neil. They stared each other down in silence until Lloyd pointed an incredibly long index finger at Neil.

"This cabin is not a democracy," he said, taking a couple of steps toward Neil. "*You*...should be well aware of that."

Neil's eyes narrowed, and he leaned forward. "What do you mean '*You*...?'"

"Suppose I just let you think about that, Mister Shepherd."

"I think I've already thought about it," Neil said.

"Tell me, then. What do you think?"

"I think you're a coward."

Lloyd bounded over and put his finger in Neil's face. "I think I misheard you. Why don't you try that again?"

Hoss: "He said you're full of *shit*, Lloyd. I heard him loud and clear. I think we all did. Didn't we, fellas?" No one answered.

"*Welp*," Lloyd said. "That's it. No canoe trip."

Complaints burst from all directions into the cabin's living area. Buck chastised Hoss again, and after that, all went quiet.

Lloyd crossed the cabin in four ponderous steps. In front of the window, his silhouette faced off with Hoss.

"Do you want to go down to Headquarters, Mr. Cartwright?" Lloyd said, leaning forward so far that Hoss actually backed off.

"Sure," Hoss said.

"Then keep it up."

"Are you sure you want to tell *me* to 'keep it up?'"

Lloyd moved in until his nose almost touched Hoss's. "Do you want to do all of cabin clean-up for the next week?"

Nothing followed.

"Mr. Cartwright?"

"No."

"Are you sure about that?"

"Yes."

"Or are you just telling me what I want to hear?"

"I'm not."

The covers in Hoss's corner ruffled for a second or two.

Mildly at first, then more severely, as though two mute animals were fighting beneath the blankets. The bedsprings squeaked. All of it meant Lloyd had put some kind of hold on Hoss during the reprimand, and Hoss fought him. Hoss's subservience meant he'd been frightened, and he wasn't going to like that.

They were motionless for a moment before Lloyd released Hoss in one last, loud squeak of the bedsprings. In another second, Lloyd left the cabin.

The quiet that followed was horrible. There was no sound other than Hoss's heavy, tremulous breathing. I couldn't tell if he was frightened or angry. But it was probably both. I wanted Hoss to say something, something sarcastic, something bad, something naughty. Something *Hoss*. Anything. Under the circumstances, I'd've been more comfortable with a good, old-fashioned *FUCK YOU, ASSHOLE!!* but Hoss said nothing.

A few seconds after Lloyd left, Bones said, "*He's* the escaped psycho."

"Yeah," Coach said. "Maybe he just left to go out to the woods, where he belongs."

"Hell, yes," Hoss said. "His breath could kill the sloth."

A loud snicker erupted from Neil's bed. And then came the giggle, deep and resonating. Quiet laughter spread through the cabin, and busy but dim chatter followed.

Too energized to settle down, I crawled to the end of my bed and peered through the old, drilled hole. The cottonwood leaves may have grown to obscure the view. I thought for a second there might be haze on the lake, blocking my line of sight, but then, I saw boat lights. They were as dim as the campfire I'd seen. Red and green lights were so close together

I could tell it was well past the lake's half-way point.

If I could see that, it wasn't hazy. In fact, it was dry out. Dusty. Had been for two weeks, since the tornado. The light in the trees just wasn't there. Maybe it was gone for good. I hadn't seen it for days, maybe a couple of weeks. Maybe Mom was only allowed to signal me a few times, and those times had already past.

I settled back onto my bed and thought about Hoss and Lloyd. Put those two in the same space, and it was like lighting a fuse. I didn't understand it.

Lloyd had taken away our canoe trip and seemed to set unintended precedents all over the place, but it didn't matter. The mystery that was Lloyd wasn't even very interesting.

Two weeks left of camp. The reality of it fell on me.

My stomach tightened. In two weeks, I'd be home. If Dad wanted me.

CHAPTER 33

THE NEXT DAY was a Saturday. It was free-rec and open-waterfront from rest period to supper, then more of the same. There were no camp crafts classes, no micromanagement that took all the fun and mystique out of the archery-range, and no swimming class that got you down into the cold when you didn't want to be there. Saturdays were glorious.

And on that particular Saturday, Lloyd was gone, too. Nobody knew where, and nobody cared. We knew he'd be back for supper, but until then, we were free. Zeke read his sloth book. Neil was down swimming laps. Hoss and Buck were off somewhere, probably tromping in the woods breaking rules. The rest of the cabin mates were out of sight and out of earshot, and that suited me fine.

It was a perfect time to cop a marker for the forbidden graffiti project. I'd copied Lloyd's roster by hand and had it back at the cabin.

By the time I got to Cabin 4, I could hear the typewriter keys. My stomach—or maybe it was my heart—leapt again. Karen and I hadn't talked much since the kiss. The prospect of seeing her outweighed my reluctance, and my pace quickened. The typewriter sound played through the woods like a symphony.

On my way to Isaac's window, I ran my fingers across the waxy bark of the big birch.

"Ted Gables, what is your position, *over*?" Isaac said from the window, his hand over his mouth. He made a scratchy sound after he said *over*. His NASA ground-control routine was a big hit in the summer of 1969.

The typing stopped.

I hid behind the tree and made a scratchy sound into my own hand. I improvised, "Houston? I'm by the big birch, heading one-niner-zero-Charlie Tango. Over?" *Scratch sound.*

Scratch. "Come again, Apollo? One-niner-zero-Charlie-Tango is not a proper heading, over?"

"Roger." I had no idea how to respond and broke character. I peeked around the tree toward Isaac's window. All my blood ran to my feet when Karen's face appeared the screen.

"Hi, Ted!" she said with not one bit of hesitation. She flashed me her pretty teeth as I stepped up to the window. When she went back to the typewriter, I studied her posture. She sat straight in the wooden chair, her hair in a perfect ponytail. Never before had a beat-up T-shirt been so elegant. Her bell-bottom jeans were two full-length skirts hiding her feet.

Isaac rolled his chair out of my chosen field of view. He took an index card and wrote something on it. He handed it to me through the window. It said:

I think she likes you, too.

I took the card and pocketed it before Karen could see anything. Isaac mugged at me.

"So what are you up to, anyway?" Karen asked, turning her chair toward me.

"Nothing," I said, "just hanging around." I pointed at the typewriter. "You, uh, writing a story?"

"I wish. More reports for Dad. That's all."

"Oh. Maybe tomorrow."

"Yep. Maybe tomorrow." She scooted her chair back into position and resumed her typing.

"'Cause you really should write more sloth stories."

Karen cast a blazing, green, thousand-yard stare. It penetrated my skull for a second, then drifted off as the corners of her mouth tightened. It was as though she'd just slipped into a nice dream.

She pulled her current page out of the typewriter and thumbed up a fresh one from a stack. Her smile faded, and she said something I didn't expect.

"You know, I wonder if I should leave the creative writing up to my sister."

Huh-UH. "No. You shouldn't."

"She's older. She's the one who got the talent. *And* the looks."

Impossible.

Maybe my surprise came from hearing Karen put herself down, which I didn't like at all. Sure, I was heavily biased in her favor, but on some level, like in mathematics in school, which you couldn't fudge, Karen was the correct answer. Her name would get the circle on my multiple-choice test every day of the year.

She loaded the paper into the machine and became the business executive again. "What do *you* think, Isaac?"

The big guy blushed.

"Isaac had a date with big sis yesterday, Ted."

"Typewriter's awful quiet back there," he said.

Karen got back to work, postured and prim. As the curl at the end of her ponytail bounced with her every move, I had my doubts about this big sister's looks.

"The summer's in its home stretch, Ted," Isaac said. "How are things down in Cabin 7?" His expression told me he already knew the answer. The coffee cup with the pencils and permanent marker stood in its usual place.

"It's a little bit of a drag in the cabin these days."

"Oh? How so?"

"New counselor."

Karen stopped typing. "Lloyd?"

"Yeah, Lloyd."

"Is he mean?" she asked.

"Sometimes."

She rolled her eyes, and her fingers went back to work on the keys.

Does anybody like Lloyd? Anybody on earth?

I never questioned any word or decision Mr. Dinwiddie made, but Lloyd seemed like a mistake.

No one spoke for a moment. The typewriter dinged, and Karen slapped the lever to move the roller to the next line. What came next was an uninvited voice.

CHAPTER 34

"LET'S GET A look at that weather equipment," Hoss said. "They've been trying to keep it from raining. You can see the weather room through this hole."

A pastime of bored campers was to peek through the knotholes in Headquarters, through one of which the bell's rope ran. The back rooms were places of legend. They'd become, through the years, the location of the lake-heater and the weather-control equipment.

"I want to see," Bud said. Hoss seemed to be taking the smaller, weaker kid for a ride.

"Just look through the hole with the rope in it."

"I can't see."

"You have to work at it."

"Lemme see through the other one."

"You're too short."

"Shut up!"

"Don't yell at me. I didn't make you short."

Bud grunted.

"I can see the equipment," Hoss said. "I can see *her* equipment."

"You can? Lemme see. Who's at the controls?"

"Who do you think?"

"Where *is* she?" Bud asked.

A shadow of protective concern crossed Isaac's face. Karen stopped typing and listened to the voices. Half-amused, and half-perplexed, she all but said, *Who are those boys talking about?*

"Kids think you control the weather from Headquarters, sister," Isaac said.

"They *what?*"

"What is she wearing?" Bud asked. Karen's grin dropped a notch.

She didn't know how much the boys talked about her. She never learned that Marty, just the week before outside of Cabin 6, told some other kid he'd been "necking" with her all summer. Mr. Dinwiddie overheard the claims and gave the privileged, North Shore brat a few choice words.

"Bikini," Hoss said, "a tight one. She just flipped the switch to warm it up outside, 'cause she's cold. You know what happens to a girl when she's cold?"

Isaac rolled back his chair and put his hands on his knees. Leaning forward as though to stand, he paused as he faced Karen.

"Omigod," Bud said. "I wanna *see.*"

If there was one moment in Karen's life in which her perceived self-image caught up with her physical form it had to be that afternoon in Headquarters. I remember it well. The awareness passed through her the moment her bewilderment transitioned to open-mouthed surprise, then something else. It was as though she had just received terrible news.

"Try harder, Bud," Hoss said. "I'm busy."

Karen's eyes narrowed above a maturing scowl.

What is she up to?

"Oh, man," Hoss said. "She's starting to breathe heavy."

"Karen," Isaac whispered.

"Is she horny?" Bud asked.

"That's it," Isaac said. He stood.

"Wait," Karen said, standing. Her old desk chair creaked. The green fire in those eyes could burn Headquarters to the ground and drove an excitement through me I could never forget or adequately describe. Isaac backed off.

She slinked out of the front room, careful not to be visible from the lounge. Without so much as a sound—the spring on the main screen door to Headquarters was the same type as the one on Cabin 7's toilet room—she exited the front door. I leaned back from the commerce window to watch her. She lifted her index finger and wrapped those beautiful lips around a *shush* I couldn't quite hear. As she disappeared around the south side of the building, Bud complained anew about being unable to see. Isaac stood and headed out front.

It was my chance. With poise and grace, as Isaac passed through the doorway, I shot my arm through the open window, grabbed the marker, and slipped it into my pocket. Isaac eased out the front door and gestured to head north toward the bell.

"Let's get a load of what Karen's gonna do," he whispered.

We strolled north from the Big Birch and stopped at a point well behind Hoss and Bud, so we could watch. Karen slinked into sight. Even with the fallen leaves and twigs all around, her feet fell without a sound. It must've been how she followed me to Mosquito Point. She positioned herself between the bell tower and the two boys, who stayed put, faces pressed into the siding of Headquarters

Bud's complaining had become incessant. "Come on,

Hoss, let me see."

"Oh, God, she knows how to use those controls," Hoss said.

"Lemme *seeeee!*" Bud bounced his heels up and down like pistons, like a three-year-old having a tantrum.

"Dig that body, man. I bet she's gonna send us a hell of a storm tuh-*night*."

Isaac tapped me with the back of his hand and pointed at Karen. Listening to Hoss carry on, I half-thought there were weather controls in Headquarters myself.

For a second, we heard nothing but the trees' breezy murmurs, ping-pong, and the waterfront. A good show was in the making, and being around Isaac made me crave movie popcorn again.

Karen silently planted one foot on the ground between Hoss and Bud, reaching for the backs of their heads.

Hoss said, "She's holding that stick with both hands..."

"*Lemme seeeeee!* I want her to hold *my* stick with both hands! Oh my G—"

That's when Karen struck.

CHAPTER 35

"OH, MY G-UH!" Bud managed to say before his forehead smacked into the wood siding of headquarters.

Karen pounced on them both, grabbing them by the hair, yanking their heads back, and lunging forward, extending her arms. The move was as graceful as any I'd seen. If my eyes had been closed—and most-definitely they were not—I'd've sworn two thrown softballs had hit the side of headquarters at the same time.

Karen's anger, power, grace, and precision at that moment will always stay with me. Right when she let go of those two idiots' heads, she took a giant step backward and stood with her hands on her hips.

Bud said, *"Ow,* Hoss! That *hurt!"*

Hoss spun around to face Karen. Surprise, then resignation, governed his face. A drop of blood squeezed its way onto his forehead.

Bud screeched when he saw Karen. "You mighta broke my skull!"

"She didn't break your skull," Hoss said. "You're gonna be fine. Look at me. Bud? Look at *me.*"

That peculiar absence crossed Bud's face. I could tell Hoss was worried—just like I was—that Bud would rage at Karen.

"Look at *me,* Bud," Hoss said again. "You're okay. *Bud.*"

Fear welling inside me, I stepped toward them.

Hoss got in front of the transforming monster and took him

by the shoulders. "You're gonna be *all right,* Bud. You hear me?" Hoss whispered in a fatherly tone that startled me. He ran a hand over the side of Bud's head, as though to calm an upset dog. Bud's distant stare changed just then. He seemed to focus on Hoss. Then on Karen. Then the bell. It was as though he'd been woken up. The monster eased back into its dark place.

With no way to know what almost happened, Karen stepped in toward Bud, shoving Hoss back a step.

"Karen?" Hoss said.

She didn't listen. Instead, she leaned in toward one of Bud's bright red ears. His scratching little fingernails dangled in clear reach of her face.

Hoss whispered in the same tone. "It's gonna be okay, Bud." He bled down one side of his nose and didn't wipe it away.

Karen said something about the weather controls. Bud slouched, extra-small next to her, a pile of TNT in sissy-blue pants and a lit fuse of unknown length. What she said to him wasn't clear. I inched closer, in case something went wrong. Hoss leaned toward Bud, ready to pounce.

A little louder, maybe so we could all hear it, Karen said to Bud, "I can make thunder, lightning, hurricanes, and tidal waves. Remember that tornado?"

Bud didn't respond.

"*I* did that. You hear me? And that fire on the beach? When my dad said 'White Birch Magic?' Guess *who*," she said, pointing into the middle of her own chest.

The red in Bud's ears went away, and his hands went limp.

Leaning even closer to Bud, she added, "I could light up

the whole forest...and whatever I do next, I'm gonna do it to *you* and I'm gonna wait till you're *asleep* to do it."

Bud never did explode in front of Karen, like I thought he would. Instead, something else happened. Something else entirely. A miracle. An irregular patch of darkness spread across the front of his powder-blue pants. As Karen straightened up to face Hoss, Bud's silent urine trickled into a puddle between his camp sneakers.

Karen pointed a finger in Hoss's face and said, "Don't you *ever* talk about me that way again."

Karen couldn't know how Hoss had just aimed to protect her. She also didn't seem to notice she'd just cast the greatest spell of White Birch Magic these woods had ever seen. Any witness to it was an immediate camp veteran. I'd do my damnedest to stoke this new legend myself, and I'd start in a minute or two with Zeke.

Nope. Karen didn't notice. She was too busy strolling toward *me*.

Her expression softened a little, but her anger was still clear. I didn't know what to do or say. Most times like that, I seemed to fall back on what was familiar. What my dad might do is drop a simple nod of acknowledgement. So that's what I did. Karen nodded back, said nothing, and went back inside.

I ached for her.

Hoss wiped the blood off his face and onto his pants. Bud noticed his wetness as I waited for Karen's muffled tears. But in a matter of seconds after the door slapped shut behind her, the only sound coming from Headquarters was the resuming chorus of typewriter keys.

White Birch Magic. She was its very source.

His face drawn out lengthwise, eyes open wide, Isaac said, "I guess…uh…don't ever upset *her*."

Another picture I've always wished I had—other than one of Bud pissing his pants—was Hoss's expression. Anyone privy to it would think maybe a stem of conscience grew out of him that afternoon. But given what I'd witness over the next hour, I wouldn't be so sure.

"Okay, you two," Isaac said, pointing to Hoss and Bud. "Party's over. Let's go see about some first aid." Strolling toward them, he covered his mouth and made the scratchy sound. "Houston to Ted? Come back?" *Scratch.*

"Yeah?"

Scratch. "Bring my marker back when you're done. Over and out." *Scratch.*

I was stunned. To this day, I don't know how he knew I'd taken it. I could only assume Isaac held a little of The Magic himself.

"*Roger,*" I said and ran back toward the cabin, not wanting camp to end.

CHAPTER 36

RUNNING BEHIND THE cabins, I darted up between 5 and 6 to find Zeke still on the bench. On the run, I shouted his name and held up the marker. He shut his book and met me in front of the cabin.

"I got a story for you," I said.

"What?"

"Tell you a little later. Let's get inside."

We entered finding the cabin empty. It was perfect. I directed Zeke on how to get into the loft. As I followed and momentarily stood on the cross ties to navigate the struts, the cabin door opened.

Again? Why someone always entered the cabin when I was standing in the rafters was anybody's guess. But as though by telepathy, Zeke scooted back, making just enough room for me to snake my way into the shadows before we were seen. We held still, hidden in semi-darkness and peered down into the cabin to see who'd come in.

Bud. Here to change his pants. It wouldn't do for that little tattle-tale to see us in the loft.

His face was red. Tears of most-certain humiliation filled his eyes. His rubescent scalp glowed through that thin mop of albino hair. Sliding his pants down to his ankles, he grimaced. His corn-tassel sprig quaked, and he broke into sobs.

I almost felt sorry for the little bastard, but I got over it pretty quick.

Zeke shrugged. I'd tell him all about Karen's miracle later. Bud took off his pants and underwear, quickly replacing them with dry ones. By the time he laced up his shoes, I wondered what Zeke and I would do if Bud decided to stay in the cabin.

But he picked up his urine-soaked garments, headed up front, tossed them in the trash can, and left.

Zeke and I wasted no time scooting toward the back wall of the cabin, just above the sinks and emergency door. Above us was a perfect rafter anchored to the ceiling. Untouched by human hands since some time in the 1920s.

"The back side of this rafter," I said. "Nobody'll ever see it."

Then the cabin door opened again. I wished Bud would just stay out. Zeke and I dutifully held still and peered down to see.

Lloyd.

Oh, God.

I had no idea where he'd come from. He scanned the living area as he clomped back toward the sinks and said "Hello?" without any trace of hospitality. "Anybody here?"

We didn't move. Through the four-inch gaps between the loft's floorboards, Lloyd had only to lift his chin to see us.

The rusty spring yelped as he opened the toilet room door. The wood-on-wood slap followed. The drop of Lloyd's zipper and especially the urine stream were comically loud. Now I was in the loft once again, watching another counselor relieve himself. Only this time, Zeke was present, and he had serious trouble containing his laughter.

Lloyd's nearly interminable stream weakened and eventually stopped. When he finished the job with two or three big squirts, Zeke slapped his hands over his own mouth. His laughing eyes welled with tears. And when Lloyd punctuated his long statement with a big, toneless fart, I thought Zeke's head might explode. He spasmed, tears rolling onto his fingers.

Then came the deafening flush. *Squawk!* went the spring, and *Slap!* went the door. Lloyd turned on the sink and stood just beneath us. He spent the next twenty seconds searching for God-knows-what out the back windows. I could've reached between the floorboards and touched his head. Humor became fear, then relief as Lloyd and his flop-footed walk headed back up front and out of sight.

Then I wondered what we were going to do if *Lloyd* decided to stay in the cabin.

For a few seconds, only outside sounds could be heard: the distant sound of a packed waterfront, the *k-dock k-dock* of Ping-Pong balls, and the occasional, and unmistakable reverberation of a wooden paddle hitting the aluminum gunwale of a canoe.

Up from Lloyd's area came a murmuring, then the sound of calloused fingers dragging across rough wood. It had to mean he was going through his shelves. He'd lost something. A curse pierced the silence.

Lloyd appeared in the living area again, ransacked my shelves and lifted my pillow. To my disgust, he pulled the cigar box off my shelves and opened it. One of the sloth story's pages fell to the floor like a stalled paper airplane. I almost said something, loft-be-damned, but Lloyd picked up the fallen page and put it back.

Then he went through Zeke's stuff, and Neil's. Zeke's face showed not an ounce of anger, only some curiosity. I've always thought Neil, if he'd been up there with us, would've favored decrying the injustice over loft-bound silence. Not just for his own things. Neil would be upset on behalf of all of us. Lloyd moved on to Sunny's and Coach's shelves. Then to the other side, toward the areas of Bones and Hoss before he made his way to Bud's, then finally Buck's.

There, he found something and mumbled, "What do we have here? Buck knife."

Buck knife, I thought. Hence the nickname. Lloyd unsheathed the blade, which was similar in length to (but definitely not the same as) Hoss's bigger knife. I didn't know Buck had one, too.

The cabin door opened again, and Buck himself strolled in. He stopped first, then froze. His face went white.

Lloyd lifted the knife. "You want to explain this, Mr. McDaniel?"

It was over for him. Buck was going home.

Outside, though, moving toward the cabin, came a full-throated, obnoxious voice, singing.

Guess who.

"Smokin' shit with CLIFF the hippie
And muh Polly AAANNNNN..."

CHAPTER 37

"S'm TIMES I get a BIG ole STIFFIE
"When she GRABS m'—

"Hey, BUUUUCCKK!" Hoss said, throwing the door open into Lloyd's shelves. The window panes rattled. *"Where you AT, BOWAHH?"*

Hoss made it through the counselor's area and toward the bunks before he found Buck and Lloyd.

"Give us a minute?" Lloyd said in his usual, accusatory tone.

"Excuse me?" Hoss said without even flinching.

Some life—I mean real energy—filled Hoss's expression and everything about him. Band-Aid on his forehead or not, he was ready to put hotels on Boardwalk and Park Place.

Zeke's eyes sparkled. The corners of his mouth lifted.

I knew Hoss too well to think he was as dumb as he was playing. Even though he and Lloyd had already gone a few rounds in the past couple of weeks, Lloyd didn't know Hoss at all. And I'm pretty sure Hoss knew *that*, too.

If Zeke could enjoy it, I guessed I could do the same. The revelation chilled me:

It's okay to like Hoss.

The way you might like a king cobra snake—with a good-and-thick pane of glass in front of it.

Lloyd puffed out his chest, seeming to make himself a little bigger, and finally answered Hoss. "Wait outside the *cabin*'s what I said."

Hoss said, "Naw...I think I'd like to stand here and watch this for a bit."

"Get out of the cabin. Now."

Hoss put his hands on his hips, cocked his head to the side, and said, "You threatenin' me with a knife?"

"No...*No*." A deep red crawled up Lloyd's neck and face as he sheathed Buck's knife.

"Because if I have to leave the cabin, I'm gonna feel like I been threatened with a knife."

Lloyd hesitated.

"He found my knife," Buck said.

"Was it hidden in your stuff?" Hoss said.

"Yeah, but not well enough to—"

"What're you doing going through Buck's stuff, Lloyd? Everybody's shelves are messed up. What're you—did you lose something, Lloyd?"

"What business is it of yours?" Lloyd said.

"You're snooping through our stuff. I'd say that *makes* it my business, wouldn't you, Buck?"

"Do you have something to hide?" Lloyd asked. "Because I'm your counselor, and I am authorized to search your shelves at my pleasure."

"I don't remember reading *that* in the camper handbook. Do you, Buck?"

"Call it executive action, Mr. Cartwright."

"I call it bullshit."

"Language."

"*Fuck* you."

The red hue deepened. "I said do you have something to *hide*," Lloyd said, placing Buck's knife on the table.

Hoss hesitated, as though thinking. "Yes," he said. "As a matter of fact, I do have sump'm to hide, and I bet you a *dollar* it's what you're looking for in the first place."

Lloyd didn't move. Buck's attention toggled between them, as though he watched the world's most important tennis match.

"I got somethin' *real* big to hide," Hoss said. He stepped around to his shelves. "Yep. You weren't too careful when you tore through here, *Lloyd-ee-oyd*."

"Watch yourself, Mr. Cartwr—"

"Shut up...*Lloooyyd*." Hoss moved his entire set of shelves and seemed to pull something from underneath it. He stood up and held the same something above his head.

This time, Lloyd was the one who froze. Then he said, "What's—"

"Oh, stop it, Lloyd. You know what this is."

"I know good and well what that is," he said, hesitating a little between words. "What I *don't* know is why a boy in this cabin would have something like that."

From our protective darkness in the back of the loft, I couldn't quite see what Hoss held in his hand, and I couldn't imagine what could scare Lloyd like that. But it was clear Lloyd seemed to make up his statements on the spot. Buck was quiet, wide-eyed. Lloyd stood near the table in the cabin's center. Hoss's back was to us.

"I'll give you a guess, Lloyd," Hoss said, holding the item

of interest high in the air, wiggling it in his hand. "This yours?"

Now I could see it. It was a flask-shaped, half-empty bottle of straw-colored, transparent liquid.

Booze. Like whiskey or sump'm.

"You're out of line, young man," Lloyd said to Hoss.

"Out of line how? For going through all *your* shit before you went through ours?"

"You have no business going through my things."

Hoss appeared to suck something out from between his upper teeth. "Call it executive action. *Llllooooooooooyydd.*"

Lloyd mouthed a couple of words, but no sound came out. As I remember, he always said more every time he was unable to speak than when he actually spoke.

"I could smell the alcohol on you every morning, Lloyd. Or almost every morning."

"I don't have any idea what you're talk—"

"Do you still think *I'm* the stupid one here?"

"You couldn't possibly know what you're saying. Let's just stop this little game," Lloyd said. "Give me the bottle, and I'll see to it that you don't get into too much troub—"

"You wanna know sumpthin'? Huh?" Hoss's speech emerged under pressure, and it was fluent. It gave me the idea the real Hoss had finally come to town. "I do know what I'm talking about. My dad drinks booze. Quite a bit of it. Then he comes home, and he smells a certain way, and he acts a certain way...

"Matter of fact, he's mean, like you. My dad is what my mom calls a mean drunk. Then he passes out and snores all night long. The more he drinks, the more he snores. Just like you, Lloyd, especially after you get back from your Tuesday nights out."

The more Hoss spoke, the louder his voice got.

"All right, young man, that's—"

"That's exactly how my *dad* is. At night. In the mornings, he smells a little different, like some kind of chemical. Just like *you* smell in the mornings, and just like you smelled the first time you ever breathed in my face."

"I've had quite enough of—"

"So don't *tell* me *I don't know what I'm TALKING about*. Sometimes you stink so bad it makes me want to puke up my goddamn scrambled eggs at *breakfast!*"

Hoss took a deep breath. He held the bottle up high and wiggled it, sloshing the booze. "Are you an alcoholic?"

"You keep your voice down. Let's just—"

"Our new counselor, *Llooooyd*, is an *al-co-HOL-ic!*"

"*Stop* it!"

"What's the matter, Lloyd?"

Lloyd suddenly lunged at Hoss and said, "Give me that!"

But Hoss pulled a lightning-quick side-step that would have gotten him away from a champion boxer. He positioned himself so the table was between them.

"You sure don't seem to want anyone to find out about this," Hoss said.

When Lloyd moved one way around the table, Hoss moved the other. I was almost embarrassed for the counselor.

"So tell me, Lloyd," Hoss said. "Do I catch a family resemblance with anyone we know?"

As the two danced slowly around the table, Lloyd's face

moistened with a thin layer of sweat. His eyes were headlight beams of pure hate. "All right," he said in what sounded more like a growl than regular talking. "What do you want?"

"Is your last name Dinwiddie, Lloyd?"

Silence.

"Well? Is it?"

"Yes, it is."

"But you're a fair bit younger?"

"Right again. Is there a point you wish to make?"

"Brother? Nephew? Cousin?"

"What do you care?"

"Come on! Tell me. There's no harm in it. Unless you're ashamed to be related—"

"No. I'm not ashamed. Mr. Dinwiddie is my older brother. Happy? Can we take care of whatever it is you—"

"So what are you, thirty? Thirty-five?"

Lloyd stopped moving around the table. "Thirty-two," he said, clipped.

"And no job? Is that why you're, you know, available? On such little notice to be our counselor?"

"I'm between jobs."

"And you don't like this one?"

"Not so much right now, I don't."

"That's okay. I'm sure it doesn't like you, either."

Lloyd breathed heavily, his lips pursed in a frown, his nose and ears nearly bright in their redness. His expression darkened still.

"So you don't give a rat's butt," Hoss said, "whether you keep this job or not. Right?"

Nothing.

"So what are you afraid of?" Hoss asked.

"I'm not afraid of *you*."

Au contraire. Everybody in that cabin was afraid of Hoss that afternoon. I guarantee it.

"But you're afraid of *something*, Lloyd, and I think that something is Mr. Dinwiddie."

Lloyd crossed his arms and blew a big breath through his nose. He was down, and Hoss was about to start kicking.

CHAPTER 38

HOSS NODDED SLOWLY, holding the whiskey bottle down to his side. Over the din of the waterfront and the *k-dock, k-dock* of ongoing Ping-Pong, I could hear the typewriter at headquarters. Just then, I wished Karen were transcribing the conversation unfolding below us.

"Okay," Hoss said. "So Mr. Dinwiddie's doing you a favor? Gave his little brother the counselor job…to get you away from all the stuff that makes you want a drink? Is that what happened? Mom says she wants to keep Dad away from the stuff that makes him want to drink. You know? Certain people, certain places? Is that what Mr. Dinwiddie did for you, Lloyd? Maybe to…get you *back* on your *feet*? Because that's another thing. Something my dad always says to my mom and my brothers. Heard it a hundred times. Says he needs something…a favor, a little money…or something like this counselor job…you know, to get him *back* on his *feet*."

The red left Lloyd's face and neck. "What do you want from me?" he whispered.

"I want you to tell us you're an alcoholic."

"Listen. I do have a little bit of a prob—I need to work on some…"

"Tell us."

Lloyd remained still, and Hoss stood directly opposite him, the table between them. Buck stood like a statue.

Voices outside. Close to the cabin. "Come on, now," Lloyd

said. "Let me just—"

"*Nope*," Hoss said, jiggling the bottle again. "Say 'Lloyd is an alcoholic'—"

"Would you please just give me the b—"

"On second thought, say, 'Hello. My name is Lloyd, and I am a *miserable* alcoholic.' That'll do."

Lloyd slumped. "Lloyd is…"

Hoss: "'Hello? My name is Lloyd?' And loud enough for us to hear it."

Lloyd rolled his eyes at the ceiling and took a deep breath. Finally, as though standing on a cold, lonely precipice, with nowhere to go but the cloudy unknown below, he must have, in his mind, jumped: "Hello," he muttered. "My name is Lloyd."

"Louder, please."

"And I am a miserable alcoholic."

"That's the way!" Hoss said with great cheer. His back was to Zeke and me, but I could imagine his big, sardonic grin.

I thought Lloyd would launch into a fiery rage, but he didn't. He just kind of sagged.

"Okay," Lloyd said. "May I have the bottle, please? Just to get rid of it?"

"No. That's not what we're gonna do here, Lloyd. You're going to leave the cabin now, and I'm going to take care of this bottle."

"Suppose I decide to tell Mr. Dinwiddie you have alcohol?"

Hoss slumped to a posture just like Lloyd's. "Is that really all you have, Lloyd? Did you just threaten to tell Mr. Dinwiddie this booze is *mine*? Whatta you think he's gonna believe? That a twelve-year-old's been hiding this bottle for six weeks? Or that you, his drunk-for-a-brother, is on the sauce again?"

Lloyd dropped his head again and cussed.

"That's what Mom says about Dad," Hoss said, bringing back his drawl. "That he's 'on the sauce.' But anyway, you're stupid, Lloyd. That's your problem, y' know. A lot of your campers are smarter than you. That's why we're in charge, and you're a thirty-two-year-old nobody who just fessed up to his campers that he's a miserable alcoholic."

Hoss waited a minute, maybe for those words to sink in, then lifted the bottle.

"You're going to leave this cabin and not come back until line-up for dinner in an hour. I'll take good care of this." He jiggled the bottle again. "And you're not going to say anything about Buck's knife. And we won't say a word about your little bottle. How's that sound?"

Lloyd took a step back and stood up straight. The red eyes, wrinkled brow, and frown could have been shame, worry, or anger. Or relief.

More voices outside. It was Coach and Sunny this time, and they were on their way in.

Lloyd quickly said, "I'll play the game."

"It's not a game, Lloyd. It's a *deal*. And it's a good one. I'd even call it generous."

"Okay," Lloyd said. "Whatever you say."

"So go on, then."

Lloyd hesitated as Hoss shook the bottle and pocketed Buck's knife from the table. Lloyd shuffled toward the front door, like a man who'd just sold his soul to Lucifer. Maybe he had.

"Oh, and Lloyd?" Hoss said.

Lloyd stopped.

"I'm gonna need you to give us our canoe trip back."

"Fine," he said, right when Coach and Sunny stepped into the cabin. Hoss held the bottle where they couldn't see it. They grabbed their baseball gloves and ran out as quickly as they'd come in.

"*Wait*," Lloyd said. "We can work someth—"

"*Five*...Four...Three..."

Lloyd stepped outside and shut the door.

When the door shut and the latch finished its short, echoey trip around the hollow structure, Hoss dropped the bottle into his baggy pants pocket. He drew his own knife out of his shirt and held it in a fighting type of pose. He whistled "Floatin' Down the Mississippi."

"My God," Buck said.

"What?" Hoss's blade carved a sideways figure-eight into the air.

"You know what. *Lloyd*."

"Oh, *that*." Hoss unpocketed Buck's knife, handing it over.

"Come on, Hoss. You gave me the creeps."

Hoss faced Buck with a thinking-man's frown, one eyebrow up. "Good. I like giving people the creeps."

"Do you think...think he's gonna tell?"

"I don't know."

"You don't *know*?"

"Just relax. Okay? After how he looked when I showed him that bottle? And especially how fast he shut me up when I said the word 'alcoholic' so loud? Come on."

Buck dropped his tense shoulders, but he didn't say anything.

"I think you're safe," Hoss said, changing the grip on his knife. "And if you go down, I swear to you I'll tell Mr. Dinwiddie about my knife. I'm in this with you. But you can bet your ass if either one of us goes down, Mr. Dinwiddie's gonna go down too."

"What? How?"

"We'll write letters to all the parents. Dinwiddie gave us his drunk brother for a counselor. And let us go on a campout and didn't even know where we were in a *tornado*. If we let fly with *that*, they'll shut down this camp and take the Dinwiddies for everything they're worth. I'd say we're in pretty good shape, all-in-all."

Hoss jumped to a defensive pose and stabbed, backhanded, into the air. "Take *that, Llllooooooyyyydd*."

Buck took out his own knife and imitated the same move.

A second later, Hoss jumped toward Buck. In one, fluid motion, he spun Buck around and grabbed him from behind. Then, as though restraining his target, his left hand on the forehead, Hoss put his knife-hand at Buck's throat. The move was too quick for Buck to react. Hoss held his knife tight in his fist, thumb up, the blade pointing away from Buck. Still holding his would-be victim's head, Hoss dragged his thumbnail lightly across Buck's neck.

"Hey!" Buck said.

"Just a quick move I'd love to pull on Lloyd."

"I told you. You gimme the *creeps*," Buck said.

"Aw, hell. You'll be okay."

"Can you teach me that move?"

"Yeah. But we gotta go get rid of this bottle."

"What're we gonna do with it?"

"I dunno. We'll think of sump'm."

They re-sheathed their knives and hid them in their waistbands.

Zeke and I held still in the loft, quiet as *two* mice. In *church*. We didn't move until Buck and Hoss buttoned their shirts and took off out the front door. Zeke and I finally got to work, vandalizing the rafter. We'd tell Neil what happened with Lloyd, but no one else.

The bottle Hoss stuffed into his pants had to be the biggest bargaining chip ever dealt at White Birch Camp. My bet was he and Buck were off to hide it in the woods somewhere. Then practice some knife-fighting, tough-guy hooey.

Zeke and I finished our own little mission, turning every member of Cabin 7 into the ghost he was destined to be. The perfectionist in Zeke made him want to record everyone's real name, nickname, and hometown on the hidden, back side of that rafter. We sat back for a second, when we were done, to admire our work.

"That's good. Isn't it, Ted?"

"Too bad it can't be out in the open," I said. "But we did what we came to do."

We were immortal in Cabin 7.

"You think anybody will ever see it again?" he asked.

"Nope," I said.

I could not possibly have been more wrong.

CHAPTER 39

THE NEXT WEDNESDAY, Lloyd came through with the canoe trip over breakfast, though his generosity wasn't exactly voluntary. A few days after the big blackmail, Hoss decided he was done waiting. Right there at Cabin 7's breakfast table, he got Lloyd's attention, mimicked tipping a bottle to his mouth, and followed the gesture with an arrogant, narrow-eyed stare. Through a haze of impending sleep and above dark circles, Lloyd was able to conjure a hateful glare.

Hoss spoke just above the usual breakfast din, audible only to those aware of the nonverbal portion of the exchange. "How was your night out last night, Lloyd?"

Lloyd's bloodshot glare intensified, and although he didn't say a word, *None of your damned business* was his message. He was positively murderous.

Hoss mocked an expression of extreme confusion and tapped the face of his watch. He then held up one index finger and shook his head. Then a peace sign, head still shaking. Then three fingers. Four. Head still shaking. When Hoss extended his thumb, his head-shake switched to a nod, and his face became serious.

Lloyd returned to the cabin at five that morning.

When Hoss mimed the use of a canoe paddle, Lloyd's baggy eyes surveyed the cabin members. Everyone was lost in conversation except for Bud, who chewed Froot Loops with his mouth open. When Lloyd's gaze rolled around to me, I didn't quite avoid his eye contact.

In a few minutes, Lloyd made his announcement. Because of Hoss, we'd canoe after lunch. Never before had anyone accomplished so much with a single pleasantry flanked by well-chosen hand gestures. Unenthusiastic as it was, Lloyd's announcement still drew such cheering from us that kids at other tables noticed. Zeke made a point of thanking Lloyd.

"You're welcome, Zeke," he said, putting down his fork and staring at his compartmented tray.

It was as easy as that. That afternoon, as the rest of Cabin Row (Lloyd, too, who didn't care to be present for the canoe trip) bedded down for rest period, all nine of us stood in our swim suits between the canoe rack and the boathouse. Six canoes lay parallel on the rack, suspended, open-sides-down, a couple feet above the sand. The rack itself was no more than two equal sets of galvanized iron pipes like giant, nearly buried croquet wickets anchored in concrete. The canoes were aluminum, and in the sun, they radiated little mirages from their flat, keeled bellies. The day was hot and beautiful, just like every day for the last three weeks.

One lifeguard stood at each end of the rack. The one near the boathouse said, "Let's get 'em unlocked." The other took a lanyard from around his neck, selected a key, and opened a padlock underneath the first canoe, releasing one end of a chain. Then he pulled the chain free. It snaked through the canoes' crossbars with a painfully loud, metal-on-metal scrape. We backed away, some of us holding our ears.

When the noise was finally done and the chain lay quietly in the sand, the guard with the lanyard said, "Cornelius

Shepherd! Do me a favor and open the boathouse."

Neil stepped over to him and took the keys. He splayed them out like tiny, metal playing cards. "Which one opens the lock?"

"They're all the same," said the guard. "Any one of them should work."

Neil opened the lock and the boathouse itself. It was a miniature of the cabins we lived in, a single room about eight feet wide and ten feet long. A slide-open window gave a view up the bluff. It was terribly hot in there, so we just grabbed what we needed and got out. The guards were off with the canoes, so Neil just put the lanyard around his neck.

An interminable lecture involving words like *keel, fore, aft, port,* and *starboard* followed. That's the day I learned the wall of the canoe is spelled g-u-n-w-a-l-e, and not *gunnel*, like it sounds. The guards beat us over the heads with rules. *Don't ruin the wooden paddle blades by getting sand stuck in them. Don't stand up in the canoes. Don't do this. Don't do that.*

It was like going back to first grade and definitely worse than any rest period.

Since Zeke was inexperienced and heavy, he partnered with one of the guards. Buck and Hoss went together, of course, and so did Coach and Sunny. Guard #2 took Bones and Bud. Bud sat like a lump in the middle of his canoe. Neil and I shared the last boat, him in front, me in back.

For the next five or ten minutes, we paddled around, either brushing up on old skills or learning new ones. Hoss and Buck were proficient, and Coach and Sunny seemed to have no grasp on even the most basic Newtonian physics. They sloshed their paddles in the water and stood still until a guard gave them a few pointers. Whenever someone hit the gunwale with his paddle, the canoe broadcast the sound.

Neil and I worked well together. I timed my strokes, just like Dad had taught me on the rivers at home, to coincide with Neil's. If he paddled on the right, I'd paddle on the left. It always amazed me how fast you could go—and how little sound the canoe made—if you did it right. Sometimes we'd focus far ahead of us, as though into the future. On other strokes, we watched the little whirlpools that swirled off the pulling blades' edges.

For a guy who'd never been in a canoe, Neil proved his natural talent. I marveled. He wasn't just a genius who read all the time. He was muscular, athletic, and a strong swimmer. Professorly as he was, when we got going in the canoe, he giggled like a kid going down a slide for the first time. When Hoss and Buck challenged us to a race, the lifeguards said it was time for us to go somewhere as a group.

"Mosquito Point!" one counselor said. "Let's go!"

The other counselor said, "You guys ever hear of Mosquito Point?" He laughed, well aware of the ordeal that cost us our first counselor.

Our canoe was pointed to the other side of the lake, and we had to turn left to go north to Mosquito Point. As if by instinct, Neil paddled on the right, and I paddled backwards on the left. Our canoe rotated like a propeller, until our heading was due north.

One counselor said to the other, "How far is it?"

"Not quite half a mile."

"Half a mile," Neil said. "How long'll that take?"

"Um…we can do walking speed for sure," I said. "Easily under ten minutes."

"Ten minutes?" he asked, sounding excited. He dug into the water with his paddle and pulled. The whole canoe lurched forward. I did the same, sure to use the entire blade with each stroke. We glided silently, blissfully across the surface. White Birch Magic shone an impossible blue from the sky, drew endless evergreens across the shores, and breathed patches of capillary waves across the lake's surface.

We pulled far in front of the group. In a couple of minutes, my peaceful trust in Neil's friendship made me pose a question.

When I asked, "You know what I wanna do?" my life took its darkest turn.

CHAPTER 40

THE SUN WAS high in the cloudless sky. On the top of the bluff, as though somebody pressed a button on the front of my imagination, an image of Karen appeared. Her apparition stepped up and sat on the bench, her hair radiating its own, brilliant, orange light. She waved at me. And maybe, just maybe, she blew me a kiss. I paddled harder.

"Hey Ted," Neil said. My picture of Karen poofed away.

"Yeah?"

"We're making pretty good time, aren't we?"

"Yeah." We were, indeed. In fact, in another minute, I could no longer see the bench through all the bluff-dwelling cottonwoods in front of Cabin 7. Those leaf-waving trees were thick as they tapered to water level at Mosquito Point.

Compared to the shallow, flat lake bottom at the waterfront, the water was darker where we paddled, and only boulders, most of them covered with algae, were visible below.

Rocks that big, just sitting under the surface, for maybe millions of years, would normally make me feel small and temporary. But that day, I felt nothing but privilege to see them. A couple hundred yards up was the tree that almost crushed Hoss.

In another two minutes, we were in line with the Mosquito Point beach. The trip from the boathouse had to be well under ten minutes. "A half mile," I muttered to myself, looking across the lake to the twin birches.

I wanted to steal a canoe and paddle there with Karen.

I wondered anew what the flickering light, absent as it had been, represented. There was no question it made me think of Mom. At night, when I peeked through the little hole in the partition, it was as though I checked, not for the light, but for Mom. And as the summer went on, her appearances were as precious as they were few.

But I guessed it didn't matter. Camp had helped me. Healed me. I liked and trusted my friends. They reminded me of how things used to be with Dad. Hiking in Brown County, fishing in the river, eating out on Friday nights.

I wondered if it could be that way again. School would start in the fall, and we'd settle into a life without Mom. It'd be a struggle, I knew, but maybe we could make it. First, Dad would have to heal, like I had. He'd have to be happy, like I'd become. For Dad to be happy…happy for *me* to be home with him?

What could I do?

"I'd do anything," I mumbled.

Neil dug his paddle into his next good stroke. "You say something?" he asked.

"Nothing really. Just thinking out loud. We did a half mile pretty fast."

"Yep. Making good time."

At our pace, a trip across the lake would take under twenty minutes, maybe even fifteen. With or without a flickering light, I still wondered about that far shore.

"You know what I wanna do?" I said.

Neil twisted to face me from the bow. "Whatta you wanna do?" he asked.

"I want to take a canoe trip to the other side."

"Other side of the lake?"

"You bet."

"Okay," he said. "Who's gonna let you do that?"

"Probably nobody," I said. "It's just a dream, but I bet it wouldn't take twenty minutes to get over there."

"We're gonna have to do that at night when nobody's looking," he said.

With his answer and a little chuckle, my wispy cloud of a dream dissolved into the sky where it belonged. Just like the reality of making the best of home, when I got there, it was time to let go of Loon Lake's other side. We had ten good days of camp left. There was no sense dreaming about things I couldn't do.

Everything was peaceful out there on the lake, even Hoss's tree. Distant waves slurped along the shore across a hundred yards of water. Birdsongs sounded, loud and clear. The splash of a jumping fish could be heard but not seen.

"I think I'm getting it," Zeke said. He was slightly out of breath, but he kept up a normal speaking volume. It took me a moment or two just to find him. His canoe was the farthest away, fifty yards or more.

"Yep. Doing a great job," his guard-partner said. "Nice going."

I was astonished at how well I heard them speak. They may have been more like seventy-five yards away. The other canoes made some headway toward us as we stopped paddling. Buck and Hoss paddled hard, closing the distance between us. In another few seconds, they pulled up alongside us.

"*Fellers*," Hoss said with a grin I didn't like. Neil and I remained quiet.

Hoss: "I'm game."

Game? Game for what?

Buck: "Me too."

Hoss: "To be sure."

Neil: "What?"

Hoss: "A canoe trip."

Me: "Canoe trip?"

"Shhh," Hoss said, his grin widening. "Voices carry over water, son. But don't worry, the counselors didn't hear about your plan..."

My plan?

"The other guys are too dumb to understand anything they may have heard," Hoss said. "Except, to be fair, your buddy, Zeke. He seems to store a pretty good brain up in his skull...but *you*, sir," Hoss said, pointing the handle of his paddle right at me, "are a *genius!*"

"What plan?" I whispered, trying to play dumb.

Hoss: "Your plan. *The* plan."

Buck, also whispering: "Nighttime canoe trip. You think we can pull it off?"

NO!! God, no.

Hoss: "Can we pull it *off*...why yes, my good friend, I believe we can. Under cover of *darkness!*"

Hoss drew out the *S* sound in *darkness* and drew on a sinister, wide-eyed face that reminded me of mad scientists in old monster movies.

Hoss: "How long do you think it'd take to get over there?"

Me: "I don't know. Hour? Hour and-a-half?"

"You said you bet it wouldn't take twenty minutes."

Shit. They heard everything. Our canoes clunked together as a couple of waves passed. Hoss and Buck held onto our canoe, keeping bows and sterns together. They whispered.

Buck: "Can't be more than a half hour, anyway."

Me: "What's the point of actually going?"

Hoss: "I just want to see it. You know? See what it looks like. Virgin forest. That's what Mr. Dinwiddie calls it. *Virgin.*"

Neil: "And suppose Mr. Dinwiddie catches you trying to get over there...under cover of darkness." He elongated the same *S* sound, making a face at Hoss.

Hoss: "We're smarter than that, Neil. I heard how you were talking to Ted. Sounds like you're game, too."

Neil: "How was I talking to Ted?"

Hoss: "We heard you say 'We're *gonna have to go there at night.*' You said '*we,*' and not '*you.*' Sounds to me like you're already pretty interested in this little excursion. Am I wrong?"

When I returned Neil's glance, he dodged me.

Sunny and Coach closed in on us.

Hoss: "The professor's in, Ted. Me and Buck are in. So what about you?"

The topic wasn't going away. I guessed there was no reason it would. After all, snowballs don't exactly roll uphill and get smaller.

CHAPTER 41

THE COUNSELORS TOLD us it was time to head back. We'd do some exercises in seven or eight feet of water, then go back to the boathouse. Hoss complained, of course.

"Time to head back *already*?" he said.

The counselors ignored him.

Then in a whisper, just for the four of us, he said, "See? We need a *real* canoe trip." Then to the counselors again, "Can't we stay out for a little longer?"

"Wish we could," said the one in Zeke's canoe. "But we need time to stow the canoes and the equipment."

"Truly," said the other counselor, "nothing excites us more than the idea of spending more time out here with you fine gentlemen, but we got places to go, people to see."

"More like 'willies to yank,'" Hoss whispered.

From that point forward, the topic of our forbidden trip would bubble to the surface of any discussion.

Back near the boathouse, Hoss and Buck got out of their canoe, and Hoss stepped over to ours. "Need any help?" he asked.

"No," I said.

"Counselor said he wants the lanyard back."

Neil still had it around his neck. He pulled it up, over his head, and gave it to Hoss.

"I don't trust him one minute," Neil whispered as Hoss high-stepped away, sloshing in knee-deep water, "especially when he's trying to look helpful."

"He's up to sump'm for sure," I said.

A guard yelled out, "Keep those paddle blades out of the sand!"

"I love it!" Zeke said, approaching the boathouse to stow his vest and paddle. "I want to canoe every day!"

When Zeke said that, Hoss threw me a grin and gestured at Zeke.

~~~

After supper, my buddies sat with me on the bench. Zeke had found a perfectly round granite rock the size of a golf ball. He held it in his hands, passing it back-and-forth as we talked. Neil dug in the sand and dirt with a stick he'd picked up.

Neil: "Ted. Have you told Zeke?"

Me: "About what?"

"Come on, man. You know *what*." He pointed his stick to the lake's other side.

Zeke: "Tell me what?"

Me: "Nothing. It's not a good idea."

"What's not a good idea?"

Neil, whispering: "Ted wants to take a canoe trip to the other side of the lake, at night. When everybody's asleep."

Zeke: "You can't do that!"

Me: "I know. That's why I'm not gonna." Neil stopped digging with the stick. "It's a fun idea. Something to talk about, but not something you actually do."

Neil: "That's all we're doing is talking. There's no harm in just *talking* about it. Is there, Zeke?"

Zeke: "I guess we can talk about anything we want."

Me: "I agree. We can *talk* about it. But if we actually *did* it, we'd have to know when to go, sneak out of the cabin, find a way to get the paddles and life jackets, unlock the canoes. You know how loud those damned canoes are, right? When you pull the chain through 'em? It'd be pretty hard to get away w—" Right then, I caught myself. I'd been working out the details.

Neil giggled when I cut myself off, then got more serious. He put the stick in the dirt he'd loosened, jabbing a couple of times. "It's hard not to think about, isn't it?"

"Hey, Neil," Zeke said hopefully. "That'd be your adventure, for sure."

Me: "Stop it."

Neil: "Wasn't there something Ted told us early on? Something about rules and dummies?"

"Look. You guys better knock it off. This is crazy talk. You don't sneak out of the cabin at night, you don't steal camp property, and you don't trespass on government land."

Neil: "Knock what off? We're just talking."

Zeke: "What do you think it's like over there?"

Me: "You guys sound like you're really thinking about this." Zeke shrugged his shoulders. "It's just like it looks over here. That's all. It's nothing special over there."

Did I just say that? Out loud? It was as though I'd taken pure magic in my hand and thrown it away. Or pushed a grow-up button. In that one statement, trying to keep a couple of good kids from using their imaginations—trying to keep them from *believing*—I devalued White Birch Magic. Hell, I devalued childhood itself. Besides, I didn't believe those words anyway.

Zeke: "Aren't you just a little curious?"

Course I'm curious. More than you and Neil put together.

Me: "You guys are ganging up on me."

"Nuh-uh. It's nothing like that."

"It's deep water out there. Real deep."

Neil snickered hard through his nose, still digging.

Zeke: "I'd be in a canoe. And if you were right there with me—"

"*Big* ole fish out there, Zeke. Big. Northern *pikes*."

Neil: "With nasty teeth."

Zeke was supposed to be frightened by that, but he didn't seem to be.

Me: "I hear the woods over there are full of Giant Sloths."

Neil's giggle pressure overcame the gates. "Shut up, man!"

In a few minutes, he turned professorly again and broke the silence. "But really...going over there, some night...what's it gonna hurt?"

Zeke: "To have a *real* adventure."

Me: "But we can't...Mr. Dinwiddie..."

Neil: "Yeah, we can. Rules and dummies. You know how it works."

Me: "I was talking about graffiti when I said that...not *this*."

Zeke: "Hey, Ted. We're just talking. I want to figure out how hard it'd be to do. Let's plan it, just for fun. You know? Like we really *were* gonna—"

"Ladies!" Hoss blurted. Neil stopped digging with the stick, and Zeke stilled the granite stone. Hoss and Buck stood right behind us. How long they'd been there was the question. We eyed them, and all was quiet.

"What's the matter with you guys?" Hoss asked, eyeing us all in turn. "I was just kiddin' ya. Let me be the first to say you're a fine group of *men*."

Buck: "What were you all talking about? It looked pretty serious."

Neil: "You know what we're talking about."

Buck grinned, and Neil went back to digging with the stick.

Hoss: "And now that all *five* of the brains in the cabin are together, we should figure it out. So what do you guys think?"

We were quiet again.

Hoss: "What about you, Neil? You still in?"

Neil froze. He raised his chin and drew eye contact with us all. He nodded. My stomach tightened.

Buck: "Excellent."

"And what about you, Zeke," Hoss said.

Zeke: "Um…we were just talking about it, maybe about planning it, like we really were gonna do it."

"Good," Hoss said. "It's gonna take some planning, anyway. So that leaves you, Boss," he said to me. "Whatta you think?"

One thing he said was true. The five brains in the cabin were right there at the bench. It was clear I was outnumbered, four-to-one. You'd think Neil and Zeke had caught whatever disease made Hoss the way he was.

Hoss: "Come on, Tedski. What's it gonna be?"

Buck: "Ted, don't feel pressured, but—"

Hoss: "Yeah. Don't feel any pressure, but there are only a

few days of camp left."

Those guys hadn't thought it through. A scroll opened in my mind, holding the list of what we'd have to do to pull off the ridiculous stunt.

The Mosquito Point Trail would keep us in the dark and help us sneak down to the boathouse through the cottonwoods. We could pull the canoe chain through quietly. It'd just take a little time. Voices carry on the lake, so we'd stick together as we paddled, and whisper if we had to talk.

But how would we get the paddles? They're locked up in the boathouse. Tighter than the canoes. The only thing the trip had going for it is we just needed one of the keys. We'd learned all three keys on the lanyard are the same. Any of them could open both padlocks—one of the boathouse, and one on the canoe chain. But we didn't have the keys, so that was that.

No way was it going to happen. Those guys were just blowing smoke.

Me: "You guys haven't thought it through."

Hoss: "Oh, but we have, my good man. Let's just say we have a plan."

Buck: "It's a great idea. It'll turn this summer into something we'd never forget."

It would indeed, but I wasn't about to ask what their plan was. It'd make me appear interested. Neil started in with the stick again. Zeke tossed the rock up and down.

Hoss: "Think about it and let us know." He and Buck stepped toward the cabin, and Hoss stopped. "Oh. I almost forgot. Hey Zeke?"

"Yeah?"

"Thanks for letting me borrow your book. Taught me more about sloths than anyone on earth would ever want to know. I think I cracked the binding when I opened it. Hope that's okay."

"It's okay. That happens to books people like to read. And you're welcome."

The nice Hoss didn't jive like the nice Zeke. Hoss was up to something again. He held the book toward Zeke, then seemed to change his mind and handed it to me.

Hoss: "Have you read it, Ted?"

I shook my head.

Hoss: "You ought to have a look inside. Learn a little sump'm."

I took the book and held it like it might self-destruct, like one of those old tapes from *Mission: Impossible*. Hoss and Buck headed toward the cabin.

I wouldn't tell the guys I'd already planned more of the trip to the other side than either of them could.

Zeke: "That was nice of him to thank me for the book. You think he read it?"

Neil: "I saw him reading it earlier."

Me: "Probably did, but he could've put it on your bunk. They were just *in* the cabin."

Zeke: "He probably just wanted to say thanks."

Coulda said thanks in the cabin.

I thumbed through the book, and something interrupted the even flow of glossy pages, the way those stiff little ads do in magazines. I opened the book, and a tarnished padlock key fell out of it.

CHAPTER 42

NEIL GRABBED THE key and jumped up from his seat. His digging stick fell against the bench and slid to the ground.

"Hey, you guys!" he said, holding the key in front of him as he ran to them.

Buck made a *shush* gesture. Hoss opened one hand, palm down, and pumped it gently in the air, his eyes proud and narrow. Neil slowed to a walk and closed his hand around the key. Hoss and Buck met him halfway.

That's when I realized Buck, who had been the definitive cabin leader at the beginning of camp, was by then just an assistant, a puppet. Hoss was in charge. Hoss the criminal. Buck was one of those guys my dad called henchmen in the gangster movies he liked to watch.

I'd seen Buck's transformation all summer, and it was complete by the day Hoss stole the key. The whiskey incident with Lloyd was when the board tipped and all the marbles rolled down to Hoss's end.

By the time Neil met the other two, Zeke and I were standing, staring over the back of the bench. Hoss beckoned us, and we went. The five of us stood in a tight circle between the bench and Cabin 7. It must've looked like some kind of meeting. A very suspicious meeting.

Neil: "Hey, man, you two are gonna have to hold onto this key, not us."

Buck: "It's all right. Nobody has to—"

"No. You're the ones who stole it. Not me."

Hoss: "It's okay. Just wanted to drop a little hint for Ted."

"But I'm the guy who wore it around his neck the entire time we were in the boats, and when they find out that key's missing, they're gonna come after me."

"Maybe they'd come after you, maybe they wouldn't."

"That's not very reassuring."

"Okay, so when they come after you, tell 'em you gave the keys to me. Ted saw you do it, and the counselors'll remember I had 'em last."

"That's not gonna work."

"Why not?"

"'Cause you can just tell 'em *I* must've been the one who took it. Before I gave you the keychain."

"Oh...*Professor*...Do you think I'd really—"

"In one damned second, you would."

Hoss's shoulders dropped. Neil had just foiled a potential blackmail plot. "All right. Gimme the key. I wouldn't rat on you like that. Besides, we don't need to worry about who they're gonna come after, 'cause they're not even gonna know the key's gone."

Me: "What makes you so sure?"

Hoss: "I can't be a hundred percent sure, but I saw where the keychain came from. It hangs in Headquarters, right inside the window. They go in there, and they grab it. When they're done with the keys, they take 'em back to Headquarters and hang 'em back up. And that's about it."

Neil: "But there were three keys on—"

Hoss: "They'll think somebody in Headquarters took the

third one, *if* they think about it at all. But they got other things to think about. Girls and nights out. Believe me. They're not gonna give a shit about some dumb *key*. But I'll take it if you want. I got some string back in the cabin. I'll wear it for a necklace."

"But—"

"But nothing. If anybody in Headquarters cries about it being missing, we'll just sneak it down to the boathouse and drop it in through the window."

"But the window's locked."

"But...but...buh-buh-*buhhhh*...I unlocked it. Come on, fellas. Have some faith."

Neil had no answer. A grin crept onto Zeke's face but disappeared when I glared at him.

It was clear Hoss had done some thinking after all.

"All right," I said, knowing they hadn't thought it through. "When's this supposed to take place? We'd have to—" I checked around me. "—sneak out."

"When's the best night to do that?" Zeke asked.

I rolled my eyes, incredulous. *Zeke* of all people, was turning criminal on me.

Buck: "We think—"

Hoss: "Next Tuesday night."

Neil: "Why next Tuesday?"

Hoss: "Because that's Lloyd's night out."

Me: "Okay. How are we supposed to do that on his night out?"

Hoss: "He'll be out of the cabin, won't he?"

Me: "How long'll that trip take us?"

Hoss: "I don't know. Two, maybe three hours?"

Me: "And in that couple-three hours, Lloyd'll come back after his night out, and he'll see we're gone."

Hoss: "He won't come back, not until late."

Neil: "How do you know?"

Me: "How can you *possibly* know what he's gonna do on his night out? Besides. There are rovers. They rove around Cabin Row at night, watching. They do that just to keep this kind of stuff from going on."

I was convinced. Never gonna happen.

Hoss: "Of course there are rovers. They're supposed to *rove* until two in the morning, but they never do."

Me: "What about Isaac?" Isaac did his job the way it was to be done. There was a morning I talked to him when he entered the cabin with his flashlight. It made me think of Cliff, that night I was in the loft, finding Karen's sloth story. Cliff had probably been roving that night he came all the way inside the cabin just to pee.

"*Isaac* stays out till two, like he's s'pose to. That's a guarantee. But the other guys don't. Or at least what's-his-name—Bill—doesn't. He doesn't even come close to staying out that late."

Bill was the Cabin 6 counselor.

"So?"

"He roves on Tuesday nights."

Oh.

Hoss had a tone of authority, or at least more than his bullshit usual. This one seemed authentic. It made me wonder how he could know all this. But then I remembered drifting off one night while seeing his silhouette in the window near his bed. From his vantage point, he'd be able to see most of Cabin 6 and know when the counselor entered his cabin.

The pre-bell squeak began.

"And Lloyd's out on Tuesday nights," Hoss reminded us.

The bell rang out, a shrill but pretty sound. It was like music compared to the painful and ugly noise of those canoes. *We'll really have to keep the paddles off the gunwales and be careful with that chain.*

"How do you know when Lloyd gets back?" I said.

Hoss's expression opened a window into some part of his past we'd never fully know. I wondered if it had to do with his apparent familiarity with mean drunks.

"I don't sleep well sometimes," he said simply. His face (and his ability, so far, to hack through every argument I'd made against the plan) made me believe him. He tapped his watch face. "The first time he came back, it was quarter-to-five. And this morning, it was balls-on. Five a.m."

Me: "So that's two nights out. What if—"

Hoss: "Three. He's been here three Tuesdays. You wanna guess when he got in last week?"

Zeke: "Five?"

Hoss: "Five a.m."

Zeke gripped his sloth book and shifted his weight from one foot to the other and back.

Buck: "What do you think he does on those nights out?"

Hoss: "Besides get sloppy-ass drunk? How am I supposed to know? I don't have *all* the answers, just most of 'em."

What a statement. *I don't have all the answers, just most of 'em.* It was something I thought I might want to say sometime, but I knew I'd never have the stomach for it.

Hoss: "Hey, Ted. Want me to tell you when Bill goes to bed on Tuesday nights?"

Me: "No."

"'Bout eleven. When it's good and dark and nobody's awake to see him not doing his job."

"That's happened three Tuesdays in a row?"

"For Bill? He's done *that* all summer."

"Does that sound like a *stand-around-and-huddle bell to you*?" Lloyd shouted from the Cabin 7 stoop. "In the cabin. Let's go."

"Speak of the devil!" Hoss said as we moseyed to the stoop.

Lloyd's face reddened. "In the cabin, gentlemen. And you," he said, his bony index finger in Hoss' face. "Get into my area. Time to have a little chat."

CHAPTER 43

WE ALL STEPPED into the cabin and went to our bunks.

Neil whispered to Zeke and me, "Hey, Ted. This canoe trip. We can handle it. Think of it like Zeke does. Let's see if we can come up with a plan. Just for fun. How would someone do it without getting caught? If they were gonna do it for real?"

And then Zeke, the cabin's latest criminal mastermind, chimed in. "Yeah, Ted. Wouldn't it be interesting to think about it long enough...to just try...to figure out if it's *possible*?"

"You guys are nuts," I said.

Maybe they *were* nuts, but so was I. Not one of us wanted to see that other side more than I did. Just thinking about it long enough to see if it's possible? I could go along with that. The only problem was, I already *knew* it was possible.

Neil and Zeke were quiet, maybe listening for the conversation we could almost hear in Lloyd's area. But I doubt it. Knowing them, their silence would be out of courtesy to me. I grabbed my toothbrush and headed back to the sinks.

As I walked, I pictured us on the lake, in canoes. Maybe just the three of us. Or maybe those two in their boat, and Karen with me, in mine. The far shore of the lake was my place, and I wanted to share it with no one else but them.

By the time I was done brushing my teeth and back at my bunk, Hoss walked quietly in from up front. He was red in the face, livid. He raised his eyebrows as he walked past. No one could hear what was said up there, and I guess it doesn't matter.

Whatever Lloyd said or did, it did no more than deepen their mutual hatred. Hoss went back to his bunk without a word. Lloyd stepped past the partition, glaring at me the way he had at breakfast. He stopped at my shelves, glanced once more at Hoss, then back at me.

"Mr. Gables. Up to my area. Now."

I thought for a second someone else named Mr. Gables was behind me.

"Let's *go*," he said.

I went. I'd never been in Lloyd's area, such as it was, and I immediately disliked being up there. It had its own smell, maybe the chemicals Hoss had mentioned. It also had some outside type of smell. Something that reminded me of autumn, but not like cool air. *Dried leaves?...No...*Something that didn't belong in summer. *Wood-burning stove* is what finally fixed itself in my mind. The smell was a mixture of wood stove and fresh air.

His area was neat, almost military, except for a dropped pile of camouflage things—a jacket, maybe; thin, white, cotton gloves; and a cloth hat with a brim—between the bed and plywood wall. As Lloyd hovered, not talking, I noticed also some fine-mesh netting attached to the hat, like something you'd get at a hobby shop to catch butterflies.

The contrast between the messy pile of clothes and military neatness didn't hold my attention long. Lloyd's stare was far too distracting. Plus, he'd gotten close enough to bite. After a few seconds, I couldn't stand it any more.

"Lloyd? Can I help you with something?"

I got nothing from him.

"Lloyd?"

Still nothing. After a few more seconds of his leaning over me and breathing heavily through his nose I decided on my own brand of *executive action* and started back toward my bunk. Lloyd grabbed my arm with enough force to hurt. I jerked away and almost yelled.

"Tell me what you know about what happened at breakfast this morning," he said, his breathing irregular and heavy, like he was dangerously upset.

"At breakfast?" I had no idea what he meant.

"Yes. When Mr. Cartwright used hand signals and spoke to me briefly. Do you know anything about that?"

As a matter of fact, I knew all about it. Hoss lifting an imaginary bottle to his face, pointing to his watch, holding up five fingers, and miming a canoe paddle? I figured playing dumb was my only choice. Being dishonest to Lloyd didn't feel like much of a crime. Besides, that colorless, smoke-and-chemical space was creepy, and I wanted out.

"Hand signals?" I asked.

"Do you intend to answer me or just repeat phrases?"

My mouth opened, but I had nothing prepared. "I...I don't understand the questions."

"The questions are simple, Mr. Gables. The gestures Mr. Cartwright made at breakfast this morning?"

All right, I thought. Now *that* wasn't even a question. I didn't like Lloyd one bit, and part of me, the part that saw him so scare Karen on watermelon night, wanted him to know it.

"Oh. The gestures. Hoss told me you got back this morning at five o'clock."

"That's just the point," he said. "Mr. Cartwright is telling lies. And this morning, you watched it happen."

"If Hoss was lying, why'd you turn right around and do just what he wanted?"

Lloyd bristled, then leaned in. I smelled his stale cigarette breath when he said, "Now you wait just one minute. That's not what happened."

I wanted to argue, but I have to admit, the hairs on my neck stood up when Lloyd leaned over me. Pleading and quiet, I asked, "What do you want from me?"

He took a deep breath. "Whatever it is you've been planning with Mr. Cartwright, if you do not intend to tell me what it is—and I'm sure you *don't*—I need it to stop."

"Uh…" I said. My jaw was slack, my eyes wide, and my mind suddenly slate blank.

"Watch your tone with me, young man."

My tone? What'd I say?

"You still have absolutely nothing to confess to me. Is that what you're telling me?"

"No."

"No? Is that to mean you have nothing to say or that I'm incorrect in saying so?"

"Yes. I mean *no*."

"I don't like being toyed with, Mr. Gables. And I don't like the way you and Mr. Cartwright…and you and"—extra contempt invaded his face—"*Karen*…are setting me up."

"Karen?"

"You think I don't keep an eye on things?"

"No. I mean *yes*. I know you keep an eye on things."

I felt my face flush, just like Hoss's.

"It appears I've gotten my point across. You're dismissed. And I'll be keeping an eye on *you*."

Something was deeply wrong with Lloyd. But I didn't know what. All I knew is that I was free to go back to my bunk, and I went. My mouth was shut for the rest of the night. As the lights went out and the remnants of daylight faded with my irritation and fear, I knew Lloyd was the type of character you're supposed to feel sorry for. But I didn't.

After all was quiet, I got up, onto my hands and knees and stole a peek through the coin-sized hole in the wall. The light in the trees was gone. I wanted Mom. Or at least a suggestion of her. Something up front went bump and reminded me how close Lloyd was. Hate is an ugly thing, but I had it for Lloyd.

In the near-complete darkness, there was only one place those thoughts could go. And with only me awake to say no to the idea, I decided the trip across the lake was on.

CHAPTER 44

THE NEXT MORNING, I told Neil and Zeke I was leaving breakfast early and heading back. Holding my breath, I sped past the fetid kitchen air. I passed the trash-filled, fifty-five-gallon drums to make the dusty stroll back to the cabin.

Footsteps followed me, but I ignored it.

"Tedski!" It was Hoss. Without Buck. I steeled myself. "What'd the old drunk say to you last night? When he pulled you up there, to his area?"

"Enough to know you and me shouldn't be seen together."

"The hell you say."

"Lloyd thinks we've been talking. Planning something he wouldn't like."

"How 'bout that," he said, appearing to marvel. "Looks like he hasn't pickled all of his brain away."

"Maybe half."

"That mean you're up for the trip?"

"Why would that mean I'm up for the trip?"

"Aw, come on, man."

"Hoss. We could get into more trouble than—"

"So think about it. Got a couple days."

I sighed. Hoss was more of a steaming locomotive than a strolling listener. I wouldn't give him the satisfaction of telling him I wanted to go, not then. Not after being run over.

"Hey, here's something," he said. "When you were up there—in his area last night. Did you see anything weird?"

"Like what?"

"Did you see the army clothes? And that mosquito face-net thing?"

So that's what that was. "I saw that stuff."

"You'd think the son-of-a-bitch would just stay inside if he didn't wanna get bit."

"Hey, guys! Wait up!" It was Buck. He, Zeke, and Neil ran up behind us. We walked together, toward the cabin and didn't say much. Lloyd was nowhere to be seen.

As we passed the waterfront, which afforded a panoramic view of Loon Lake, Hoss said, "Sure looks mysterious over there."

"Yep. It does," Zeke said, patting me on the shoulder. Where did that boy find all his boldness? It was as though paddling the canoe had made him taste something good for the first time, and he suddenly couldn't get enough of it.

I took off in a jog, deciding to stay away from Hoss.

~~~

The rest of the week went by quickly. People talked about the end of camp. *One week to go*, guys would say. *Be time to pack soon*. Somebody even mentioned school.

White Birch Camp would change ethereally, the luster of magic turning like autumn into a melancholy that can only be felt, not described. The occasional hot, dry breeze through the treetops would issue its own good-bye. Each time it did, I wondered if I'd ever hear it again. Many of us began to miss our friends, as though we'd already gone. We were all, slowly but surely, transforming into ghosts of Cabin Row, like Cal

Owen. I wanted to take Zeke and Neil home with me. They could live down the street. We could ride bikes to school.

But I couldn't. We'd separate at the end, and I knew it. The ache about separating from Karen came so strongly I wondered once or twice if I'd actually throw up.

On Saturday, Zeke said "Six days left," and his permanent smile faded dead away. He seemed afraid to meet eyes with Neil or me. I'll never forget that. Ours was a very adult and peculiar kind of sadness only the end of a summer camp season can thrust into the heart of a kid.

A new legend emerged before it was all over, and that was the Drought of 1970. Mr. Dinwiddie said he had never seen anything like it. As the days wore on, dust devils swirled through the waterfront. The anguished cottonwoods dropped cracked, yellowing leaves in the sand. Except for the heat, you'd think it was October. I spent a few collective hours on the bench studying, of course, the other side. Whitecaps agitated the surface on some days, and not on others. The shore beckoned. Karen even sat with me there one day. I almost reached for her hand once, but I didn't. Should have. Those moments were both thrilling and painfully sad.

The last camp weekend faded into history, and Lloyd's last night out approached. No one talked about the trip for days. The excitement (or pressure to go through with it) seemed to recede. But on Monday night, when just the five brains of the cabin were together, Lloyd off somewhere else, Zeke asked the question.

"Is the trip still on?"

I clenched my fists with the rush of anticipation. I also

clamped shut with dread.

"I don't know," Hoss said. "What do you say, Ted?"

Buck showed me a neutral kind of patience. Zeke's face was childlike and pure. It was as though he had too much natural goodness to see anything wrong with the plan. If Zeke wanted to do it, I thought, how wrong could it possibly be?

Still, part of me wanted to go to Headquarters and tell Isaac. *Lloyd stays out too late on his nights out. He drinks. Someone needs to talk to him.* That would have slammed the book shut. I could have done that. But I didn't. Instead, I heard Zeke's simple question, saw Neil's *I'm with you either way* expression, and I uttered one syllable.

"Yes."

Hoss's lips stretched tight and separated, showing those perfect, white teeth. In his face, I saw the devil and should have run.

"All right," Hoss said. "You wanna go over the plans?"

Neil: "Wait a minute. Who even knows about this, besides us?"

Buck: "Just us."

Neil: "We *are* planning on the nine of us going?"

Hoss: "Hell yes. Have to. No idea what those other four dip-shits would do with us gone. Who they'd tell and all that."

Buck: "Yeah. Definitely all of us."

Hoss: "Especially Sunny. He'd cry a river if he didn't get to go on an adventure with Buck, our fearless cabin leader."

Fearless cabin leader. That was indeed what Hoss wanted everyone to think. No one much liked Hoss, but they *loved* Buck. Where Buck went, Sunny wanted to go. With Sunny would come Coach, the amiable sportsman. Bones would go along, because that's what he seemed to be put on the earth to do.

"What about Bud?" Neil said. It was a good question. What *about* Bud? Our only real liability. Our little question mark. The stick of dynamite that could light itself.

Hoss included Buck for the appearance of leadership. But Buck just gaped back.

"We'll handle him," Hoss said. "All we gotta do is tell him at lights-out. Tell 'em all at lights-out. Make it sound real fun. They'll go. We'll take care of Bud."

I said, "Tell Bud he better go or we'll tell everybody he peed his pants."

"Everybody already knows," Hoss said.

CHAPTER 45

TUESDAY'S WAKE-UP bell, line-ups, activities, and meals came and went. Lloyd disappeared for his night out sometime before five, even before his usual time. All was going perfectly, except that Karen wasn't in Headquarters like she usually was after dinner. The rest of free-rec was uneventful. Call-to-quarters came around just as expected. The Tuesday-night rover, Bill, would tuck us in around five minutes before lights-out. He was a nice guy and would cause us no trouble. We'd be without a counselor for that evening, and without any supervisor after Bill went to bed.

The way Hoss saw it, White Birch Camp had two rule-breaker counselors, and it was our dumb luck that both of them perpetrated their crimes on the same night, week after week. It seemed safe enough to count on Lloyd not being back until around five in the morning. Bill would probably knock off at ten-thirty or eleven, in lieu of the faithful performance of *his* duties. Leave it up to Hoss to find a way to take advantage of it.

Hoss lifted a key on a piece of red string and dropped it over his head. He tucked the key into his flannel shirt. Part of me hoped the trip wouldn't go forward. But then, Hoss nodded at Buck, who said, "Hey, Guys. Got something I want to run past you." Sunny and Coach attended to him quickly. So did Bones. Bud drifted along.

"Tonight," Buck said, "We're going on a little trip."

He stated the plan. We needed to be in bed, clothes and boots at the ready. Three flashlights, no more. We'd go when Bill turned in at his too-early time. We'd be alone, and everyone on Cabin Row would be in bed by then.

And that was that. The four others took to the idea just as though Mr. Dinwiddie himself had hatched the plan. Such was the power Buck held in the cabin. The bigger and hidden problem was the power Hoss held over Buck. But things were smooth. The evening's pages turned like a script.

Until Isaac showed up. He blew through the door like a stiff gust. His broad shoulders and enormous frame almost filled the space in the partition. His eyes seemed sunken in his face again, like when he has a *famous migraine*. But he managed to remain chipper. "Cabin seven! How you guys doin'?...Don't everybody talk at once."

In my mind, I shouted. *Lloyd's a drunk! He'll be out all night! And Bill doesn't ROVE! We'll be all alone! We're not safe!* That'd fix the canoe trip problem.

"Um," Buck said, "yeah. Fine. I thought Bill was rov—"

"He was," Isaac said. "But I'm taking over…"

That was it. The trip was off. A part of me, but only a shockingly small part, was relieved. The rest of me was disappointed. Neil and Zeke kept poker faces.

Hoss said, "Sounds pretty fair," and nodded casually, incriminating his deep talent for deception.

"…at least," Isaac said, "until Bill gets back from town. Should be in a few minutes."

And just like that, trip was back on. My buddies exchanged glances. Zeke squeezed his fists together.

I'll never know exactly why those guys so wanted to take such a chance, but I decided if their reasons were good for them, they were good for me. I wanted like crazy to see what was on the other side, but my real hope was to get home to Dad and see about putting things back where they'd once been. I was starting to think we could do it.

Isaac spoke. "You guys need anything?"

No. We didn't.

"If you do, just gimme a shout. I'll be out in front of The Row." He left the cabin, and the door slammed like it may never open again. The incessant, call-to-quarters chatter from Cabin 6 bled in through our windows.

No one said anything before we heard Isaac's booming voice: "Cabin six! How you guys doin'?—Hey! Bill's back. You ready for the duty?"

Isaac meant the roving duty. We didn't hear Bill say anything, but Isaac said, "Groovy, man. My wagon train's headin' to the ranch."

We were pretty sure 'the ranch' meant Headquarters.

"Have a good night," Isaac said. In another moment, Cabin 6's door slammed shut, just like ours.

Hoss took a little swipe at his light string and nodded at Buck, who then said, "Let's get those lights out, fellas." And out the lights went, one by one.

After that, Buck and Hoss sat on their bunks, waiting for Bill to cheat and go to bed early. At night, Cabin Row burned two lights. One was the naked bulb just above Isaac's window. The other towered above the beach house and cast a shallow cone of light all the way down Cabin Row.

For the next ten minutes, no one made a sound in Cabin 7. We heard Bill yell at Marty to pull his light string in Cabin 6, and it eventually went out. It was dark and quiet on Cabin Row, save for the glow from down at the waterfront. Hoss leaned toward his window and narrated in whispers the mundane story unfolding outside. Bill left Cabin 6 and went to the bluff. He lit a cigarette. That's what he always does, Hoss told us: lights-out, quiet, smoke at the bluff, sneak back inside and go to bed.

So far, since Isaac left Cabin 7, things had gone exactly as Hoss said they would.

I lay back on my bunk, jeans and boots on. Zeke slipped out of bed and laced up his boots. So did Neil. And quietly, so did everyone else.

I thought about the Emergency Door at the rear of the cabin and figured I'd better grab a piece of notebook paper.

CHAPTER 46

"*PSSST!*" CAME A sound from Hoss, no doubt a cue for Buck.

"Bill went inside," Buck whispered harshly to the cabin. "Wait five minutes. Get ready."

Bud started to say something, which came out in a regular voice. He produced one syllable before Buck, Hoss, and Sunny shushed him.

"Okay," Buck said a few minutes later. "No jumping from the bunks. Everybody ready?"

A flurry of soft affirmatives.

"All right, then," he said. "Let's line up at the door."

"Don't go out the front," I said. "Out the Emergency Door. We'll be in the shadows back there." I remember thinking we'd never even make it to the canoes—much less across the lake—if Buck were actually in charge.

Hoss offered, "Good idea, Ted."

I led the way to the back door. Not trusting anyone to open it quietly but me, I turned the knob and pushed, trying to keep the door from rubbing on the frame. Motioning for the guys to file out of the cabin, I reached for the notebook paper in my pocket while Sunny went to close the door. I told him to stop.

"There's no knob on the back," Sunny whispered.

"I know."

"How we gonna get back in? Through the front?"

"No," I said, still folding the paper, "I'll show you—"

"Buck!" he said. "How we gonna get back in?"

"Prop it open with a stick," said somebody else.

"No," someone answered, "It'll swing back open."

As the unenlightened debated quietly, I stuck the folded paper over the latch and shut the door, securing it in place. "Nice thinkin', Tedski," Hoss said. "What's next, Boss?" he said to Buck.

Buck faced the fronts of the cabins and took two confident strides toward the river of light the beach house spilled down Cabin Row.

"Wait!" I whispered. Buck stopped. I wanted to kick him out of the Five Brains Club. "Gotta stay behind the cabins and go around back, to Mosquito Point trail."

The quicker we got around to the back of the cabin, the better. All it would take is Marty peeking out his window and seeing us all out there.

Sunny pointed to the woods north of Cabin 7. "Uh, Mosquito Point's that way?" he said. Then, pointing toward the bluff, he added, "And the canoes? Well, they're *that* way."

I said, "Mosquito Point Trail's in the *dark* and goes close to the bluff's edge about twenty yards down. We could go down the bluffs there and never get into the light until we're down by the water. If you want to go straight to the boathouse from here, you'll get us all nailed."

"Hoss," I whispered, shrugging my shoulders as though to say *Sunny's your problem. Fix him.*

"Yeah, Sunny," Hoss said. "Listen to Ted. And leave the smartass comments to the professionals."

I took Zeke's flashlight from him, the one like Hoss's. Sunny's was the third of three flashlights. After explaining some brief signals, I stole toward the back of the cabin and the trail. After a carefully chosen light signal from me at the trailhead, we all made it to the trail, leaving a quiet Cabin Row behind.

Even so, the sense of extreme visibility never went away. There was more moonlight than I would've liked. The cottonwoods wagged their puppy-tail leaves, just like during the day. *Here, guys!* they seemed to say. *Over here! The water is down this way!*

We gathered where the Mosquito Point trail bent near the bluff. Beyond around ten feet of dirt and pine needles, we found the deep sand, where the cottonwoods were sparse enough to give us an easy path down to the water. The upper limbs of the tallest ones whooshed in a dreamy, comfortable way. A small part of me still wanted to be back in my bunk, drifting off to those beautiful, comforting sounds.

Otherwise, it was quiet. So quiet, really, I wished someone would say something.

"Hoss," I said, "you want to go first? Me and Zeke can bring up the rear."

"No," Hoss said, and then, still specifically to me, "you know the way. I'll stay in the middle of the group, and Buck and Zeke can be in back."

It seemed like a good-enough arrangement. I started down, weaving between the cottonwoods. My position on the bluff afforded me a view I'd never seen. There was just enough light to make out the silhouette of the far treetops and plenty to guide us down to the water. A full moon floated in the sky across the lake. It lit up the sand and cast a broad beam across the water.

Right when we headed down our serene path, we heard a rustling up toward the trail. A twig snapped, and Bud's mouth let out something that might pass for a weak scream. Hoss pounced and in a strange, almost nurturing way, shut him up.

Bud: "What was that?"

Buck: "It's okay, Bud, it's nothing."

Sunny: "Had to be somethin'."

Zeke: "Probably a squirrel or raccoon."

Bones: "Loon Lake Sloth."

Bud: "Nuh-*uh!*"

Buck: "Quiet, you guys."

Sunny: "Escaped psycho."

Sunny's was the comment that brought no response. Leading the way, I stopped. The group's energy somehow changed as a tiny landslide swaddled my feet and ankles in sand. Everyone froze in place, in a drawn-out *S* form, among the cottonwoods. Escaped psycho. The topic we'd all tried to ignore was up for discussion.

Hoss grabbed Sunny by the shirt and said, "Nobody wants to hear about that. It's just some crap Isaac made up."

"I could've done without hearing it," Neil whispered.

"Me too," I said.

Coach asked, "There aren't really any psychos out here, are there?"

"No," Buck said. "No one would let a camp be out here otherwise." That's what Buck said, but his voice cracked a little when he said it. In a short gasp of wind, the trees shivered.

The thought of a killer on the loose scared me like no science fiction ever could. I'd much rather fear The Sloth. I stepped down to the water, and there it was.

The light in the trees.

I couldn't believe it. On past the far end of the moonbeam, where the trees darkened the other side, where the twin birches would shine in the setting sun, the shimmering glow was unmistakable.

Mom spoke. *Ted...if you have to do this...please be careful. Do you hear me?*

Yes. I heard her.

That instant, I forgot the fear. Sloths and psychos didn't apply. We had only the lake and the padlocks to get through. In silence, the others followed me to the strip of wet sand separating the black water from the dune grass. The tiny waves soothed the shore, like fingers on skin, as though lulling it off to sleep.

In the bath of fluorescent light, the boathouse cast a long shadow. In it, we were just as invisible as the water. Until a flashlight came on.

CHAPTER 47

I SNAPPED, "LIGHTS off!" in a whisper that startled Neil and Zeke. Sunny switched off his light. "Buck," I said, like a fed-up mother, "take his flashlight." Buck did as he was told, and I felt like the leader I didn't want to be.

We pushed on to the rear of the boathouse. The water sloshed on its concrete supports and took the comfort out of the waves' rhythmic massage. A vague dread told me no camper should ever be in a position to hear those waves on that concrete, especially at night.

As the others gathered there next to us, it was the first time I realized someone would have to venture into the blaze of light. The moon hung in the sky. Even in the boathouse's shadow, I no longer felt invisible. The next few minutes would be critical.

"Damn!" Hoss whispered, feeling at his neck with both hands.

"What," Buck said.

"I forgot the key!"

Just enough moonlight showed behind the boathouse to see the surprised faces. We all seemed to exhale and not breathe in again. It was the deathblow to our adventure. Hoss. He got us started on this thing, and he'd finished it. I dropped my head forward.

"Just a kiddin'," he said, holding the key on his makeshift, red-string necklace. "Here it is." I thought about punching him square in his perfect teeth.

But when he showed us the key, a peculiar sense of relief snapped open in me like a parachute. Or maybe it was just excitement. Up in the cabin, when Zeke and Neil were happy to hear Bill was back to take over roving duty, I knew I'd do the trip for them. But when Hoss showed us the key, the excitement was all mine.

I guess there's rarely any contest between certain safety and the promise of adventure.

Zeke said: "What do we do, Ted?"

I didn't hesitate long. "Hoss," I said, "somebody's gonna have to take your key and unlock the boathouse. And the canoes. And who's gonna drag that chain over all those thwarts?" Several guys gasped when I said that.

Imagine that canoe chain after lights out.

The din would chop clean through the moonlit night. And those guys hadn't even thought of it. The plan should've felt doomed right then and there. But it didn't.

I continued. "Let's get that door open and the canoes unlocked before anybody else steps out of this shadow."

Hoss took off his key-necklace and darted around the bluff side of the boathouse. My heart jumped into my throat when he went, but then I figured, even if we went around the side facing the water, he'd be standing in front of the door in two seconds, anyway. Hoss whistled and worked the key into the lock. He was inside in no time. I sent Zeke and Neil around to get the paddles and sneak them to the lake-side of the boathouse. They were steadfast and serious and inspired me to feel the same. Hoss stole toward the canoes, dive-rolled under them, and worked on their lock.

"Hoss is gonna need help with the canoes," Buck said.

Just then, Bud, Sunny, and Bones darted out to help. If Cabin 7 had three members who hadn't yet thought about the dead-waking racket that chain would make, it was them.

"Get them back here!" I hissed at Buck, and took off toward them. If someone had to bet on who those guys would let boss them around, I'd put all my money on Buck. I had no real say. Buck wrangled them, and I ran into the bright, wide-open of the beach.

We'd just spared ourselves, and everyone asleep within a half mile the most horrible racket these trees had ever heard at night. What I hadn't thought of is each canoe's size. They were big, round, metal, and even shiny in the light of the beach house and moon. They looked like the backs of sleeping dinosaurs.

"Okay," I said to Hoss. "I'm gonna get under the canoes and feed the chain through. Just make sure those other guys stay behind the boathouse."

I dropped onto all fours and crawled. It felt nice to be back inside a shadow. All six canoes sat on the rack, each teeming with noise potential. I got Hoss to hand me his flashlight. Holding it up, inside the canoe, I was able to see how the chain was set without spilling too much light. The chain spiraled through the front thwart of each boat in loops, each loop wrapping around one of the iron, croquet-wicket canoe racks. I was able to wind up the chain and pass it noiselessly over the thwart of the first canoe. Sliding back in the shadows, I steeled myself to do the same with the rest. One false move is all it would take to get Isaac and Mr. Dinwiddie running toward the bluff.

I wound up the chain to pass it through the second canoe. Then the third and fourth. Hoss watched, having wisely crawled into the canoes' protective shadows, and even cheered me on.

In some strange way, his words of admiration came as far more of a compliment than I would've guessed. It was as though I'd been teaching a camp-crafts seminar. *Week 1: Tying a Sheepshank Knot. Week 2: Pitching a Tent...Week 8: Stealing Canoes at Night—Without Making a Sound.*

I prepared the chain for the fifth canoe, when Hoss told me we only needed four. *Huh. Even I haven't thought it all through.* We'd need four canoes for eight paddlers, and Bud could just sit, like the lump he was.

All four of the canoes were free of the chain and ready to lift off the rack. But then, of course, with a dark pragmatism no twelve-year-old deserved to be saddled with, I remembered something.

One summer, as I lifted a canoe, it slipped out of one hand, rotated, and fell onto the rack. When it did, you'd think someone had just smacked one of those noise-makers with a baseball bat.

Hoss and I crawled back to the first canoe and hunched in the shadows. I shot a glance up the bluff. The bench was empty, its arms wide, welcoming, without a trace of scorn for my misdeeds. I felt unworthy.

"Time to bring 'em down," Hoss said.

"Don't drop 'em," I said.

"'Don't drop 'em.' *There's* some good advice. Thanks,

Ted."

"Nuthin' wrong with a little reminder, smartass."

Hoss dropped a grin of undeniable approval.

CHAPTER 48

THEN HE DROPPED one of the canoes.

Just before we stepped out from under the shadows, back into what seemed like the brightest light that ever shined, I wondered, more deeply than ever before, why we were really making the trip. The simplest answer anyone would ever come up with, and probably the most honest, is that we were able to figure out a way. I had my own, unspoken motivations, and Hoss had a strong will to get away with something.

Once we were on the water, we'd be a lot safer, and I was pretty sure we'd get back and undo what we'd just done and just as quietly. A sense of true adventure returned.

"Okay, man," Hoss said. "You ready to pull those babies down?"

"I guess."

"Oh, come on," he said. "You're a natural at this. Next stunt I pull, I want you right there with me."

"Natural?" I'm a natural at pulling stunts?

"Aw, hell yes. You're a regular criminal."

The thought of my mom being out there, somewhere, to hear Hoss say so, made me cringe.

I positioned myself at the end of the canoe nearer the water, Hoss at the other end.

"One, two, three, lift," I said, and we both lifted. The canoe elevated from the rack without so much as a little scrape. I walked backwards into the shallows, boots and all, mindless of the water filling them. I tilted my head, indicating which way to turn the canoe on its axis to put it, keel-down, in the water. Zeke and Neil were there to drag the canoe to the far side of the boathouse. Hoss and I did the same with the next two canoes, then readied ourselves for the fourth. "One, two, three, lift," I said.

Then Hoss dropped his end. Its tip glanced off the rack and plunged into the sand. I winced and listened for an echo as Hoss jumped back and did some kind of strange dance. As he hopped from one foot to the next, his heels off the ground, he let out a series of vowel sounds, most of them *E*s. He brushed wildly at the inside of one arm. Then he stopped dancing and cursed.

"Something was crawling up my arm," he said.

Daddy Long-Legs spider, probably. They love the insides of top-down canoes. I wouldn't care if Hoss's body was covered with tarantulas. My main thing was to wonder why the canoe hadn't sounded much louder. It must have been how the boats' tips were built. The ends were sealed with flotation devices. It appeared that striking the ends of the canoes might just not reverberate so much when struck. But that night was no time to test the theory.

Hoss picked up his end of the canoe, and we launched it with the rest of them. Neil and Zeke had already recruited the other guys to help hold the floating canoes still. For a short time, all nine of us and four canoes stood in relative safety behind the boathouse, and I had another thought. In fact, I was sure I'd been doing more thinking—or worrying—than all the others combined.

For every minute we were gone, save for the inside of

Cabin 7, Cabin Row would be quiet and unchanged except for one thing: those shiny, sleeping dinosaurs were going to be gone with us. An almost-empty canoe rack would sit in their space. If anybody, and I mean anybody—Bill heading to the bench to burn another cigarette, for example—stood at the bluff for any time at all, he'd notice, and that'd be it.

He'd search the cabins right away. Or get Isaac or Mr. Dinwiddie, *then* search the cabins. We'd be sent home from camp. If I hadn't thought of it, no one had. I added the empty canoe rack to all my worries.

I pinched away an image of Lloyd, whether drunk and hobbling or not, coming back early and finding a cabin of empty bunks. The fullness of the risk we'd decided to take landed on me like that canoe in the sand.

Buck said, "Okay. Four canoes. We need strong paddlers in the stern of each one. That means me, Hoss, Ted, and who else?"

"I'll do it," Neil said. As the natural he'd been with me, he was the best choice. Plus, Neil as stern man meant each canoe had at least one good brain in it.

We did debate some over partners, though, during which time Zeke inched his way over to me. He said, "I have to go with Ted."

"Why?" Buck asked.

"'Cause he's the only one heavier than me."

That worked for Zeke and me. Neil, though, didn't fare so well. The only combination that worked for him was to have Bud and Bones in his canoe. Buck took Coach, and Hoss took Sunny.

Zeke held the canoe for me, and I stepped in. Then he got in without any trouble. We were set to go. The others wrestled with their paddles and banged the gunwales once or twice, but all-in-all, we shoved off quietly. The soundless gliding and freedom it brought were the jewel we'd mined through all the risk we took that night.

For a beginner, Zeke feathered his paddle beautifully. The moonlight glinted off the drops and their elegant, concentric little splashes sliding past us.

In no time, we were well beyond the waterfront, maybe a quarter of the way across the lake. For a whole minute I forgot what we were up to. The sneaking and stealing, even the mystical light in the trees, disappeared from my mind. A sudden pang of sadness was the only feeling I had. In a couple of days, Zeke was going home. We all were. He'd go to Missoula, Montana. Neil would go home to Ann Arbor. I faced the reality that neither of them was going home with me.

I wondered hard, right then, and right there, gliding across that peaceful water and into the moon beam, if I would ever see Zeke or Neil

(Karen!!)

again.

Bonds like the friendships we built that summer come only once every lifetime. White Birch Camp taught me that lesson by age twelve.

I wondered with more doubt than I wanted, if I'd ever canoe with Dad again.

CHAPTER 49

WHEN I CHECKED to see where the other canoes were, I gasped. A little light shined from between Cabins 1 and 2. A flashlight.

"Zeke!" I whispered loudly.

"Huh? What's wrong?" He shifted in his seat to face me.

"Flashlight. Up between the…"

"What do we do?"

"It's not…*wait.*"

"It's not what?"

"Not moving."

"What?"

I hesitated.

"Ted?"

"Wait a minute."

"What."

"It's not moving at all…Oh, God…It's the light on Headquarters, right above Isaac's window."

"Oh." Zeke said. "That scared me half to death, Ted."

"Me too."

"What now?"

"Just keep paddling, I guess. The farther away we get, the better." Coming back, it'd be *the closer the worse.* We squared ourselves in our seats and paddled. The guys behind us were quiet enough, and I relaxed some. Zeke's silhouette against the moonbeam was nice enough to be stamped on a postcard.

We must've been a third of the way across the lake by then. The breeze was steady and warm and perfectly nice.

"Hey, Ted?"

"Yeah?"

"What about the life vests?"

We'd only brought paddles, not life vests.

"I figure if we've been this stupid so far, we might as well risk drowning, too."

"Okay," Zeke said, digging his paddle in for another mighty stroke.

He didn't speak for a few minutes but soon started again. "Ted?"

"Yeah."

"What if that was a flashlight back there?"

"It wasn't. Don't worry."

"But if it was, do you think—"

"No way would that light reach all the way out here."

Zeke was quiet for another minute, paddling.

"Ted?"

"What, Zeke."

"What time do you think it is?"

"Maybe…'bout eleven-thirty? Quarter to twelve?"

"Does anybody but Lloyd have a night out tonight?"

I'd thought of that and hoped no one else would. "I dunno. Why?" The question got me thinking again about Lloyd, on some fluke, getting back to the cabin before us. If Zeke wondered the same out loud, it would ramp up my worrying ten-fold.

"Just asking. What if they do look out here?"

"They're not gonna," I said, hoping it would stick.

They probably wouldn't look out here at all. Unless it's extra pretty out on the lake…nice enough to be a postcard. Pretty moonbea—

"Zeke!"

"What?"

"Turn! Turn left!"

He switched hands and paddled on the right, pulling hard, just like I said. And only then did he ask.

"Why?"

"We're in the moonbeam! Anybody on Cabin Row can see us!"

We paddled hard, due north, the same direction we traveled to get to Mosquito Point with the lifeguards.

The other three canoes were still headed straight to the other side.

"Turn left!" I said to them in a loud whisper, doubting my voice would carry that far, lifting my paddle above my head like it was a chin-up bar and thrusting it toward the north. I experimented with a soft, regular speaking voice. No reaction. Then a little louder. And louder, the same voice Hoss heard from a distance days before.

"Shh!" said someone in the group of three canoes.

"Shut up!" It was Hoss's voice. "What's wrong, Ted? Everybody shut up and listen!"

"Turn left to get out of the moonbeam!"

Quick murmurings and a few expletives carried across the water. The lagging group's paddles all started moving in different directions, and quickly. In about two minutes, paddling at top speed, all four canoes met and stopped, like four horsemen in the desert. We floated serenely there, well north of the water that was between the moon and camp.

Pointing somewhere over to the far side of the lake, Bud said, "Why did we come all the way over here if we want to get over there?"

We did our best to explain the moonbeam thing to him, but he didn't get it. Bud was dense. Even more dense than usual. Maybe because he was tired. So Buck said, to our collective relief, "Just believe us, Bud. We're okay now. That sound good to you? We're okay now. Time to head over."

Like the desert horsemen, we found our bearings and headed east, toward the light in the trees. Zeke leaned into each stroke, working hard. I wondered what thoughts ran through his mind as he did. Neil's thoughts, too. Did they think about the end of camp? Were we going to write each other? I pulled my paddle strongly. Maybe they thought about home. Their families. Their bedrooms. I'm sure, as we plunged our paddles' blades in a hypnotic rhythm, they thought about their moms.

I'm so proud of you, Mom said to me. *And you know that pretty girl back there? Karen? She is absolutely darling. You know what else, Ted? I think she likes you. And who wouldn't? You're such a nice boy.*

That's where Mom would've hugged me. I could feel her grip around my back, her kiss on my head, above my ear. She told me, the way she always did, she loved me.

Those little fantasies used to tear me apart, but I got used to them and learned to like them. By the time we stole those canoes, I'd even learned to crave them and to hope they never went away.

With only a short way to go, I saw the twin birches were actually three trees. Two close to shore, and a third, deeper in. Zeke and I stopped paddling, more or less at the same time. The other canoes drifted up next to us. My cabin mates' forgettable conversations waned as we gathered maybe fifty feet from shore. The chilling and steadying breeze carried the peaceful smell of autumn.

"Hey look!" Bud said, jerking to his feet in Neil's canoe, "A fire!"

"Sit your ass down!" Neil said.

Bones pushed up on the gunwales and lifted his butt up to adjust his position. When he released his grips to let himself fall back into the seat, Bud lost his balance, as though slipping on ice. He tumbled out of the canoe and splashed into the lake, gone, beneath the black surface.

CHAPTER 50

NOTHING. NOT A hand, foot, or gasping mouth broke the top of the water. Zeke grabbed at his flashlight. Working to switch it on, he fumbled it. He reached, palms up, and connected with his flashlight two or three times. But it splashed into the water and disappeared.

"Where the hell is he?" Hoss yelled about Bud.

Neil said, "Right there!" as an arm jutted through the surface. Then another. The hands alternated in their slow, reaching movements.

"He's gonna drown," Neil said. Sunny leaned over, sticking his paddle out there, toward Bud's climbing arms. Bud's head poked out a little, his neck extended. Sunny's paddle was right there for the grabbing, but Bud, gasping and bubbling, didn't take it. Sunny leaned a little farther, and Hoss leaned forward, reaching, groping for one of Bud's arms.

"Just a little more," Hoss said, "I can get him!"

The rest of us just seemed to sit there, our mouths open, not speaking. I knew Bud couldn't think to grab a paddle.

"Hold still, Bones," Neil said. "I'm jumping in."

But Hoss and Sunny leaned too far to the same side, and their canoe capsized. They both went under, head first. Their boat slowly righted itself as Sunny came up, gasping. Hoss didn't come up before grabbing Bud around the waist. Both their faces broke the surface, but only their faces.

"Hoss can't swim!" I said.

Neil jumped in. Hoss held onto Bud and struggled, reaching for something, anything. Neil grabbed Hoss's arm and pulled it to his canoe. "Bones!" he said. "Lean the other way, so they don't tip us over."

Bones did so. Neil maneuvered over to Bud.

"Let go of him, Hoss," he said. "I got him."

Hoss let go quickly and grasped the gunwale of Neil's canoe with both hands. Bud coughed and sputtered before taking a deep breath. Then he seemed to expel all the air in his lungs in a visceral cough that echoed around the entire lake.

"You okay?" Neil said.

"Huh-uh!" Bud said with a full voice.

"Jesus," Hoss said.

All told, I'll bet Bud wasn't under water more than a few seconds. I wondered how anybody passed his twenty-minute test. Hoss and Neil struggled to get Bud back into his canoe, but they did, and he sat there, cross-legged, just as before. He let out one, final cough.

"My flashlight!" said Sunny, who held onto the side of Neil's canoe. He reached into his submerged pocket. His light was dead.

"There's only one flashlight now, guys," Buck said.

Two of our three flashlights were in the one canoe that capsized. Sunny's was dead, and Zeke's was gone. By some good grace, Hoss's floated in the canoe, and someone grabbed it. Losing two of our flashlights was the next in a growing list of things we hadn't planned.

"Now what are we gonna do?" Sunny asked.

"I guess you just try to paddle it," Buck said. "It has floats in either end, you know. It won't sink."

"That'd be some pretty slow going," Neil said.

"It'd take all night and half of tomorrow to paddle that thing back," I said. "We need to get the water out of it."

Defensive-sounding, Sunny said, "How are we supposed to do *that*?"

"It's not hard," I said. "We can do it right here, in deep w—"

"Do you have any idea how heavy that canoe is with water in it?" Sunny asked.

"Yeah, but if we turn it ov—"

"Somebody has to go back to camp. We need the rescue boat."

No one bit on Sunny's proposal.

"Any *other* ideas?" Hoss said, facing me.

As a matter of fact, I did have an idea. In 1968, I witnessed the counselors righting a swamped canoe in deep water. They told me almost no one with a capsized canoe seems to think you can get the water out of it by turning it upside down.

I supposed we could paddle the thing fifty feet to our destination, but I decided to hot-dog it and fix the problem in open water.

"Hey, Neil?" I said.

"Yeah?"

"Let's get your canoe out of the way, and get Hoss's over by ours."

Without question or hesitation, Neil grabbed a hold of the gunwale of my canoe and pushed on it so he could draw his canoe backwards. Bones helped him.

"Okay, good," Hoss said. "What's next?"

"Get the bow over here," I said. "Get it pointed right at the middle of my canoe, like we're making a big letter *T*."

"What good is that supposed to do?" Sunny asked.

"Just shut up and listen to him," Hoss said.

They did it. Coach even helped push the stern of that canoe to get it lined up. Nobody knew the purpose of the maneuver yet, but everybody seemed to contribute.

"All right," I said, "turn it over, keel up, like on the canoe racks." They rolled the canoe over. "Zeke. Scoot down to the middle of the canoe with me." He and I crouched together in the middle of our boat. "Let's stay real low. Hoss and Sunny. Each of you get on opposite sides of your canoe. Grab our gunwale with one hand and lift that bow up, over *our* canoe." Zeke and I leaned to the opposite side to offset the pressure trying to pull us over.

"Good," I said, when the bow was up on our boat. "Now all four of us. Let's slide the whole thing up, over top of ours. And watch your fingers." We slid the canoe, sleeping-dinosaur position, up and over the top of ours, until the two boats crossed at their middles. The letter *T* became a big *plus* sign. I moved back to the stern of my canoe and rolled the upper one, free of all water, onto its keel, and we slid it back into the water, empty.

"Voilà," I said. "Empty canoe. Now you guys just have to get back in without tipping it over."

Hoss and Sunny struggled and grunted but eventually climbed back in.

Sunny said, "I've had about enough excitement for one night. I think we should go on back now."

Hoss snorted, mean-sounding, like a bull ready to mow down a matador. "What? Are you nuts? We're almost *there*."

"Yeah," Sunny said, "but things just seem to keep happening. I don't like it. I don't know who's burning that f—"

"Shut up," Hoss said. "Who do you think's in charge of this trip, anyway?"

Now there was the question. No one said anything for a moment. Not even Hoss seemed to know the answer. But then, he said, "What do you think, Fearless Leader?"

"I say let's go," Buck said. "I'm getting to that other shore tonight. Not going back."

"Yeah," Bones said.

Sunny interrupted. "You guys, it may not be a very good idea to..." His voice trailed off.

"Good idea to what, exactly?" I asked. "To sneak out of the cabin at night? Break every waterfront rule? Steal the canoes? Paddle right through a big, fat moonbeam? Without life jackets? And *still* decide to go over to the other side of the lake and almost get one of us killed? Is this the first time you thought this trip might not be such a good idea?"

Sunny didn't answer.

"Huh?" I said, my voice getting away from me.

"Hey, Ted?" Neil said.

"What kind of grades do you get in school, Sunny? My *God*. I can tell you what this trip is. It's not just 'not a good idea,' it's stupid. *You hear me? STUPID!"*

"Ted." Zeke said. "Sunny's starting to—"

"But here we are, maybe fifty feet from there." I pointed

toward the fire. "And suddenly you—the guy who thought we better go back and wake up Mr. Dinwiddie to bring a *MOTOR BOAT* over here to rescue us in the middle of the night decided to wonder about *what's a GOOD IDEA?*"

Then Dad's voice: *If you let yourself get mad, it only makes you—*

"*Shut UP, TED!*" Sunny said, his cracking voice loud enough to echo. He was crying, and at the time, I was glad I'd done it to him.

"Damn, Ted," Hoss said.

"Okay," I said. "It's a stupid idea, you guys. Sunny's right. We shouldn't be here."

"It's the smartest idea," Hoss said. The distant fire lit up the sincerity in his eyes.

Zeke said, "We all know it's a bad idea, but I think that's why it's good. We're twelve. We're supposed to do stuff like this. Right, Neil?" Zeke's voice gained strength as he spoke. "I heard you talk about this trip, Ted, and Neil did too. We knew it would break rules and all. But it would be worse not to do it. Wouldn't it?"

"Can you imagine turning back now?" Neil said.

"It's one of those things. You get so close, and if you don't actually do it, you wonder about it for the rest of your life."

"We've come this far."

The forest floor glimmered like a stage, just for us. Zeke dug his paddle into the black water and pulled. Neil did the same. Soon, we were on our way.

They had me all along, but that fire made me shiver.

CHAPTER 51

You could almost mistake the setting for peaceful. When we were close enough to see the fire's glow on the tree trunks, the moon was high in the sky. It shined between the peaks of two big evergreens. Their feathery tufts of needles, even in silhouette, identified them as white pines, bigger than any I'd ever seen up close, a hundred feet tall or more. Even though the moon was bright, more stars than I could ever imagine shined in the sky.

"Hey Ted?" Zeke said.

"Yeah?"

"Who do you suppose built that fire?"

The canoe stopped in an instant, to the sound of a loud scrape. I slid forward, and Zeke slipped all the way off his seat and fell down on his knees. His paddle tumbled into the water. It hit flat, handle-first, and torpedoed ten feet to shore.

"My paddle!"

"Yeah, I saw it. It'll float, but we sure can't lose it. Gonna have to get out of the canoe and get it."

Zeke grabbed the gunwales and peered over each side. The bottom was like the one that caused Hoss trouble on Tornado Night. It was clear our canoe had run aground on a shallow boulder and stopped on its keel.

I could see the paddle, pitching in the tiny waves. It was caught up in the sagging grasses growing between the water and the low forest floor. The night's strongest gust shot through the whole area and made the trees rock back-and-forth at their peaks.

"Whoa," someone behind us said. The air current pushed two of the canoes off kilter. The shimmering, mirror-like surface blurred in certain areas my dad calls cat's paws.

Zeke said, "Okay, I'm gonna get the paddle."

"Be careful. I don't know how deep it is here. We're on big rocks. Might be pretty deep otherwise."

Zeke hesitated.

"You want me to get it?"

"No," he said. "Let me do it." He held onto the gunwales with his hands, his grip firm. He stood into a crouch and swung his left leg over the side, making no purchase beneath the surface. When he tried the other side, he found a safe foothold. Pulling his other foot into a standing position on the rock, he kept his other in the canoe for balance. The canoe lurched and slid out from beneath him. It was instantly too late. One foot on the rock and the other in the canoe, Zeke fell backwards into the lake.

"Zeke!" I half-shouted.

The boy who had spent the lion's share of the summer afraid of deep water was down in it and out of sight. I tried to stand and thought better of it.

"Zeke!" I said again. His hand shot up and grabbed the wall of the canoe. His other followed immediately. A foot popped out a few feet away and seemed to grab at the rock. The canoe moved—more by seeming magic than a well-executed move Zeke performed—toward the boulder.

His head popped up so I could see his face.

"Are you—"

"I'm okay."

"Jesus!"

"No," he said, spitting out some lake water, "it's just me."

"You need to be more careful."

"Next time," he said.

I have to admit, for the next half a minute, or so, at least until the other canoes showed up, I couldn't breathe. Funny none of that worry happened to me when Bud fell into the water, or *either* time Hoss did. Zeke tested his footing on the rock and easily retrieved his paddle. He torpedoed it back to me and told me to stow it in the canoe. From the water's edge, he was able to walk a little north and found a sandbar.

"Zeke," Neil said. "You all right, man?"

"Yep. Okay, you guys," he said from the sandbar. "Bring your canoes over this way. Don't try to get out where Ted is, or you'll fall in. Ted. Can you paddle over here?"

I could, and I did, following Zeke, the leader. I was proud to be his friend. Sunny and Hoss scraped into the sandbar.

"Lemme tell you, Sunny," Hoss said. "It woulda been a shame. A *crime*, really, if we didn't come the rest of the way here. Sure, it's risky and all that, but hey. It's worth it. And I'll tell you what else. Mr. Dinwiddie? If I get caught and he sends me home? Who cares. I'm not coming back here anyway. Any more summers up here'd be boring next to this one."

No one seemed to address Hoss.

Zeke told Sunny to get out and pull the canoe into the sand. The others followed.

Bones, as Neil's canoe scraped into the sand, said, "So

where are we going, exactly?"

Buck: "Ashore. That's where were going."

Hoss: "Yes, my boy, we're going ashore."

Bud: "I don't like it."

Neil: "It doesn't like you either."

Bud: "Shut up!"

Neil: "What. It was a joke. Somebody had to say it."

Bud: "Shut *up*, I said."

Zeke: "You shut up, *Bud*. He was just kidding you." Zeke put up a hand as though to tell Neil to stop messing with Bud. Neil nodded and gawked, clearly incredulous. Where'd Zeke get this stuff all of a sudden? Coach and Buck stowed their paddles and got out of their canoe.

But Zeke didn't stop there. "I hope you feel lucky nobody's beaten you up this summer," he said to Bud, grabbing the bow of my canoe and giving it a quick hoist onto the sandbar. Then he added, "Except Karen Dinwiddie."

Bud launched his seethe-and-quake routine.

"Yeah," Zeke said. "I heard about that. I heard *all* about that."

Bud's breath quickened, and he started in with his little growl-thing. Ready to explode, he was no threat. The whole cabin was ready to stop him until his sanity (what little of it he ever had in the first place) returned.

Eyes on Zeke, Hoss's mouth hung open.

"And I thought it was *funny*, what she made you do," Zeke said. "But don't come after me. Like you did that one time. Because I'm ready for you now."

It was as though Clark Kent had fallen into the dark water

and emerged as Superman. Zeke gave me a quick shrug and a wry grin. I liked the old Zeke, and I liked the new one at least as much.

"Damn, Zeke!" Hoss said. "Tell the little punk who's boss! I'm headin' in. Who's comin'?" Hoss high-stepped toward the fire, crunching through brittle, fallen branches and dead saplings.

"Come on, you," Buck said, patting the corn-tassel shrimp on the shoulder. He extended his hand until Bud grabbed it. Buck pulled him to a stand. "Let's give these guys a break, huh?"

The three of us watched as Buck walked into the woods toward the fire. Bud must have felt like a ball and chain to him. All four others tromped after Hoss, who even yelled *Yoohoo! Anybody home?*

No one answered.

The three of us were alone and quiet for a bit, until Zeke whispered, "What should we do now?"

"You hear Hoss?" I asked.

"Yeah," Neil said. "He's crazy. Certifiable."

"He is, but I meant back here, when his canoe pulled up. You hear that crap about 'If I get caught'?"

They didn't answer.

"It's like I finally learned all about him. 'If I get caught.' Not 'If *we* get caught,' but 'If *I* get caught.' He's not doing anything for anybody but himself. I mean…he's all he cares about. Just wants to stay out of trouble."

Neil: "We *all* wanna stay outta—"

"Yeah, but it's like this. People *like* Buck, so Hoss uses him to get people to do what Hoss wants them to do. And Cliff. Hoss used that marijuana thing to keep Cliff quiet. And the whiskey thing. He used that to get the canoe trip. Or maybe just to be mean. It's like we're just tools in a box."

"Used *you* to get us over *here* safely," Neil said.

"Yeah," Zeke said. "I guess he did."

"All right," Neil said.

"All right what?" I said.

"We're over here. What're we gonna do?"

"Who built that fire?" Zeke asked.

CHAPTER 52

The flames were probably three end zones away from us, or a little less. There was no real path to the clearing that appeared to surround it. Whoever built the fire may have come from deeper in the woods, which unsettled me into wordlessness. Hoss was already there. Tall and thin, he stood next to the flames. Bones, Sunny, and Coach arrived there just behind him. Bud stepped to the other side of the fire and stood next to Hoss. Buck stayed near the other three.

In no time, he grabbed two small logs, each a few feet in length. He threw them onto the fire, turned back for more, then threw *those* in. He found another branch as big around as a man's arm, maybe six or seven feet long. He pushed it up on one end and let it fall like a felled tree, into the flames. Orange sparks drifted upward. Buck fed the fire as he did on Tornado Night.

The other guys milled around, some throwing little sticks into the flames. Hoss found a cross-sectioned tree trunk the height of a seat. It was the only sign of inhabitation on the far shore, other than the fire and the clearing around it. He stood on the stool, arms akimbo, proud, as though presiding over a tiny slice of creation—or a slice of hell, since it was Hoss. The canoe incident had left him with a ripped-open shirt. Bare stomach showing, Hoss emerged as a complete savage. A savage with a necklace, adorned not with sharp teeth, but with a single padlock key.

Near where Bud stood, behind the fire, an enormous white pine with knobby, black bark jutted out of the ground and into the dark canopy above.

At the big pine's roots, a rotting tree from yesteryear lay on the forest floor. Maybe two feet in diameter, it was a rich substrate for dozens of little pine and oak saplings. The oak leaves had grown large in the shade and sagged in front of the dead tree. They were thick enough to create a shadow in the fire's light. Subtle greens and browns, the colors of decomposing plant matter, occupied the shadowy space.

The three of us tromped through the woods, parallel to the shore, as though wanting to see behind the fire without having to get closer to it. When I finally started toward the clearing, the other guys followed, but Zeke stopped, and soon, his righteous liquid stream roiled on the forest floor. Zeke stood, head down and back to us, his arms seemingly missing, his parabolic urine stream unwavering. "Ahhhh," he said. "That's better."

With that kind of stimulus, I thought I might not get my fly open in time to do the same.

"Probably the only good idea tonight," Neil said over the *Zip!* of his own fly. The three of us had found another way to bond. Zeke giggled, and his parabola shook.

Jumping up and down and shimmying to clear the last few drops before zipping, Zeke was the first to stop laughing. "Ted, who do you think built that fire?"

So far, as a cabin, we'd done a laudable job ignoring the topic. Something in me didn't want to know. But there were questions someone in his right mind might ask.

If someone built that fire, and I know someone did, who is he? Or she? Much more, where is he? Might that someone return to the fire and ask us our names? What we're doing out at midnight with no adult around? Is he someone who might know we're from White Birch and report us? Or a law officer who had no choice but to report us? Might someone like Bud or Sunny just give us all up by name?

I should have said *no* to the whole trip.

But we were there. And we had no plans. No goal. Nothing to tell us we were done and that it was time to go. We'd all talked about how much we wanted to *be* there, but no one talked about what we'd do when we made it. It was as though we'd taken a big trip to a football stadium when we knew there probably wouldn't be a game. Once we reached our destination, the only thing to do was leave and go back.

Somebody's hiding from us.

Neil started toward the fire, and we followed.

"Gotta get out of here, you guys," I said.

"Yeah," Zeke said. "Now it really *does* feel like a bad idea."

In the five minutes we were there, the flames doubled in height. But even still, Buck threw sticks, long and short, onto the burning stack, one after the next. The firewood pile was nearly gone. The fire itself was a feeble, wooden building alight, nothing left but a frame on the verge of collapse. At its base was a bed of coals maybe eight feet across. They scintillated, orange to white and back to orange. Buck eventually walked over to Hoss. The other guys backed up—probably from the growing heat—but continued to face the flames.

The wind kicked up again, and the trees swayed. *Be careful*, their needles and leaves said to me. The fire responded by leaning, briefly, with the air current. A ball of flame, as ephemeral as it was ambitious, leapt from the burning pile, into the gush of oxygen, and disappeared.

Something caught my eye. A glint. A reflection. Something wrong with the shadowy, twig-and-leaf landscape down by that big, rotting log. It changed in some way. Or maybe my perception changed as we got closer to it. Something was out of place, the way the Empire State Building would appear on rolling, Midwestern farmland. The out-of-place something reflected the fire's light. It wasn't there before.

Did something move?

The jumping flames lit the area from so many, fleeting angles that almost everything appeared to move, to dance. Everything, even the knobs on the big white pine shape-shifted. The leaves of the saplings growing on the decaying log swayed in the heat and curled. Something made me head that direction. Neil and Zeke followed.

"It's spooky over here," Zeke said.

"Damn right it is," Neil answered.

As I studied the shadowy place, Hoss jumped down from the log and strolled over by Bud, who dropped his wet jacket and stood dumbly by the giant white pine. Hoss appeared to see something. In fact, he approached the same place that bothered me. Buck hopped up on the stump and turned his back to the fire. Bud watched Hoss.

Neil said, "Let's get Buck to start rounding everybody up."

I barely heard him and said nothing.

"Ted?"

I walked faster. Hoss inched closer to the shadowy area, bending at the waist, concentrating. The out-of-place thing, the glinting object, was no longer visible. Something was wrong. Something *was* moving down there in that shadow.

"Do you see that?" I asked.

I heard Bud say, "Hey Hoss. Whatcha lookin' at?"

Something in the fire popped, and a spark shot maybe ten feet out from the flame. The pop was loud enough to startle everyone else and draw his attention toward the fire.

"Get out of the way," Hoss said to Bud, waving him off.

The glinting object appeared right when I heard a deep groan. Bud screamed. The sound he made wasn't one of his cutesy, attention-grabbing yelps. This one was real.

Zeke, Neil, and I froze on the edge of the clearing as Bud paused to take a deep breath. Then, he let out another scream, took two running steps, and kicked. His kicks, one-after-the-next, thumped into the shadowy area.

Suddenly, Bud's body went horizontal in mid-air, as though levitating. A section of the dead, sapling-covered tree seemed to writhe and come to life as Bud landed in a cloud of dust.

"Bud!" Hoss said.

Bud stood immediately and dived into the writhing thing, screaming still, his behavior the exact same as when he attacked Zeke at the beginning of camp.

"Stop it, man!" Hoss said, reaching for Bud. "You're gonna get—"

Then Bud shot three or four feet to one side. The moving thing scrunched into a ball-like position.

Hoss stood, feet apart, knees slightly bent. His arms were out a little from his sides, his shoulders up in a shrug. It was the same stance he had right before his flight across the cabin. The moving part of the dead log stood. It was a man.

"*PSYCHO!!*" yelled Coach, who ran for the shadows, toward the canoes. Bones went with him, but Sunny stayed behind.

Bud lay on the ground, squirming, out of the way. The man was a head taller and assumed very much the same posture as Hoss.

The man's face was invisible. In plenty of firelight, it just wasn't there, where the face should be.

Hoss changed position suddenly, as though surprised, then drew back his right arm and yelled, *"Son of a BITCH!"*

Bones and Coach were long-gone. Sunny, standing on the other side of the fire, picked up a remnant of the woodpile and side-arm heaved it. About two feet long and as thick as Sunny's wrist, the stick helicoptered through the top of Buck's flaming structure. The psycho took a massive swing at Hoss's face.

Without changing course, the spinning stick launched three or four flaming twigs far outside the limits of the clearing, into the dry pine needles.

An odd thought came to me as my brain seemed to want out of the situation. The light in the trees wasn't Mom. How silly of me to think it was. It was just some psycho's campfire. That's all it ever was. The other side wasn't magic after all.

Just as the psycho's right fist connected with Hoss's head,

Sunny's stick made its impact, almost knocking the man down. The psycho pivoted on his feet and took one running step toward Sunny, who screamed and sprinted toward the canoes.

CHAPTER 53

THE SATELLITE FIRES caught quickly in the growing wind. Flame wrapped little fingers around the rotting log from behind. On the clearing's other side, a thoroughly dead cedar tree soaked up the flames. In no time at all, the cedar was alight and threatening a much-larger tree.

It was past time to head back to the canoes. Zeke seemed to struggle with the idea of not at least *trying* to put out the fires, but Neil got him going back.

I was the last one to the boats. Buck and Hoss settled in their canoes. I dropped Bud's jacket into his cross-legged lap, but he didn't seem to notice. My cabin mates' faces danced with false expression in the fire's dynamic, orange-white glow. The heat would soon be overpowering. No one spoke. We made a frantic but oddly organized group effort to launch canoes and grab paddles. I made sure everyone still wore his boots.

Coach broke the silence. Pulling his canoe into the water, he asked shakily, "What caused the other fires?"

"Sunny threw a stick at the psycho," I said. Hoss returned my glance.

"Is the psy—is he following us?"

"No."

"Are you sure?"

"Yeah," Neil said. "Ran the other way. Sunny scared him off."

"I did?" Sunny asked.

"Yeah, you did."

"Way to go Sunny!" Coach said, his voice barely audible over the wind and the fire.

"Let's get the hell outta here," Hoss said.

"You think the…that guy will be okay?" Coach asked. "I mean…in the fire?"

"Oh, yeah," Hoss said. "He will. He ran away. *Other* way, I mean. Pretty fast. But the fire'll get *us* if we don't get outta here."

Fresh, live pine needles lit and curled as we talked. Animals bounded away from the heat. In the growing wind, flames would reach the water's edge in minutes at the rate they were moving.

We shoved off, kept our canoes close together, and headed straight for Mosquito Point. Wind at our backs and efficient with our paddles, I'd swear we made the rocky shallows in fifteen minutes.

After we headed toward the boathouse, hugging the shoreline, the choppy waves ran parallel to us and rolled our canoes. We lost some time because of it, but I'll bet we made it back to the boathouse in five minutes. Under other circumstances, we could have been proud.

The dry, steady wind continued. By the time we were half way from Mosquito Point to the boathouse, the distinct fires on the other side had spread into one. Silent lightning flashed in the east, beyond those woods. Some lit the whole sky, like flashbulbs, and others were discrete, jagged bolts.

We made it to the boathouse, staying, as best we could, invisible behind it. The wave action on the beach and on the canoes was constant. The boats pitched and rolled in the waves. Everyone worked—except Bud—to keep them from banging together. Hoss and I put them on the rack soundlessly, one after the next. As only the fourth and final canoe remained, Hoss and I walked to get it. When he got in front of me, I almost fell down when I saw the back of his head.

"Hoss," I said. He didn't hear me. "Hoss!" I repeated, grabbing his arm. When he stopped, I reached for the back of his head with one hand and held it, palm-up, to show him. His eyes opened wide. He raised his hands to the back of his head.

"What's that?" Coach asked. He'd come out of nowhere.

Hoss bent to wash his hands in the water. "Soot," he said. "We have soot on us from the fire. We can't bring that back to the cabin, not with"—he pointed at the forest fire—"*that* going on."

Zeke came over and pulled Coach back to the boathouse. Hoss suggested we put up the last canoe before he cleaned himself off.

I pictured policemen and my own father inspecting the boats. "No. Do it now. You can't touch the boat with those hands."

A sense of realization seemed to strike him, and he went to Buck to check *him* in the light. Buck's face was dark with it. The two of them dropped into the water and scrubbed their faces and heads. It would have been comic if it were something else. They scrubbed and checked, then scrubbed some more.

Soot.

When Hoss and Buck finally stood up for good, Hoss said to him, "We need to get rid of all these clothes." His flashlight fell out of his pocket, and Neil picked it up. Everyone's movements were automatic, collective, efficient. And then, as an afterthought, Hoss said to the group, "You guys, we need to throw out all our boots. Footprints."

I'd thought of that but hadn't said it yet. There'd be hundreds or thousands of footprints over there from nine sets of feet, some of them kid-size, and a summer camp right across the lake.

How does Hoss know to think like that? My dad was a prosecuting attorney and talked about crime scenes all the time. That was my excuse. What was Hoss's?

After Hoss and I racked the last canoe, the keel-up, sleeping dinosaurs were back where they belonged. The top of the bluff was quiet. I scrambled beneath the boats to run the chain. The waves and wind made enough noise to cover up some sloppiness, but I was careful and quick.

Doing my damnedest to cover up what we'd just done, I suddenly wondered, near-paralyzed with guilt. *What's wrong with me?* Zeke and Neil were my two best friends and innocent bystanders. My interest in protecting them kept my mind in the moment and on what we had to do to get back to the cabin.

The open padlock, in its own simple world of sand, aluminum, and steel, clicked nicely as I locked the canoes to the rack. I moved onto the next task. *The paddles.* In even the thinnest illusion that no one took a canoe trip that night, those paddles had to be put away. We should've worked in parallel, some stowing the paddles, Hoss and Buck rinsing off in the lake, me running the canoe chain. But we didn't.

Zeke, bless his heart, took two paddles to the boathouse

door, dutifully keeping the blades out of the sand. The door was closed, padlock in place. It was locked. Zeke asked Hoss for the key. I took a few, hurried steps into the open.

The others stood passively, gaping at the fire, awaiting instruction. We were all exposed in the beach house light, and no one seemed to notice.

Hands at his throat, Hoss's fright scared me.

"I don't have it," he mouthed.

CHAPTER 54

THE KEY. HOSS had lost the key. And he wasn't joking this time.

"Where did you have it last?" I asked, immediately figuring he'd come back with some smartass answer: *If I knew that, it wouldn't be lost* or *Half past a monkey's ass and quarter to his nuts* or *I left it at your mom's house last night.* But it was no time for games. Not even Hoss was trying to play.

"I don't know," is all he said. The possibilities seemed to stream through his head, like they did mine. The key could be in the sand. If it fell, it'd be buried, but the string wouldn't. It could be on the other side of the lake, in the sand. It'd melt in the fire, wouldn't it? To the point of being unrecognizable? "Maybe it fell off when I fell in after Bud."

That'd put the key safely in the depths of the lake. Maybe it did, I thought for a minute, but that wasn't right. "No. It was around your neck. Over there." It was when he stood, bare-chested, on that log-stool.

"Oh, God," he said, and *Oh, God* was *all* he had to say. *Oh, God* didn't help us. It could be the key was over on the other side, lying in the dirt, waiting to be found. Next to all our footprints. Who knew? I wondered again if the fire could possibly melt the key to the point of no longer fitting into the locks. Or *maybe*, I remember wondering, that key was lying over there, perfect as can be, hungry for a ray of sunlight to shoot into some investigator's eye. I thought of the fictional boy-sleuth, Encyclopedia Brown. Encyclopedia would find the key and try it in every padlock on the lake. And on Loon Lake in 1970, the list of padlocks wouldn't be very long.

I decided not to share my immediate thoughts with anyone. Instead, I told Hoss, "You need to make sure you're cleaned off. Buck, too. Just go take another rinse. For good measure."

Hoss did what I said, and he did it right away. He took Buck with him. I didn't notice that Zeke and Neil disappeared. The paddles were gone, too. Not lying in the sand or floating in the shallows. They were just gone. Something thumped in the boathouse. I checked the bluff-side of the structure and found Zeke passing the last two paddles into the open window.

Hoss had unlocked that window.

Neil's face appeared in the frame.

"They're all back where they belong," he said.

"Did you get the sand off the handles?" Zeke asked.

"Yep."

On his way out, Neil started headfirst, curled into a tiny ball, pulling his feet out, over the sill. Grabbing the ends of the rafters beneath the roof overhang, he slowly elongated his body, and let himself fall, standing, into the sand. We darted around to the shadow where the other guys stood. Hoss and Buck finished rinsing and joined us. I spun them around and ran my fingers through their hair. They were clean.

"No more soot?" Coach asked.

"No more soot," Hoss said.

No doubt about it, I was in charge. Everyone followed my every command. I was the chief of *The Big Lie of 1970*.

Sunny had his arm around Bud's shoulders, and Bud

seemed to be calm. Sunny would take care of him, get him back okay. Bones and Coach stood still, watching the fire.

"What'd we do?" Coach said, his lips pressing together, his eyebrows tenting on his forehead.

"You followed us, Coach," I said. "You didn't do anything." Zeke patted him on the shoulder and urged him north, toward the cottonwoods.

Coach said, "But the fire."

I grabbed his shoulders and tried to speak gently. "I know. It's okay—well, no, it's not okay. But let's just get back to the cab—"

"How'd you guys get away from the psycho?" he asked. Sunny stilled his walk with Bud and faced us.

"Sunny threw a log at him and hit him," Neil said.

"Scared him away?"

"Real scared," Neil said.

Firelight-tinted skepticism crossed Coach's face. "You're sure he got away okay?"

"Yep," Hoss said.

"Shh," I said. "Let's talk later. Okay?"

"Yeah," Hoss said. "Let's get back to the cabin."

Coach and Bones walked toward the cottonwoods. Sunny guided Bud. Buck and Hoss headed north, just behind them. I thought about what Coach asked. I wasn't sure who knew what.

Quiet, distant lightning flashed in the sky. The next wave crashed. Growing, orange light pervaded our world. Right at that moment, until the gentle roll of thunder stopped, I hated us all.

Coach and Bones climbed back up to the Mosquito Point

trail. The ribbon of sand had vanished underneath the waves. I caught a whiff of campfire smoke. The waves and wind were nothing like on Tornado Night, but a light gale would feed the hell out of that fire.

"The window!" Neil said. Without another word, he ran back toward the boathouse, leaping up and over as many waves as he could. He entered that blinding wash of beach house light and closed the window he'd left open.

I hadn't noticed the window. Judging by Zeke's expression, neither did he. *What else did we forget?*

Neil loped back to us.

For the moment, we as cabin mates had enough to do to keep us from thinking much about what happened. Another, impressive bolt of lightning struck the other side as the three of us started up the bluff with the others.

Zeke said, "One-Mississippi...Two-Mississippi..."

Weak thunder rolled at *ten-Mississippi.*

"Two miles," Zeke said, part way up the slope of deep sand. "A little farther away than last time. Maybe half a mile farther."

"Okay?" Hoss said.

"The closest lighting may be getting farther away."

"So what?"

"That means we might just get a lot of wind without any rain."

"How do you figure?"

"Don't worry about it," I said. "Let's just go." I pointed up the bluff. "It's time to be quiet, now."

We took to climbing again. Neil fell in the sand. So did Bud, and so did Hoss. Zeke fell twice. We all did as well as we could, but we were in deep sand and soaked to our skin.

The cottonwoods' leaves waved at us, and I tried not to pay attention. If the trees actually *could* speak to us, I'd hate to hear what they had to say. The triangular leaves rocked back and forth in their lazy figure-eights. Swishing left-to-right, left-to-right, they chanted:

I know what YOU did
NAH-nah-n'NAH-nah.

Damned trees. We climbed and finally conquered the bluff.

"Lotta sand," Buck said. "Let's brush it off as much as we can."

Too much sand in our inspection-winning cabin would rouse suspicion. Brushing the front pocket of my jeans, I realized it was empty.

"What's the matter?" Zeke asked.

"Nothing. Let's get back."

CHAPTER 55

AFTER TWENTY YARDS of trail, we stood at the trailhead. Cabin Row arced to the waterfront in its quiet, breezy night. As a finishing place, Cabin 7 was supposed to be a kind of salvation—the successful completion of a harmless stunt—not some brooding doorway into the rest of our lives. I wanted to puke.

Hoss held up his hand at the trailhead. He stood there, peering around the last tree, checking if the coast was clear. I wondered how many of the guys thought Hoss might be protecting them, as though he thought of anything other than *If I get caught*. Cabin 7, to Hoss, I was sure, *was* the salvation. It was *still* going to mean the finish to a successful, mainly harmless stunt. I fell to my knees. A little burp came first, then a big heave. Nothing came up.

Neil and Zeke knelt down to see what was wrong with me. I told them I was all right. A dry gust tousled my hair, and the trees whooshed.

A couple sticks cracked in the woods, and nobody so much as flinched. If only we were on a campout and a giant, prehistoric, man-eating sloth were after us, felling trees with its scythe-like claws. No one was worried about what might be in the dark. We'd already been through—or done—the worst thing these woods had ever seen. But the real fear was yet to come, and we didn't know it yet. We would fear, we would dread, we would have dry throats, and we would taste copper in our mouths.

Doubt would creep in. We would even doubt ourselves. Each of us. We hadn't even begun to wonder if, over the last three days of camp, we could keep our lies consistent. We hadn't yet worried if we would remain safe from each other.

Except Hoss, I was sure.

Hoss beckoned me to the front, and I went. Someone was going to get us back into the cabin, and I was the only one I trusted to do it.

"You guys wait here," I said.

I ran to the back, far corner of the cabin. As the darkest corner, it was then visible in the orange light. All eight faces were now clear at the trailhead. I ushered them back. In full darkness on the cabin's back wall, we inched our way to the Emergency Door. I poked my head around to the other side of the cabin, breaking back into the orange haze. The piece of paper we'd used to jimmy the latch was still in place. Since I'd last seen it, an entire lifetime might have passed. Or at least an entire childhood.

Then the Cabin 6 bathroom light popped on.

I stole back to the darkness. Someone in Cabin 6 tinkled into the porcelain megaphone. The toilet flush was loud enough to give me gooseflesh. I imagined all the lights in the division clicking on, string-pull after string-pull, hushed voices turning to shouts, the Headquarters bell ringing, prison alarms, sirens, and red-spinning lights.

But things did, again, quiet down.

"So open the door," Hoss said in a whisper.

Open it yourself, you shit-ringed butt-pucker.

I was able to get my fingers between the door and the frame, one hand above, and one below the latch and pulled. By the time I noticed the wood-on-wood scrape and wanted to stop pulling, the door opened, and Zeke took the folded piece of paper.

The relative safety of the cabin's darkness seemed to pull on us. Boots, I thought. Boots on the floor. Which lummox cabin mate was going to clop his boots in there just like it was time to run out and play capture-the-flag? Who was going to step in and daintily pull a light string because he couldn't see? Who was going to stretch the spring on the toilet-room door and send its angry squawk echoing through all of Cabin Row?

Sunny clomped a boot onto the wooden stoop, grabbed the door to pull, and said, "What are you waiting for? Let's g—"

I stuck my arm straight in front of him and told him to wait.

"What? Why?" Sunny asked, and I didn't have an answer. I just wasn't ready for someone like him to be the first to go into the cabin.

"Because we need to take our boots off," Bones said. "And our clothes. We can't have sandy, wet clothes all over the place in the morning. They'd nab us for sure."

It was more than I'd heard Bones say all summer. I no sooner expected him to have a knack for deception than Zeke.

"What?" Sunny said. "That's—"

"Do what he says, Sunny," Hoss said.

Zeke and Neil unlaced their boots. So did Coach, then everyone else. I stripped down to my underwear and wondered about Bones and his apparent criminal instincts.

Share a cabin with Hoss all summer, and maybe you, too,

could learn to lie and cheat.

I blocked the doorway to take everyone's boots and shoes.

That's when a big, ripping snore filled the cabin and shot out the Emergency Door.

CHAPTER 56

I ALMOST COLLAPSED. We all quit breathing. My heart may have stopped in mid-beat.

"He's already back?" Sunny hissed.

"Oh, God," Buck said.

"He wasn't supposed to be back early," Zeke said. "Was he, Ted?"

Neil shook his head.

I met eyes with Hoss, who had nothing to say. The snoring must have wiped his mind clean of ideas, like it did mine.

"Yeah," Zeke said. "We're just gonna have to be quiet. As long as he snores, he can't hear us."

Our choice was clear. We had to enter the cabin, no matter what.

After Hoss finished stripping, all nine of us stood in the growing orange light, wearing nothing but our underwear. Could we possibly be the only ones awake on Cabin Row? Nothing around us moved or made a sound. I hoped Bill was fast asleep, not roving, like he was supposed to be. If it'd been Isaac, he'd still be out, roaming through the shadows. But he'd already hitched up his wagon and driven it back to the ranch for the night.

As a group, we were our own little wagon train. Some of us were horses, and two or three were drivers. Hoss and I appeared to share the reins. The two lead horses were Zeke and Neil. Reliable as could be, they didn't need a driver at all.

Coach and Bones were good, second-row workers. Buck and Bud even cooperated some. But Sunny was trouble, the sullen child in the back of the wagon. He didn't like it when I drove. When Sunny caused problems, Hoss took over.

"Okay," I said, surprised I could even talk. "Everybody get in here. Wipe your feet off when you come up the step."

"Wipe them where?" Sunny asked, shitty as can be. "We don't exactly have a doormat."

"Use your *hands*, you dumb fuck," Hoss said.

Buck made it up the step and dutifully wiped the sand off each foot with one hand. He stopped and asked me, "When did he get back, do you s'pose?"

Of all the answers I couldn't find, I opted for the safest, simplest, and most true: "I don't know."

"You think he knew we were gone?"

"No," Hoss said. "If anyone knew we were gone, this place would be a circus. All the lights would be on. Dinwiddie'd be up and around. Searching all over for us. There would even be cops, probably."

What Hoss said was true. Buck wasn't thinking clearly. No twelve-year-old, under the circumstances, should.

"And besides," Bones whispered, "he'll be drunk off his ass. Won't wake up at all."

"Yeah," Hoss said. "That, too."

Heeding the mandate of soundlessness, the near-naked members of Cabin 7 tiptoed up the steps and through the door, holding their bundles of clothes and boots. We must have looked like prisoners heading to our cells. Or maybe something unspeakable from World War II Germany.

Then I thought of something else.

"You two," I said, nodding to Buck and Hoss, holding my own pants in front of me, as though ready to step into them. "Stuff your clothes down my pant legs."

They did what I said, not questioning.

"How come?" Coach asked. "Why *their* clothes?"

Hoss answered before I could. "All that soot on us, Coach. If there's a fire over there, we can't have—"

"Okay," Coach said, stepping carefully into the cabin.

"Zeke," I said. "Go open the toilet room door. Real slow, so the spr—"

He got the door open quietly.

"Everybody, quiet as you can, put your clothes in the shower."

"And be quiet," added Sunny, who I decided to leave alone.

"Okay, Sunny," Hoss said. "We'll do our best."

The complete absence of sarcasm in Hoss's response bothered me. He'd yielded into Sunny's attempt to gain some power. The terrain had smoothed for the moment, and Hoss had handed Sunny the reins. It was, after a moment's thought, a brilliant move. Let the troublemaker drive the wagon. Or at least let the troublemaker *think* he's driving. It would keep him close to us, engaged, part of the team. It would keep him from dissenting. Dissent, and you divide the group. Divide the group, and someone says something to somebody else. Talk about what we'd just done, and the lies become inconsistent.

Hoss's acceptance of Sunny's leadership may have saved us. Somewhere in our dark leader hid a talent for dealing with people, solving problems, heading off trouble before it begins.

We all put our wet and sandy things in the shower and gently closed the plastic curtain. Zeke slowly closed the toilet room door. The nine of us huddled in front of the sinks. The snoring was the only thing we heard.

Hoss addressed the group. "Okay. Listen up. Tonight, we just have to go to bed. If your skivvies are wet, go back to your bunk and change 'em. Be as quiet as you can be getting in your bunks. If that snoring stops? You freeze until it starts again. Understand? And try not to talk. Don't think about what happened tonight. Best thing to do is try and forget about it."

"We set the forest on fire," Coach whispered.

"I'm afraid we can't help that now," Hoss said. His tone was fatherly and convincing. After all we'd done, Hoss still surprised and frightened me.

The tall trees surrounding Cabin Row rocked in the breeze. The wind sounded like a distant train rolling down the tracks. Soundless lightning flashed.

Hoss went on. "Buck. Take the little guy and tuck him in." Hoss paused until Bud was safely out of earshot, then whispered to the rest of the guys.

"So if you're worrying about how to handle this whole thing, let me tell you. Anybody talks about it, and we all get in trouble. And you know we did more than just break a couple rules."

Everyone listened to him closely.

"Until we *are* sure how to handle all this," Hoss went on, "and until all of us agree on it, nobody should talk about it. To anybody. Understand? Not even each other. We'll work out the rest in the morning. Anybody has any questions, you talk to me or Ted."

"We have to be a team, you guys," Sunny said.

"Sunny's right," Hoss said. "And thanks for taking care of the clothes, Ted."

Snoring.

It occurred to me as I pulled up a dry pair of underwear and got into bed that Hoss was the wagon's only driver. He'd parceled out control of the reins as he saw fit. He'd just given them to Sunny to prevent a fuss. He'd given *me* the reins all night, and he'd been inviting Buck to drive all summer.

I was in awe of Hoss's power, his ability to *control*.

I hated him.

CHAPTER 57

AFTER WE WERE in bed, when I squeezed my eyes shut as tight as they would go, an image of Cal Owen came and went. Then Mom took his place. She had a sympathetic frown and a drawn brow that told me she couldn't help me. She wasn't angry, just afraid for me.

I flipped in my bed and felt the tears squeezing through. My stomach and face both tightened painfully, and a kind of wall seemed to break down. I sobbed into my pillow.

Panic bloomed when I felt a hand on my shoulder.

"Ted?" It was Zeke.

"You okay, man?" whispered Neil, who had also climbed out of bed.

"No. Not really." I rolled over to see them and sniffed.

Neil: "I'd ask you what's wrong, but I don't suppose that's necessary."

I had no way to apologize for getting them into such a mess. For ruining their summers. For putting a horrible scar on their childhoods. I wanted to take it back, but I couldn't. My stomach spasmed again, and I let out one last, quiet sob. Zeke patted my shoulder, and Neil put a hand on my covered foot and squeezed.

Zeke: "Hey, Ted. I'm so sorry we made you go. I really wanted to. Just to paddle the canoe some more. That was what I wanted."

Neil: "Yeah. I think we put a lot of pressure on you. We knew you didn't want to go over there."

Zeke: "It sounded like such a good idea."

I sniffed and said, "I thought this was something I did to *you* guys."

They shook their heads and both said, "No."

No one spoke for a minute. We could barely see each other's faces. The wind in the trees continued, gently enough. The counselor area went quiet for ten or fifteen seconds before a loud gasp pealed like thunder. Then came more, regular snoring. The glow of orange made some of the trees visible outside, through the screened windows.

"What's goin' on over here?" asked Hoss, calling to order a whispered meeting.

Neil: "Ted was just upset, and we wanted to see what we could do."

Hoss: "We can't talk about it right now."

Neil: "We have to talk about it."

Zeke: "It's hard to ignore."

Hoss: "I know it is, but listen. The less we talk—"

Neil: "The better off we'll be. We know all that shit, man. We also have to know some other stuff."

"Like what?"

"Like do you think Coach and Bones really think that was soot in your hair?"

Hoss dropped his head and lifted it again. He asked Zeke and Neil, "How much did you see?"

As Hoss and I prepared to rack the last canoe, and I put my hands in his hair, what came back and shone in the beach house light was *red*. Smeary and full of little clots, it covered our hands and Buck's face. I even smelled the iron in it. How those guys could believe it was soot, I don't know, but I was sure they had. They'd want to *believe*.

Me: "They saw it, Hoss."

Hoss: "Saw what?"

"They saw everyth—"

Neil: "The psycho. What Buck did."

Hoss froze. "You and who?"

"Me and Zeke. You were unconscious."

"I was *what?*"

Zeke: "He hit you in the face and knocked you out."

Hoss rubbed the left side of his face.

Zeke: "Does it hurt, Hoss?"

Hoss: "Let's figure out who knows what."

Neil: "Coach and Bones ran away after Coach yelled 'Psycho.'"

Zeke: "So they only know about the fire. Right?"

Me: "Right. And Sunny…"

Neil: "He threw that stick and ran back to the canoes."

Hoss: "When? *Before* it happened?"

"Yeah."

"Are you sure?"

"Definitely. The guy acted like he was going to run after Sunny."

"Okay, so we're the only ones who know. Plus Buck."

Me: "And Bud."

Hoss: "In the morning, Bud won't know what planet he was on."

I supposed that was probably right.

Zeke: "His clothes caught on fire, Ted…"

Hoss: "They did. Buck had no choice."

Zeke: "…they just burned. And he didn't do anything about it."

Neil: "Hey, Zeke. We shouldn'a been over there, but Buck saved Hoss's life. That guy—the psycho or whatever you want to call him—he was gonna throw Hoss in the fire."

It was true. Buck had, in a grotesquely bloody way, saved Hoss's life.

Zeke: "I just don't know how somebody can burn like that and not even try to—"

Hoss: "He's dead, Zeke."

"*I know it,*" Zeke hissed, scrunching his face without crying. "I just don't like it."

I just don't like it.

Zeke said it all, right then and there.

"We can't talk," Hoss said. "You hear me? Bones, Coach, and Sunny just know there's a fire. Bud won't remember shit. Buck? We don't know. Right now," he said slowly, staring right at me, "we just can't talk."

I thought about the blood shooting from the open wound, Hoss falling damned-near into the fire, scrambling to keep from being burned. It was a self-defense killing, to be sure. Sort of. Buck had defended Hoss. What would the police—what would *Dad* call it? Justifiable something-or-other. At least that's what I'd tell myself as we kept quiet and waited for the sun to rise.

I'll never forget the sight of a grown man collapsing, face first, into that overbuilt fire. He made no attempt to protect himself as his full weight crashed onto a bed of coals as big around as the hood on Dad's GTO.

An enormous flock of orange sparks took flight. The impact catapulted two burning sticks from the campfire. One landed on the forest's red, pine needle carpet. The other came to rest at the base of the rust-colored, long-dead cedar tree.

Hoss stood, as though he'd put an end to our little conference. But then he put his hands on Zeke's shoulders and pulled him close. He did the same to Neil. Hoss leaned over my bed and put his nose just above my ear, where my mom used to kiss me, and he breathed in. He straightened quickly.

"You smell like smoke," he said. "We *all* do. We shoulda rinsed off in the lake. All of us."

We'd gotten rid of what visible evidence we could think of, but no one had thought about how we smelled. We'd make the entire inside of the cabin smell like a campfire, and there wasn't a thing we could do about it. "Probably shouldn't talk any more tonight," Hoss said. He disappeared to his bunk. Only one little squeak made it out of his bedsprings as he slithered beneath his sheets.

The trees rustled outside, and the snoring went on.

I couldn't believe we'd made it back to the cabin, but that was not all there would be to it. Somebody might find something—Hoss's lost key, maybe—and connect it to the boathouse, then to us. Maybe the waterfront counselors would find the paddles out of place. Footprints on the other side. The impressions our canoes had made on that sandy spit where we'd landed over there. Someone would smell us and start to wonder. The only thing between us and what we'd done was *one fleeting thought*. All someone had to do was think about it. Just once, and this frail illusion we'd begun to create would poof away, like Cliff's tendril of pot smoke in a breeze.

All stayed quiet for what remained of the night. I don't know if Zeke or Neil slept, but I hoped they did. I hoped they took a few hours to spare their minds the thoughts that went through mine.

Those thoughts were the first taste of the real trouble, the trouble that would come when we had no urgent task. Since we'd made it back to the cabin and were quiet in bed, we had nothing left but to stew about what we'd done. That orange light bled onto the outside world, and I had nothing else to think about.

That light glowed through the peephole next to my shelves. I used to have to squint through that thing for the slightest prayer of seeing it. Its meaning had changed immeasurably. The light in the trees had reached across the lake, shined on the cabins, washed everything in orange, and poured through the peephole.

That night, the light in the trees came looking for *me*.

CHAPTER 58

A FEW HOURS later, I couldn't tell the difference between forest fire and the daylight, but the wind picked up a notch or two. A few, dry cottonwood leaves blew past Buck's window. Our campfire smell had filled the entire cabin. Coach even coughed once or twice. A hot bulb flashed in my chest as bedsprings squeaked mightily up front.

My mind was an anxious blur.

"Oh, muh…" Shuffling. Pants going on over legs. Clomp. Putting on shoes. Clomp. The door opened, and then closed abruptly, its windowpanes rattling.

Hoss peered out his window, then right to me. Did we drop any clothes on the ground? A pair of pants from when we stripped and entered the cabin almost naked? A shirt? A single *sock*? Wouldn't take more than that to rouse suspicion. God forbid…someone might pull back the shower curtain.

Sunny got out of his bed without too much noise, and I wondered if he'd seen anything other than the fire. Coach and Bones stirred. Hoss sat on his bunk, arms crossed, staring at the floor. Zeke jerked awake. Coach slipped out of his bunk and headed up front with Sunny. Without a sound, Bones followed them. Buck's head lay on his pillow, eyes open.

The guys up front whispered.

Coach: "Why'd he leave so fast?"

Hoss cupped a hand behind his ear. I listened carefully.

Bones: "Fire, probably."

Coach: "Why'd he get back so early last night? Hoss said he'd be out till five in the morning."

Bones: "He'd been asleep here long enough to not know about the fire till right n—"

Sunny: "Doesn't matter. He never knew we were gone. That's all I care about. Let's just keep quiet like Hoss said."

Coach: "God. Look at that thing burn." What he said next was a whisper I couldn't hear.

Sunny: "Hoss said he got away. Ran away. I'm sure he's fine."

Coach mumbled some acknowledgement. It appeared those guys had bought the stories we'd sold them.

Hoss nodded at me, a satisfied grin on his face. A curl of smoke passed between Cabins 6 and 7. Someone down Cabin Row coughed. Then someone else.

Smoke.

It was everywhere. The whole place would smell like it. Not just us.

Zeke and Neil sat up in their bunks, and Hoss strolled over.

CHAPTER 59

WE WERE QUIET for a time after the bell rang. Buck rolled a little before jerking into a sitting position and staring through his window. Soon came the other cabins' counselors yelling *Time to get up!*, younger voices complaining it's too early, the hollow thumps of kids hopping out of bed, onto the cabin floors.

From Cabin 6 someone yelled, "Holy *SHIT!*"

"Marty!" Said Bill, *"I told you to watch your m—OH MY GOD!"*

A moment later, from down The Row, I heard someone yell it.

"FIRE!!"

Front doors of cabins burst open, and chatter filled the world outside our bunk space.

I got dressed and wordlessly ambled up front. The fire was at least twice as bad, twice as big as I could have imagined. The steady wind blew the smoke and heat our way. Under that swollen bruise of a sky, whitecaps and a few rolling breakers dotted the lake's dark and upset surface.

Isaac appeared in the doorway. "Mornin,' Boys," he yawned. His eyes were sunken. "What's the matter? Haven't you seen a conflagration before?"

I could smell the smoke on him.

"A what?" Bud asked.

"A big fire," Hoss said.

"That's right," Isaac said. "Forest fire. Line-up's in a few minutes."

"What's with the fires?" Bud asked.

Isaac didn't so much as blink when Bud said that. But I did. Someone may have sucked in a deep breath. Bud's use of the plural—*fires*—proved he did remember something and sent a clear message about how tenuous our situation was. We didn't have to leave clothes lying around outside, smell like smoke, or leave our footprints anywhere. All we had to do was take one word, a word like *fire*, and add an *S* to the end of it. Doing so might make somebody wonder if we'd seen several little fires before they spread into one big one. Our tight spool of deception was about to pop. I was sure of it.

In his usual cheer, Isaac said, "The fire'll be there when we get back from breakfast. You boys still have to eat…" When he added, "…no matter what happened across the lake," my spine iced over. Isaac's sentence hung before us like bait. I could just see Bud taking it: *What did happen last night, Isaac?*

But Bud asked something entirely different. "Where's Lloyd?"

Isaac hesitated. Maybe his head hurt too much to answer immediately. But maybe there was something the staff hadn't told us. "We had to borrow a few counselors to make some phone calls. Some kids are coughing because of all the smoke—it's a health hazard, you know—and we have the counselors calling parents. Some of you may be going home a little early.

"We also borrowed Alex from Cabin One and just now sent Bill from Six to man the telephones. I have to go ring the bell.

Can you guys handle getting to line-up by yourselves?"

But we just got up. Everybody. Just got UP. How had they coordinated all that activity so quickly? Something (if not quite throwing open the gates of Hell on Loon Lake's other side) was wrong. There was something Isaac wasn't telling us.

As Isaac finished his speech, a gust of anxiety consumed me. We pretty much kept to ourselves, getting ready to go. I laced up my one pair of tennis shoes. No one had boots—ours were all wet and hiding behind a flimsy, plastic shower curtain, waiting for us to do something with them. Just as easily as someone might put the *S* at the end of the word *fire*, some staff member, any staff member, could stroll into the bathroom, pop open the shower, ask us about all the wet clothes, and that would be it. Even if they didn't see the bloody ones stuffed into the legs of my pants.

And as if on cue, as I finished my second shoestring knot, Isaac strolled back toward the sinks, then into the toilet room itself. He was within a couple feet of the shower.

We were all silent. I waited for the scrape of curtain rings on the iron bar. But when I heard the toilet flush, the spring, the door slap, and water running out of a faucet, I let out a chest-full of held breath.

"Okay, guys," Isaac said, "be just a couple minutes 'til the bell rings, so be ready to go."

I headed out front. Half the Cabin Row population stood atop the bluff, staring over the water. Their outlines were hazy in the smoke. Some had their hands over their mouths. It was daylight, but the sky was, indeed, dark. Two strange boats motored from the state park's boat ramp. They were not pleasure-craft, and it was no time for boating. Not under that sky, and not in that choppy water. They headed for the flames.

In a couple of minutes, the bell rang.

When we got down to the big birch, Mr. Dinwiddie emerged, straightening his hair with his hands. Karen, who usually emerged with him, didn't. Line-up was sluggish and disorganized.

"Good morning, fellas," Mr. Dinwiddie said. His face was long, drawn. His eyes didn't smile. His daily greeting— *Gentlemen!*—never came. A little guy from Cabin 1 coughed into the voiceless silence.

"As you know," Mr. Dinwiddie started, "there's the fire."

"What started the fire?" someone blurted.

"That's a good question. We don't know, but there's been lightning since at least early morning. It's been awfully dry these last few weeks, and we think the lightning may have struck something over there.

"In any case, we find the smoke a bit of a problem. Some of you are coughing, and some of you have asthma. We certainly do not want anyone getting sick because of this. That's why we're dividing this morning, to call your parents. You'll notice some of your counselors are missing. Two are using the phones in Headquarters and the others are in the office, up by the highway.

"The summer of 1970 at White Birch Camp is almost over, and now we have the fire. Because of the health hazard the smoke presents, I tell you with some sadness we've decided to give your parents the option of picking you up early."

At this, some kids gasped, and some cheered. Some seemed

worried about camp ending soon. The members of Cabin 7 didn't react at all.

Sunny stood in front of me and whispered to Hoss, "At least we don't have to worry about smelling like sm—"

Hoss backhanded Sunny's shoulder. "Shut *up*," He hissed through clenched teeth.

It didn't matter, I supposed, that Hoss was maybe a little too confident, that Sunny seemed to think something was funny, or that Buck hadn't said a word all morning.

It didn't matter, because if the staff weren't onto us already, they probably would be soon. It wasn't perfectly clear we'd been found out, though, until after breakfast, when we returned to find Mr. Dinwiddie waiting for us in the cabin.

CHAPTER 60

WE TRUDGED ALONG to breakfast, a chain gang of hush-mouthed crooks. Not just crooks. We were killers. Quiet, sleepy, and resigned killers. I ate some of my breakfast, just to keep up appearances. Zeke and Neil did the same. Isaac was up half the time, answering other campers' urgent questions.

Mr. Dinwiddie left, and Isaac followed him. Just a couple counselors managed us all. When Zeke, Neil, and I got up to head back to the cabin, I felt a rush when I remembered the shower. About that, something bothered me, other than the obvious trouble a pile of bloody clothes in the shower would bring if someone found it. This was something big, and I didn't know what it was. As we stood, so did Hoss. He whispered something to Buck, probably to get him to keep the other guys quiet.

"Ted," Hoss said to me as the three of us shot past the hot kitchen smell outside. "Wait up." He checked behind him and nabbed a couple of the extra trash bags from a little cubby behind the bag-lined trash drums. He folded them dutifully and shoved them down the front of his pants, just like he'd already made half a career of hiding incriminating evidence.

Something about those bags in the front of his pants bothered me horribly, the same as the shower had. Maybe just *everything* at that moment bothered me.

"We need to talk about what to do," he said.

"What to *do*?"

"What I mean is we need to figure out how to handle this."

"Who to tell first?"

"Tell? I don't think so. We need to meet as a cabin so we can figure out—"

I stopped, and so did they. "Didn't you say not to talk about it at all?"

"Yeah. Not till after breakfast."

"Oh. So now we're talking after breakfast. Who're we gonna talk to?"

Hoss narrowed his eyes.

If I get caught.

Neil: "Ted. I don't think—"

Me: "I vote we tell Mr. Dinwiddie."

Zeke: "Ted?"

Me: "What, Zeke?"

Hoss: "We can't tell Mr. Dinwiddie."

Hoss stepped back. I'd made him nervous. I liked that and stepped into a walk toward Cabin Row. They followed.

Hoss: "Isaac, either. We can't tell anybody."

I didn't want to tell anybody at all, couldn't even imagine it, not then. But I pushed on. My anger at Hoss grew as I went.

Me: "We can't? What if I do anyway?"

He took a deep breath. Neil and Zeke walked close by, watching.

Hoss: "Look, Ted. Do you really want to tell them, or are you just trying to be hard to get along with?"

"What if I want to get *you* caught?"

"You'd get us *all* caught."

"But it's yourself *you're* worried about."

"Of course I'm worried about it. So are you, and don't tell me you're not."

Zeke: "*I'm* worried, Ted."

Neil: "Me, too, man. But remember. That guy was trying to kill Hoss. He has just as much, you know, civil right as anybody, but—"

Hoss: "It's Buck I'm worried about."

I stopped. "Buck?" The four of us stood on the south side of the waterfront. Smoke wafted between us.

"Yeah. Buck. I mean. He's the one who"—Hoss checked around him quickly—"*did* it."

Yes. Buck did it. I remembered what he did after Bud went on his rampage and Sunny threw the stick. "Okay," I said. "What do you want to do about Buck?"

"You have any idea what'd happen to him if we got caught?"

I guessed I didn't know. Right then, I didn't care. "I didn't think you were worried about anybody but yourself."

"Listen. And don't forget Buck saved my life."

"So let's hear it. Tell me about *Buck*."

"'Kay," Hoss said. "I got older brothers. They drink and smoke pot and all that. They're all at least eight years older than me. They tell me I was the woopsie-baby, the mistake or the *accident*, that Dad didn't pull out in time. That kind of stuff. They're basically assholes. Except my second brother. He was always nice."

"What does that have to do with—"

"Just listen. This one brother of mine, his name is Jake, got in trouble when he was about fifteen. I was maybe five, but I remember his friend telling me what happened. Jake never really got in trouble like my other brothers did. Stealing fishing lures out of the hardware store and smashing the glass on the fire alarms in school. Jake didn't do any of that. He was quiet and pretty much behaved himself. He got picked on a lot at school. Problem was, no one knew how strong Jake was. He could wrestle just about anybody down, but he kept to himself.

"So anyway, there was this tall kid, big-shot basketball player. He was bigger than Jake, you know, and between classes one day, he got Jake backed into a corner by the lockers. Giving him a hard time, calling him names, calling our *mom* names. That kinda shit."

Hoss had a knack for speaking quickly when excited.

"So Jake—he had a lot of muscle, you know, but he liked baggy clothes, so nobody knew, right?—is backed into the corner? And the tall kid starts shoving him, punching him in the arms and chest, saying mean things. The other kids were standing around, watching, egging on the mean kid. And that day, for whatever reason, Jake just kind of exploded. He either got mad or scared, or both, like something that filled up and had to break open. And right then in front of all those kids, he did. He just tucked his head down and plowed into the tall kid like a linebacker or something. Jake hit him so hard they both fell and slid like ten feet across the floor.

"It didn't take long before everyone crowded around so tight no one could even see what was going on, including the teachers, you know? The kids cheered like they do when there's a fight. Jake punched the kid in the face a few times and pulled a wrestling move. Flipped him over on his stomach and started hitting him in the back, then in the side of the head with his fist. There was blood on the floor, all over the kid's face, and all over Jake.

"Before the teachers could break through the crowd, Jake got up and stood on the kid's shoulder. Grabbed one wrist and pulled. Hard, until the arm bone snapped in half."

"Oh, no!" Zeke said.

"No shit, Zeke. By the time the teachers got in there to stop the fight, Jake was about to break the kid's other arm. When the teachers pulled the two apart, Jake didn't have a scratch on him, and the big-shot basketball player had a broken arm, two broken ribs, a blood-gushing nose, a fat lip, and a concussion."

"Wow," I said. "That sounds really bad, Hoss, But I still don't see how it—"

"Lemme tell you. Jake got expelled from school. They made him see a—"

A couple of kids from Cabin 3 walked by, watching the strange boats, which seemed to be spraying water that didn't quite reach the flames.

After the boys passed, Hoss spoke a little more quietly. "They made Jake see a…a shrink, you know? And the mean kid's parents got pissed, too. They did everything they could to hurt my brother. He got sent into a special hospital for a couple weeks as some kind of punishment. They called it treatment." Hoss screwed his face up when he said the word, *treatment*. "And he didn't even remember what had happened in school that day. He just lost his mind for a little bit. He went nuts."

"Like Bud?" Neil said.

"What?...Yeah. I guess. Something like Bud. But big and

strong."

"Okay," I said, "so finish your story about *Jake*."

"All right. When he was in that treatment place, somebody tried to stick him with a needle, a nurse, I guess, and he said no, and she tried to do it anyway, and he said no again, and, well, one thing led to another, and she ended up flat on the floor, and the next thing you know, four great big guys in white jackets pinned him down with leather straps and stabbed him with all *kinds* of needles.

"They just put him on medicine after medicine. And when he finally made it back home, he just wasn't the same person. He was dull, didn't seem to want to do anything, wouldn't throw a ball with me, just seemed half pissed off all the time. Then he flunked out of school. Smart guy, too. Smarter than all his teachers, and all those people who rotted his brain with that medicine."

We started toward Cabin Row again, walking slowly.

Hoss continued. "Didn't take long for Jake to learn how to hide his pills in his cheeks when our mom gave them to him. To get off those pills, he had to cheat, and he had to lie. He lied to his doctors, and he lied to Mom and Dad. He went back almost to normal. But as a cheater and a liar. And a high-school dropout with a job at a car wash. And my Dad didn't like that. He'd get drunk. And when he was real drunk, he'd hit Jake."

Three more kids ran by us to stand at the top of the waterfront, facing the lake.

"So Jake," Hoss said, checking around him, "with his new friends, started drinking, and taking drugs, even selling—"

"Okay," I said. "That's bad. I get it."

"It *is* bad. My point is, Buck—"

"What happened to Jake, Hoss?" Zeke asked.

"Jake's twenty-two, and he's in jail now."

"What for?" asked Neil.

"Got drunk and took a bunch of drugs and beat my dad half to death. Dad was in the hospital. Just got out in May. Jake broke both his legs."

Bullshit. I gave it a moment's consideration but rolled back. *He's making this up.*

"They arrested Jake, and Dad's letting them, you know…"

"Press charges?" I asked.

"Yeah," Hoss said. "That. And Mom? She didn't know what to do with me while she took care of Dad at home."

Liar.

"So what'd they do with you?" Zeke asked.

"Told me they were gonna send me to some camp."

"Oh," Zeke said absently, as though to the lake. "*Oh.*"

"Now picture that happening to Buck," Hoss said. "Can you picture Buck strapped to a bed in some nut house with four big guys in white uniforms stabbing him with needles? Selling dope on the street? And being beaten up by a drunk?"

That explained at least why Hoss hated Lloyd so much.

"Because that's what he's gonna get if somebody talks about this. And the only difference between Buck and Jake is that one of them defended himself from a mean guy, and the other one defended somebody else. And that somebody else is *me*, in case you haven't noticed."

"And that psycho was trying to *kill* you," Neil said.

"Hell yes, he was. Buck is my friend," Hoss said. "I don't

want to see him go through all that."

I wasn't sure what to say. It was like being in a room with two doors, one labeled *Hoss is lying*, and the other, *Hoss is telling the truth*. I figured...pick a door and move on. It shouldn't be any mystery which door I picked.

"So let's get these trash bags back there," Hoss said, "and take care of those clothes in the shower. What do you think?"

He adjusted the trash bags in his pants, right where his...his knife...

BUCK'S KNIFE!!

The fire blazed, the lake churned, and I ran. "You guys get back to the cabin and start cleaning. I'll be right there." I stole down Cabin Row and onto the Mosquito Point trail.

CHAPTER 61

BUCK'S KNIFE IS what nagged me at breakfast. I'd picked it up over there after he'd dropped it. I'd sheathed it, pocketed it, and meant to throw it into the lake. But I'd been distracted, paddling back, and I never did. Because the knife barely fit in my pocket, the hilt poked out the top. When I took my pants off and told Buck and Hoss to shove their clothes into my pant legs, the knife was no longer there to worry about.

There was a chance I'd dropped it under the canoes as I struggled to put the chain back in place. A knife with that blood on it was worth a million footprints.

I ran past Cabin 7 and darted into the hidden safety of the trail. A picture in my mind appeared. In it, Buck was strapped to a hospital bed, trapped in a dingy corner, surrounded by pale green tile. Brutes dressed in white stabbed him full of needles.

"Complete bullshit," I muttered, grabbing a cottonwood tree to control my descent down the deep sand of the bluff. "There's no brother named Jake."

Stealing down to the canoes at night was easy. During the day, when a fire drew everyone to the bluff's edge? It'd be a little more difficult. When I got down to the flat, wet sand, I shot over to the north side of the boathouse, keeping my eyes peeled for the knife along the way. We'd left breakfast early, hadn't we? Maybe everyone was still there. Almost everyone, anyway.

Taking a chance, I peeked around the bluff side of the

boathouse. No one was up top. The longer I waited, the worse the risk. My sprint through the deep sand seemed horribly slow, but I got to the boat rack. Diving to the ground, I went crab-style, beneath the canoes' safe cover.

It didn't take long to find it. The knife sat in its sheath in plain sight, under canoe number three.

"Ho-lee shit," said Marty, from Cabin 6.

I froze. What was he? Ten feet away? Twenty? *Down by the boathouse?* But no, he was up on the bluff. From between the canoes, I could see him.

"Marty," said another counselor, who'd taken over while Bill was off making phone calls to parents. "Come on, man, you have to get inside and clean up, like the rest of your cabin mates."

"Those guys aren't even back from breakfast."

"Marty, get back in the cabin. *Now.* I'm not like Bill. I won't put up with your shit. There's still plenty of camp left to make your life good and painful. *Now move your ass.*"

Marty went without a word. Someone had finally spoken to him in a language he could understand.

That's just what Hoss needed. A language he understood.

I waited ten or fifteen seconds. With a flood of boys returning from breakfast, I'd soon have no chance to get off the waterfront without being seen.

For a moment, I stood, alone on the waterfront, bloody knife in hand. I dropped it into my pocket and ran toward and past the boathouse. The hilt and belt-loop of the sheath reached the top of my pocket. Climbing the bluff in that sand was arduously slow, but I made it without trouble.

The knife sat safely in my pocket as I stepped up to Cabin 7's closed and quiet door. Getting rid of the knife would be only a minor challenge. I didn't trust throwing it in the lake so close to shore, and I didn't have time to bury it in the woods properly, at least not before inspection. The cigar box could serve as temporary storage.

Of course, as I reached for the knob, I thought of Mom. Did she know what I'd done? And Dad. I was sure I'd dashed any remaining hope of a relationship with him. I hated the sneaky cheating, but it seemed necessary until we figured out what to do and how to do it.

I wrapped my trembling fingers around the doorknob and opened the door. Inside, Isaac and Mr. Dinwiddie stood in the middle of the cabin. Isaac crossed his arms. Mr. Dinwiddie's spread like an eagle across his face, but his eyes didn't change a bit.

CHAPTER 62

THEY LOOKED MOURNFUL. Regret-filled. The tip of the sheath rested at the bottom corner of my pocket. I brushed my hand over where I feared the hilt might bulge or even poke out the pocket's top.

"Come on in, Ted," Mr. Dinwiddie said, waving me in slowly. "We've been waiting for you. Have a seat on your bunk."

All of Cabin 7's campers were present. *Who* had already said *what* I could only imagine.

"We need to have a very serious talk," he said.

I sat down. Hoss's gaze drilled into me, and I kept my eyes on Mr. Dinwiddie. What little breakfast I'd eaten tried to crawl its way back up. Mr. Dinwiddie let out a deep sigh and seemed to try to be himself, but his unsmiling eyes were tired.

"It is with great disappointment," he said, "that I tell you Lloyd's journey with White Birch Camp ended yesterday."

A couple guys let out incredulous *What?* sounds. I couldn't believe it myself.

"Good," Bones said. "We didn't like him, anyway. Did you fire him or something?"

Bones shocked us all. It seemed he'd held all his comments until the end of camp. It made me wonder if he even knew Lloyd was Mr. Dinwiddie's brother.

"So he's *not* up making phone calls?" Sunny asked.

"No, Sunny," Isaac said. "He's not."

"Then why did you say he was?"

"I didn't. Not really. I danced around that question a little, because it's Mr. Dinwiddie's place to tell you what happ—"

"Did you sleep in the cabin last night?" Coach asked.

"Yes. Came in late…"

Isaac. What? He would have had to enter the cabin after we left and before the fire was big enough to notice. Not only that. He would have to have entered the cabin and gone to bed without noticing we weren't there. That didn't sound like him at all. He'd always checked on us when he roved. Why wouldn't he check if he was the one going to sleep in the cabin?

"I hope I didn't disturb you," he said.

Oh, God. They know. They're just not telling us.

Isaac yawned.

UNLESS…unless…

"I had one of my famous migraines and just had to get to bed."

I didn't know whether I could believe him or not and may have let out an audible whimper.

"Let's turn the floor over to Mr. Dinwiddie," Isaac said.

"Thank you, Isaac," Mr. Dinwiddie said. "You see, gentlemen, our most important job is to help you have a meaningful experience at White Birch Camp. Isaac is here to do that. For the rest of this season, he will serve as your counselor."

"Why'd you fire him?" Buck asked.

Mr. Dinwiddie dodged the question.

It didn't matter, really. Most likely, the campers' questions were out of curiosity, not disappointment. No one loved Lloyd.

Nobody liked him. Most in the cabin didn't seem to care either way. I was numb. Had the directors seen the shower?

Mr. Dinwiddie continued for a minute or two, apologizing to us in his brand of colorful speech. He was sorry he'd given us, not one, but two counselors who had to be fired. But of course, he described them as gentlemen who would wander...in their respective journeys...away from the meandering path White Birch *Camp* would take into the *future*...and blah, blah, *blaahh*. Mr. Dinwiddie was a master of euphemism, but his speech that morning was overworked, like a funeral parlor with too many flowers.

As he talked, he touched on how unusual the 1970 season had become. The tornado, the drought, the fire. A tone of regret or sadness colored his voice. He apologized for the mark a bad counselor would leave on our summers. He was sad for *us* in that way. Another part of his sadness, I'm sure, lay in his being responsible for Lloyd. Without question, the last and probably biggest wedge of his complex sadness was a deep anger that grew out of the reason Lloyd was fired in the first place.

The guarded secret behind *that* was never supposed to reach us.

Mr. Dinwiddie explained no further. Seeing so much happiness drain from that great man's face was heartbreaking. Our silence about the fire and the other issue on the far shore was awful. Dress it up however you wanted, but that silence was a lie. And lying to him? I hated it. Wondering when I had my first chance to get that bloody knife out of my pocket made it that much worse.

Mr. Dinwiddie said, "Isaac and I will leave you now, O

Champions of Inspection this summer, to do your thing. We'll inspect just before lunch." Isaac waved to us and followed Mr. Dinwiddie.

I was dumbstruck those men hadn't been in Cabin 7 to tell us they knew everything.

Just as they stepped out, and the door latched, Hoss bounded out of bed, yanking the trash bags out of the front of his pants. He said something about inspection and getting to work. He took off for the shower and took Buck with him. The door spring squawked, and the door slapped shut behind them. I waited until the iron rings squeaked across the rusty curtain rod. I didn't want anyone to see me transfer the knife to the box. I was on outdoor detail and grabbed the rake from the back of the cabin. Everyone was busy, giving me my chance. I carried the rake to my area and reached into my pocket.

That's when Mr. Dinwiddie stepped around the partition and said politely with the same, unsmiling eyes, "Ted?"

I stopped.

"May I have a private word? Out front?"

Hoss's muffled voice wafted up, between the slats in the loft's floor and through the cabin. I heard, among them, the phrases *hold the bag*, and *boots're gonna be heavy*.

I stood with my mouth open until Mr. Dinwiddie made a *follow me* gesture, and I went with him.

CHAPTER 63

MR. DINWIDDIE LIKED me. He trusted me, and I was sure he didn't trust Hoss. The director had brought me outside to prevent Hoss from interfering. That was my take. It was clear Mr. Dinwiddie, in his position and the grace in which he held it, kept up all manners and gave me every benefit of the doubt that surely grew in his heart.

The sheathed knife stabbed so severely into my pocket I could practically count the stitches on the sheath by feel.

"I want you to walk with me, Ted," he said. "Let's chat a bit."

He decided to cut between Cabins 6 and 7. Whether or not he was headed for our Emergency Door occupied my every thought. I was certain he was toying with me, trying to get me to break and confess like some under-oath criminal in Dad's courtroom drama movies.

Might Mr. Dinwiddie have seen a few dozen footprints back there, by the Emergency Door? Fresh footprints in bare feet, maybe hundreds of them, huddled by the steps? And that's why he came after me? I scanned the area, trying not to alert him by turning my head, but I couldn't see anything. We strolled half the length of the cabin before he said anything more.

"So, Ted."

"Yeah?"

"Have you had a good summer?"

THE LIGHT IN THE TREES

"I guess so." Nothing seemed to jump out at us from near the Emergency Door. You'd have to get pretty close to see the footprints or the…

"I want to ask you something."

…*THE RED STRING!!* I heard something from inside the cabin. Whistling. "Floatin' Down the Mississippi." Hoss's victory theme. I knew it meant he had filled the bags with the sandy clothes and boots. I wanted to dart over and grab that string before anyone saw it. The director and I passed the back of Cabin 7. I wasn't sure where he was going, but I wasn't about to break rank with him.

"Ted?"

"Huh?"

"What do you think?"

"About what?"

"Oh, just—I need to ask you something."

I needed not to forget about that string.

"Forgetting something?" he asked with a vexing grin.

He knew I was forgetting the string. I was about to crack under questioning. He almost had me. "I don't know," I managed to say. Right then, I'd've told anyone just about anything.

"The rake," he said. "You don't want to carry it all the way to Headquarters."

"Oh," I said. The rake. "Right."

Wait. Headquarters?

I ran the rake up to the cabin and leaned it near the Emergency Door. Among the one-thousand barefoot prints, the string was there. All I had to do was bend over and pick it up.

But I ignored it. Direct Mr. Dinwiddie's gaze down there, and that would do it. I ran back to him no faster than I'd run to put down the rake. My stomach churned, and I tingled all over.

One element of my fear, in this case, is no crime had to be proven. The proving part would be easy, judging by what I knew from listening to Dad. There's always evidence, he said. Always. The crooks can almost always be connected to their crimes. Floating near Loon Lake's far shore, a flashlight said YASKO in permanent marker. The nearby sand recorded fresh keel marks. Hours-old footprints spoke silently of a dubious recent history outside the Emergency Door. Fresh blood dirtied our clothes. A quarter-million boot prints placed us right next to the uh…

Dead body.

And the knife that killed him. Sat right there in my pocket.

All anyone had to do was suspect us. A single, well-placed question would finish it all. How come nobody in here has boots any more? Why do all you boys seem so tired today? You guys see anything funny last night? Anything at all? Now, Mr. Dinwiddie was taking me down to Headquarters to ask some questions.

"Boy, Ted. I have to tell you I'm disappointed."

"You are?"

Paralyzed, my legs somehow kept walking.

"I'm so terribly sorry your cabin has been through so much this summer."

"So much…what?"

"Change. Not the least of which is that you're now on your third counselor. If I may, I want to tell you I sincerely hope it hasn't tarnished your or any of your cabin mates' experiences here."

"It's okay," I said, flying blind. "I like Isaac as counselor."

A weary smile crossed his face. "I like Isaac, too."

His words were casual, but his tone and demeanor were not. I could hardly stand it. Two or three times that morning already, I'd nearly collapsed into full confession.

We strolled behind the lazy arc of Cabin Row. The big birch and Headquarters became visible. What could he possibly want with me at Headquarters? One boy each raked the ground outside his cabin, clearing it of twigs for inspection.

When we got to Headquarters, Mr. Dinwiddie held the main door as though for me to step inside. No camper entered Headquarters. Unless Mr. Dinwiddie took him. Inside, a cork board posted a few weekly schedules: Nighttime *Roving. Lifeguarding. Forced fun monitoring.* The boathouse lanyard, brandishing its two tarnished keys, hung silently on a hook.

Good for you, Ted! Mom's voice told me. *You even left evidence in Headquarters!*

"Step into my office," Mr. Dinwiddie said, gesturing to the fabled wooden chair. Toad's chair. "Have a seat."

I sat down. The birch waved a few wary leaves from a perspective I now shared with Toad. In a minute or so Isaac opened the screen door and appeared in the office doorway. Mr. Dinwiddie reached into a drawer and pulled out a white envelope.

"Ted. I want to ask you another question. Isaac, come on in and close the door." When Isaac shut the door, Mr. Dinwiddie stepped between me and the desk. Leaning against it, he

317

crossed his arms and narrowed his eyes a little.

I felt like a half-empty sack, a pillowcase, as though all my bones had disappeared, and I was about to slide to the floor. I was one hundred percent sure the knife's hilt had poked out of my pocket.

"I trust you, Ted," Mr. Dinwiddie said. I sat face-to-face with his pleading eyes. "You're here because I'm a little worried about something."

Here we go, I thought.

CHAPTER 64

IT ALL CHANGED the night before, when Hoss yelled *"Son of a BITCH!"* Everything took on a sudden meaning. Karen's story in the loft, the campout on Tornado Night, saving Hoss from drowning, tackling Mr. Dinwiddie, and voices carrying over open water. It all culminated.

Hoss lunged toward the tall, staggering figure, swinging a mighty punch to the no-face. Hoss didn't seem to bluff; he'd obviously intended great harm. The no-face collapsed for a split second and enveloped Hoss's fist. It was as though he'd just punched a melon-sized lump of green dough. The Psycho's head shot back, but only for a second.

My awareness and understanding limped along.

The psycho wore blue jeans, a green and brown jacket, and a hat. The glinting thing was a bottle rolling into the firelight. I finally understood.

Lloyd seemed to awaken fully when Hoss punched him in the face. Bud stood up and took another shot, but Lloyd shoved him away a third and final time. Hoss stepped back, pre-emptive in his stance. Lloyd took one big swing and connected with Hoss's face, snapping his head to one side.

Hoss collapsed to the dirt about the time Sunny's helicoptering stick cracked into Lloyd's shoulder. A second or two later, Lloyd took a threatening step toward Sunny, and Sunny retreated to the canoes, screaming.

The mosquito net still in place, Lloyd seized Hoss by the

back of the belt and lifted him off the ground with one hand. Lloyd wrapped his other arm tightly around Hoss's throat and carried him toward the fire. It appeared Lloyd, too, intended great harm.

Hoss suddenly kicked. His left arm was free and reached behind his own head. Gasping, eyes bulging, Hoss grabbed for anything. His movements grew more and more frantic as he made no purchase. Soon, maybe even inevitably, he groped at his own stomach, just above the belt. His knife was gone. Lloyd hesitated a few steps from the fire and tightened his grip. When Hoss's panicky face became an open-mouthed stare, each leg slowed to little more than a dangle. It was clear what was about to happen.

Since my mind told me part of the dead tree had broken loose and started to move, I had no conscious thought. None while Bud went horizontal in mid-air, none while Hoss took out a lifetime's-worth of anger on mean drunks, and none while Lloyd squeezed the life out of him. When Lloyd carried Hoss toward the fire, there was nothing left to do, not a single thing on this earth, but run toward them. I didn't see Buck doing the same.

"Stop!" I shouted in a dead sprint. *"STOP IT!!"* I slid to a stop close to Lloyd, who'd suddenly faced me. In the firelight, I could see his eyes through the net's mesh. Dinwiddie eyes. Just one expression short of rising suns. There may have even been a little Karen in them.

Our counselor let out an *Oooff!* as Buck glommed onto his back. Lloyd staggered hugely, almost falling into the fire. The three of them together were a bobbling, two-legged monster with three heads and two faces.

Buck's expression, as his elbows propped on Lloyd's shoulders, was a vacant mix of fear and shame. His left arm reached Lloyd's forehead and pulled back.

Something, somewhere in the forest, let out a primal moan. That booming voice might have been the sloth itself, but it changed. It lost volume and became a bubbling gargle. A wheeze followed, then a few gasps. Lloyd dropped Hoss, who skittered away from the small mountain of orange-white coals.

A red mist filled the air in front of Lloyd and Buck.

Two jets of dark fluid burst in parallel, a few feet skyward, one pump after the next. Buck let go and slid off Lloyd's back to his feet. Lloyd stumbled forward to the fire's edge and stiffened for a moment. Then, like a tall, slender building imploding from its base, he toppled forward, gained speed, and crashed face-down into the fire.

The feeble, disorganized structure collapsed easily under Lloyd's weight, and he hit with a splintering thump. A blinding flock of orange sparks took flight when he hit the coals. His impact launched two hula-dancer torches in opposite directions, well beyond the edges of the clearing.

His legs kicked once or twice before he lay, motionless. His forehead rested on the biggest, orange-glowing log. Blood dripping from his gaping neck sizzled on the coals just inches beneath the wound. His jacket and hat went up almost immediately, even before the fire's upper structure settled on top of him. Something sputtered, and something hissed. In a few seconds, he sounded like raw meat that'd just been dropped into a searing pan.

As Buck stood still, his knife dripping Lloyd's blood, he wore the same, vacant stare. The initial sputters-and-hisses gave way in a few seconds to a rhythmic, dripping sound: *Pssst!*

It sounded a little like Sally Michaels at home, trying to pass a note in class.

Pssst!

Zeke and Neil stood motionless, right were I'd left them. Bud was still on all-fours, slowly getting back to his feet. Hoss rubbed the front of his own neck, and Buck was slow to emerge from his trance.

Sunny, Bones and Coach were nowhere to be seen. I stepped over to Buck right when a deathly scream filled the woods. Bud stood, facing Lloyd. Screaming.

Hoss leapt over to him and said hoarsely, "Bud! Be quiet, okay? It's not what you think. It's all okay. Bud? You hear me? Let's get back to the canoes. It's gonna be just fine."

Bud went silent and slapped his arms around Hoss's middle. Hoss stood still for a second before simply hugging back. He held Bud in a way that would keep him from seeing the fire.

"Don't look at that, okay?" Hoss said. Bud broke the hug.

"That's the way," Hoss said. "We're all gonna be *oh*-kay."

A crowd-like gasp waved through the treetops in an unexpected gust.

Hoss pointed at Buck and said, "Ted. You take care of him, all right?"

The fire's heat burned at my skin, and I thought Buck might sizzle where he stood. His shirt was open, plaid tails untucked, his bare stomach showing. I called his name, and he blinked.

The knife dropped out of his hand. He pulled the sheath from his waistband and dropped it near the knife.

"Neil!" Zeke said. "Help!"

Zeke stood, trying to pull one of the hula torches away from a dead tree, a rusty-brown, fifteen-foot cedar, already its own fire. Another gust wafted the new flames into a nearby, drought-anguished pine. Its live needles popped and curled in orange singes. Across the clearing, an unsteady, orange light glowed beyond the sapling-covered log. Even at that early moment, those fires were out of control.

The treetops drew in a labored breath, then whooshed hoarsely, speaking to me. They had a lot to say. *Look what you've done, Ted*, they said. *You've set us on fire, and you're going to run away. And leave us here to burn.*

"Ted," Zeke said, his face contorted into a crying frown. "Can you help?" His voice devolved into a desperate cry. He squeezed his eyes shut as the cedar's fire spiked up to maybe forty feet. Proper flames reached the nearby pine.

I realized only later that Zeke's fixation on the trees was his way to escape the bigger problem, the way I'd once wracked my brain to figure out who'd borrowed Mom's car, because it just couldn't have been her in that crash. Neil took hold of Zeke's upper arms and urged him to go. I told Buck to go with them, and he did.

CHAPTER 65

BY THE TIME I was twelve, I had heard my dad utter the phrase *crime scene* more times than I could count. It made me head back toward the fire, the sapling-covered carcass of a tree, and the giant white pine. At the base of that pine was Bud's jacket. I told Zeke and Neil I'd be right with them, and I ran to get the jacket. By then, the delicate saplings' big leaves waved frantically in the heat, the fire reaching for them. A little evergreen burned behind the dead tree.

I picked up Buck's knife and sheath, scanning the area for anything I might've missed.

Pssst! Lloyd said.

He faced downward as before, his clothes aflame. The sizzles and pops were almost unbearable.

Pssst!

Lloyd's final word to me—with just the two of us there— was his most memorable.

The knife had blood on it. I thought about wiping it on my pants, or Lloyd's. I couldn't bring myself to do either, so I stuck the blade into the sheath, then into my pocket. I took one last glance around for anything we'd left behind. The near-empty whiskey bottle would stay right where it was.

Dad had other common phrases, like *obstruction of justice*, and I figured with some awful nausea, that taking evidence away from the clearing might qualify.

Another whoosh of air brought a combination of familiar

smells: campfire, burning plastic, and frying bacon. I bent at the waist and dry-heaved. When I felt myself wanting to cry, I ran toward Zeke and Neil.

The trees and brush—and the encroaching flame—seemed thicker on my way back to the canoes. Getting back to the edge of the forest was like trying to run in a dream. At the sandbar all nine of us and all eight paddles were accounted for. Hoss directed the canoes be boarded and launched.

"No paddles hitting the gunwales," he said. "And stick together." The *Buck's-in-charge* game was over. Hoss seemed to have everything together but didn't appear to wonder about Bud's jacket or Buck's knife.

When I asked if everyone had his shoes, I thought, *Maybe Hoss is right. Maybe I am a regular criminal.*

As we shoved off, the high moonlight revealed the riveted, keel-gouged molds the canoes left in the sand. Bootprints, too. The flames behind us grew in a steady eastern wind. Hoss faced me as he stood in the shallows and launched his canoe last.

I'm not sure exactly what was going through his mind that night, right there by the canoes and the inception of what was sure to be known as the Great Fire of 1970, but I knew he didn't trust me. It was clear he wouldn't trust anyone for the rest of camp. Probably not even Buck. *If I get caught* is what that stare said to me.

"Gotta go," he said to Sunny, pulling their canoe off the sandbar.

The criminal in me could not stop wondering where Hoss's knife was. I wondered if he'd even thought about it.

You're a more careful criminal than Hoss, Ted, said

Mom's pretty voice. *I'm so proud of you.*

I had other pretend conversations, too. *Dad? Do you think Lloyd felt the fire when he landed in the coals? Or was he already dead, do you think?*

Distant lightning flashed. It would be a few minutes before we felt the tail wind and the wave action beneath us.

As we all dwelled and paddled, making Mosquito Point in record time, my mind asked, *Dad? When somebody dies...you know, the way Lloyd did, when do you stop saying* him *and start saying* the body?

Right when he's dead, sweetie, Mom said.

Yeah, Buddy-Boy, Dad answered. *Right when he's dead. And you can just about bet Lloyd's good and dead.*

Really?

Yep. You can start calling him 'the body' now.

I sure don't know what you're going to do, though, Ted, Mom said. *Not too many kids go to summer camp and kill their counselor.*

~~~

And there I sat. In Toad's chair. The director leaned against his desk, facing me with Lloyd's unsmiling eyes. My heart pounded as I tried to appear comfortable. I ran another nervous hand over my pocket and found the knife's hilt was still fully covered.

Pssst!

"Ted," Mr. Dinwiddie said, "The reason you're here is that I'd like to tell you something. I'm a little worried about what may have happened with Lloyd last night."

The master of euphemism.

If I hadn't been so afraid, I'd have cried. And if I'd cried, it would have led me somewhere I didn't want to go. At least not yet. But either way, I hated the hiding and the sneaking. I was in a safe room with two men I loved and trusted and had begun, with my silence, to betray.

That instant I decided I would tell the truth and tell it fully.

CHAPTER 66

JUST NOT TO them. My dad was the one I wanted to tell. But not for the protection he might provide as an attorney. He was simply the only one I wanted to tell. There would be no other way to see his initial reaction. No way to see where I really stood with him. If I'd ruined a relationship that was going to heal otherwise, I wanted to be the first to know.

It came to me, clear as crystal, as I sat in that chair. Dad was the most important thing there was, no matter what I was to him. I wanted him terribly.

"The reason I've chosen to speak to you over your cabin mates, Ted," Mr. Dinwiddie said, "is because you're level-headed, genial, and the more senior veteran in the cabin."

It felt like the kind of compliment adults start with when they're about to say something horrible. My eyes were dusty, granite stones scraping around in bony sockets.

"I want to know something," he said. "That is I *need* to know the truth. About Lloyd...as your counselor. Isaac and I have just learned some things about him that concern us."

His gaze darted toward Isaac, then back at me. He cleared his throat.

"Do you know of any...anything *inappropriate* between Lloyd and any of your cabin mates? Anything that might make anyone...uncomfortable?"

Slicing Lloyd's throat open and leaving him to cook in a makeshift barbecue could be construed as inappropriate. And it *did* make us pretty uncomfortable. Especially *him*. I kept my answer simple. "Like what?"

Mr. Dinwiddie breathed in deeply through his nose. "Anything, I suppose. I was referring to, say, any kind of"—he tented his eyebrows—"*touching*."

"You mean like, maybe, hitting?"

"Any kind of touching. Other than something like shaking hands or patting someone on the shoulder."

Mr. Dinwiddie's words fell flat. I was twelve in 1970 and slow on the uptake for the subject matter. My dad tossed around the word *pervert* a hundred times when I was a kid—much to Mom's dismay—but I still didn't get what Mr. Dinwiddie was trying to say. It was imperative that I come up with something, though, or he might give up on me and put another one of us Toad's chair. "He, uh, grabbed Hoss's arm once."

"Mr. Cartwright," the director said.

"Lloyd…yelled at us quite a bit," I said. "We don't like him very much…just because he seemed pretty mad most of the time. We talked about him a lot as a cabin because of it. But other than Hoss, I never heard of him…*touching* somebody in some bad way."

A deep sigh and what seemed like a great weight fell from Mr. Dinwiddie when I said that. His shoulders dropped, and at least *some* of the sunrise returned to his eyes. He wasn't near ready for the striped suits and straw hats of the barbershop quartet, but he was far better than he'd been.

The envelope in his hand crinkled.

"Oh," he said. "Ted. Karen wanted me to give this to you."

Karen. I filled with anxiety at the mere mention of her

name. The Lloyd situation and everything that went along with it marred most of what I could allow myself to feel for her. But I felt it just the same. Where she'd been I didn't know, and it hurt.

He handed over the sealed envelope, on which she had written *Ted*. Off to the side, a pencil-drawn long-eared rabbit stood next to a tall, leaning mushroom that somehow seemed ready to tell the rabbit a secret. I remember wanting to hold the envelope up to my nose to check it for Karen fragrance.

"I told you she likes you," Isaac said.

"She *is* quite fond of you, Ted," Mr. Dinwiddie said.

I figured I'd better save the envelope for later, but I opened it right there. Inside was one sheet of stationery with a few, handwritten words.

8/11/70

Dear Ted:
I'm sorry I didn't get a chance to say good-bye when I left.

"Why did she have to leave?" I asked.

"We thought it best," Mr. Dinwiddie said. "And I'm afraid we have to leave it at that."

"She wanted to say good-bye, Ted," Isaac said.

I read the rest of the short note.

I had a fun time getting to know you, and I'll miss you. Dad gave me your home address so I can write. And you please write to me.
Love,
Karen

Karen settled my mind for a minute. As I stood to pocket her letter, the knife's hilt dug into my groin. Right then, a sheriff's patrol car pulled up between Headquarters and the big birch. Cold fingers of brand new terror crawled up my back.

The car seemed to lurch to a stop with clouds of dust growing from its wheels. A pot-bellied, uniformed deputy sheriff stepped out. He had a revolver, handcuffs, sunglasses, and a pen in his shirt pocket.

Mr. Dinwiddie put a hand on my shoulder and said, "Let's head outside."

You can only be terrified so many times in fifteen minutes before it feels routine, but my bowels loosened when he said that.

Isaac herded me out front as I put Karen's letter in my other pocket. The spring groaned as he opened the door.

"Good morning," the deputy said, not an ounce of cheer in his voice.

Robotic and full of fear, I said, "Good m—"

"Head on back to the cabin, Ted," Isaac whispered, leaning down to me and patting me on the upper arm. The deputy pulled out a notebook and introduced himself to Mr. Dinwiddie. I wanted to run, but I couldn't. I just walked.

I listened as I went. *Fire's just too big to even look for him* was one thing the deputy said.

Look for who? Did Mr. Dinwiddie know Lloyd was over there?

Dread squeezed at my stomach as I pictured what Dad would say about it all.

The flames consumed the far shore and the fireboats

sprayed, still doing no good. The sky—at least what parts of it were visible through the smoke—positively sagged. It couldn't be much longer, I thought.

When I remembered the red string and the footprints by our Emergency Door, I took off in a sprint for the rake.

CHAPTER 67

AS I RAN, I heard another engine. Gaining on me. I ran faster and made it back to Cabin 7 before the V8's growl and the rattling stopped. A beat-up old truck pulling a canoe trailer sat on the bluff, next to the bench.

Two maintenance men, there to collect the canoes for the off-season—*if only they'd picked the canoes up yesterday*—got out of the truck and descended the bluff.

As they worked, I jogged over to the Emergency Door of Cabin 7. The red string was still there, and I grabbed it. It was a single string about two feet long, frayed at one end, snake-like in its position. A piercing, sonic chill scraped my bones.

The canoe chain.

The string was evidence. When I bent to pick it up in my latest *obstruction of justice*, I noticed its buried end had a little weight. A fat knot grabbed and lifted the key, which I pocketed next to the letter.

The key wasn't around Hoss's neck when we got back to the boathouse. But it was when he stood on that sawed-off log. It must have fallen somehow, when Lloyd had a hold of Hoss, and slipped into the front of his pants. Its position there survived the canoe trip back, the blood-rinsing, and the climb up the bluff. When we all undressed before sneaking back into the cabin, the key fell in the sandy dirt.

I grabbed the rake and dragged it through all the footprints as I did my inspection duty. I hated what I was doing. Each voiceless stroke of the rake felt like a big, fat lie. I guess it was. But I didn't stop until the footprints were gone.

The rake drew a field of parallel lines as I dragged it to the cabin's front. I stopped to watch the men carrying the canoe, one at each end. As they topped the bluff, the man walking backwards tripped on a half-buried granite rock that had always seemed part of the bench. He fell back, dropping his end of the canoe. Its point crashed onto the rock and landed between his legs, maybe an inch from his crotch.

The canoe announced its landing with a God-awful sound and shook like a diving board someone had just jumped off. The guy who fell cursed, then apologized to me for his words.

I couldn't help but stand and watch them work. They didn't drop any more of the canoes. On the fourth, our first to put on the rack from the night before, I saw something. Right near the float, one hand's width in front of where the maintenance man gripped, two dark smudges, each shaped like the heel of a hand, obscured the registration stickers.

Hoss's handprint in Lloyd's blood.

Hoss must have scratched the back of his head before we racked the first canoe. The evidence mounting against us was ridiculous. In a couple of minutes, after they'd loaded all six canoes, the men drove away. Their route would take them past headquarters and the police car.

With a pull I couldn't possibly ignore, I went toward where the man fell. The care I'd have to take for Dad to hear our story first was overwhelming.

The canoe left a little bit of itself on the stone. The aluminum scrape was almost iridescent.

"What's up, Ted?" Hoss said quietly.

Startled, I still held the rake.

"I snuck the bags down to the cans behind Cabin Four," he said. Those were the trash cans on the utility path between Cabin Row and Campout Circle. No one used them very much, since they were not so convenient, but the trash truck picked them up weekly, just the same.

"You see the scrape on that rock?" I said. "That's where they dropped one of the canoes when they came to get them." Hoss didn't register anything. I said, "There'll be a fresh scrape on one of the boulders over there." I hitched a thumb toward the fire. "The one me and Zeke ran into last night. Remember that?"

"So what."

"Somebody's gonna see it."

"No they're not. Nobody cares."

"Look at that scrape. It practically shines like a light. You think they'll not care when they see ours over there by the fire?"

"No."

"The fire and the dead body?"

He cinched his eyebrows.

"You think they'll care when they see all the footprints over there?" I asked.

"Shut up, Ted."

"And your knife. Where'd that go?"

I'd scared Hoss, and I liked it.

"Did you drop it over there? Right by the fire, maybe?"

The boy who could talk a mile a minute seemed unable to speak. I pressed on, enjoying what I was doing to him. Enjoying being Hoss's bully. An image of mom's face appeared. It made me not *like* that I liked what I was doing. But I wasn't able to stop. "And that key you dropped? The padlock key? You think about *that* this morning?"

"Been thinking about it *all* morning, Ted."

"When they find the key, they'll find those padlocks."

"I'm pretty sure I dropped that key in the lake. When I fell in and pulled Bud out of the water."

"It didn't fall off then. I saw it around your neck when we were over there. When you were standing on that stump."

Again, Hoss didn't have an answer.

"You think Lloyd ripped it off your neck?"

"No," he said. He squinted at me and asked, "Are you screwin' with me?"

"It's the only thing that makes sense, man. Maybe your key's on the ground over there, right next to your knife. And right next to Lloyd. What happens when they find *that*?"

"Shut up."

"The canoes are gone," I said. "Some guys came to get 'em."

"Good. One less thing. Take 'em to store them over the winter?"

"Probably. Unless the deputy sheriff down at Headquarters wants 'em."

His expression fell as the blood drained from his cheeks. His pupils may have popped open a little when I said the word *sheriff.*

"Stop it, Ted. I mean it."

It was as though I'd given Hoss the beating of his life. I

thought about mentioning the bloody handprint, and I'm not completely sure why I didn't. Maybe because I wouldn't kick a man while he was down, the way Hoss had with Lloyd over the hidden whiskey bottle. Or maybe my conscience—for deliberately scaring Hoss—was starting to get the best of me.

"Just being careful," I said. "It's important to talk these things through."

"It is, I guess. But we shouldn't tell—"

"Because all somebody has to do is *wonder* if we were involved."

Something—an acorn, maybe—hit Cabin 7's roof with a weighty *splat*.

"And then they'll find out," I said.

"They're not gonna find out," he said.

Another acorn hit the ground.

"They will if they have something to wonder about," I said. If anyone saw the bloody handprint, there'd be a lot *somebody* would have to answer for.

"They're not gonna *wonder*," Hoss said.

Another acorn. Then another. They hit the roofs, the ground all around us. Something smacked me in the face, just below my left eye.

Rain drops, not acorns.

A fat one splatted on Hoss's shoulder. Then, the sky opened. A watery bombing raid assaulted Cabin Row and Loon Lake. The choppy waves flattened as the water took on a greenish color. The splattering rain turned to mist above the dock and beach house. The noise filled our ears.

On the granite stone, the iridescent aluminum scrape

337

remained as the ground cratered around it. The rake marks I'd made disappeared. The canoe truck's tire marks would soon follow. In one minute, any obvious trace of our having been across the lake—save for the forest fire and Lloyd's dead body, of course—would disappear. But I didn't share the thought with Hoss.

Across the lake, a battle waged. Rain versus fire and wind. The assault from above soaked us clear to the skin, and we made no effort to correct our situation.

"Not gonna find any footprints now," Hoss said without the winning mug I would have expected.

"You and Buck ever find *his* knife?" I asked.

Hoss glared at me.

"Gotta talk these things through," I said. "It's gonna be a miracle if we ever—"

"You fellas nuts?" Isaac asked from beneath an umbrella. Hoss and I spun toward him as his voice boomed through the white noise of the rain. "Let's get inside!"

We huddled under Isaac's umbrella and walked with him to Cabin 7. I dragged the rake behind me, thinking as we went. If ever anything was suspicious, it was a pair of smart twelve-year-olds too distracted to quit standing in the rain.

338

CHAPTER 68

HOSS AND I slopped into the cabin, dripping. Sunny said, "Where you guys been? We still have to finish cleaning the shower."

"You boys gotta do something about those wet clothes," Isaac said.

Wet clothes.

Buck snapped his attention toward the cabin's front. Zeke and Neil flinched.

Hoss said, "So we've been out in the rain, you guys. We gotta get outta these wet clothes. Shower's clean, Sunny. If you'd get off your butt and check for yourself—

"Don't worry about inspection, fellas," Isaac said. "It's cancelled. It's really coming down out there. Be lunch time before too long. It's free-rec until then. You'll have to find some stuff to do in the cabin. Sounds to me like a good opportunity to pack. Except your raincoats. Those, you might need."

Tepid affirmatives wafted toward Isaac, and he continued. His voice was very businesslike and clipped, but still a hundred percent *Isaac.*

"Couple things. You know how we've been calling your parents? Some news on that. You guys listening? Okay. Bud...Bones...Coach. You're going home early. Bud. Your parents might be on the road already. Lincoln, Nebraska's what. Twelve hours from here? Be here late tonight, they said.

Okay? *Bud?*"

"Huh?"

"Your *parents*. They're coming to get you *tonight*. Okay?"

"Okay."

Isaac shook his head. Bud did seem oblivious, which meant he was himself, and that was good.

"Coach."

"Yep."

"Where you from? I forget."

"Sheboygan, Wisconsin."

"Oh, that's right. So it's what for your parents? Ferry from Manitowoc to Ludington? Then up here in a couple-three hours?"

"Sump'm like that."

"All right. Your Mom's raring to get you, too, okay? She and your dad may be here as early as evening."

"M'kay."

"Good enough. *Sunny*. Your parents are getting you a new one-way flight. Traverse City to Chicago, then on to San Diego. Leaves tomorrow morning. We'll getcha to the airport. You got that?"

Sunny nodded.

"Okay, then. Get packin'," Isaac said. "Gotta get going. Somebody'll come check on you here in a bit."

I wished Isaac had been our counselor all along. With him, none of this would have happened. I wanted to think I could have prevented it, but I didn't. Instead, we were packing to leave camp, disposing of forensic evidence, acting way too casual for a bunch of boys who'd just killed their counselor and set the forest on fire.

Zeke concentrated on his sloth book. That book represented the innocence of days long past. So did Zeke. The nicest kid who ever walked. He was supposed to come to White Birch, meet his friends, question a time-tested camp legend, send away for a textbook, read it, draw conclusions, and grow in the process. His whole life had been that way, and what a perfect young man he'd already become. A part of me wept for what being my friend had put him through.

"You two," Isaac said to Hoss and me. "Put on some dry clothes and hang your wet stuff over the sinks. I'm heading over to Cabin Six to tell them who's leaving early. Be soaked to the bone before I get back to H.Q."

In a second, Isaac opened the front door, popped open the umbrella, and sloshed down into the wet sand. Hoss and I went up to the windows. The rain descended, less in individual drops and more as though being poured out of a bucket.

"You think it's raining that hard across the lake?" Hoss whispered to me.

Through the cottonwoods and the haze of the downpour, the orange glowed. "We better hope," I said.

"No footprint could survive this."

I leaned his way and whispered, "The rain'll probably even wash your bloody handprint off that canoe."

That comment got rid of him. He went back to the sinks. I finally managed to get that knife out of my pocket and into the cigar box.

For the rest of the morning and through lunch, none of us said very much. Sleep came to most of us over rest period. I

341

woke with such a start that Neil asked me if I was okay. Zeke slept, and I hoped his dreams were better than mine.

~~~

That night, Cabin 7 bid farewell to its first departing camper. Coach. Before he left, he thanked me for letting him use my bed as a couch and offered me a stack of *Mad* magazines. I accepted them and was even a little sad to see him go. Coach was not a big part of my summer, before or after Lloyd, but I liked him. It was hard to acknowledge that I'd never see him again. Such were the ways of season's-end at White Birch.

You meet a kid and get to know him a little. And when he leaves, you wonder about him. What is he made of? What are his passions? After three summers at camp, I understood losses like Coach. The end of each summer marks at least a dozen such little tragedies. In my library of acquaintants, Coach would be a good book who would probably remain on the shelf.

Before Coach slung his duffel bag over his shoulder, Hoss spent a little time with him, one-on-one, in the front of the cabin. I overheard the spiel Hoss had prepared. In giving it, he was careful to refer only to the fire. In another brilliant move, he left out the part about Jake. Doing so, I figured, was to keep from singling Buck out to a camper who didn't even know there was a body.

When we all said good-bye to Coach, I knew he could walk away never knowing anyone died that night. Hoss seemed self-assured after Cabin 7's first departure. It was as though he'd checked a box on a to-do list. I shrugged, a gesture meant to say, *You never know who's gonna talk when they get home.*

Late that night, just after sundown, which was about nine-thirty in mid-August, Isaac came to get Bud. There's a kid I was happy to see go. I didn't like him, didn't care what he'd become, didn't even wonder. He was neither asset nor liability. He was just gone. Hoss and Buck both vetted Bud and ended up thinking he remembered almost nothing. I would've crossed Bud off that to-do list myself. He was a book I didn't want in my library, but into the shelves he went.

The next morning, Sunny went before breakfast. He gave the due handshakes to Buck and Hoss, nodded at the others, and ignored me. That suited me fine. Hoss and Buck never had a more loyal follower. Sunny was a check in their *Win* column. After his ride to the airport pulled away in the steady rain, Sunny staring forward like a mannequin, only Bones and the five brains remained.

The rain calmed to a common, summer shower. By bedtime that night, the orange glow was gone. Only little curls of smoke twisted up from the forest's charred remains.

Mom and Dad were no longer there. The light in the trees was and always had been a sham. I drifted off to sleep that night resenting Lloyd for his role in it. And myself, for wanting to *believe* in the first place.

CHAPTER 69

RAINCOATS WERE STILL standard dress on Friday morning. Cabin Row's herd thinned after news of fire, smoke, and coughing fits spread across the country. Between Wednesday morning's revelation and Thursday evening, half our population had already gone.

I sat at Cabin 7's usual table in the dining hall. The black, denuded trees stared right back at me. Very few had leaves or needles with which to talk in the wind. The enormous, knobby white pine tree, the one next to the sapling-covered log, still stood, presiding over its fallen brothers and sisters.

Several boats were anchored at the far shore by then, in much calmer water. Men wearing something like space suits entered the remnants of the forest.

Neil and Zeke whispered something as we left Bones, Buck, and Hoss at the table. Isaac had already left for Headquarters. Neil and Zeke ran ahead of me as I walked. Their even-temperedness through all of it let me know they were as numb as I. They stopped at Isaac's window and Neil reached in, up to his shoulder. He craned his neck and scowled like a professor as he reached. When his face softened, he emerged with a stubby pencil and a small stack of scratch paper. He and Zeke wrote feverishly and beckoned me to join them. As I caught up, Neil told me to write down my home address.

The time had come. My two best friends and I were going to part at some point very soon. They were their own group, towering in their importance to me, above the dozen-or-so guys I never got to know and was vaguely sad to see leave forever. Neil and Zeke were not going to leave that way. Not with me, and not me with them.

As books in my personal library, these gentlemen would remain unshelved and frequently studied. We huddled at Isaac's window, and I wrote my address twice, once for each of them. When I slipped their addresses into the front pocket of my pants, I thought of something and got ready to run back to the cabin. I needed to beat Hoss back there.

"Hey, Ted?" Zeke said.

A sheriff's patrol car pulled to a stop at the top of the waterfront, followed by a second. The other three Cabin 7 members stared at them from the bluff. Bones pointed at the deputies and Hoss hurriedly pushed Bones's arm back to his side. Buck didn't seem to know where to go. Hoss gestured toward Cabin 7 and started walking. Buck and Bones followed.

A couple of counselors, including Hank, the waterfront director, carried life-rings and other equipment from the beach house. They stepped up to the top of the waterfront just in time to see Hoss grab Bones's arm. But they kept walking. They were busy storing the waterfront equipment for the off-season.

The deputies got out of their vehicles and stepped toward the main door of Headquarters. One of the deputies headed straight for us. We got out of his way as he peered into Isaac's window. The other knocked on the main door. On the other side of the waterfront, coming back from the dining all, was Mr. Dinwiddie, his pace quickening.

The deputies stepped down to greet him, holding their hats

in their hands, adjusting their grips. One of them put his hat on, as a kind of umbrella, I'd guess, but he took it off again. Mr. Dinwiddie broke into a slow jog. From beneath the hood of his raincoat, he warmly greeted them.

Before anyone said another word, Mr. Dinwiddie's expression melted a little. He slowed to a walk. Isaac opened the main Headquarters door and ushered the three men inside. Not one of them said a thing.

Our course back to the cabin lined us up with Hoss and Buck. Bones had lost himself in the view of the lake and the other side. Mr. Dinwiddie's drooping face and the sheepish behavior of the deputies consumed me. I knew what it meant and could hardly think. I stopped and leaned on the back of the bench, having forgotten who was around me. Twists of smoke rose from the ruins.

"Ted," Hoss said. "What's the matter?"

Breathless, as though in another one-on-one talk with Hoss since the fire, I said, "I think they just found Lloyd."

Neil: "What?"

Hoss, in a breathy whisper: "Oh, shit."

Zeke: "Lloyd? What do you mean?"

My gaffe was, bar none, the most careless thing any member of Cabin 7 had done since our little cover-up began. Buck dropped to his knees, as though he'd already suspected it.

Zeke: "Ted?"

Neil, whispering, eyes wide: *"That was LLOYD?"*

Buck threw up his breakfast. Hoss dropped next to him and asked if he was okay. He put one hand on Buck's shoulder, and used the other to brush sand and dirt over the vomit.

Neil and Zeke collapsed onto the bench. I moved in front of them, watching their expressions.

Neil: "Are you sure?"

Hoss: "Buck. Can you get up?"

Me: "He was wearing a mosquito net."

Hoss: "You gotta get up, man. Somebody's gonna see you. Can you do it? 'S gonna be all right. Buck?"

"Hoss," I said. "Let's grab his arms and get him sitting on the bench."

Neil and Zeke scooted over.

Right as we got Buck sitting down and stepped back, Hank and the other counselor emerged from between Cabins 4 and 5. If they were ten seconds earlier, they'd have seen Buck throw up. Hank's face showed something I'd call curiosity as the boathouse lanyard dangled from his index finger. He and the other guy descended the bluff without a word. They'd be taking the paddles and life vests to storage.

"I'm sorry, you guys," I said to my friends. "I didn't want you to know."

Zeke didn't answer. Neil's initial, hard-at-thought scowl relaxed. His eyes roved for a few seconds, and he exhaled. Then, he did something I didn't expect.

He nodded.

It was almost too subtle to see, but he did it. I got the feeling a big portion of his anxiety had just been doused, like the fire by the rain. No innocent victim died over there. It was just Lloyd. Neil's face was very adult-like. It was clear he made a decision when he heard the truth, and it was almost instantaneous. His little nod rapped a gavel on a court's bench.

Zeke's attention volleyed between Neil and me. His mouth hanging a little open, he showed no obvious fear or indecision. Then, as though Neil and I urged him to jump into the water for his twenty-minute swim test, Zeke nodded, too.

I'll do it for you guys.

The moment we shared chilled me, but it also made me feel a respect, trust, and friendship in a depth very few people ever get to experience. It was a moment we should have shared alone, just the three of us.

"That's the way, fellas," Hoss said. He checked to see how close Bones was to the bench. "Buck. Let's get up. Back to the cabin. Can you walk?"

We went back to wait for the next surprise.

CHAPTER 70

BUCK WENT TO his empty bunk and collapsed on Bud's vacated mattress. He hunched forward and sobbed.

Hoss: "Jesus, Buck. Hold it together, okay? Bones is coming. Be here any second."

Zeke: "Hey, Buck."

Buck, taking in a deep, wet sniff: "Yeah?"

"You did what you had to do."

Hoss: "Forget about it, Zeke."

Zeke: "You saved Hoss."

Buck: "They're gonna find out. They're gonna know."

Hoss: "No. They're not."

"Yes, they are! They're gonna find out, and they're gonna—"

"Gonna find out what?" Bones asked.

Hoss: "It's nothing."

Bones: "You guys know something I don't?" None of us matched his gaze.

Buck: "We have to—"

Hoss: "No, we don't. Whatever you were gonna say, we don't have to do it. We don't have to do anything."

Bones: "Have to *what*?"

"Keep our mouths shut," Hoss said. "That's what. It's just a few more hours. Once we're out of here, we're gonna be fine. If they, you know, wondered, they'd've said something by now, and they wouldn't let us go. We just have to hold it together."

I thought of why I wanted to get back to the cabin before Hoss. I slunk back toward the drying pants still hanging over the sink. In hiding the knife, I'd forgotten all about the key. I retrieved the key, string, and Karen's letter, and I hid them in the cigar box.

Buck took another deep sniff and stood up.

"It'll be all right," Hoss said. "Right, fellas?"

No one said anything.

Hoss tried again. "I said, 'Right, fellas?'"

"We heard you," I said, slipping the cigar box into my duffel bag.

My words echoed in the cabin until I heard a deep but quiet voice from up front say "Cornelius Shepherd."

Buck wiped his eyes.

"Cornelius Shepherd!" boomed Isaac's voice through the front door. "You have a visitor, Young Man!"

Neil stepped toward the front. "Dad! Mom!"

"There's my boy!" yelled his father.

I peeked around the partition. A heavily muscled man with a flat-top and horn-rimmed glasses stood on the stoop. He was Neil in thirty years. Neil's mother stood there, too, elegant and stately. With a handkerchief, she dabbed away a tear.

"Hello, Baby," she said to Neil, as he hugged her so tightly she laughed.

Isaac stood by.

Neil introduced Zeke and me. His parents gave us their complete attention through the introduction and actually thanked the two of us. Neil had written them letters about us, and I guess he must have said some nice things.

Isaac asked Zeke and me to help get Neil's things. The Shepherds' car was right outside the door. I grabbed Neil's duffel, and Zeke took his box of books. The elder professor opened the trunk of the car, and we put the items in. He said "Thank you, gentlemen," then asked Neil if he was ready to go.

Neil said he was ready, and there was no doubt in my mind he wanted to leave the camp and never come back. He opened the car door but stopped. He was suddenly more unsure than I'd ever seen him.

I'll never forget it. His face betrayed a naked, ugly surprise. It was the very moment he realized he was saying good-bye to us. His lips pressed tight, and another set of lenses appeared behind his glasses. As he reached to shake our hands his eyes squeezed shut. Two tears rolled down, one on each side. Zeke dispensed with the hand-shaking and hugged his friend. I did what seemed right and hugged them both. Neil's wiry and curly hair pressed against my cheek, and I felt him sob twice, but then he stopped. He took one step back and nodded at Isaac, who bid him a fond good-bye. He got into the car and closed the door.

Professor Shepherd took us into his benevolent gaze for a moment, shook Isaac's hand, and then sat behind the wheel of Neil's family car. The Shepherds took their son away from us. Zeke and I ran to the back of Cabin 7 to watch the car pull away. Its taillights disappeared around the bend of Cabin Row. It was a hard moment.

Neil had just become Cabin 7's latest Cal Owen.

Zeke and I headed back inside to what was left of our areas. I had my packing to do, and Zeke had nothing left but his sleeping bag and pillow on his bare mattress. He picked up one of Coach's *Mad* magazines and flipped through it. I busied myself, packing socks and underwear. In a minute, Zeke whispered to me, unhidden pain on his face. "When are you leaving, Ted?"

"I don't know. Sometime tomorrow, maybe."

Bones packed. Hoss held the pants he'd just taken from the sink. Buck sat still, his elbows on his knees, his cheeks resting on his fists.

Isaac appeared, carrying the 1970 cabin plaque, two nails, and a ball pein hammer. He dragged a chair to use as a stepstool as I thought of the graffiti linking our souls to the dubious memory of 1970.

As Isaac hung the plaque, he was more quiet than usual. The men in the white space suits had, in fact, found Lloyd's body. Lloyd made a habit of camping on the other side, and Mr. Dinwiddie knew so. Lloyd went to the far shore the night he was fired, and with the forest fire, Mr. Dinwiddie would have put two and two together and called the sheriff's office about it.

It all made sense. Around the time Cliff's life-journey (or whatever Mr. Dinwiddie had called it) diverged from ours, the light in the trees shone less and less. In fact, after Lloyd blessed us with his presence, the light only burned on Tuesday nights. It sickened me that my secret connection to Mom had been nothing more than Lloyd's campfires all along. It was a hundred times worse than when I was six and learned the truth about Santa Claus. It was the biggest dose of ugly truth that ever shoved me toward adulthood.

As Isaac stood on the chair, checking to see if the plaque was straight, someone new stepped through the door.

"Hoss Cartwright!" said Hank, the waterfront director, in a voice that made Isaac sound meek. Hank stood in the partition between the counselor and main areas of the cabin. "You wanna tell me what your flashlight's doing in the boathouse?"

CHAPTER 71

HANK HELD THE L-shaped flashlight, and he clearly wanted answers. I got a little lightheaded, but I was ready. Ready for it to happen. Ready for the truth to come out. Ready for any consequence. My only regret would be that I didn't get to tell Dad the story the way it needed to be told. Hoss's face was blank, and Buck's turned as white as Bud's hair.

Hoss had dropped the flashlight. Neil picked it up and still had it when he climbed through the boathouse window to stow the paddles. He'd climbed in and out of there in such a hurry he forgot to close the window and had to go back. The window, apparently, wasn't all he forgot.

Isaac stepped down from the chair. "Good question, big guy."

Hoss stalled. "What? *Where'd* you find that?"

He'd been bested. Even *Hoss* couldn't think his way out of this one.

"It was in the boathouse," Hank said. "Why would it be there?"

"I, uh, don't...are you sure it's mine?"

"Says 'Cartwright' on this piece of tape. Pretty sure it's yours."

The cabin was quiet.

"Bud threw it down the bluff," I said with a coldness that startled me.

Hoss's gaze darted to me.

"He was pissed at Hoss for something," I added. "Grabbed his flashlight and threw it down there. I bet somebody found it and put it in the boathouse because they didn't want to mess with it. And then they forgot about it."

"When?" Hoss asked me. "What was he so mad about?"

In all my years, I've never seen a more cunning, thinking-on-his-feet liar. Hoss's transition from caught-red-handed to surprised-and-convincingly incredulous was seamless. If opportunistic deception were an academic discipline, Hoss would be its founding scholar. And me? I appeared to be his star pupil.

"Heck if I know," I added. "Bud always seemed mad about something."

Isaac held his arms out, palms up, hammer in hand, shaking his head. It was clear he believed the scenario. After all, he'd seen Bud wet his pants and be taken in by every ridiculous story he ever heard. Bud was crazy, and the flashlight story fit him well.

But Hank didn't really know Bud. He narrowed his eyes and glared at everyone in the cabin before fixating again on me. "Is that what I'm supposed to believe? Kid got mad and decided to throw a *flashlight* down the bluff? That doesn't make a *damn* bit of sense."

My mouth parched. The ruse wasn't working. My relationship with Dad was about to end. I swallowed dryly and tossed up a Hail Mary. "*Bud* doesn't make a damn bit of sense."

All we needed is one staff member to become suspicious. And right then, Hank was that guy. He was in a cabin full of nervous kids, hearing a half-cocked story about a flashlight.

Even *if* he didn't see Buck puke up his breakfast, and *if* he didn't see Hoss keep Bones from pointing at the deputies, Hank could probably read—if he thought about it—how uncomfortable Buck was, just sitting still.

We'd put up a forest of spinning plates on sticks. When the first crashed to the floor, the rest would follow. Tension built up in Cabin 7 and seemed to choke us. Buck drew in a deep breath. The first words of his complete confession formed on his lips.

"Hank," Isaac said. "You didn't know Bud very well, did you?"

"No. Pretty weird kid, was he?"

"Pretty much. Take what these guys say, add fifty percent, and that's Bud."

Hank seemed to ease a little. Or maybe he just got bored. "If you say so." He tossed the flashlight to Hoss and walked out.

Buck bowed his head as Cabin 7 released its pressure like a let-go balloon.

"All right, fellas," Isaac said, heading toward the door. "Check out the 1970 plaque. I'm headed back up to Headquarters until the next weird thing happens. Keep packing."

Hoss was still. No one said anything. Isaac shut the door. In another half minute, no one had moved, and the door re-opened.

"Hoss Cartwright!" Isaac said. Buck jumped. "Time to saddle up! Wagon train's a leavin' town!"

It was Isaac being Isaac and nothing more. He'd barely had

356

enough time to step out the door before someone came to tell him it was time for Hoss to go.

"You, too, Bones," Isaac said as he stepped into the main room. "Both of you have the same flight to Detroit and separate flights after that. Headed to the airport soon. You both packed?"

They answered *yes*. Isaac stepped out front, and Zeke followed. We'd walk Hoss and Bones down to Headquarters. Hoss stepped toward me, as though to say something. I'll never know what he wanted to say, because I spoke first.

"Don't worry about the flashlight," I whispered, so no one else could hear.

"What? My flash—"

"No. Zeke's. It's just like yours, remember?"

"So?"

"It floats," I said. Maybe it was over there, just bobbing around in the lake, next to all the fireboats. A yellow flashlight so freshly dropped nothing green could yet be growing on it. And maybe, just, "*Maybe*...it's even Yasko-side-up."

Bald-faced horror lit onto Hoss's face.

"But it'll probably sink," I said. "So like I said. Don't worry too much."

"Why are you—"

"If I was you," I said casually, "I'd worry about the two knives you and Buck lost over there."

He picked up his duffel bag, and the two of us walked toward Headquarters. He'd already spoken his last words to me.

CHAPTER 72

"C'MON, YOU guys," Isaac said through the open door. "Grab your stuff, and let's head out. Let's walk 'em down. See them off."

A station wagon waited for Hoss and Bones at Headquarters. The driver put their duffels in the back. Bones climbed into the back seat, and Hoss followed. Never had I seen him so uncomfortable.

Isaac leaned through the windows and shook their hands, told them to have a good off-season. Hoss glanced up at Buck through the open window. He opened his mouth to say something, then closed it. A peculiar distrust grew in his eyes when he rolled them my way, along with a hint of threat. His was the kind of face you shouldn't make in public. Then he shut me out and faced the front of the car until it drove away.

Hoss was gone.

He was another book for the library, one I'd never want to read again, couldn't afford to throw away, and wanted to keep hidden high on some shelf. But something told me the *Book of Hoss* would stay on the table with Zeke's and Neil's.

Bones was gone, too, an interesting and slightly scary, dime-store mystery for the cobwebby, pulp fiction section.

I should've known Isaac would, in turn, identify the object of Hoss's ugly stare. But I didn't. For a second, while the station wagon pulled away, its steamy exhaust rising in the drizzle, I locked eyes with Isaac. He knew immediately there was something between Hoss and me. So soon after the issue with Hank and the flashlight and what had to be the recent discovery of Lloyd's body, all that strange behavior could doom us.

Zeke stood by, having waved good-bye to Hoss. While I had my uncomfortable eye-lock with Isaac, Zeke walked over to the big birch and ran his fingers over its bark. Buck stood nearby. A few cars parked above the waterfront and a dozen parents moved around in the rain, quickly carrying trunks and luggage.

"So Ted," Isaac said. "What's with Hoss?"

"Huh?"

"He stared at you. Looked real mean. What's going on?"

"Nothing anymore. He's gone."

"I can *see* that...but why the ugly mug from him?"

"He's a jerk, and I didn't like him."

"Okay," Isaac said, now walking alongside me. I'd always liked time with Isaac, but not just then. I needed to get back to the cabin without him. We left Zeke behind, transfixed in a world of tiny knobs and white bark.

"You'd think," Isaac said, "he'd just flip you off if he wanted to give a parting gift. Right?"

I didn't like the questions. Wasn't quite sure how to answer them. Buck followed, silent. All Isaac had to do is ask Buck what was going on, and Buck would fold. I figured I'd better keep talking.

"He already flipped me off this morning at breakfast," I said. A lie, of course, but it was okay. "Hoss is just a jerk is all. He was mean to Bud, mean to Neil and Zeke. *Zeke* of all people." Hoss had been a little mean to Zeke at the beginning of camp but had been respectful the rest of the time. "And he was mean to *me*. I'm glad he's gone."

"J'you flip *him* off? You know? Return the favor? Maybe with both hands?"

"Prob'ly *should* have."

"I'd'a turned the other way if I saw you do it."

I laughed before realizing when I left White Birch, I'd lose Isaac, too.

"All right," he said, booming-of-voice again. "You guys all packed?"

"Just about," I said.

"Then hop to it, young man. I'm headin' back to H.Q."

The last thing the remnants of Cabin 7's citizenry needed was for Isaac to have a *mono y mono* with Buck over this ugly stare business.

"C'mon, Buck," I said. "Let's get back there. I got somethin' to show you." Buck followed me toward the cabin, and Isaac headed back toward Headquarters and the big, white birch.

CHAPTER 73

BUCK AND I went back. Just the two of us were there, alone, in a position to talk about the summer and the cabin. It was just like the first day, before I ever talked to Hoss. Even before I met Zeke, and while Neil hadn't even arrived at camp. Buck was helpful and outgoing that day, straight and true. But as the summer wore on, under pressure from Hoss, the iron of Buck's constitution weakened and eventually bent. By that very last day of camp, Buck was broken and lost.

The cabin was quiet.

"Hey, Buck?"

Even after everything that had happened, the kid still extended me a pleasant expression and seemed patient, waiting for what I had to say.

"I have something to tell you," I said.

"You do?"

"Yeah. Couple things, really." He nodded and gave me time. "Hoss's knife fell out of his pants when he fell in the water after Bud. Pretty sure it did, anyway. I got rid of your knife, too. They're not over there somewhere to be found, like I told Hoss. And the key? The one to the padlocks? I got rid of *it*, too."

"But Hoss said…"

"To hell with Hoss. *I* told him all that stuff myself."

"Why?"

"'Cause he got us into this, and all he cared about was

himself."

"But we all went along with it." He ran his fingers through his hair.

"We did, but he did a pretty good job persuading us."

"We each did our part," he said. "Some more than others."

"But you saved Hoss's life. Don't forget that." I lowered my voice to a whisper. "Lloyd was gonna kill him."

"We shouldn't'a gone."

"I agree with you on that, but we can't do anything about it now. I wanted to scare Hoss a little. You know, for what he did." I shifted on my feet. "And I wanted to tell you the truth when he was gone."

He shrugged, or rather, his shoulders seemed to shrug themselves, once, twice, then over and over until I realized he was crying.

Hoss ruined him.

I told Buck it was going to be okay, another lie. I'd just tell the truth when I got home.

What'll happen to Buck when I tell Dad? What'll happen to Neil? And Z—

The cabin's front door swung open. Zeke hurried inside. His face was red, and he was breathing heavily.

Isaac got to him. Oh, God, oh God.

I'd protected Buck, but I didn't protect Zeke.

"Ted?"

"Hey, Zeke."

His mouth seemed too try to move, but it wasn't very successful. He looked as lost as Buck had, just moments before. Then with a cracking voice and a quivering chin, he said, "My wagon train…"

My hands popped up to the top of my head. What Zeke had to tell me was, for some reason, the last thing I expected to hear. His eyes filled with liquid lenses, just like Neil's. Isaac didn't get to him at all. It was just time for him to go.

No.

He and I busied ourselves, checking his shelves for anything he may have forgotten. When we were done, and there was nothing left for us to do but walk him down to Headquarters, he gave me a hug. I'm glad he did.

Buck stood by that time, wiping away tears of his own. He patted me on the shoulder and said, "C'mon. Let's carry Zeke's stuff."

I carried his duffel bag. As Zeke left Cabin 7 for the last time, a black squirrel darted in front of us. I remember seeing the glow of White Birch's most innocent Magic when I took my first walk down Cabin Row in June, with Karen. As we walked to Zeke's ride, I watched him secretly. He glowed with the Magic.

I don't even remember Zeke getting into the car, but we'd already said good-bye. He made sure he had his copy of my address and showed me it was in his pants pocket. The car drove off. To Isaac, Zeke was another successful departure. Another camper to the bus station or airport. To me, it was— just different.

I hated crying, but sometimes it happened. I stood, alone, trying to be inconspicuous. But when Isaac stepped over to put his arm around my shoulders, I leaned into him and just let go. Some sadness just can't be described. Leaving camp and saying good-bye to your best friend isn't quite like suddenly losing your mother, but it carries its own, seasonal brand of anguish. The feeling was common at White Birch. For one day a year, in those northern Michigan woods, it rained tears.

Mine weren't just for Zeke leaving, though, but for every kid who lost his best friend at the end of camp. Time, unrolling just the way it's supposed to, can be tragic. It has a way of reminding you what you haven't done that you wish you had, and maybe no longer can. What I wouldn't give to be an innocent twelve-year-old again for an hour, sit on that bench, and kick at the dirt with Zeke and Neil. We'd talk about the woods, The Sloth, the teeth on a northern pike. And whatever else twelve-year-olds talk about.

When I finally calmed down, I knew Zeke's car was gone.

"I bet *Zeke* didn't flip you off," Isaac said, holding onto my shoulders, eye to eye.

I sniffed and said, "Nope."

Facing another direction, as though to move onto the next task, he said, "You two guys remind me what's so important about White Birch." He lifted a hand to his face, maybe to wipe away a tear of his own. The end of camp gets us all, even a big guy like Isaac. Another car pulled up, another set of parents.

"Oh, my word," I heard a mother say when she got out and saw the far shore of Loon Lake. My time to say good-bye to Zeke was over.

CHAPTER 74

AFTER A WHILE, Buck would thank me for telling him the truth about the knives and the key. When he got into his own little wagon train and rolled away with a sincere nod and wave, I was the only one left. I spent the next hour outside Headquarters, my duffel packed and ready to go. The cigar box was secure inside it. Every time I moved my bag, I heard a sliding thump and remembered I'd stowed a sample of Lloyd's blood in my things. I left the duffel at the stoop beneath Isaac's window.

I stood among the trees behind Cabin 4 and studied the bell on the north end of Headquarters. I traced the rope in through the knothole and pictured Karen there, leaning in for leverage, popping Hoss's and Bud's heads into the wall. It seemed to have happened so long ago.

Wrapping my hand and wrist around a pine tree six inches in diameter and leaning out from it, I let it hold my weight. Walking around the tree like that, leaning out, and feeling the bark crumble under my hand killed a little time. The bench didn't have anything for me anymore, so I stayed away from it. For me, that summer, all the essence of White Birch Camp— except Isaac—was gone.

A certain V8 engine rumbled. It was no distant boat on the lake. Down the way, past Headquarters, rolled Dad's GTO. My heart quickened, but not because of what I had to tell him. It quickened because he was there. He'd come to get me. It's still amazing how much of me thought he wouldn't. I stood up straight, let go of the tree, and thought about running to him.

What if he doesn't want me to run? What if he's here to get me but doesn't really want to?

Only one thing was certain. I wanted him to be happy to see me. I was tired of worrying about whether he'd dumped me off at camp to get rid of me.

His car pulled to a stop beside Cabin 1, where I couldn't see him until he walked back toward Headquarters. Dad could've been a puppy that didn't know which way to go first. He scanned the faces of the younger boys running and playing, biding their time as parents trickled in from around the country. Dad seemed to recognize Isaac, who stood near the big birch, and bee-lined to him.

Dad continued to search as I walked toward him. After a few steps, I couldn't stand it any more. I ran as fast as I could. He was anxious, and he was after *me*. And finally, he found me. As he did, he jumped, separating his feet and bending his knees. He threw his arms out wide.

"*TED!!*"

My grin was so wide it hurt. I crashed into him and wrapped my arms around his middle. He laughed and picked me up and squeezed. His shirt smelled like his aftershave, a dash of cigarette smoke, and just...him.

He came to get me.

He'd come after all. I was safe and secure. All those months of doubt washed away forever. It was the happiest moment of my young life.

CHAPTER 75

AFTER TWO WEEKS at home, I was used to waking up without a bell. I was in my own bed with the smell of clean sheets. Breakfast was downstairs, not a quarter-mile away in a noisy dining hall. Since the end of camp, Dad and I had already hiked in Brown County, fished in the Blue River, and gone out to eat on Friday evenings. We watched Saturday afternoon movies on Channel 4 and listened to Dad's forty-fives on the record player.

Each record, I noticed like never before, had two sides.

Each morning, my clean feet would hit the sand-free carpet on the A-side, and on the B-side, I'd picture a dead cedar fully alight with flame. I'd greet my friends at the Lafayette Street Park, and I'd see Zeke telling me his wagon train was about to leave. I'd chat with Dad over breakfast, then out the window see a charred, smoky dreamland with a dead body in the middle of it.

On Saturday, the twenty-ninth, the afternoon was muggy. I watched Dad sneak out to the mailbox. The grass teemed with moisture and life. When the breeze wafted just right, I could smell flowers on one side and decomposition on the other. Lush and humid, southern Indiana made White Birch Camp look like a desert.

Dad walked in through the kitchen, carrying a package in brown paper. It was fastened with stringy tape that could withstand shipping over a distance. Four times that week, those packages came, and four times, he stole away with them to his den. He didn't mention them, and I didn't ask, but with each one since the first, my curiosity doubled.

Still, though, I had bigger things to worry about. For two weeks, I'd been home, watching Dad, gauging his mood. He was clearly back to his old self by the time I came home from camp. I didn't worry any more about how he felt about me. He had a glint in his eye and seemed to enjoy patting me on the shoulder or tousling my hair when he walked by. His general way since I'd been home solved a lot of problems and answered a lot of questions. Dad was happy to have me home, and I knew it.

That record's other side played a nagging kind of song. It grew in my mind, creating a pressure that squeezed out other thoughts and blurred my vision. I had to tell Dad about Lloyd. Each moment I didn't felt like a lie. I couldn't take it any more.

Lloyd was a mean drunk, and he'd tried to kill someone, even if it was just Hoss. He slapped the table when Zeke made an innocent comment, and he didn't like Neil. (Lloyd's blatant racism has come to my attention over time.)

There in the kitchen, in view of brown-paper package number-four, I pinched from my mind all images of Buck strapped down, being shot full of medicines. It was time for Dad to know, and he had to hear it from me. For two weeks, I'd held it in, fearing, not Dad, but for his happiness. The news would disappoint him.

No. It would crush him.

I'd been home long enough to know there was no such thing as a good time to break it to him. But it was just a matter of time before someone in uniform came along and took my choice away.

The familiar snaps of his briefcase clips echoed through the front hall before he entered the kitchen. In blue jeans and a t-shirt, he looked a little funny carrying his briefcase. My mouth was dry, and it tasted like wet pennies. Setting the case flat on the counter, Dad scrunched up a wad of brown paper, the package's wrapping. As he did, a wry grin spread on his face. It was an expression I was about to wipe away for good. He pulled an envelope the size of a birthday card from his pocket.

"Hey, Buddy-Boy," he said to me, studying the envelope, "got something for you. Came in the mail. 'L - L - S,' it says. Lake Ann, Michigan. Isn't that near White Birch?"

"Yeah, it is." Lake Ann. Karen's home. But I didn't know what *L - L - S* stood for. He gave the envelope to me.

"Has a drawing on the front," he said. "Looks like one of those little arms off a *Tyrannosaurus rex*."

The envelope was springy with folded-page thickness. Adorning the front was a cartoon drawing I pegged as one of Karen's. An arm with curved and razor-sharp claws appeared to slice through the air. *L - L - S. Loon Lake Sloth.* She had written me. The envelope filled me with joy, and Karen's absence made me ache in the usual way. Side A, Side B.

Dad's eyes teased. "It's a girl's handwriting, you old dog."

Karen was the one who wrote the letter, but it seemed clear Dad was proud of *me*. It was no time to crush him. The urgency to tell my story receded as it had so many times in the previous two weeks. Only the very laziest nagging remained.

"Gonna have burgers on the grill tonight," he said. "Headed

out to the store to get the meat and some corn or something. You still like corn-on-the-cob?"

"Sure," I said absently, still studying the envelope.

"Good."

Dad tossed his car keys in the air and caught them as they fell back down.

"Hey, Ted?"

"Yeah?"

"I want to tell you a secret."

Oh, yeah? I have a secret, too.

He reached for my shoulders and pulled me into a hug. I wrapped my arms around him. Dad was always pretty big with displays of affection. He'd put an arm around my shoulders or mess up my hair, or kiss my head like Mom always did. Those displays seemed to go away for a while after Mom died, but they'd kind of sniffed their way back home.

"What's your secret?" I asked, my voice muffled against his shirt.

"I never wanted you to go to camp."

"You didn't?"

"I just about refused to take you up there in June."

"You did?"

"Sure did."

"Why?"

"Because I knew you wanted to go. You love that place." He squeezed me a little tighter, and the brown paper in his hand crinkled. "'Nother thing is...I was...kind of afraid you wouldn't want to come back."

I couldn't believe what I was hearing.

Don't cry, Ted.

"I did want to come back."

At the drop-off in June, when I first talked to Karen, Dad had seemed quiet, standoffish. But he wasn't. Not at all. The head cold that popped up out of nowhere. That had to be Dad on the verge of tears. He'd been afraid to let me go.

Dad and I hugged for a time until he let go and stepped back.

"All right," he said. "Gonna go to the market. 'Bout a half-hour." He strolled out the back, tossing the wadded wrapping into the carport trash can as he went. The GTO burst into life, and he took off. The first thing was to race upstairs to put Karen's letter safely on my bed. Investigating the brown-paper packages was more urgent, and I could only do so while Dad was gone. I skipped down the stairs, back through the carport door, and out to Franklin Street to make sure the GTO was good and gone.

I grabbed the scrunched-up wrapping from the trash and unfolded it. Written in permanent marker was *Roy Gables* and our address. A red-ink stamp saying Traverse City Record-Eagle served as a return address. I could already smell the newsprint on the wrapping. The mystery packages had been newspapers from Traverse City.

The papers were sure to be squirreled away in Dad's den. He always encouraged me to go in there and look at his books or sit at his desk, but I didn't want to *snoop*. Maybe, I thought, I could just stick my head in the door and find a short stack of newspapers. If they were there, I could read them, and it wouldn't be snooping.

But then, there was his briefcase. He'd taken the package into his den and emerged with the case. He probably meant to put it in his car and forgot. I thought for a second, then grabbed the case, releasing both spring-loaded clips at the same time. Under the lid, staring me in the face from inside was the *Thursday, August 27, 1970 Record-Eagle*.

The headline said something about the Sleeping Bear Dunes Park. On the lower half of the front page was a minor headline.

Fire Victim: White Birch Camp Employee

Clutching that paper like it was the last thing to read on Earth, I read the entire article there at the kitchen counter. *The victim has been identified as 32-year-old Lloyd Dinwiddie.* That sentence wrapped around and cinched me uncomfortably. Certain phrases arose from the text. *...near-empty liquor bottle* was one. *...alcohol intoxication...* was another. *...charred remains...* shined out like a beacon, and *...enough remaining teeth to identify the body with dental records...* made me a little sick. I didn't know at the time somebody could burn badly enough to make his teeth fall out of their sockets.

I made some sense of the article's use of words like *history of heart rhythm problem* and *unconsciousness.* The word *alcohol* came up more than just a few times. An interview with an investigator yielded things I understood: *thermal burns* and *asphyxiation.* There was even something about a *.38 caliber* *revolver...found next to Dinwiddie's bag* (must have been hidden with him next to that dead tree) and *all five rounds are thought to have discharged in the heat of the fire.* The article said nothing about gunshot wounds.

Buried in the text was the phrase *death is thought to be accidental,* and glaringly absent was any discussion of a crime. There was nothing akin to *...throat slit open...,* *...knife wound...,* any word like *murder, manslaughter,* or *homicide.* The article mentioned the Grand Traverse County Coroner's office, but very little about law enforcement. It mentioned nothing other than the folly of a drunk man alone in the woods with a campfire and something about a heart condition.

We members of Cabin 7, dispersed across the country for all time, with scant record to connect us ever again, had officially gotten away with what happened at camp. There was nothing left to worry about.

Other than the truth.

I wondered. How was the Dinwiddie family? How smug and victorious would Hoss feel if he read the same article?

Or would he feel something else? How I'd tried to worry him in the last couple of days of camp didn't sit well with me. The behavior didn't seem like mine. The idea that Hoss had fundamentally changed me flitted by, and I didn't like it.

I want you right there with me, he'd said when we launched the canoes to head to the other side. *You're a regular criminal.* Maybe a regular criminal, a liar, and a cheat is what I'd become. Every inch of my skin tingled at the thought.

Damn, Ted, said Dad's voice, *I didn't say 'tell the truth' just to hear my gums flap. This is the kind of crap that happens when you—*

Roy. Be gentle with him. Ted? Sweetie? You need to tell your father, and you need to do it soon.

I willed away the chin quiver as I stared at the headline and as the majestic V8 rumbled into the driveway.

Hastily, I put the newspaper back into the briefcase and slid the case into the position in which dad had left it on the counter. The GTO idled into the carport.

You need to do it soon.

The article in the paper sealed our success in concealing what we'd done, but any sense of liberation I felt came from my commitment to tell the truth anyway.

THE LIGHT IN THE TREES

CHAPTER 76

CHEESEBURGERS with pickles and fresh, Indiana tomatoes were our entrees. Corn-on-the-cob was the side, and for dessert, we decided to make s'mores in the back yard. After dinner, Dad had something he wanted to watch on television, and later, we'd build the fire, like we did sometimes with Mom. To kill time, I stepped out back and hopped onto my Schwinn, its handlebar grips feeling good in my hands. I rode up and down Lafayette Street for a few minutes, zig-zagging, even doing a few wheelies. I thought about the fire Dad would build. It made me think of Cliff carrying the...

Idiot Box...Mosquito Point...the sloth story...holding hands with—

Karen.

Karen's letter. I U-turned my bike to go home. Karen. Mr. Dinwiddie. *Lloyd.*

Pssst!

As I rolled into the carport to park my bike, I pictured Hoss punching Lloyd through the mosquito net. I ran up the stairs and couldn't help seeing white and orange-glowing, hot-coal teeth dropping out of Lloyd's flaming skull.

The evening sun shined through the high part of my window and cast a sharp beam onto Karen's letter as it sat on my bed. My pulse quickened. When I opened the envelope, no small number of single-folded pages the size of a stenographer's notebook slid out. Pages dense with ink pen impressions, the words were written in Karen's hand.

8/25/70

Dear Ted:

How are things at home? Do you miss camp? Do you miss the sand?? Has school started yet? Do you like it??

Do you like how I'm writing all these questions? That's to get you to write me the answers.

An entire museum of memories opened: typewriter in Headquarters…her red hair down over one eye…holding hands at Mosquito Point…our one kiss in front of everybody.

But Ted? Remember how you told me I should write more stories? This is one, but it's not about the Loon Lake Sloth. This story is true, and it's not going to be very fun to write. Okay? Some of this I can't even tell my parents, not after what's happened to Lloyd. (If you don't like what you've read so far, please return this letter for a full refund.)

If you're still reading now, don't say I didn't warn you.

Do you know why Lloyd got fired and didn't even have the chance to take his stuff out of Cabin 7? I don't know why I'm asking you, because I'm sure you don't.

They fired Lloyd for trying to do I-don't-know-what and using some words Dad said no one should ever call a girl, especially me. About a day before the fire started, I'd been typing for Dad. You know, all those reports. I needed a break, and it was nice out, so I decided to go down to the waterfront to get some sun. I got about half way there, and I realized I forgot my suntan oil in Headquarters. When I went back to get it, Lloyd was in my room, going through my sock and underwear drawer. I asked him what he was doing, and he was so surprised, you'd think someone had just blown a horn in his face while he was asleep.

Then I got mad. I told him he had no right to be in there. When I told him to put down my underwear, he shushed me. I should've screamed, but I didn't. Instead, I walked over to him to take the underwear out of his hand and put it back where it belonged. Then he asked me if my panties were as tight as my bikini.

(I'm sorry you have to read this, but I've heard it's good to...tell upsetting things to someone you trust.)

Anyway, when Lloyd asked me that, his face scared me. Then he said he was sorry and wanted me to hug him. That's when I tried to get out of the room. He grabbed my wrist when I did. I'm not sure what he really wanted, especially when he grabbed me and started pulling. When he put his other hand on my bare back, I guess I kind of panicked. I slapped Lloyd across the face, pretty much as hard as I could.

That reminded me of how Karen bashed Hoss's and Bud's heads and made Bud wet his pants. To know she slapped Lloyd for doing what he did? My God, how proud of her I was.

It surprised me how loud the slap was. Isaac's chair squeaked and rolled all the way across the room. Lloyd called me something bad and tried to slap me back. I yanked away from him and ran toward the door. Isaac was there and went in after Lloyd. As big as Isaac is, he can move like a cat if he wants. He got Lloyd in a bear hug and kind of wrestled him out of my room.

I didn't want to sunbathe any more. Instead, I put on a pair of jeans and a long-sleeved shirt and just stayed in Headquarters until Dad got back. Lloyd always gave me the creeps, but that afternoon, he made me feel a way I've never felt and hope to never feel again. I hate him for that. And I'm mad at him for making me need to hate something.

But anyway, the next thing I knew, Lloyd was gone. Isaac, I guess, fired him and told Dad what he knew about what happened, which isn't near everything. When Dad came to see me, he didn't know whether or not he was supposed to try to hug me. Can you imagine? Lloyd made it so my own dad didn't know if it was okay to hug me. (I hate Lloyd for that, too.) So I hugged <u>Dad</u>. He told me it was time for me to go home with Mom, and he took me.

The fire happened that night. Dad worried Lloyd had caused it, since Lloyd camped over there at least once a week during the summers. Once he found out about Lloyd, Dad was more upset than I've ever seen him. He says making Lloyd a counselor is the worst mistake he's ever made. I hate seeing my dad upset—and confused—and angry with himself! He's just not supposed to get that way. You know what I mean? He's my <u>Dad</u>!! He was so upset that he told me some stuff I probably shouldn't know.

Like Lloyd ~~has~~ had a drinking problem. (One time, he even had to go to the hospital because I guess he got so drunk it made his heart go too fast or something and almost killed him. Another time, the drinking made Lloyd talk about shooting himself.) Dad thought Lloyd had quit drinking long before you guys needed a new counselor. When Isaac kicked Lloyd out of the camp, Lloyd went over to the other side of the lake, built his fire, got drunk, and had that heart problem right at the wrong time. You know what else? They found a gun over there with him. Dad said Lloyd might've been planning to…you know…but nobody could ever be sure. Anyway, whatever happened (and please don't think bad things about me for saying so, Ted) I think Lloyd did the world a great big favor.

Is that terrible?

I will say this to you and only to you, Ted, just because it's not good to hide things. I'm glad Lloyd is gone. Or at least, I'm glad my dad is with us and Lloyd is the one who isn't.

That's where you come in. What I have to say to you is it's because of <u>you</u>, Ted, that Dad is here. You saved his life, and because of that, he's here with me. So <u>THANK YOU!!</u>

You know, it's funny. As long as Dad's here, I find myself not caring at all about Lloyd. He doesn't deserve to be cared about. Maybe I'll be able to forget him altogether. For Dad and me, things are getting back to normal, and I'm happy about that, because I love him.

He's here because of you, Ted. The only thing I would change right now is to be able to see you and say ~~good-bye~~ <u>hello</u>.

Now, then. You better write me!

Love,

Karen

I read the letter three or four times, each time hearing Karen's voice. I was proud of her for taking care of herself. My chest ached for Mr. Dinwiddie being sad or confused or mad at himself. Still holding Karen's letter, I thought for a bit. Given that Lloyd really *was* trying to kill Hoss, I figured he didn't mean to live very long himself. Mr. Dinwiddie was probably right about that gun. Buck slit the throat of a man who was about to kill himself anyway.

In five minutes, maybe. Or even five seconds. Maybe Hoss was the distraction that made Lloyd take the gun down from his head. Lloyd would've done the world a big favor either way.

If we didn't take our little canoe trip, I'd forget all about Lloyd and Buck and the other guys. Even Hoss. I'd be pals with Zeke and Neil, and I'd write letters to Karen with not a worry in the world.

I dreamt about that little *what if* for a whole minute. But the nagging B-side song played on. I wasn't sure how my friendships would play out when I told D—

Dad called in through the carport door that the fire was burning and ready for us to cook marshmallows. It was also time to talk to him. I put the letter in the cigar box and took out something else.

My heart ached again when the next image of Karen appeared. Maybe, I thought, telling the truth would fix what hurt so much. But it didn't matter. Dad simply deserved to know. I reached for the doorknob and steeled myself. The first few steps down the hall were surprisingly easy, and the next few, down the stairs, were even easier.

In my mind, Karen winked. *Lloyd did the world a great big favor*, she'd said, and I agreed. When I walked out to the back yard, Dad hummed some silly tune and snapped his fingers. He was a happy man that evening. A righteous man, a man who'd made it his business, his career, and moral imperative to find the truth.

He's such a good dad, and he's happy.

That's all I wanted for him, all summer long. Too bad I was about to destroy it. The sun set, the air cooled, and the fire gave off enough heat. On lawn chairs, Dad and I sat side-by-side. It was supposed to be nice. He told me stories about work, fishing, his buddies on the police force. I listened, waiting for the right time.

That time came when Dad went inside to get another chocolate bar.

I reached into my pocket to get what I'd grabbed from the cigar box: the birch tree medallion Mr. Dinwiddie had given me. I ran my fingers over it one last time and tossed it into the fire. The bark around its circumference burned immediately. In the hot coals, the birch wood caught a little more slowly. The words

**Integrity
&
Courage**

obscured as the medallion burned. Dad returned, humming again, and put the Hershey bar on the little table behind us. In the fire's heat, those two words, *integrity* and *courage*, disappeared forever.

But that was only the B-side tune.

A passage from Karen's letter is what played on Side A of *that* particular record:

As long as Dad's here, I find myself not caring at all about Lloyd. He doesn't deserve to be cared about. Maybe I'll be able to forget him altogether. For Dad and me, things are getting back to normal, and I'm happy about that, because I love him.

I leaned into Dad's side. He put his arm around my shoulders as Karen's pretty song played in my mind, again and again. After a short while, I figured I'd just sing along.

THE END

Thank you for spending your valuable time reading *The Light in the Trees*. If you think others may like this book, please tell them or post a short review. Word-of-mouth—in either form—is the author's best friend. It'll help our stories reach others' hands.

I'm sure the young Ted would thank you for following him. He'd probably shake your hand (with the right amount of squeeze) or nod like his dad taught him. He'd remember your help as his years rolled by, as he tucked his chin and steeled his gaze. As the first flecks of gray entered his hair, as he worried about his aging dad's health, and as uninvited memories of White Birch Camp came to visit. All the while, he'd be mindless that his story is not over, of course. But he'll find out soon enough; *White Birch Graffiti* is set for publication in August, 2018.

About the Author

Jeff Van Valer and his wife, Luci, live in Fishers, Indiana, and parent Martha and Joe, who make them proud. Jeff practices Neurology and Sleep Medicine and rides mountain bikes. On his commutes to and from work, his imagination runs wild with fiction.

Acknowledgements

Special thanks go to my family, especially to Luci, for tolerating the at-first inexplicable time I've spent (at my writing station) in a basement corner.

My beta readers include my friends, Caroline Arbuckle; Sara Coers; my sister, Kim Van Valer; author, editor and friend, Joanie Chevalier; and Karma Lei Angelo. Thanks also for the valuable opinions and advice from my sister, Lynn; Clabe Polk; and Emma and Joanie from Emma's Detail Shop: Author Assistant Specialists; and of course, my Blue River, Indiana buddies: Jason, Jay, Matt, MaryAnn, and Scott.

Cover art is by Jake Clark at jcalebdesign.com.

Questions for Discussion

Did Ted go through a fundamental character change in this story? If you think so, which changes did he undergo?

Who, in your opinion, is the primary antagonist in *The Light in the Trees?* Why do you think so?

Do you think Ted will be able to forget about Lloyd? What effects might Ted's final decision about the truth have on his well-being?

How did Karen evolve during the story? Hoss? Zeke? Neil?

At the story's beginning, Ted is convinced he's being dumped at camp. He feared that after his dad tastes his freedom for two months, "maybe he'll want to keep it." In what other ways might Ted have misinterpreted things? How did these misinterpretations affect how the summer unfolded?

Ted narrates *The Light in the Trees* as a middle-aged man. In what ways does the distance between the experience and the telling influence how the story was told?

Made in the USA
San Bernardino, CA
24 March 2018